Three
In A Bed

Carmen Reid

CORGI BOOKS

THREE IN A BED
A CORGI BOOK : 0 552 14947 0

First publication in Great Britain

PRINTING HISTORY
Corgi edition published 2002

9 10 8

Set in 11/12pt Palatino by
Phoenix Typesetting, Ilkley, West Yorkshire.

Corgi Books are published by Transworld Publishers,
61–63 Uxbridge Road, London W5 5SA,
a division of The Random House Group Ltd,
in Australia by Random House Australia (Pty) Ltd,
20 Alfred Street, Milsons Point, Sydney, NSW 2061, Australia,
in New Zealand by Random House New Zealand Ltd,
18 Poland Road, Glenfield, Auckland 10, New Zealand
and in South Africa by Random House (Pty) Ltd,
Endulini, 5a Jubilee Road, Parktown 2193, South Africa.

Printed and bound in Great Britain by
Cox & Wyman Ltd, Reading, Berkshire.

For Thomas and my sisters,
Natasha and Sonya

Acknowledgements

Thank you, Thomas Quinn, for total support in the decision to quit the day job, have babies and write novels. You are a brave and lovely man and I couldn't have done any of it without you.

Thank you also to my fantastic agents at the Darley Anderson Literary Agency. This book would never have happened without Darley's encouragement and inspired advice, and Carrie Neilson's absolute faith in it. I can't thank you enough and know I'm in very good hands.

I'm very grateful to everyone involved at Transworld for being so enthusiastic about Bella, especially Diana Beaumont.

I owe a huge debt to my friends and family who have been so helpful in all sorts of ways. Thank you to everyone who read drafts, took photos, looked after Sam, or simply made me believe it would work out.

Much love to the people I leaned on when the going got tough: my parents, my sisters Tash and Son, Scott and Dorothy Luke, Mairi Mallon, Glyn Pugh, Lucy Rock and Jo Sewell.

And finally, a big kiss for my little son, Sam – a daily inspiration.

Chapter One

It was 6.29 a.m. The digital alarm clock beside the bed was about to go off. Just as it started up with its nasty little beeping, the bedside phone began to ring too.

Bella leaned over to click off the alarm and answer the phone.

'Hello?'

She heard a distant 'Hello!' far from the other end of a crackling line, followed by singing.

'Happy birthday to you, happy birthday to you . . .'

'*Don*!' she shouted and heard it echo back at her.

'Hello Bella, wake up, I love you, I want phone sex now.'

'I love you too,' she said laughing.

'What? It's a terrible line.'

'I love you too!' she shouted. 'When are you allowed to come home?'

'Ah ha . . . well I'm phoning you from Grozny airport. By the time you get back from work, I'll be there.'

'Yeah?! I can't believe it! That's bloody brilliant!'

'My job here is done,' he said in mock superhero voice. 'Seriously, it's been a nightmare and it's getting dangerous now, so they're pulling me out. Plus I told them it was your birthday and I had to get home, or else a fate worse than a rebel gunman awaited.'

'Are you OK?' she asked.

'I'm very tired, it's been three weeks from hell. Oh bugger, hon, I have to go now, I'll see you tonight and I am so looking forward to it.'

'Me too. Take care.'

'Missing you already,' he joked, then the line went dead.

She was smiling hard, was going to be smiling all day long, she thought, as she got out of bed and started on Operation Bella. The difference between Bella and other women whose looks were somewhere between moderate to good on the scale was that she tried harder. In fact, 'tries hard' was a description that had peppered her report cards since she was tiny.

At the very start of her career, she'd spent a long summer on assignment in New York and it was there that she had found her spiritual sisters, the immaculate New York women who jogged, gym-ed, power manicured and treated sex as just another way to business network. Her eyes had been opened and she always joked that she'd checked all her insecurities in at JFK airport and never bothered to check them out again. This wasn't exactly true, the insecurities were still there, she'd just learned to hide them well.

She pulled on her running clothes and trainers now, because Monday to Friday, she jogged for twenty-five minutes every morning with NO EXCEPTIONS. She loathed almost every second, but it was the only way to shake off any remaining booze from the night before, stay on the slim side of curvaceous and guarantee that she got some exercise crammed into her day.

After the run, she showered, shaved, dried off and moisturized. Then, with her hair wrapped up in a big white towel, she stood in front of the bathroom mirror.

She stared hard at her face. Twenty-eight years old today. Pulling a smile, she looked at the tiny crinkles radiating out from her eyes and the very first hint of bagginess on her eyelids. It was obviously all downhill from here.

She sponged a generous squeeze of foundation from collarbone to hairline and loaded up a powder brush to dredge over her face. She thanked God every morning for make-up. Then she shook her hair out of the towel and blasted it dry, before bundling it up into the loose chignon which she thought made her look older and more serious for work.

Back in the bedroom, she pulled open her underwear drawer and rifled through it. Don was coming home! He'd been away so long, he'd find her a turn-on in greying pants and a jogging bra, but hell he deserved a treat. She took out her newest pink and black underwired lace bra and matching G-strings, then opened the wardrobe. She slipped into a crisp shirt and hold-up stockings then buttoned on a black suit with tightly fitted jacket and a narrow skirt which fell to the knee.

She checked herself over in the long bedroom

11

mirror and approved. Of course, since New York, nothing about Bella's workwear was left to chance. She'd taken the hair and make-up lessons, been colour-consulted and image madeover. Her perfectly appropriate outfit, about to be perfectly accessorized, was supposed to scream 'woman headed for the top'.

She fished about in her jewellery drawer for small chic earrings and the tiny platinum pendant Don had given her, fiddled to put them on then grabbed high-heeled leather pumps from the shoe rack and hurried into the kitchen.

Two oranges were blitzed in the small electric squeezer. She put the glass of juice and a pot of yoghurt onto the tiny marble-topped table in the kitchen, then went to the front door of the flat to bring in the newspapers. She sat down and studied the *Financial Times* carefully as she had breakfast, then flicked through Don's tabloid until she found his latest report, and read every word.

At 7.45 it was time to go, so she collected raincoat, briefcase, laptop and keys and headed out to work. As her left hand pushed shut the heavy wooden and glass front door of the mansion block, her eyes fell on the thin platinum band, sparkling with tiny diamonds on her fourth finger, and she couldn't help smiling. God! Marriage was still such a novelty.

Just one birthday ago, she'd woken up in yet another unfamiliar 'loft-style' bedroom, with make-up caked deep into her pores and the roots of a truly monumental hangover taking hold in her skull. Her nostrils had burned suspiciously and she'd been repulsed to see a fleshy, snoring equities trader, whose name she couldn't recall, fast asleep beside her.

She had retrieved her underwear, pulled on a dress stiff with sweat from the night before, picked up her bag and shoes and crept out of the flat. Three heart-attack-inducing espressos later in an Italian café on the corner, she'd come to the realization that it was time to put as much effort into her personal life as she'd put into her career. And about a month after that, all psyched up to stay away from men and sex and one night stands until she'd got her head together, she'd bumped smack bang straight into The One. After a thirteen-week romance, the longest she'd had for years, they got hitched. Fear of commitment, ha!

She had crossed that line, made the jump, taken the plunge. Well, actually, Don had seen straight through the tough City-girl-shagger defence to the person underneath, the one who hadn't dared to fall in love since Big Romance Number One had gone all horribly wrong. Don had taken her hand and convinced her this was the real thing. He'd urged her to make the leap with him and when he'd slid the slim ring onto her finger, she'd felt a surprising solemnity. She'd felt terrified of it too. But there was so much love just radiating out of him, she had committed, signed on the line, sealed the deal.

She turned away from the front door into the lukewarm May sunshine. In the distance she could hear the gentle roar of traffic: anther day in the capital was already under way. She unlocked the door of her low, cream-coloured classic

Mercedes 280/SL soft-top, threw her coat and bags onto the passenger seat and climbed in, smudging her right calf with oil on the door frame.

'*Damn,*' she said out loud, then leaned over to the tiny glove compartment and popped the button, causing half a dozen packets of black hold-ups to slide out onto the floor. She held her leg out of the car door, whipped off the smudged stocking, rolled on a new one then, tossing the spoiled one into the back, she fired up the engine and set off for the office.

At 8.25 a.m., juggling coat, briefcase and laptop with the packet of twenty Marlboro Lights and large bottle of Evian from the shop round the corner, Bella arrived at Prentice and Partners, one of the City's smallest, but sharpest, firms of management consultants.

'Morning, Kitty,' she said as she walked in.

'Hi, Bella.' Kitty looked up from her desk in the large reception area.

'Is Susan in?'

'Of course.'

'Girls first. Are the boys in to play today?'

'Yup, Hector's due in any time and –' Kitty checked her screen – 'Chris will be in for the afternoon meeting but he might be earlier.'

'OK. I'll just go through my diary and put the coffee on then I'll be ready for you,' Bella said with a smile.

She went into her little office and settled in, hanging up her coat and filling the coffee machine before she took out her laptop, checked through her e-mails and clicked open her schedule.

MAY 8

Tuesday

* Happy Birthday – just in case you've forgotten. Old Bag.

* Put in follow-up call to Petersham's office to answer/reassure on queries/nerves/cold feet.

* Prepare for meet with Merris.

* BOLLOCK Hector.

* Chris and Susan meet 2 pm – Petersham's and Merris details.

* Get pregnant?

What???! She re-read that last bit. God, why had she put that in there? It was on her mind, but that didn't mean it had to be in her diary. She hit delete. It was off the screen, but not out of her head. She knew she wanted a baby: really, really wanted one. Something that had begun as a vague interest several months ago had now grown into a fully-fledged desire. It was weird.

Why did she want one so much? She'd tried to analyse her reasons endlessly: maybe because her own parents had made such a mess of things and she wanted to do better, maybe because she worried a lot about what the future held for her and Don without kids. He was thirteen years older than her and she couldn't help imagining herself growing ancient, all alone with deranged, incontinent cats for company instead of children and grandchildren.

Bella also worried that it might take a very long time to have a baby. Her own mother had given birth to her at 29, then spent eight years enduring miscarriage after miscarriage before finally giving up hope of a second child. She remembered the little cradle and the boxes of baby clothes, all carefully labelled, in the upstairs loft room and how sometimes as a small girl she would find her mother up there, weeping furiously.

But Bella's biggest problem right now was that when she married Don seven months ago, he didn't want children – said he was too old, too independent, too set in his ways – and she'd agreed 'no kids' with him. But now she knew she hadn't meant it, hadn't really thought it through.

The idea was beginning to form in her mind that if a pregnancy were to happen 'accidentally', Don would of course be shocked, but she was sure he would come round to it. Anyway, her mother's experience had left Bella with the belief that conception was a million miles away from actually having a baby. So, would it be so bad to get pregnant and see what happened?

There was a knock on the door and Bella was interrupted from her thoughts by Kitty.

Bella poured them both coffee and, as usual, teased Kitty about her latest office outfit, in between briefing her for the day.

Kitty, small, spiky red-haired and generously curved, was crammed into silver hipster trousers, a tiny purple T-shirt and a silver padded waistcoat. Platform-soled trainers with flashing lights completed the look.

'When is the mother ship due to land?' Bella asked with raised eyebrows.

Kitty looked at her blankly.

'You do not speak the language of earthlings?' Bella added.

'Shut up, Bella.' A grin split Kitty's face. 'Just because you like looking like an airline hostess, you twentieth-century throwback.' She ignored Bella's exaggerated gasps of horror and added: 'Silver is so *now*.'

'But are you dressed for success, Kitty? I think not,' Bella answered.

'You are such a corporate clone! Power dressing does not equal power,' Kitty snapped back. 'Where are you headed Bella? Straight for the glass ceiling.'

'Oh God,' Bella groaned. 'It is way too early for a radical feminist rant, *please*.' She cracked open her pack of cigarettes and lit up, closing her eyes with pleasure for the first drag of the day.

As it headed towards 9 a.m., Bella shooed Kitty out of her office and started on her calls. She was in a gap between two big contracts and restless to drum up new business. After she'd made the first call, the phone on her desk buzzed.

'Hello. Bella Browning,' She answered.

'Bella, it's Kitty, I've got a very angry caller for you. Do you want me to say you're busy?'

'No, they'll just ring back. I might as well face the music. Who is it?'

'Tom Proctor at AMP.'

'OK, give me just thirty secs then put him through.'

She closed her eyes and took a deep breath,

willing herself to stay calm as she slowly put her finger over the flashing extension button to connect him.

'Hello Tom, how are you?' she said.

'Don't call me Tom, you bitch,' he shot back at her. 'You know perfectly well how I am. I'm fucking sacked. Sacked after seventeen years of working my arse off for this company only to have you come in here for eight weeks and pull the entire thing apart.'

This was the worst part of her job, the part that racked her with guilt. Tom was 53 with three kids in full-time education and a very expensive lifestyle to maintain. He did not have a great track record and was going to find it hard to get another job as good as the one she'd had him fired from.

'Have you any idea how much damage you've done here?' he raged. 'My colleagues, men with families and young children to look after, are packing their things into bin liners and leaving in tears.'

She swallowed hard, really not wanting to hear this.

'Just who do you think you are?' he screamed down the phone. 'I'll tell you – you're some cocky little graduate with a bollocks business degree whose only idea of cost-efficiency is sacking people and you probably only got your ludicrously over-paid position by sucking every cock in the city.'

Christ, that was way too much.

She answered coolly: 'Mr Proctor, I have a starred first in Economics from the London School of Economics, where I was top of my MA year. I spent four years working for the biggest consultants in the country before I joined Prentice and Partners. And Susan Prentice is a woman, so I certainly didn't need to suck her cock.'

Undeterred, he shouted back: 'We didn't fucking well need you lot of bloodsuckers in here. You've destroyed us. I'm going to make sure you never get another contract in the City again, you smug cunt.'

She couldn't believe she was hearing this. She stood up at her desk and her voice began to rise: 'If you were even half as good at your job as I am at mine, AMP would never have needed to call consultants in. Without my help that firm would have gone to the wall in two years max and everyone would have been laid off without the kind of generous redundancy payout you've received.'

Just for good measure she added: 'How dare you phone up to insult me? You kept telling me one day you'd move to the country and restore antique furniture, so why don't you sod off and do it?'

Damn, she instantly regretted that, but *cunt*! Cunt? How dare he?

At that moment, she glanced over to the door and saw Chris grinning at her and giving her the thumbs up. That was all she needed, Susan's number two listening in on this. Quickly she added: 'Mr Proctor, I'm very busy, you'll have to excuse me. Thank you for your call.'

She heard an astonished gasp, but put the phone down before he could say anything else.

'Phew, you tell them Bella,' Chris grinned at her. 'Just sod off to the country and restore antique furniture. I must remember that the next time someone calls me a cocksucker.'

'Chris, you heartless shit,' she said, relieved he was treating this lightly. 'I'm really embarrassed you heard that. Are you going to fire me now?' She asked with a little arch of her eyebrows.

'No,' he paused for effect, 'but I may have to get very firm with you, Ms Browning.' Then he added: 'Just try not to make too many enemies for life. Anyway, how was your weekend?'

'Good,' she replied. 'Don wasn't around so I did girlie things, you know, drank ten pints of lager, did three lines of coke, shagged a complete stranger in the toilets.'

He gave her an intrigued look.

'I'm joking, Chris.' Then the penny dropped. 'Oh!! You actually did that. Well you're a lucky boy, but at your age you have to think of your health, you know.'

'I'm only 34!'

'Mmm, but you have the added stress of being a senior partner,' she teased.

'A job you would probably kill me to get. Which is why I never send you out for sandwiches.'

'I'd never go!'

'Bella –' he reached for the door handle. 'It's been a pleasure as always, but we have lots of work to put together before this afternoon's meeting. Merris, Petersham, any queries, I'm next door, watching you through my spyhole.'

'See you later,' she said and he was gone, leaving her with a slightly too flirtatious smile on her face.

There was another knock on the door.

'Come in.' She knew it was Hector. Hector, the fresh out of university new boy who seemed never to tire of telling them about his heroic Highland pedigree. And that was just one of his many annoying qualities.

'You wanted to see me?' He poked a tousled head round the door.

'Yes,' she said.

He came in, looking arrogantly crumpled, as usual. He still bought into that boho tweedy suit, pashmina, I'm not going to conform or try too hard kind of look. He was a very brilliant guy: why else would he be working here? But he really was going to have to get it together.

He sat down on the chair opposite her desk.

'So, what is this piece of crap?' She tossed a thick, spiral-bound report onto the desk.

'Ah, I was wondering if a few inaccuracies might have crept in.'

'A few inaccuracies!!' She picked the report up again. 'Let me just open it at random . . . 32 per cent of £586,000? That is . . .' she barely paused, '£187,520. Yet unbelievably, you've got £28,500 down here. Totally, utterly out of the ball park.'

'Well, I suppose I'm not a mathematical genius like you, Bella,' he had the nerve to reply.

'What does that have to do with it? Why don't you buy yourself a sodding calculator?' she snapped. 'In fact go and buy a proper sodding suit while you're at it. It's about time you sharpened up.'

He looked up at her rather surprised, but she continued: 'You've been here for four months now and you don't seem to have learned anything. This report is about a major company, you were working out their profits, their losses, their expenses. Your mistakes could have cost hundreds of thousands of pounds, could have cost people their jobs. This is not a game, Hector, this is not a theoretical problem you discuss in a tutorial. Christ. It's all very well having potential if you're 10. There comes a time when you have to prove it.'

There was a long pause.

Hector wondered why Bella was holding the report right in front of her face and shaking slightly.

'Are you OK?' he asked.

He was surprised to hear a snort of laughter emerge from behind the pages.

'Oh God,' she put the report down on the table. 'You really deserve a strip torn off you, but I can't do this with a straight face.'

'Er . . . I'm sorry. Do you want me to do it again?' he asked.

'No, I've already sorted it. Will you just try and concentrate hard on the next thing you get from me?'

'Yeah, sorry.'

When Bella was on her own in her office again, she laughed at herself. 'Potential is all very well if you're 10' – she suspected she'd read that on a bill-board somewhere.

She lit up another cigarette, took a deep drag and massaged her temples. This was turning into one hell of a day.

There was another knock and Kitty came in with an enormous bouquet of flowers.

'You thought we'd all forgotten, didn't you?'

'Forgotten what?' Bella asked.

'Your birthday, you idiot.'

'Oh God . . . thanks.' She went over to take the flowers, reading the note signed by all four of them.

'Thanks,' she said again, looking round her room and wondering where to put them.

'There's a vase at reception, shall I keep them out there till the end of play?' Kitty asked.

'Yeah, you're a star, Kitty. I bet everyone else would have forgotten.'

Nine hours later, after hundreds of calls, calculations and a gruelling meeting with Chris and Susan, Bella was finally tapping in her last memo and tidying her desk for the day. It was 7.15 p.m. when Chris appeared at the door to ask if she was coming for a drink over the road.

She declined because, at last, it was time to get home to Don. The traffic was infuriatingly slow all the way back across town, so she redid her make-up, sprayed on perfume and flipped through her CDs before giving up in disgust and enduring the radio. She couldn't wait to see Don again. Three whole weeks: it was the longest they'd ever been apart.

When she finally made it back to the block she swung open the front door, ran to the lift and impatiently jabbed on the button over and over again until the doors pinged open.

In the flat everything was still and for a heart-crushing moment she thought Don hadn't been able to make it back. Then she saw his bag and his battered oilskin coat in the hall. Quietly she walked through to the bedroom. The curtains were closed and Don was lying in bed fast asleep.

She was so happy to see him she felt her stomach flip. She moved closer to take a long look at him. His face was brown against the white pillow, but tired and drawn. His thick steely-grey hair was rumpled and still wet from the shower he must have taken. His glasses were on the bedside table and he looked deliciously clean and freshly shaven.

She was sure he was naked under the duvet and she couldn't help herself, she longed to feel his body against hers. She put down her bags and coat, took off her shoes and undressed, then slid into the bed beside him, curling her naked body up against her husband's warm, naked back. Wrapping her arms round him, she put her nose to the nape of his neck, breathing in the smell of the sandalwood soap she'd been using too because she missed him so much: 'Hello Don,' she whispered.

He stirred a little and answered with a 'hmm' so she moved closer. She ran her hands down his warm, fuzzy chest and stomach until she reached his sleeping cock.

A longer, throatier 'mmmm' came from him now as she held his cock in her hands.

'Hello,' she said. 'Aren't you going to wake up and say hi?'

'Oh yes,' he answered, surfacing from sleep now. He rolled round to face her and kissed her on the lips.

Then he smiled, creasing the skin round his eyes and looking at her with so much love and longing she felt a lump in her throat.

'Hon, I'm so glad to be back, you have no idea,' he said in a voice still thick with sleep.

'I've missed you too.' She kissed him back, winding her legs round his, pulling him so close their pubic hair brushed together and she could feel

24

his cock stir against her as he moved his hands down from her waist to her buttocks.

'I still can't believe I'm married to you . . .' he said, in between small hungry kisses, 'and you're naked!'

He kissed her properly now, squeezing her into him and parting her lips with his tongue. She tasted his hot, minty mouth.

As he pulled her up against his hard erection, she wound her fingers into his hair and placed teasing kisses on his neck and round his ear.

'I have missed you so much,' she whispered.

'I've missed you too, especially your breasts,' he said with a smile, gently stroking and licking at her nipples and the soft white skin around them.

They felt and touched and kissed and licked until she rolled over and pulled him on top of her. Watching her face, he pushed inside and slowly moved in and out all the way along the length of his penis.

'You tease,' she murmured, holding her hands on his hips and moving him faster until they were gasping together in a fast and frantic fuck.

When they fell apart, they were slightly sweaty and breathing heavily.

'God you're good,' she said with a smile. 'I still can't believe you're my husband. I mean husbands are meant to wear slippers and wash the car, not give a girl multiple orgasms.'

'All in a day's work!' he answered.

'Hey!' she sat up, loving the fact that he couldn't take his eyes off her breasts. 'You better not have forgotten it's my birthday today.'

'I phoned you first thing, remember.'

'Yeah, you phoned, but where is my large, expensive present?'

25

'Bella, I've just come back from a war zone, there wasn't much to buy . . . give me a chance.'

She didn't know what to say. Maybe she was being unfair. What could Chechen Duty Free have had to offer?

'But . . .' he leaned over to fish about under the bed, 'I did get you this.' He handed her a big, khaki green furry hat with earflaps. 'Genuine Russian Army issue,' he said with a mischievous smile.

'Oh! Thanks.' She tried to look appreciative, then added, 'My first ever birthday present from you. Next year, remind me to get a different husband.'

'And –' he reached under the bed – 'I can't tell you how hard I had to barter on the black market to get this.' He turned round and presented her with a glossy pink box tied with ribbon.

'Happy birthday.'

She untied the ribbon and lifted the lid. Inside was an extravagant set of lilac and black silk under-wear. A lace-trimmed bra and G-string, a camisole top and French knickers. She picked the bra up and looked at the label – correct size. She was impressed. Black market ha, ha.

'Is this a present for me or for you?' she asked, but before he could answer, said: 'Thank you very much. You're very sweet,' and kissed him on the mouth.

'Oh good, I'm glad you like them, because I *really* like them. Now stay there,' he said, getting out of bed and putting his dressing gown on.

'I'm opening the wine, ordering Chinese, and I'm going to try and persuade you to spend the whole evening in bed with me.'

26

'Well, OK then, since I now have the outfit for it,' she said, lifting the camisole out of the box.

They ate the food in bed and made each other laugh, Bella talking about work and Don telling war stories.

'God, I do wonder if I'm getting a bit old for it, though,' he said, serious for a moment.

'Will you stop it?' she told him. 'You are not old, you're 41, you're very fit,' she leaned over, letting her dressing gown fall open and kissing him on the forehead.

'In many ways, you're like a man half your age,' she teased.

He pulled her across so she was sitting in his lap. 'Thank you for your vote of confidence darling,' he kissed her on the mouth.

'Yeuuck, black bean sauce.' She screwed up her face in mock horror.

'I'm going to kiss you somewhere else then.' He dropped her down onto her back and began to kiss her breasts and her stomach. Then he moved down to her pubic hair and blew on it gently. She drew one foot up, bending her knee.

He pressed his tongue onto her small nub of clitoris, listening to her sharp intakes of breath, then rolled her hard nipples between his fingers and thumbs. She said in a soft voice: 'Mmmm. This is what every girl needs on her birthday. It's much nicer than cake *and* less fattening.'

He pulled himself up over her and she moved her legs apart so he could enter.

She tensed every muscle for his thrusts and he felt her coming underneath him, clinging to his body to soak up the pleasure of his every move.

He took much longer and finally came as she was screwing up her eyes and whispering to him: 'I can't do this much longer . . . I can't . . .'

She kept him on top of her, feeling his penis slowly fall out of the spermy wetness between her legs and a huge sense of satisfaction welled up inside her as she thought about how she would not be taking her pill tonight, because she wanted to get pregnant.

Chapter Two

Flicking through her e-mails in the office, she was trying hard to think about the contract they were making a final pitch for next week, but her mind was wandering.

She couldn't believe three months had gone by and she still wasn't pregnant. Each period had been a surprisingly crushing disappointment.

Oh well, they'd just have to have more sex. Hardly an awful prospect.

'Bella? Bella, hello!' Kitty was at the door, in pink dungarees with a fluffy white cat apliquéed on the front pocket.

'Yes?' Bella stared at the cat.

'Susan's ready, you can go in now. Chris will be along in a minute.'

'Thanks, hon . . . but what's with the cat?' Bella asked as she gathered up her papers and headed for Susan's office.

'Post-postmodern,' Kitty replied.

Surprise, surprise, Susan was on the phone. She waved Bella in and pointed to a chair.

Bella's one-time mentor and now her boss was in

her forties, a rapier-thin, control freaky workaholic. She had scarily huge hair and only ever dressed in very expensive beige. She was married to an equally successful man. No kids.

Susan had been one of the stars at Laurence and Co., the fuck-off, major league consultancy firm Bella had joined after university. But Susan had left to set up on her own after a row with one of the MDs. There had been an almighty fuss, she was taken to court for breach of contract, they'd tried to drag her through the dirt, but it had all just made scary Sue even more determined to succeed. She'd finally agreed to let Bella join her a year later.

No matter how early Bella arrived at the office, Susan was there first and she always stayed late. Her only look was 100 per cent perfect and because she was constantly on her mobile, it was clipped to her waistband with a dainty headset which ran from her pearl-studded ear to her beige-brown mouth. This allowed her to tap into her tiny, shiny, titanium-cased laptop without a break in conversations.

'Hello, Bella,' she said as she finally ended the call, but didn't take the headset off.

'I was just speaking to Anne, you remember from the job last year? She's just had a baby so I'm supposed to be all thrilled and excited for her. Good grief, I'm so glad you're not planning to sprog. That's why I hired you, really. I needed another woman, a good one. But I didn't want someone who was going to go off and do the whole baby thing on me.'

Barely pausing for breath, she added: 'No matter what working mothers tell you, no good career woman is ever the same afterwards. They just haven't got their whole mind on the job once they have children. In fact,' she paused to give a little sarcastic smile, 'They haven't got their whole mind.'

Bella forced herself to return the smile, but suspected it had come out like a Cherie Blair grimace. She remembered exactly when she'd told Susan she didn't want children. It was when she'd first approached – make that pestered – her for a job. Obviously it had never entered Susan's head that now Bella was married, she might have changed her mind. It amazed Bella that Susan was often guilty of the most appalling sexist crap no male boss would dare to utter unless hidden in a pall of cigar smoke in the safe confines of a gentleman's club.

Luckily she was saved from having to make any sort of answer by Chris coming in. The meeting kicked off.

It was a little short of 5 p.m. when they finished, but there wasn't much else to do, so Susan sent them away early.

Bella headed for the car. The traffic looked grim but the sun was shining and she was going to drive with the roof down wearing her new sunglasses, so suddenly it didn't seem too bad a prospect. She was in a long queue at a roundabout, when she gave Don a call on the mobile.

'Hello, hon, it's me.'

'Hi Bella – do I hear traffic in the background? God, you're not out of the office, are you?'

'Yes, out early for good behaviour.'

'I'm in town,' he said. 'Job's nearly over, but I won't have to go back to the newsroom now, so

31

d'you want to meet up? We could go out for dinner round here somewhere.'

'Uh-oh, you've forgotten about the drinks party!'

'Errrrr . . .'

'Drinkies, darling,' she trilled in a silly voice, then added, 'At eight-ish with Mel, Jasper, Lucy and somebody's client. I can't remember who's paying for this one.'

'Ahh,' said Don, not at all disappointed. It was always fun going out to play with the City boys and girls.

'I'm going home to get dressed up. Are you coming back as well? Or d'you want to meet there?'

'I'll meet you there,' he said.

She gave him the details and they said their good-byes.

When Bella and the gang had all worked at Laurence and Co. together, they had been an incredibly close little group. They had seemed so exactly the same: young, precociously clever, ambitious, impatient to get ahead. They had worked hard and played harder in an inseparable band with their own private jokes, code words, pet hates and games. Even when they had all moved on to different companies, the intimacy had remained for a long time.

But over the past few months, Bella had noticed that she no longer really felt part of it – a difference she could only put down to marriage. She didn't want to be out socializing all night, every night. She wanted to go home to Don. She was starting to find the gossip dull, all the 'who's sleeping with who tonight/last night/tomorrow night' and the 'who's been hired, who's been fired' and how much their bonus was worth.

Even worse, Bella knew her little gang had picked this up and now thought of her as a slightly honorary member. She kind of wanted to be out of it, but was still hurt that they had sidelined her, closed ranks without her. It also really pissed her off that they didn't get Don at all, couldn't fathom what she was doing with a man who wasn't interested in *money*.

It did not take Bella long to get ready. She showered again and picked out a tried and tested outfit. Her get-dressed philosophy was simple – work the good stuff. She liked her face, her breasts and her hair and her legs from the knee down, so she never wore trousers except at the weekend and she always did heels and cleavage of some sort. Her long, dark hair was either piled up in a big chic bundle or let glossy-mane loose.

She walked into the smart little function room shortly after 8 p.m. and could see Don perched on a stool by the side of the bar already but, before she could get over to him, she was leapt on by Mel.

'Daaahling' – kiss, kiss – 'how are you? Looking foxy.'

Mel looked pretty slinky herself in a tight crimson number.

'Now come over here, Lucy wants you to meet the mob she's working with at the moment and Jaz is around somewhere.'

Bella managed a wave at Don before she was bombarded with a flurry of introductions. She set her face to interested smile and prepared to handshake. Network, network . . . that's what it was all about.

Almost an hour had passed before she finally made it over to see Don.

'Hello.' She put her arms round his waist and kissed him on the mouth, tasting whisky.

'Hi Bella, you look lovely,' he said.

'Well you know, it's my version of "Speak softly and carry a big stick".'

'What is?' he laughed.

'Speak like a financial whiz but wear a see-through dress,' she answered.

'Killer combination,' he agreed.

'Irresistible,' she said and lit a cigarette.

'D'you want to stay much longer?' he asked.

'A bit longer. I'll go speak to Jasper and his new buddies, then we'll make a move. You're not too bored, are you?'

'Nooo,' he answered, 'I'm chatting to everyone who drifts past.'

'D'you want to come and speak to Jasper?'

'OK, if you like.'

He stood up and followed his wife through the throng, watching the glances she was attracting, dressed in her tight black satin skirt topped with a dark green chiffon blouse which looked demure, but on closer inspection turned out to be entirely transparent with the merest wisp of bra underneath.

It pleased him to think how surprised the fleshy faces in pinstriped three-pieces would look when she left with him – the oldest and scruffiest man there, in a badly creased suit and scuffed suede boots.

Finally they got out of the place and crammed

into her tiny little car to race back home, Don marvelling at the fact that she could actually drive in those heels and that she'd restricted herself to two glasses of champagne – he hoped.

As soon as they were back at the flat, Bella pushed him playfully up against the front door for a long, probing homecoming kiss. She felt him relax as she leaned into him. Slowly Don ran his hands down from her shoulders to her hips, pulling her in close to him.

As they kissed, he felt for the zip at the back of her skirt and tugged it down so the satin slid into a heap at her feet. He moved his hands down, registering his appreciation that beyond the stocking tops, there was no underwear.

'Oh God, I want to fuck you,' he whispered into her ear.

'Well . . . OK then,' she said, putting her hand in his trousers.

Later in bed, she lay curled up beside him and felt a flicker of guilt. Would he really forgive her if she got pregnant? She could reel off a list of reasons why he was not exactly a great Dad candidate: he was the chief reporter with a tabloid newspaper, so he worked really long hours, was away a lot, and liked a good drink with the lads. Even worse, he was in his forties, his own dad had left when he was just a small boy *and* he didn't want kids.

Christ. She leaned over to get a cigarette out of her handbag.

He'd told her before they were married he didn't want to spend his fifties dealing with a teenager and his retirement paying for a student. And yet . . . somehow she was convinced she could change his mind because she knew he was a good man and he loved her.

'Don't smoke in bed,' Don groaned.

'Don, please . . . I need a cigarette.' She sat up now, so he could see her breasts bounce lightly against her chest, and put the cigarette between her lips. She clicked the lighter and took a deep drag, causing the end to glow and crackle.

'OK, I'm going for a shower.' He got up, leaving her in the bed in a pale cloud.

Bella didn't care; a warm plume of smoke was hitting the back of her throat and nicotine was surging into her veins. She lay back against the pillows and daydreamed about the gorgeous little baby they were going to have.

Chapter Three

Bella let her hair down and brushed it through. She checked herself over in her small handbag compact and decided to apply the full-on red lipstick.

How many times do we go out to celebrate winning a £500,000 contract? she thought to herself, smiling smugly. The Danson's job was finally in the bag and it was due to her. She had met the company director socially and she had reeled him in.

She was buzzing with excitement, too much nicotine and the small vat of coffee she'd consumed. The test she'd done this morning confirmed it was something else too – she was about to ovulate and by the law of the jungle, she should be hunting down a mate.

The word put David Attenborough into her head . . . *And here we have the Bella. She is 28 and she has to mate this season or her chance could be over. She will be cast out of the herd and the bull will reproduce with younger, more fertile females.*

God, listen to me, she checked herself. I'm still years away from my prime. Isn't it scientifically proven not to kick in till 36?

She knew she was looking good today in a smart but more than slightly sexy black, very tailored suit (which had cost about three times more than she'd ever intended to spend. Ooops). Her red silk shirt was casually unbuttoned to reveal a diamond slung onto a short chain and just a hint of cappuccino-coloured lace if she leaned over.

She checked the time: 5.30 p.m., surely it wouldn't be unreasonable for everyone to down tools and start the celebrations now? She e-mailed Chris.

Can we go yet? you lovely sweet man. I've got bugger all else to do and I'm gasping for a nice cool glass of wine.

Hello Bella – OK fine, so long as you're still wearing that very hot suit you had on earlier.

Of course I'm still wearing it. I don't often prance around my office naked getting changed.

Shame.

When the alarm clock went off the next morning, she woke with a pounding head and a disgusting taste at the back of her nose and throat.

'Oh God,' she groaned. The worst thing was, it was Friday today so she would still have to go for a jog and back into work to face the music.

How could four professional people have made such a mess of a night out with the boss? Of course they had all drunk far too much. Susan had kept them waiting at the restaurant's bar for three hours. And it wasn't just drink.

She didn't know if it was Hector or Chris who had brought the coke in to spice up the celebrations, but Bella and Kitty had been passed a wrap and had sneaked off to the loos for a dose. Bottles and bottles of champagne, and cocaine as well. Bella cringed when she remembered what they were doing when Susan finally arrived – holding a farmyard noises competition.

Somehow, with intense concentration, everyone had managed to sit at a table, order food and attempt to eat it. But Hector and Kit kept taking turns at getting up to go to the loo, sniffing heavily when they came back.

Then they went off together and didn't come back at all. Bella and Chris had been left at the table with Susan and she remembered trying to keep the sinking conversation afloat, painfully aware of the fact that she could hardly control her lips.

Finally Susan had slammed her platinum Amex down on the table, paid the bill and left in obvious fury. And that was when the real trouble had begun.

There was a newly opened bottle of champagne on the table and Chris had topped up their glasses, insisting it shouldn't go to waste. Bella couldn't remember much of a conversation, Chris had just reeled off drunken compliments and silly stories and she had giggled a lot.

When the bottle was empty and it was time to go, he had of course suggested they share a cab as they lived in the same part of town. She had fallen back into the cab seat to find his arms around her and without a moment's hesitation she had turned her face up and snogged him all the way home.

Oh God. She closed her eyes but she couldn't shake the memory. It had been so much fun. Despite the night of boozing, he had smelled and tasted good. They had spent the twenty-minute taxi ride entwined in long, probing, teasing kisses.

Even worse, she remembered telling him: 'This isn't really me, Chris, my hormones are on overdrive and I have to mate.'

CRINGE CRINGE. Why could she never have a memory blank like every one else seemed to when they got that drunk?

She had arrived home to Don, legless, coked up to the eyeballs and probably with smeared lipstick and an unbuttoned shirt. Not surprisingly, he had been quietly furious. He had forced her to drink about three gallons of water then sent her to bed.

She had absolutely no intention of saying anything about the snogging unless Don had already guessed and asked her first. A fresh wave of guilt broke over her: there was now an indelible blot on her marriage copybook and they hadn't even been married a year, for God's sake.

It was one thing to have a little crush on someone in the office: quite another to go ramming your tongue down their throat.

She got to work late, harassed and feeling awful. She hurried into her office and flicked on the computer. Among the e-mails waiting for her was:

Bella, I'm out at a client's all day. But I just wanted to let you know I've ordered a whopping bouquet for Susan this morning to atone for our sins. Good plan? Chris

She sat down and sent him a one-word reply.

Genius.

She was sure he would not leave it at that and she was right. Just minutes later, her in-box was flashing.

Oh hello, I'm glad you've finally appeared. I wouldn't have said last night was a complete disaster . . .

Chris, I think we all drank an awful lot. I'm trying not to think about it, I'm not sure I can remember the entire night.

Well that sounds truly pathetic she thought as she hit the send button.

Fine.

She stared at the word on the screen and realized it would be best to leave the conversation there.

'Hi.' Kitty was at the door, looking pale, blotchy and lanky haired in a strangely sedate grey outfit, which meant she must be ill.

'Oh darling,' Bella winced. 'Sit down and I'll pour you some coffee from my lovely little machine over here and you can tell me all about your night of passion with Hector, you evil girl.'

'He is lovely, isn't he?' Kitty said wanly, sinking into the seat.

'Yeah – gorgeous.' Bella hoped she didn't sound too insincere.

'I've fancied him for ages.' Kitty picked up her coffee cup with a trembling hand. 'We had coke and a grope in the Ladies but he didn't come home with me, which I'm taking as a very bad sign. And he's not in yet, so I don't know what to think?'

'Hmm,' said Bella.

'And what about you and Chris?' Kitty added. 'For a married woman, you looked very flirty.'

'I did not!' Bella launched straight in on the defensive. 'We were trying to distract Susan from the fact that two of her staff had *vanished*. Chris is sorting out flowers for her this morning to apologize.'

'He has a point,' said Kitty.

By four in the afternoon, Bella realized her work had been punctuated all day long with thoughts of Chris. He had such an indecently full mouth. She just needed to think about their long kisses to feel a little adrenalin hit.

'I have got to get a grip,' she told herself. '*Just stop this*. I want to have my husband's baby, not an extra-marital fling.'

But she could not silence the little voice in her head that kept telling her this was it – her last chance. Chris was one final opportunity for the wild abandon of a hot affair before she fully embraced motherhood and responsibility.

'But I've already embraced responsibility.' What the hell was this?? Nerves? She was married, she owed it to Don not to sleep around, not even once, not even if there was hardly any chance of him finding out.

Over lunch Kitty had confessed in whispered

42

giggles to licking coke off Hector's dick in the loos and Bella had felt a stab of jealousy.

Then she thought of Don and felt guilty. Married life was brilliant, but just occasionally she did hanker for the sexual adventure of singledom. Yes, it was like eating McDonald's: you really, really wanted it, you enjoyed most of it, but you felt crap afterwards. Still, she thought marriage would suit her perfectly if she was allowed just the very occasional indiscretion. She would be so very discreet about her indiscretions.

But the flip side was she would have to allow Don to do the same and she knew she could never, ever let him. She'd already warned him if he ever strayed, she'd snip his testicles off with nail scissors.

What on earth was she doing messing around with Chris? For one thing, he was Susan's partner, Bella's immediate boss, and she'd always made it a rule not to sleep with the people she worked with. Even if she was single. *I'm not single*, she reminded herself sternly.

Chapter Four

All the way home, she thought about her ovulating eggs. The weekend was going to be one long 1960s style love-in, John Lennon eat your heart out. It was time to think about Don, and Don alone . . . being in love with Don, having Don's baby.

Chris was a donut on a passing sweet trolley and she was *not* going to eat him. She was going to say No Thank You, I don't think I'll have dessert today . . . or ever again.

It was a baby she wanted now. *Baby*, baby, think baby thoughts. No more sexual hedonism, unless it's with that lovely man wearing your ring on his fourth finger.

Dashing through the supermarket that evening, she'd felt almost out of control when she saw babies and toddlers bundled into trolley seats. She was overwhelmed with the desire to pick them up and squeeze them, push ripe banana into their adorable chubby little hands.

This was becoming weird. Here she was buttoned into her expensive designer suit, zipping home in her successful career girl car, but in the depths of her butter-soft, hideously extravagant leather briefcase was the ovulation predictor kit she was now organizing her life around.

A future without a child now seemed utterly unbearable.

But nothing went to plan and by Sunday she was furious. She was left pacing up and down the flat, barely knowing what to do with herself. Over on the windowsill of the large, airy sitting room she saw her cigarette packet. Only three left, damn.

So much for a love-in. The weekend had been a complete disaster. On Friday evening Don had gone on one of his legendary marathon drinking bouts and there was nothing she could say, shout or even scream down the mobile at him to make him come home.

He hadn't staggered in till the early hours of Saturday morning and then he'd spent most of the day asleep. She had been monumentally angry with him and he couldn't really understand why.

They had gone out for dinner on Saturday night, but Bella had spent most of the meal ranting at him for the night before and it wasn't until Sunday morning that they had finally had make-up sex.

They were still in bed when the phone rang and she knew as soon as Don had reached for a pen that he was being sent out on a job. He'd left for Wales soon after, telling her he could be away till the end of the week. She felt powerless, frustrated and furious. She was going to have to wait another whole month before they could try for a baby again.

She threw herself down on to the sofa and lit up. After a few drags, she decided to phone Tania.

It rang for a few moments before Tania picked up, sounding breathless.

'Hello?'

'Tani.'

'Bella!'

'Are you doing anything this afternoon that you can't get out of?'

'Hmm . . . sex?'

'You can get out of that!'

'Depends. How urgent is it?'

'Pretty urgent. I've been abandoned by my husband for the week and I haven't seen you in a towel for ages.'

'Gym it is, then.'

'When can you get there?'

'Three-ish??'

'I love you, Tan.'

'Sod off, I'll see you later.'

'Byeeeee.'

Tania and Bella's usual routine was a gruelling workout in the gym, followed by a swim, a sauna, then a long, gossipy meal with gin and tonics to start and a bottle of wine to follow, which undid all their hard work.

They had been friends since university where Bella had taken one look at Tania, the only other girl in their maths tutorial group, and fallen in love.

Tania was the most glamorous thing 18-year-old Bella had ever seen. She wore tight, short dresses, had masses of highlighted hair, two boyfriends, a French mother, and contact lenses. She smoked Marlboros, giggled in a tinkly, flirtatious way and drove to class in a scarlet, open-top Beetle.

Newly out of a feministy all girls school in Oxford, Bella could not have been more different. She wore jeans, Dr Martens and dark jumpers, accessorized with short hair, glasses and about ten pounds of excess puppy fat. She always took the tube and was virginally single.

Bella had assumed there was absolutely no hope of Tania ever talking to her, let alone becoming a friend. But she'd been wrong. Tania was, like the rest of the class, in awe of Bella's freaky maths genius and determined to get to know her better. Underneath the dweeby, spec-wearing exterior, Tania found Bella a surprisingly funny, upbeat, ambitious kind of girl – ripe for a makeover and had seen her as something of a project.

Tania had taken her to the gym, the hairdresser and even out shopping with her impossibly chic mother, Valerie. Bella still followed Valerie's make-up advice: 'Always Chanel darlings, anything else *rrrruins* the skin – and take it off with cleanser, not this terrible soap.'

By the time Bella left university she was slimmer than Tania, had longer hair, eyes which had been surgically corrected and was madly in love with Daniel, her boyfriend of two years. She also knew exactly where she was going next – straight into a graduate traineeship with Laurence and Co.

Her own parents had been horrified at the transformation, especially her mother. Celia Browning, the wife of an Oxford professor, had put her own academic ambitions on hold to have children. She had settled on a career teaching maths at a very good school but had always felt disappointed with her choice, especially as she'd only managed to have one child and she'd had to watch her husband's stellar academic career from the side-lines.

What she'd always wanted for Bella, who had even more ability than her, was the prestigious university path she'd turned down. But Bella had deserted that for a job in the City! The City! Where you didn't even need a maths O Level to get on. It still made her feel physically ill. No matter how hard she tried to analyse it, she basically didn't understand Bella, had no idea why her gifted daughter had wanted this sort of career. She thought it deeply unsettling that Bella worked shoulder to shoulder with the City sharks, squeezing companies and having people sacked, all in the pursuit of a vastly inflated salary.

She understood Bella's fascination with herself even less, although Celia never mentioned this now. Her daughter's long hair, painted nails, high shoes and short skirts made such a mockery of all the ideals she had tried to instil in her.

Their one argument about this had gone very badly, because Bella had been furious enough to bring up the G-strings. One afternoon when she was about 13 years old, Bella had been poking about in her parents' wardrobes trying on jumpers and jackets. There was never anything sparkly or fun to be found in her mother's side of the cupboards, just grey, black and beige knitted separates and trouser suits. Her schoolmarmish mum had the plainest, frumpiest taste in the world.

Bella had put on one of her father's tweed jackets, turned up the collars, stuck her hands in the pockets and pulled out a pair of pale pink G-strings. On closer examination, she saw they were stretch cotton and unwashed. They were nothing like the sensible white Sloggi briefs her mother kept in the underwear drawer.

With rather stunning naivety, she'd actually shown them to her mother, laughing and teasing her about how uncomfortable they must be.

Celia had snatched the knickers out of her hands and in a shaking voice demanded to know where Bella had found them. When Bella said in her father's jacket pocket, her mother had turned white and without the need for another word, Bella had received her very first painful lesson in her father's fondness for fucking his poetry students.

So, years later, when Bella and her mother had argued furiously about the rights and wrongs of dressing to impress the boys, Bella had of course been angry enough to bring up the G-string incident, telling her mother that if she'd tried a bit harder, maybe her dad wouldn't have looked elsewhere.

It had been an unforgivable thing to say, she'd known that as soon as she'd said it. Her weeping mother had accepted her apology but Bella knew she'd done something she couldn't take back.

Neither of Bella's parents had yet reconciled themselves to her whirlwind marriage to a forty-something tabloid journalist. They had argued and argued against it, racking up monster bills on the telephone from their retirement villa in Italy. They had not come to the wedding, had refused to meet Don, and Bella had not seen them since, although once a month or so they spoke awkwardly on the phone and Bella e-mailed them a little more often than that.

It had not helped Don's case that her father had once ended up in the Sunday tabloids after a disciplinary hearing about an 'improper' relationship with a student. 'Professor Perv' they'd labelled him, of course. And how Celia had rallied to the cause, standing by her man and claiming it was all untrue.

Her father had moved sideways into a different department, just for a term, and once the fuss had died down, Celia had suffered a very quiet nervous breakdown and gone into therapy, which had lasted for years. It was her dad who'd fucked around, but her mother was labelled 'the problem'. The injustice of this still enraged Bella.

So, when she'd moved to London and discovered Tania and a whole new way of life, she'd cheerfully stuck two fingers up to her supposedly liberal-intellectual upbringing and decided to rebel.

After their gym session, Bella and Tania went back to Tania's new flat. All her friend's fussing over paint shades and curtain fabric made Bella realize how much she wanted to have a home of her own. How did she get to be so old without ever owning property, she wondered?

She didn't exactly envy Tania her love life, though. Bella made the mistake of admiring an exquisite gold and diamond bangle Tania was wearing and Tania dissolved into tears.

'What's the matter?' Bella asked, putting an arm round her shoulder.

'Oh darling. It's bloody Greg. This must be about

the fifth time he's brought home a pale blue box from Tiffany's and I've thought "Thank you God, he's finally going to propose" . . . only to open it and find a bracelet, a brooch, a necklace . . . any bloody piece of jewellery you like, apart from a ring.'

'Does he know you want to get married?' Bella felt she had to ask the obvious.

'Well, it's not just something you come out with, is it? I bloody well want to be asked. I don't want to propose to him. It should be damn well obvious I want to marry him. Otherwise, why would I still be with him?'

'Maybe he thinks you're happy not being married. I mean you're not even living together,' Bella said.

'He's the one who insists we have our own flats. He says it's a better investment and he only lives around the corner from this place. That's why I moved.'

There was a pause, then Tania quickly wiped her eyes and tried very hard to stem the flow of tears.

'God, I'm sorry. I hate sounding like some sad woman obsessed with getting a ring on my finger like you used to be,' she joked.

'No I did not,' Bella replied. 'I never wanted to get married at all. It was Don who insisted . . .' *Shut up, shut up, you're not helping*, she told herself.

Spookily Greg and Don were the same age. She'd always wondered if Tania hadn't been in search of a Don of her own when she found Greg. But whereas Don was a free-thinking, rolling stone, rebel 41, Greg was a bloody boring, banking, masses of personal finance plans 41. Maybe Tania craved the security, but he didn't seem to give her that either,

51

and it was weird the way he wasn't even hinting at marriage. Men like him were usually desperate to get all traditional and settle down.

'Let's talk about work,' Tania broke the silence. 'I'm brilliant at work, you know. In fact, I have a client who's looking for a good consultant, I must give you his number.'

Bella got a very good idea of how well Tania's PR company was going when Tania named the client. Hugely impressed, Bella passed the information on to Chris when he came back to the office on Wednesday.

'You realize we're going to be late tonight?' Chris said, as he headed back to his room. 'They need those proposals stitched up by start of play tomorrow.'

'Yeah, it's no problem, I've nothing else planned,' she told him, thinking that it would be their first time alone together since the night in the taxi.

By 8 p.m. everyone else had gone out and Chris asked her to set out papers and plans on the big table in the communal office space while he finished off some other work in his office. She was leaning over to study one of the charts when he came out and walked over to stand right beside her. She didn't look round, but felt the hairs on the back of her neck move.

'I do remember exactly how the office night out ended, you know, and I suspect that you do too,' he said in a low voice. 'I just need to know how you feel, Bella.'

She turned then and looked into the dark eyes riveted on her and somehow the words 'Chris,

I'm married' just did not want to come out.

She parted her lips to say something, but Chris had already moved in and they were kissing, then biting, grabbing at each other, teeth banging together.

Chris broke off from her lips to suck at her neck then moved down, pulling open her blouse buttons. He pushed up against her so she was wedged tightly between his hard-on and the edge of the table.

He was pressing his hips into hers and she was on fire. The blood pounding in her ears overruled every sane objection. She closed her eyes, felt for his belt buckle and could only think about the thrill of having frenzied sex on the office table.

An incredible rush was starting to take hold of her. She gripped the warm skin under his shirt and moved against his erection. 'Oh God,' she heard herself whisper. She could feel nothing but adrenalin surging through her veins, she was that junkie finally giving in.

She unzipped him and put her hand inside, hearing him groan. His hands were under her skirt now, rubbing the skin at the very top of her thighs while he kissed and licked at her mouth.

Her heels lifted off the floor as he slid his fingers under her knickers and moved them around, feeling how wet she was. She was so turned on, she could barely breathe.

As his finger ran up and down her clitoris, she kissed him and tasted coffee. Dizzy with pleasure, she let him lift her onto the table and pull up her skirt.

'Is this OK?' he whispered, pulling her knickers

to one side as he pushed his warm cock up close.

'Oh yeah, yeah,' she murmured and then heard the unmistakable ping of the lift doors opening in the hall. SHIT.

They jumped apart, hurtling back to reality, and scrambled to sort out their clothes as Susan walked in.

Shit, shit, mega shit. Susan must have guessed. How could she have missed it? The two of them must have looked like startled rabbits. SHIT.

However, Susan gave nothing away, she simply said: 'Hello, working hard I hope?' and went into her office, but pointedly left the door ajar.

There was nothing Chris and Bella could do apart from shakily get down to work again. Several hours later, when Chris was on the phone, Bella took the chance to slip out.

The cool night air hit her like a slap in the face. What the fuck am I doing??? Fuck, fuck, almost completely fucked, she thought. Opening the low door of her sleek little car, she flung in her bags before scrambling in, then slammed the door shut and shouted at herself: '*Bella*, you slut. You totally idiotic slut.'

The reality of the situation was beginning to sink in. She had just cheated on Don. Why? What for? A few minutes of tabletop action with one of her *bosses*. Thank God Susan had walked in.

She fired up her engine but for a moment could only see blur in front of her eyes before tears spilled down her cheeks. She was the worst person in the world. 'What is the matter with me? Am I out of my mind?'

Her mobile began to ring, she picked it up and

saw the call was from the office. She switched it off and sped out of the car park before Chris could catch up with her.

Somehow by the time she put her trainers on and started pounding the pavement early the next morning, the situation did not seem nearly so gruesome. OK she had come within a hair's breadth of an enormous, big-time, major mistake, but she hadn't had sex with Chris, quite, and now she knew she absolutely should not, *no way*. She was married, committed, trying to get pregnant for God's sake, and anyway, Chris was a boss. It was totally against the rules.

When she got into work, there was of course an e-mail waiting for her.

Bella, I'm out of the office all day today and tomorrow, but could we talk? Is there any chance of meeting for a quick drink tonight? Chris

She was going to have to nip this straight in the bud . . . but very nicely. She opened a new file and started typing.

Chris, what can I say? That was a lot of fun, totally unexpected. But I feel really bad today. Really bad. I'm married. And I'm sorry if I've made you think, well, what can I say?

I love working with you and I would hate to have spoiled that. Can we possibly put last night behind us and be 'just good friends' again? I'll meet you tonight if it would help, but I don't want to give you the wrong idea. Bella.

Just minutes after she had hit send, the inbox flashed. She felt a flicker of nervousness as she opened the file. Chris was her boss, after all and she was blowing him out big time.

Friends????? Oh. OK.

I am a bit hurt.

But you are being very sensible. Forget tonight, I'll see you soon.

She sent back a simple 'thanks' and crossed her fingers that things were going to be OK, then she got down to the only thing that would take her mind off all this madness. Work.

Don came home close to midnight on Friday. His story had finally come off and was splashing in the paper tomorrow, so he was in a fantastically good mood. She met him at the front door showered, wrapped up in her silk robe and smelling delicious.

'Hello, fantasy wife,' he said giving her as much of a hug as he could without squashing his armful of goodies.

'Hi, I've missed you loads,' she said, feeling the stab of guilt hit her right on the breastbone.

'This is for us.' He waved a champagne bottle.

'This is for me.' He jiggled his takeaway bag.

'And these are for you.' He held out a scruffy bunch of petrol station roses.

'Thank you. These are for you,' she laughed and pulled open her gown to flash her breasts at him.

He plonked everything down on the floor and moved in for a proper kiss.

After a few moments, he broke away saying, 'It's no use, Bella, I am going to have to eat first, I'm absolutely starving.'

He ate the takeaway in bed, drinking champagne with her and telling her the week's adventures. When he'd finished, he leaned over, kissed her on the forehead and apologized for the weekend before.

'Don, I've already forgotten about it.' He had nothing to apologize for compared with her. But in her experience, unprompted confessions were always a mistake.

'You're so self-contained and self-sufficient,' he said. 'I sometimes forget that you might want me around more. I'm not going to dare suggest that you might "need" me around.'

'Of course I need you,' she said, wrapping herself around him. 'We all need to be loved and held and brought to incredible sexual climax.'

He smiled broadly. Putting the foil dishes on the floor, he said: 'OK, can we start making up now?'

Her dressing gown slid down over her shoulders as he kissed and touched her slowly.

She helped him out of his clothes until they were curled up naked together on the bed where they made love tenderly, looking deep into each other's eyes and Bella realized how much she loved him. What the hell had she been doing? This was where she belonged. Don was her real life action hero, he went to war zones, had even resuscitated someone from a heart attack, for God's sake. Next to Don, most other men seemed pretty tame. Her infatuation with Chris suddenly made her want to laugh.

She also saw that it was crazy to be trying to get

pregnant without Don knowing. They needed to figure this out together, they needed to buy a house and anyway, work was about to get very busy again. Two major new clients had been taken on and she was going to be doing at least one of the restructurings herself for the first time.

The next day Bella went into town and bashed her credit card buying a scarily expensive new work suit, just to underline her new resolve.

Chapter Five

It came as something of a shock when she double-checked her dates and there was no doubt about it: her period was five days late.

At lunchtime she slunk out to Boots and bought The Test, feeling rising panic as she handed over the cash and stuffed the box into her briefcase.

By 6 p.m. she couldn't stand the tension any longer, so she e-mailed round the office that she had drinks with a prospective client, and left.

She rushed back with the test burning a hole in her bag all the way home. By the time she finally made it through the door she was so desperate to get this over with that she went straight into the bathroom.

She dumped her briefcase and laptop on the floor, then fished out the Boots bag.

OK, pee on stick, watch result come up one minute later. Not exactly rocket science, then.

So, once the stick was peed on, should she sit watching it for a minute or turn it over and wait? She went with turning it over. She looked at her watch: no second hand, she would have to count.

Suddenly she felt unable to breathe, let alone count. She stood up, pulled up her knickers, smoothed down her skirt and jacket and hung her coat up on the bathroom hook.

Hell, it must be time by now.

As she put her fingers on the stick, she noticed that her hands were trembling. She turned it over and there it was, the second thin blue line that meant yes. She was totally shocked.

She slumped back onto the loo seat with the result in her hands and stared and stared at it. Her mind went blank.

She'd thought she'd wanted a baby . . . but did she really? Now? Starting now . . . possibly arriving in nine, God no, eight months' time? And like this? With Don not knowing? Oh God, this did not feel right at all.

Too shocked to cry, she stuffed the test into its box and went to the bedroom where she hid it in a drawer. She could hear her mobile ringing and went to find her briefcase.

'Hello?' she said, trying to sound bright.

'Hi, hon, it's me,' came Don's voice.

'Hello, are you on your way back?'

'Yeah. What shall we do for supper?'

'I don't know, I haven't thought about it.'

'Is there stuff in the fridge?'

'I'll have a look. How's your day been anyway?' she asked, heading for the kitchen.

'Not too bad. You?'

'Yeah, OK. Right . . . chicken breasts, some peppers, onions. I think we have noodles. Would that do?'

'Fine, I'll see you soon then.'

'Byee.'

'Bye.'

Bella was so distracted that evening, Don wondered if she was OK.

'Just tired,' she kept telling him when he asked. But she seemed too fidgety and restless for a tired person. Finally, she said she was taking a bath and going to bed early, but he noticed she took her laptop with her into the bedroom.

Almost an hour later, he went in to check on her and found her propped up in bed, staring at the screen. 'What's up?' he asked gently. 'Is it work?'

'No, no,' she looked up at him with a surprisingly sombre expression, 'I was just e-mailing Jenna . . . you know, my friend in New York, but I don't know, it's not flowing tonight.' She gave a forced smile.

'How is she?' asked Don.

'Very well. She's got a great new job and she's moving to California and it looks as if her man might be moving with her, but she's a bit scared I suppose. She e-mailed me the other day asking about you and marriage and how would she know if, you know, he was The One . . .' Bella trailed off.

'Ah-ha and you're sitting there stuck for words about us?' Don smiled at her. 'Come on, move over, I'm the wordsmith.'

He sat down beside her. Their conversation had lasted just long enough for Bella to have quietly deleted all the soul-searching about the pregnancy she'd written to Jenna.

'OK.' He pulled the computer into his lap and tapped in his rapid two-fingered type: 'How You Know If It's Love' as a heading, then underneath:

'You just know. You'll feel it somewhere between your breastbone and your stomach. No individual details matter: looks, height, hair colour, job description – that person makes you happy, gives you a warm glow,' 'No,' he hit delete. 'That sounds like Ready Brek'. 'Gives you security, comfort,' he typed, 'makes you laugh, makes love like it really matters. You'll go the extra mile for them and you know they'll do it for you.'

'Oh, that's so sweet,' Bella said reading over his shoulder.

'Sweet?' He was smiling at her. 'I set out my philosophy of love and all you can say is sweet?'

'Errr . . .'

'You're embarrassed, aren't you? Do you love me even half as much as I love you?' He was still smiling but she detected an undertow of seriousness.

'Of course I do, Don, of course.'

'That's OK then.'

She put her arms round him and kissed him on the mouth, but she couldn't sum up the courage to tell him.

One week later, she still hadn't told him she was pregnant. She was scared. This was going to be a monumentally big thing for him – his life was about to take an entirely different turn than on the route he had mapped out with her. As she lay in bed beside him, she wondered if she really knew him well enough to guess how he would react.

Almost exactly one year ago now, they'd rushed into marriage at the Chelsea register office. It had been a cool wedding with not a shred of the white or traditional about it. Well, there hadn't been time to arrange all that for a start. As soon as she'd said yes, Don had fixed up the first available date at the registrar's, convinced she might change her mind.

She'd worn a long, tight, wine-coloured lace dress with her hair up. Don was in slightly rumpled black linen and somehow ended up carrying the flowers.

There had been just a small crowd – close friends and as few relatives as they could get away with, made easier by the fact her own parents didn't come. Everyone had taxied to Claridges for a monumental lunch, then Don and Bella had sent the guests on their way so they could start their honeymoon.

In their wonderful room, they had filled the enormous bathtub to the brim with hot water and foam and moved in there for hours swigging gloriously expensive champagne out of the bottle, singing love songs and having giggly sex, trying to avoid impaling each other on the taps or causing too disastrous a tidal wave.

It had been so romantic. Lying in the dark now, Bella couldn't help smiling as she cuddled up close to Don listening to him breathe. Everything about him coming into her life had been romantic, interesting and full of fun.

It was such a fluke they had even met. She had been in a crowded, noisy bar with workmates. A bar she'd never been in before and would never have gone back to. As she had tried to spark up her zillionth fag of the evening, her lighter had died.

She'd tugged at the sleeve of the nearest person to ask for a light. It was Don who'd turned around and glanced at her, then held the look with obvious interest.

She'd lifted her cigarette, raised her eyebrows and said: 'Light?'

His reply, with just a hint of melting Scottish burr, was: 'I knew one day I'd regret not being a smoker.'

She had smiled wide and warm and they had looked each other over approvingly.

'Too bad,' she'd said. 'D'you want to buy me a drink instead?'

'Yes, please,' he'd answered, 'Why didn't I think of that first?'

She'd been unable to stop herself from adding archly: 'It's OK. Most girls don't like a man who's always first.'

They had stood at the bar and talked while the attraction between them built up to bonfire level.

He was clearly gorgeous, intelligent, very interested, ringless. His hand had been round her waist before they had finished their first drink together. She had immediately liked everything about him. He was tall, in a nice suit but he made it look casual with his unbuttoned shirt collar revealing a beaten-up white T-shirt. She'd noticed his clumpy crêpe-soled boots and black plastic diving watch.

He seemed so relaxed and refreshingly individual – a journalist, not another financial clone. She could tell he was way old, in his forties, but it made him more interesting. She'd liked his face, comfortably worn in and full of character. His humour was dark and cynical but he seemed to like her upbeat optimism and she'd never met a man who could quote Machiavelli and Woody Allen back at her.

'God, aren't you a bit young to be a fascist?' he'd asked her with a grin.

'But I'm so attracted to the style, you know, polished leather boots, white marble, geometrically perfect haircuts,' she'd shot back.

They'd looked at each other, laughed and almost kissed right then, but both their mobile phones had gone off at once.

'Whooo . . . synchronicity,' Don had said before answering.

'So what do you do?' she remembered him asking and when she'd answered 'Management consultant', he'd looked utterly appalled.

'Oh God,' he'd said. 'You are quite the City girl, aren't you? So you get paid stacks of money by the big boys to go in and sack people?'

'*Hey*!' she'd rounded on him. 'Just a minute. I've turned loads of companies around that would have gone under costing everyone their jobs. And anyway, I only work for medium-sized finance companies and I have a lot of principles, thank you. What about you? Mr Supposedly Free-Thinking Rebel, you work for Totally Evil Global News Inc!!' she teased. 'And I bet you wear Levi's and Nikes, and look, you're drinking Budweiser and probably do Starbucks three times a day so, hey! Don't talk to me about selling my soul to the big corporations.'

'OK.' He was startled now and pulled a frightened face at her to make her laugh, but it didn't work.

'God,' she'd continued angrily: 'Why do people get so Luddite about big businesses? They're just made up of people, people with mortgages and families and ideas. And if you don't get big companies to change and treat their employees well and not devastate the environment, where do you start?'

'Sorry . . . I'm surprised you've given this so much thought,' he'd said, then wished he hadn't when she answered: 'Why? Because I'm a well-paid girlie??'

'Look I'm impressed . . . it's OK. God, you don't drink Starbucks?' He'd tried to lighten the tone.

'*No*. I make my own coffee!'

'At work?'

'Yeah.'

'I'm very impressed. And you don't wear trainers?'

'No, well, unless they're made in the EU – *don't laugh*! The people who made these shoes,' she'd held out her foot, showing off high-heeled mock snakeskin, 'are entitled to sick pay, trade union membership, a year's maternity leave . . .'

'Ah, but what about the tobacco growers?' he cut in, pointing at her cigarette.

'Well . . . OK, you have spotted my Achilles' heel there. I mean I've tried the ethical, additive-free ones but, just not the same.' She'd taken a hefty drag and smiled at him. He was lovely.

After their final drink, she'd decided to throw to the wind all her advice to herself to stay off men for a while and had asked him: 'So Starbucks drinker, would you like to try my coffee? Very strong espresso, keeps you up all night.'

'Yes please,' he'd said and steered her out of the bar.

They'd kissed for the first time on the pavement outside, then over and over in the back of the cab. She'd been so turned on, she'd found it difficult to unlock the door to her flat. When she finally got it open, they had rushed in and were eating each other up in the hallway, throwing coats, bags and jackets to the floor.

Then Don had slowed down to kiss her with surprising tenderness. Gently he had unbuttoned her blouse and slid her bra straps over her shoulders so he could kiss her nipples. They had made love for the first time standing up in the hall. It was incredibly passionate and yet went so smoothly.

For once she'd been wearing a skirt which wasn't too tight to hitch up, and Don had braces on so his trousers didn't fall down round his ankles.

It could still make her pulse rise if she thought about how helpless, how loose-kneed with lust she'd felt when he had moved a finger expertly between her legs to feel for her clitoris for the very first time.

It was his relaxed assuredness, his complete confidence in himself that she found the most incredible turn-on. He even had a condom on him which he had taken out of his wallet, murmuring 'You must think I'm such a slut' into her ear. And every hair from her ear lobe to her shoulder blade had pricked up with pleasure.

'Likewise,' she'd whispered back, closing her eyes, leaning back, impatient to be kissed fiercely, penetrated, pushed up hard against the wall by such a good-looking, virile man.

He'd lifted her just slightly onto her tiptoes to

take him inside. And as he'd entered her for the first time, she'd let out a sigh of pleasure. For a moment she didn't know what the sensation was, then she realized that he was a breathtakingly perfect fit.

He'd whispered, 'God this feels so right. You're incredible.'

Throughout that fantastic first fuck, in which they had come almost together, she had allowed herself to think the forbidden thought – that she had finally found her match.

Don had stayed with her for the rest of the weekend and had teased her relentlessly about her bare flat.

'There is nothing here, have you just moved in?' he'd asked, looking round on Saturday morning and taking in the sitting room furnished only with a sofa, TV, side table and stack of pink *FT*s and business books.

It was a lovely flat though, two big rooms, large floor to ceiling windows, a galley kitchen, bathroom and a tiny roof terrace.

'Well, five months ago. I'm not here much,' she'd said defensively, knowing he was guessing at her astronomical rent.

'Nope, you're not.' He'd opened her fridge. 'Is that it?!' he'd asked, seeing just yoghurt and oranges.

'I suppose I eat out lots or take away. I'm a complete workaholic, you should know that about me,' she'd answered.

'Should I?' he'd said wrapping his arms around her and gathering her up in a sexy, protective way. 'You mean, if we're going to take this any further.' He'd smiled at her.

68

'How much further is there to go?' she'd teased back.

He'd answered: 'Oh a lot. A lot further. I really like you.' And she'd felt deliriously happy.

They spent the rest of the weekend talking and talking, in cafés, in bars, in the park, in bed – in between the marathon sex sessions – and both of them felt an amazing connection.

It wasn't that sort of cliché-d liking all the same things, but a fascination for how different they were. Grown-up, cynical rebel versus young, go-ahead, corporate girl. He wasn't at all interested in money, which intrigued her because she aspired to being fantastically rich, which in turn intrigued him. He adored his mother, she . . . well it was complicated. He'd left school at 16, she'd been steeped in over-education since the day she was born.

They were so interested in each other it had felt as if they couldn't ever know enough. A lifetime of talking wouldn't be enough. But when Sunday night finally arrived and Don said he would have to go back to his flat and get ready for the week, she'd had a flicker of doubt. Could this really happen? Would he call? Would they ever see each other again?

Just as she'd prepared to face the melancholy of a Sunday night alone after two unbelievable days like this, he'd said: 'Why don't you come with me? Pack your overnight bag and drive me down.'

She'd flung her work clothes into a holdall before he could change his mind.

Of course he'd been *über*-impressed with her car. 'They don't cost that much,' she'd admitted straight away. 'And I got quite a bit of money on my 21st.' Aaargh. Too late.

'You still have your 21st birthday present?' He'd sounded shocked,' Oh my God, I'm dating a child.'

Oh yes, dear reader, it was only day two and he distinctly said 'dating'. Now it was her turn to be shocked.

'Cars are very important,' she'd told him as they'd pulled out into the road and she'd recovered the power of speech.

'Why?'

'They're like clothes – the outward expression of our inner desires and aspirations.'

'And I thought they were quite a good way to get around.'

'Yeah, right. And let me guess exactly which type of large, chunky off-roader you drive, my friend.'

He was really surprised now.

'See! I'm always right. Some people can guess star signs. I can guess cars. I'm seeing large, dark colour, mega-horsepower, very thirsty jeep-type. I'll go for the classic Cherokee.'

'I must have told you that!'

'You did not!' she was mock indignant now.

Of course, his flat had been the opposite of hers: a low-ceilinged dark basement, crammed full. Every wall was lined with bookcases stuffed not just with books but with old cameras, mini tape recorders, PC disks, candle ends, ornaments, light bulbs, mugs filled with pens, photos, framed and unframed, socks! Jesus, not even her cleaner could help him now, he needed a feng shui expert or maybe a skip.

But it wasn't grubby, thankfully. Doing the

guided tour, he'd showed her his room and she'd seen clean white sheets. In the contrastingly spartan bathroom there was evidence that someone had done all the essential cleaning jobs not too long ago.

She admired his hardware – top of the range stereo, widescreen TV and two very sleek computers, 'One's from the office,' he'd explained.

He had made her tea in a patterned china teapot with loose leaves and it was really good, even though she only ever drank coffee. Then he got out an ancient-looking bottle of whisky and they cuddled up on his shabby sofa, with a worn tartan rug flung over it, and got mellow-drunk together.

She'd sat up to light a cigarette and moved to face him, cross-legged, as she smoked it.

'So, what are you like? What do you like to do?' he'd asked.

'Hey big scary journalist,' she'd teased. 'Is this your standard prospective girlfriend interview?'

'Maybe . . .' he'd smiled.

'OK, let me think . . . I mainly work. I love my job. If I'm not working I'm either out eating, drinking or smoking. I go gym-ing or shopping to relax. I used to spend a lot of my spare time having sex with unfamiliar people in unfamiliar places. But I'm trying to cure that habit and apart from the occasional relapse . . .' they'd both laughed, 'I now spend a lot more time reading. Newspapers – but not yours – business books, books from the dodgy "Mind, body, spirit" section. Why am I telling you this?' They'd laughed again.

'I'm not going to pretend I go to the theatre or art shows,' she added. 'Who has time to do that in London? Just tourists and the unemployed.'

'Heretic!' he'd said.

'God . . . I'm always so disappointed by the theatre and postmodern art, or post-postmodern or whatever the hell it is these days, don't get me started!'

'Why do people your age always make me feel so young?' Don had asked. 'You're so grown-up and sensible. I bet you have investments.'

'We didn't all have the luxury of growing up in an economic boom, you know, when teenagers like you could just grow your hair and head off into the sunset in sandals,' she'd said.

When he laughed at this, she'd asked: 'Did anyone you knew at school have their family home repossessed? Didn't think so.'

There was a pause and Bella had changed the subject, not wanting to dwell on how much older he was. 'How long have you owned this place?'

'I've been here two years. I rent it, actually, from a mate.' That had surprised her.

'It's a bit of a hole,' he'd added. 'Damp, the odd mouse, not very warm in the winter. I think I'll move in with you.' This was meant as a joke but they'd looked at each other and just knew it was going to happen.

When she'd reached up to kiss him, he'd responded so passionately that within moments they'd been fumbling with each other's clothes desperate to make love again. And the sex was so good, it was almost a disappointment when it was over and they were too played-out to do it again. Later, she'd told him they should take two weeks to think about it. He'd said she was being wonderfully sensible and that was what he loved about her. The L-word within 48 hours!

Two weeks later he'd moved in – minus most of his stuff. That had been her other condition.

As Bella lay in bed, remembering their first weekend together and the wedding, she knew Don loved her, would love her no matter what. She wondered why she had been so nervous of telling him about the baby. It was time for him to know. She'd tell him tomorrow, on their wedding anniversary.

The next evening, 10 October, they went out for dinner at the restaurant they'd been to on their first proper night out.

Bella decided to wait until she was a couple of glasses of wine down before breaking the news. But then the starters came and she thought she'd hang on a bit longer. Once the waiter had cleared their plates, she took a few more hefty swigs from her glass and brought her cigarettes out of her handbag to steady her nerves.

'You're not going to smoke now, are you?' Don asked with a frown. 'We're in the middle of our meal.'

'Don, we're between courses. Please don't nag. I've had a very long day and I'm just trying to unwind.'

'It's just so anti-social.'

'Oh shut up, will you. I never vowed to give up smoking when I married you, so stop nagging.'

Silence. Oh bloody great, thought Bella, why don't I just start a row? That'll really create the right atmosphere for a pregnancy announcement.

'I'm sorry, Don. Let's talk about something else.'

She took a last long drag and stubbed her cigarette out in the ashtray. 'What do you think about buying a house together?' she asked.

'I think it's a great idea,' he said then reached over and took her hand. 'I know I've always said I was happy renting and I didn't want all the baggage of owning a place, but now I think it would be really nice. I'd like us to have a home.'

'Oh, that's so sweet,' she said.

'I know. Sickly,' he smiled.

She could feel her eyes start to swim. She took a breath and was on the verge . . . but the waiter interrupted the moment by arriving with their food.

There was silence between them as they ate the first mouthfuls.

'Delicious,' said Bella.

'Brilliant,' Don agreed with his mouth full.

After another long pause, Don looked up at her and asked: 'Is there a problem at work? You seem really tense tonight.'

'Umm . . . no,' she answered. 'It's something else.'

She looked up at him and tried to sound calm: 'There's something I've got to tell you. I'm sorry I haven't told you before, but I've been really worried about how you would take it.'

'OK . . .' he was smiling at her, wondering why she looked so deadly serious.

'You've reached the limit on your credit card,' he said, still smiling, then when she didn't laugh, added: 'It can't be that bad. This is me you're talking to, I'm sure we can handle it.'

'Well . . .' This was it. She took a deep breath then blurted out: 'I'm pretty sure I'm pregnant. No, make that, I am pregnant.'

Nothing but absolute, expressionless silence from Don. Whole minutes seemed to go by, then he said in a quiet voice: 'Christ Almighty. Do you want to keep it?'

Of all the replies she'd anticipated, this had not been one of them.

They sat there motionless, staring at each other, and Bella realized she was close to tears. She asked in a raised voice: 'How could you ask that? Of course I do.'

In confusion, she stood up to leave but Don grabbed her by the wrist and pulled her down into her seat again. He was shouting at her too, but in a sort of whisper: 'Jesus, how do you expect me to react? I can't believe it. How did it happen? I thought you were on the pill.'

She didn't say anything, so he want on: 'I just asked that because you looked so unhappy. I thought you were going to tell me you wanted to . . . terminate. You've always said you didn't want children. You're mad about your job and everything. I mean, have you really thought about what a baby will mean?'

She couldn't bear to hear this any more. She wrenched her wrist free and stood up, hissing at him, 'Yes I have, Don. Yes, it's a surprise but I was beginning to think it was a good one. I'm sorry you don't feel the same way. Fuck . . .'

She picked up her bag and headed for the coat check, trying not to stumble in the blur of tears.

A little later, the waiter went over to the table. He picked up Don's empty plate and Bella's cold, almost untouched one. 'She didn't like it?' he asked with a sympathetic smile.

'No, she didn't like it one little bit,' Don answered. 'I think I'll have a large whisky, please.'

'Of course, sir.'

As he sat in the restaurant drinking, still in a state of considerable shock, Bella was in the back of a taxi. She didn't really want to go home, but she couldn't think of anywhere else she wanted to go either.

Just as the cab approached the flat, she got the driver to pull up outside the wine shop on the corner. She jumped out and went to buy a very expensive bottle of white and 20 Marlboro Lights. She paid with the one credit card in her purse she'd never used before – card number two on Don's account which he made her carry just in case she needed money when all her own cards were maxed – and that made her feel slightly better.

She planned to down a few glasses, have a couple of cigarettes, cry a bit more, then sleep on it. She felt sure Don wouldn't dare approach her again until the morning.

Once she finally fell asleep, she slept for a long time and didn't wake up till late. The bedroom was exactly as she had left it, Don hadn't been in at all. But she could hear the shower running, so he was home.

She lay in bed wondering what they were going to say to each other. She didn't feel angry any more, in fact she felt calm. They were going to work this out: they had to. She tied on her dressing gown and opened the bedroom door. The hall was full of roses, about six enormous bunches of them – red, white, yellow, pink. The sitting room door was open and she could see even more flowers in there.

Roses were crammed into vases, cups, mugs,

teapots, even the kettle. Pink and red carnations had been threaded onto string and pinned to the wall, which looked ridiculous, but she appreciated the sentiment.

Well, kind of. It was a bit cheesy and it did cross her mind to get out the scissors and snip all the heads off to show Don she wasn't going to be mollified by a bunch of flowers, no matter how big. The shower was off now and she decided she might as well go and hear what he had to say first, then decide if the flowers should be decapitated.

Don was standing in the bathroom, dripping wet with a towel round his waist.

As soon as he saw her, he said: 'Sorry, Bella. I'm really sorry. I don't know what else to say.'

'Thank you for the flowers,' she said.

'Oh yes. I had to buy them to get a lift home.'

'What d'you mean?'

'I spent hours walking around town and I got completely lost. I finally met this guy setting up his flower stall and I said I'd buy the lot if he took me and the flowers home. We need more vases, you know.'

She gave a little laugh at this.

Then he added: 'I was walking all night thinking about you and us and . . . a baby.' He moved to put his wet arms around her. 'And I still can't get my head round it.'

That didn't sound good. She waited, wondering if he was going to say anything else.

'I still think of myself as young with so much to do before I settle down. The reality is, I'm going to be 42 next year, I'm married and I'm going to be a father. That's quite a shock.'

'You haven't got the monopoly on being worried, you know,' Bella said.

'I need to think about this.' He put his hand on her hair. 'I mean, I think it's going to be OK. I think it will be fine . . . if you're sure it's what you want.'

'Yeah,' she whispered, 'I think so.'

'Well OK, let's try and get used to the idea.'

'OK, that's fine Don . . . that's fine.' She hugged him tightly.

Chapter Six

She dropped her knees down and stared at a crack
in the ceiling, trying to relax as she felt the cold steel
go in. How did this whole cervical smear thing
start? she wondered. Did women campaign for
this? Or did doctors invent them?

God, even root canal work would be better than
lying here on an examination couch being terribly
polite and civilized as some nurse she'd never met
before cranked open her vagina with a speculum
and scraped at her with a wooden spatula.

She had finally made it to the doctor's and sitting
down on the little chair opposite Dr Wilson's vast
desk, she had told him her period was 26 days late
and, well, it looked like she was pregnant.

He had looked at her slowly over his glasses
obviously trying to decide if she was being funny
or merely stupid and said in his usual mono-
tone, 'Hmmm, here's a specimen bottle, shall we
check?'

And surprise, surprise, she was definitely still
pregnant. About seven weeks, he told her.

Then he weighed and measured her, took her

blood pressure and sat her down for a little 'lifestyle' chat.

She didn't hear anything she didn't already know – fresh fruit and vegetables, moderate exercise, lots of water, folic acid tablets – good. Alcohol, cigarettes, too much stress – bad.

'How much are you smoking a day?' he asked.

'About ten,' she lied.

'Well, you'll have to stop. If you absolutely can't stop, you'll have to cut it to below five. It's very dangerous for the baby, never mind what it's doing to you.'

'Well what about cocaine then?' She felt the mood needed lightening.

He didn't miss a beat, just said, 'We don't recommend it.'

He then asked her which hospital she wanted to go to.

'Hospital?' She was confused.

'For the birth.'

'Oh God. But it's not till next June. Do I have to decide now?'

His reply was a long 'Hmmmmmm.' Followed by: 'No. But it makes it easier for me.'

'Well, you're not the one having the baby, so I'll get back to you on that,' she said, delighted that for once she was going to come out of the doctor's surgery with the upper hand.

But then he had flicked through her notes and said, 'Ah, I see we are due for a smear test. If you let reception know, the nurse will see you in a few minutes.'

The next morning she got up very early to fit in her morning run before going all the way over to Hammersmith for day one at Merris Group.

Merris was her first solo project. She had won the work and Susan had assured her she was ready to handle this contract by herself. Of course she was nervous, make that very nervous, as she pounded along the pavement trying to pump the anxieties out of her system. It was a personal finance company, she reminded herself, her speciality . . . yes, but 'so *old* . . . so *establishment*,' came the little anxious voice. She ran faster to try and blot it out.

It was her job not to be scared, to be confident and absolutely sure of herself otherwise the whole business of advising companies on how to make far-reaching changes just didn't work. Her clients were like wolf packs, they could smell fear a mile off and hunted it down.

After her shower, she donned the armour for battle – serious make-up, a scraped-back bun and her smartest work outfit, white shirt, most expensive black suit, black stockings and high black shoes.

She'd been warned to leave her car behind, because there wasn't much parking space, so she picked up her papers from the stack at the front door and set off down the road to join the throng of cross-town commuters on the tube.

God, she'd forgotten how crowded and warm the trains were even this early in the morning. She took off her coat and managed to squeeze herself into one of the last seats left. Ten minutes later, she was feeling sweaty and nauseous. She put her papers down and closed her eyes, willing the journey to go quickly.

By 8 a.m. she was in Hammersmith feeling

unusually dizzy and drained. She could not face the ten-minute walk to the office so hailed a cab. She arrived at the stately-looking building and braced herself for the day ahead.

Come on, Bella, she told herself. Get it together.

Gathering up laptop, briefcase, handbag and coat, she somehow, with a third hand, paid the driver, then clacked up the marble steps and through the revolving door. At reception she announced herself and was told to join the executives upstairs for their breakfast conference.

In the lift she checked herself over in the mirrored wall. She felt queasy and extremely nervous, but thanks to the generous application of cosmetic aid, she looked groomed, professional and moderately beautiful. She took a deep breath and let it out slowly, then the lift pinged open and she headed for the conference room.

Opening the heavy door, she took in a large mahogany-panelled room, an enormous table with twenty or so heads swivelled in her direction and a side buffet heaped with plates of bacon, eggs, kedgeree, fried toast, croissants and steaming pots of coffee.

Nausea rose up in her throat like a hard ball and she broke out in a cold sweat. She could feel beads forming on her top lip and suddenly she knew what this was. Morning sickness. All eyes were fixed upon her and she was rooted to the spot, unable to open her mouth, convinced she was about to throw up on the highly polished parquet floor.

Somehow she managed to swallow the ball down and say: 'Hello everyone. I'm Bella Browning. Where would you like me to sit?'

She wobbled over to her seat while Mr Merris made the introductions. She accepted a cup of tea and as she sipped it she began to feel a tiny bit better. She glanced at the men around the table – all men, all older than her, all definitely thinking, What is this girl going to be able to do for us?

'We'll just run through our usual business first, shall we?' Merris said. 'Give Ms Browning time to get her feet under the table.'

Bella listened carefully, knowing more could be learned about a company in one meeting than in weeks of figure analysis. She easily spotted the people who were good at their job and those who were fudging. Immediately she could tell this was a company dominated by formality and attention to procedure, so she guessed that new ideas, new objectives and goals were needed but were not exactly going to be welcomed with open arms. God, she still felt awful.

When the conference was finally over she was shown to her own small office, where she unpacked her computer and files and made a few calls.

Later on, she managed to get her doctor on the phone but as she'd suspected, he told her it was normal, there was nothing she could take and it would probably wear off in about six weeks or so.

Six weeks!! Six weeks of feeling like this was frightening. And why the hell was it called morning sickness when it seemed to last all day?

She didn't manage to get out of the office until 8 p.m., and day two at Merris got off to an even worse start. She walked into the breakfast conference room and as her gaze fell on the platter of congealing fried eggs, she could barely contain a retch. There was nothing she could do apart from sit down in her chair feeling overwhelmingly sick and weak. When she reached for her teacup, she noticed that her hand was trembling. Even worse, she knew other people had noticed it too.

After conference there was a second long meeting to get through before she could finally hole up in her office. She had barely sat down and lit up a cigarette in the hope of a quick energy buzz when there was a knock at the door and the human resources director, an American called Mitch, appeared and asked if he could come in.

'Yes, of course,' she said and waved him in, fanning smoke around the room. They shook hands and introduced themselves properly then he shut the door behind him, but didn't take up her offer of a seat.

'To be honest,' he said with a serious look, 'I'm here because we're all a bit concerned about you. Forgive me for saying this, but you don't seem very well.'

She suspected she hadn't been hiding it brilliantly. He carried on: 'We do need a consultant, but we need someone who is going to be here for us 110 per cent.'

Bella felt a twinge of irritation now, but carried on listening.

'I'm beginning to wonder if you are the right person for us,' Mitch continued. 'Well, what I mean is, er . . . you seem to have a problem.

'Mitch,' she said, fixing her eyes on him. 'What are you talking about?'

'Well, you've turned up here every morning pale, weak, hands shaking. You only seem to come round after you've been in your office on your own. You know, some of the guys are even hinting at a drink problem.' He gave a brief laugh to distance himself from the suggestion, although it didn't seem *so* far-fetched.

Bella was stunned. It was all she could do to keep her jaw from dropping open. The Merris executives thought that their thousands of pounds a day, A-list consultant was turning up with a hangover and drinking in her office.

There was only one response. She snorted with laughter at Mitch, then added: 'I've never heard anything so ridiculous in my life.'

She put out her cigarette with a single stab and told him: 'I have a perfectly straightforward medical condition I'm not prepared to discuss which will make long tube journeys and greasy breakfasts difficult for a few more weeks. No-one has ever accused me of having a drink problem before and it's certainly not going to start now. I am the most hard-working, 110 per cent person you're ever going to meet. In fact, if you or your colleagues so much as whisper "drink problem" between yourselves again, I'll have you up on a libel charge.'

It was Mitch's turn to look stunned. He realized he was going to have to patch this up pretty quickly.

'Look, er . . .' he fiddled with the knot of his tie, 'I hope you'll accept my apology. Obviously a complete misunderstanding. I'm sure it will be fine for you to come into morning conference a bit later.' He smiled. 'But you should eat something, you know – protein-based breakfast equals better productivity.'

'Oh really!' she said, but he missed her sarcasm.

'Yeah, I thought you'd know that,' he said. 'You're all about improving performance, you should take every little factor on board.'

That was too much.

'How about the fact that people working 12 hours a day, five days a week, tend to under-perform, leave their jobs sooner, take more days off in illness and suffer higher levels of depression,' she shot back at him.

'So, we're in too early for you,' he replied. Ouch, this was getting nasty.

'No,' she answered in a conciliatory tone now. 'I think you all stay too late. From 5 p.m. onwards, hardly anyone in this building does anything constructive. It would probably do you all good to go home to your families.'

'Yes, well . . . that would be nice,' he said with a smile.

'Do you have kids?' she asked because it had recently occurred to her that she didn't know anyone her own age who did.

'Yeah . . . two boys, Mickey five and Joel, three.'

'Nice names,' she said.

'Thank you.'

'I do appreciate the offer of coming in after breakfast. That would work much better for me, thanks,' Bella smiled now.

'Bella,' Mitch smiled back and ran a hand through his sandy hair, 'I don't want us to get off on the wrong foot here. I've looked into the work Prentice and Partners has done recently and you do seem to be able to turn companies around amazingly fast. God knows we need a shake-up, but I have no idea how you'll get this lot to take on anything new.'

'Well, you'll just have to watch and learn.' She arched her eyebrows.

'I look forward to it. Where do you live, by the way?'

'Belsize Park, north London,' she said.

'It's just that Geoff has a driver pick him up from Swiss Cottage every morning, maybe he can collect you en route.'

No more tube. Thank you, God.

The following morning, a sleek black limo pulled up at 7 a.m. A limo! she thought as she climbed in; that will bloody well have to go when the new management plan comes into action.

Geoff, the finance director, was already in the back but fortunately not desperate for conversation. They sat companionably together, reading their *FT*s and passing the odd comment.

On arrival at Merris Group, Geoff went into breakfast while Bella hid in her office for twenty minutes eating yoghurt and drinking water. The sickness was still there, but it was bearable, so for the first time that week she was starting to feel slightly more optimistic about the job ahead of her: turning this dinosaur company around before it became completely extinct.

Later in the day she scrolled through a raft of new e-mails to find a message from Chris:

Darling, how is it going all the way over there in rural Hammersmith? Merris will have to do without your brilliance for a few days because we are off to pitch for work together in Birmingham.

Chris, hello. B'ham?? Really?? I didn't know anything about this. When? Where? Who?

Ah! There you are. Express orders of the boss. Three days of meetings in the next week or so at the wonderful Salwood House Hotel in the country- side. You, me, hard work, fine wines. It's going to be lovely. Client is Bensons. Small finance company over here with a big partner in the States.

OK. Well, phone me next week with the details and I'll sort it out. It better be a good job.

Let's just say if we get this, we'll all be upgrading cars sweetie.

I love my car.

It's so old!!!!!!!!!!!!!!!!!!!!!!!

It's a classic. Now go away, some of us have work to do.

Byeeeeee. Looking forward to B'ham.

Oh God, it wasn't exactly hard to work out what he had on his mind . . . and now she had it on her mind as well.

She clicked back to the file she'd been working on and tried to focus.

Chapter Seven

Bella threw herself onto the bed and listened to her heart thudding in her chest. What the hell was she doing? She had wedged a chair under the door handle, not because she was worried that Chris might try and force his way in, but to stop herself from getting out again – well at least not without thinking twice, three times and maybe once again before doing it.

Here she was trapped in luxury, country house hotel splendour with a dark and handsome colleague who was on charm offensive. It was only Wednesday and they were here together until Friday. She didn't trust herself any more; how could she after what had happened?

She had met Chris on the stairs earlier in the evening as they'd come down for dinner. He'd been looking particularly edible in a dark, close-cut suit and fat glossy tie and had leaned over to kiss her on the cheek saying: 'I swear, I'd be soooooo discreet.'

She had answered with a flirtatious laugh and given him the arched eyebrow thing because she didn't want to say 'yes' but still hadn't learned how to say 'no'.

They'd met the clients in the bar and gone through to the dining room where Chris had manoeuvred himself next to her and throughout the exquisite meal had held his hand oh so gently on her leg, running his finger up and down the inside of her thigh, daring to get to the top of her stocking and feel his way along the skin exposed there.

Above the table, she'd been holding her own in a heated financial debate and below, she was considering a red hot invitation. The combination was intoxicating, her conversation was getting faster and more passionate and she was knocking back glass after glass of wine.

After dinner, they'd all retired to the library for brandies, then the clients had gone to hold a phone conference with the American office.

Chris, Bella and another round of drinks were left alone in the quiet room where Bella had sunk back in her leather armchair and was staring into the fire.

'I don't care how long it takes, Bella, I know I'm going to wear you down,' Chris had said to her quietly. 'We could sneak back down here to the fire later on. Imagine the thrill. Someone walking in on two financial superbrains writhing naked on the carpet in unbridled passion.'

She'd laughed, swallowed a sip of brandy, then said, 'It would be against the Code of Conduct, Chris. But would it improve my chances of promotion?'

He'd looked at her, smiling with that soft, expressive mouth: 'Well, if I was a total bastard, I'd say yes. But the truth is, you're probably going to become a partner much sooner than you think. You're a very clever girl.'

'I already know that,' she'd answered.

'And you're bloody sexy as well.'

'Ah ha, I happen to know that too.' She'd drained her glass. 'And use it to full advantage.'

'Can I walk you to your room?' he'd asked and there was no need to guess what he meant.

'Why not?' she'd answered, stepping lightly out of the chair and across the room. She'd walked quickly across the hall and suddenly it had felt like a chase, so she'd run up the huge staircase two steps at a time, hearing Chris start to run after her.

She'd turned down the long corridor and raced for her door, giggling, with Chris belting along close behind her. At the door, she'd turned to face him. They were both breathing hard with effort and excitement.

He'd leaned towards her and they'd started to kiss, just softly on the lips for a moment, then, as she pulled him against her, their mouths had opened hungrily.

She'd pushed her tongue deep, tasting wet warmth and brandy and she'd begun to shudder with the pleasure of it. Her arms were round his waist untucking his shirt, so she could feel the warm, soft skin on his back as he nudged an erection against her and began to unbutton her blouse.

Her eyes closed, she'd leaned her head back and felt him kiss her breasts while her heart pounded almost painfully in her chest and she knew she was

91

very close, very close to the point where it would be impossible to . . .

'Chris, I just can't,' she'd forced herself to say.

'Ssh!' he'd whispered 'Ssh! No, no, no, no . . . You know you don't mean that.'

And he was so right, she didn't mean it. She could, she really could. She just absolutely shouldn't.

'I'm sorry . . . I'm sorry, I do.' She'd said this gently, pulling away from him.

He'd opened his eyes and held her gaze for a long moment, then snapped: 'What is the matter with you? You are going to drive me completely insane.'

Holding her tightly round the waist he looked far too fuckable to turn down, but she had to get a grip: 'I'm sorry, Chris, I'm sorry. I've got to stop doing this. God, I'm married . . . you're my boss. This is ridiculous.'

He hadn't said anything, so she'd added, 'Look, I'm just going to say good night now, I don't want to make things worse.'

His arms had fallen from her waist. 'OK, fine,' he'd said finally. 'Good night it is, then.' He'd turned on his heel and she'd watched him walk down the corridor.

She'd gone into her room where she was lying on the bed now, full of remorse. What is the matter with me? Haven't I messed things up enough already? she thought. She was pregnant, for Christ's sake. Pregnant!! Hello!! Was she completely mad? She wondered if, in the words of Mitch, she needed help.

If she could just be faithful, she'd get to keep Don for ever – it really wasn't such a bad deal, was it?

But the thought of lifelong fidelity scared her. She was like a reformed alcoholic who had to take it one day at a time.

She had been utterly faithful to Daniel, the first love of her life, but he'd broken her heart and since then every man who'd even thought about falling in love with her had been dumped or cheated on. Until Don.

Don had convinced her to take the barriers down and trust him.

But sometimes she wondered if Daniel had taken some non-returnable piece of her heart with him. The scar had healed up nicely but sometimes it ached. It ached for a time when she'd thought love was perfect and unbreakable, not this extremely intricate and complicated machine which needed daily tuning and maintenance or else all kinds of crap was liable to get in there and mess it up.

Christ, she was so tired of always having at least three men in her head – the one she was with, the one she'd left and the one she wanted. It was time to put a little faith in the lovely man she'd married. She'd trusted him, she had to go on trusting him and stop trying to fuck the whole thing up.

It was 1.15 a.m. but she dialled her home number.

'Hello?' came Don's groggy, sleepy voice at the other end of the line.

'Hi, darling,' she said gently. 'Sorry to wake you. I'm really sorry I didn't call you earlier.'

'It's OK,' he said. 'Busy night?'

'Yeah . . . I love you, Don.'

'I love you too. Are you OK?'

'Yeah, I'm fine. I just wanted to hear you. You better go back to sleep.'

They said their goodbyes and rang off. She felt a little better.

The next morning, she woke early and ran, nervous at the prospect of facing Chris again.

Sober grey skirt, pale grey skinny rib jumper and her least frivolous shoes were picked out of her bag. This was definitely a no green signals day. She felt queasy as she went down to breakfast – a mixture of mild morning sickness and nerves.

In the dining room, Chris was already at a table so she went over and said a guarded 'Hello there.'

He smiled back, 'Hello, darling. The scrambled eggs are delicious. Grab some, sit down beside me and tell me what we are going to blind our boys with this morning.'

'Thanks, Chris,' she said. She couldn't help but be grateful for the fact that he was happy to file last night away in the stupid mistake drawer and try to go back to the flirty, matey work relationship they'd had before all this lust started floating to the surface and causing havoc.

The day went well and ended with the two of them in the library together again, but the mood was very different. Surrounded by leather-bound books and wood panelling, Bella felt at ease. Apart from a residual flirtiness, the sexual tension in the air between them had diffused. They were even sitting side by side on the same sofa and it didn't feel dangerous. They were talking work and bitching about the clients.

'They may be brilliant, but they are so dull,' said Bella. 'Their idea of fun is a novelty golf club cover.'

Chris laughed at this, but then turned to her with

a serious face and said, 'Bella, why can't I shake the feeling that you might be the one person in the world who's perfect for me, but I got there too late?'

For a moment she was too surprised to answer, but she realized he was waiting for a reply.

'Erm . . . thank you, that's very nice . . .' she said, 'but I can't be your perfect person, because she'll feel just the same and make herself available no matter what.'

Bella swirled the brandy round in her glass and added: 'I'm married. Liking me is just another symptom of your commitment phobia. I know this because I'm a bit the same.'

'Really?' He was surprised now.

She took a long drag on her cigarette, then said: 'I'm really in love with my husband. He's definitely the best thing that ever happened to me. I want us to have kids, grow old together, the whole thing. But I still haven't got out of the habit of pushing the self-destruct button whenever things are going well.'

She stubbed her butt out into the ashtray to hide her filling eyes and immediately took out another cigarette and lit up again.

'It's OK,' Chris said. 'It never happened, OK? We'll just hit delete. You're happily married with a clear conscience . . . no consequences.'

Bella smiled; it was a nice thought, but the guilt didn't go away quite so easily.

After a long pause, Chris finally said, 'OK, maybe you're right Bella, I'm 34, I've got to sort my life out and find a good woman. And I don't want to be going to her wedding three weeks after I've met her.'

'Ah! I'm sorry . . . I don't know what to say. This is all ridiculously flattering,' she said.

He leaned back with a sigh. 'OK, that's it. I'm going to give up on you, then . . . for the moment anyway.'

Chapter Eight

Bella was sitting in the sauna with Tania. They had managed to drag each other out on this freezing cold, grey December Sunday to get to the gym, and now they were relaxing.

'God, you are filling out, Bella,' Tania said, in the blunt matter-of-fact way that only best friends can get away with. 'Is it all the weights you're doing?'

'No you complete cow, it's because I'm almost four months pregnant.'

Bella was enjoying the look of shock on her friend's face.

'WHAT!!!!!!!!'

'Yup. I've been absolutely dying to tell you. Don and I are, fingers crossed, going to have a baby. And you better be pleased, because I want you to be godmother.'

'Oh my God. I can't believe it. You and Don . . . Parents!!!' She gave a little shriek, then leaned over to give Bella a big sweaty hug and a kiss.

'That is absolutely amazing. I just can't believe it. You?? Bella, mathematical genius, financial whiz-kid and career girl. You're going to be a mummy.

My God! You're still so young! Bloody hell! What are your plans?'

'Take maternity leave then go back to work.'

'Of course. But it's so brave of you to take on all that extra responsibility. I'm so busy right now, I barely remember to feed my cat.'

'Not helping Tania.'

'God, I'm still in shock. You and Don . . . I can only picture you together in a bar drunk. You're obviously doing a brilliant job of domesticating each other. My God, he's going to be pushing a pram. What does he think about it?'

'He's fine,' Bella answered. 'He's being very mature. I think he's finally realizing he's a grown-up.'

'This is so amazing,' Tania said, 'Where are you having it?'

'I don't know yet.'

'Do you know if it's a girl or a boy?' Tania could barely contain her excitement.

'No, not yet.'

'We'll have to go shopping for gorgeous glamorous maternity clothes for you and cutesy baby things. *Oh my God*, do you know what this means – I'm going to be thinner than you! Yes! Yes! *Yes*!' Tania hugged her again. 'This is going to be so much fun.'

Bella beamed back at her. Tania was taking this much better than expected. Bella had dreaded Tania disapproving or being jealous, or somehow making her feel it would drive a wedge between them.

'Have you told your parents yet?' Tania asked.

'Well no. You're the only person who knows

apart from Don, oh and the doctor, obviously.' Shit, she still hadn't rebooked the last cancelled appointment.

'You should tell your mum and dad,' Tania told her.

Bella let out a heavy sigh. 'I know, I know. I'm absolutely dreading it. You know how weird mum is about pregnancies and they still haven't met Don yet. I just don't want to make things worse than they already are.'

'Well, try not to worry about it,' her friend said. 'It will work out, I promise. Grandchildren seem to have this way of resolving all kinds of problems.'

'Ha, well . . . we'll see,' Bella replied.

'Gosh you are looking well. They're obviously taking care of you over at Merris Group.'

This was Susan's idea of a hello when Bella met her for lunch a few days later.

Her boss was obviously desperate to say: Look at the weight you've piled on. Are you eating too many business lunches? Just to make her point, Susan ordered salad. But there was no way Bella could restrain herself, she was permanently starving. She ordered carrot soup with crusty brown bread, then followed with salmon steak, new potatoes drenched in butter and a side salad.

She would have loved to eat dessert too but Susan had looked so horrified at the suggestion, Bella decided to pass.

She had thought a cosy lunch with the boss might have given her the opportunity to break the baby news, but Susan was in a dreadful temper and just wanted to talk shop. She wanted a detailed progress report on Merris Group and then asked Bella about moving over to the Danson's job in the spring, much earlier than planned.

Bella couldn't believe it. How the hell was she to fit maternity leave in? 'I thought Danson's didn't want us in till August at the very earliest?' she asked.

'Well, they've had a rethink,' said Susan. 'They now feel they have the budget to go ahead in May or June. Are you expecting Merris to overrun? Is that the problem?'

Bella tried to fudge it: 'Well, obviously I should be available if Merris doesn't overrun. But you would be best to tell Danson's if they really want me, they should make it August. I suppose I could do some preliminary reports, but get down to it in late July, August. I really want that job, Susan, I worked very hard to get the contract.'

'Merris is never going to run past April. Have you got something else lined up for Spring?' Susan asked sharply.

'Well . . . er . . . there is something I haven't mentioned to you because it is in the very early stages,' she began, but then her courage deserted her 'It's . . . um . . . someone I'm trying to woo over to us and they already have consultants booked in for May/June, so I'm trying to pinch that slot.' She willed herself to shut up, she was making this worse.

'So who's that then?' Susan looked interested.

'Well, I'd rather not say.' For a dangerous moment, Bella thought Susan was going to press the point but instead she dismissed the subject with: 'Well, OK, I'm sure you'll tell me when necessary.'

How right she was.

Susan snapped shut her dinky laptop and flicked her Amex onto the table to pay the bill.

'You're a very able consultant, Bella. You are going to be one of the best. I don't want to lose you. If anyone makes you any offers, please come and talk to me first. In the meantime, you're getting a healthy raise come January and I promise you won't be disappointed with your Christmas bonus.'

Bloody hell, thought Bella. 'Thanks Susan, that means a lot,' she said.

OK, she hadn't told her about the baby, but generally the lunch hadn't gone too badly.

When she got back home that evening, Bella stripped down to her underwear and looked in the mirror. Her breasts were enormous: they were spilling out over the top and sides of her C cups. Her stomach stuck out in an alarming pot belly and her waist had completely disappeared.

She didn't look pregnant, she looked fat and frumpy and she wasn't happy about it at all.

She heard the front door slam. Don was home. 'Bella?' he called.

'I'm in the bedroom.'

'Lucky me.' He stood in the doorway looking at her.

'I'm depressed.' She threw herself down on the bed. 'Look at me, I'm fat all over. My clothes are straining at the seams.'

He flung himself right down beside her.

'Hey, gorgeous,' he said, kissing her mouth

tenderly. 'Look at your cleavage though, it's fantastic.'

He slipped her bra straps down over her shoulder and kissed the tops of her breasts.

'I look fat,' she wailed.

'You look perfect to me and you're doing a great job. You're making a whole new person in there.'

Funny how she hadn't even begun to think of it like that. She wasn't just 'pregnant', she was actually making a baby. It was very weird. She pulled him close and smelled the slightly sweaty, grimy scent of a day's work on him. It was very sexy snogging him when she was naked and he was still dressed in his suit.

'How are you?' she asked.

'Oh, I'm OK, I've got some very nice things I'm going to cook you for supper.'

'Oh yeah. I think your kitchen skills are the sexiest thing about you,' she teased.

'Really . . . well, in that case, I'm going to chop, grate and stir-fry.'

'Oh yeah,' she pretended to pant. 'And what about marinading or casseroling? I'm getting shivers down my spine!'

Her naked body was pressed close up against his and as he tasted his way around her mouth, her hands were undoing his belt. 'What can I do to make you feel better about your lovely body?' he asked.

'Mmmm, I can think of a few things,' she answered.

*   *   *

102

On Saturday they went shopping together because she needed new bras to accommodate the increasingly heavy breasts.

Don perched on the little stool inside the changing room with instructions to be quiet. But the sight of his wife slipping in and out of underwear in a semi-public place proved too much to bear. He kept pulling her over, whispering, 'Bella, you have no idea. I'm living out one of my favourite fantasies here.'

For someone hitting 42 next year, he had an impressive sex drive, she thought, looking at the bulge in his trousers.

There she was in the most white and frumpy bra she had ever tried on in her life – welcome to the 'maternity' section – and she suddenly felt the need to thrill Don, to let him know she was still the shockingly sexy girl he'd married.

So she knelt down beside him and unzipped his trousers, freeing the large hard-on inside. Moments later, he came quickly with an impressively quiet gasp.

Bella thought of England and swallowed. Before either of them could say anything, a shop assistant was at the cubicle curtain wanting to know how she was getting on.

As Don fumbled with his zip, Bella stood up and put her head round. 'Haven't you got anything a bit less, well, maternal? These are just hideous,' she said.

The assistant stepped into the cubicle and eyed Don sitting self-consciously in the corner, then she looked at Bella, dressed in a white bra that seemed to stretch from way below her bust all the way up to her collarbone.

'You will need the support over the next few months,' the saleswoman said, adjusting the donkey pannier sized bra cups.

'The breasts get very heavy and if they're not supported, they will droop. We don't recommend underwiring, so you'll have to wear a supportive soft cup.'

'Right,' Bella said, somewhat shaken at the thought of inducing breast droop. 'I'll take two of these monstrosities for day wear then, but I want the nicest, silkiest underwired 34DDs you can find me for special occasions.'

The woman came back with an armful of bright satin and lace. This was more like it.

Bella chose lime green, peach and cappuccino all with matching G-strings, to make up for the horror of the maternity wear.

Don scooped the lot up to take to the till: 'My treat, Bella,' he said, still completely bemused.

Chapter Nine

Bella was in the doctor's waiting room flicking anxiously through old copies of *Tatler*. What for? God knows, she had stacks of files in her bulging briefcase she could be looking through instead. But she was on the verge of being nervous now and she knew she wouldn't be able to concentrate on the finer points of the Merris Group investment return figures.

She was four months pregnant and had been cancelling doctor's appointments almost every week because she had been so busy at work. Finally, overwhelmed with guilt, she'd taken a whole day off to coincide with antenatal day at Dr Wilson's surgery.

But she was fidgety at the amount of time she was wasting.

'Miss Browning,' the receptionist called. 'Dr Wilson is ready for you now.'

She gathered up her handbag and briefcase and strode over to his office, saying 'It's Ms' to the receptionist as she passed.

'Hello, Bella, how are you?' Dr Wilson didn't look up immediately.

'I'm fine, thanks.'

'So . . . Four months pregnant. You're not showing it at all,' he said when he saw her.

'Believe me, my bra is about five sizes bigger and every waistband is straining,' she replied.

'How are you feeling?'

'I'm feeling fine. I'm over the sickness and I feel normal, my usual energetic self.'

'Hmmm,' was his reply. 'OK, you lie on the couch, I'll do a quick examination then I'm going to turn you over to Declan.'

'Who's that?' she said, arranging herself on his couch and lifting her top, so he could feel her stomach.

'Our midwife,' the doctor answered gently squeezing and pressing down on her lower abdomen which felt surprisingly tender.

'Oh right,' she said, wondering why she felt slightly strange at the prospect of a male midwife.

'The midwife will see you now, Mzzzzzzzz Browning,' the receptionist said after Bella had spent another ten long minutes flicking through more magazines in the waiting room then reading all the uplifting notices on the walls: 'How to spot meningitis', 'How to treat a heart attack', 'Saturday appointments are for emergencies only. A cold is not an emergency.'

She opened the door at the end of the corridor and clapped eyes on Declan, who was not at all what she had expected. He was a wiry little elf of a man with short frizzy hair and twinkly eyes.

'Bella Browning. Lovely name,' he said, instantly

106

revealing which side of the Irish Sea he was born on.

'Hello.' She shook his outstretched hand. 'You don't look nearly old enough for this job.'

'Oh, don't worry, I'm 31. I've been doing this professionally for ten years,' he replied. 'But I actually delivered my first baby when I was 12. Sit down and relax. You're not due for months, so we've plenty of time to get acquainted and go through your options. Now, first of all do you mind explaining exactly what you're doing pitching up here at sixteen weeks, when you should have had a booking appointment with me a month ago?'

'Well, I'm a very busy girl.'

'Yes, you and every other woman who pokes their little Italian shoes into this surgery.' That surprised her. He went on: 'Antenatal care is a serious business, for which you are entitled to official time off work.'

'Yeah, *if* you've told your work you're pregnant and *if* they don't dismiss you on the spot for showing "lack of commitment".' She wondered why this was irritating her so much.

'I'm sure you're aware there are laws against that kind of thing.'

'I'm sure you're aware that there are ways around those laws,' she shot back.

'OK, so let's put a big S for stressed in your book here, shall we?' He turned back the cover of a blue booklet.

'Was the pregnancy planned?' he asked.

'Is that anything to do with you?'

'Look, I'm trying to fill in your maternity book

107

here, this is an official question. You don't have to answer it if you don't want to.'

'Yes, it was planned,' she snapped, still not sure why she felt so angry. She watched him tick the 'yes' box.

They went through the list of questions – age, allergies, illnesses – then he asked if she smoked. To her astonishment, Bella found herself bursting into tears.

When Declan instinctively put an arm round her and asked if she was OK, out it all tumbled – the guilt at telling Don it was an accident, the terrible worry that she would have miscarriage after miscarriage like her mother, not even wanting to tell her mother about the pregnancy because it would upset her. All the fears Bella had not even properly admitted to herself and here she was coughing them out to a complete stranger.

'Have you been pretending to yourself that you're not really pregnant at all?' Declan asked in the kind voice which had made her crack up in the first place.

'Yeah, I suppose so.' She was frantically dabbing at her eyes and trying to stop the tears.

'Smoking too much, because you're so stressed about it?' he asked.

She nodded, starting to weep again.

'Drinking too much?'

She put her head in her hands.

'Look, it's OK.' He patted her back. 'You've got to 16 weeks, that's a really good sign, there's no point worrying about what you've done. But it's time to look after yourself a bit better now. If you can't stop, cut down, OK, and try not to worry

108

about everything so much.'

As she calmed down, they talked about hospitals, screening tests and scans and he rolled up her sleeve to take blood.

When Bella got home that evening, she was determined not to give in to the desire for a drink and ten cigarettes. In the kitchen, she poured an inch of white wine into a tall glass. She swirled it round so it had coated all the sides, then tipped the wine out into the sink. She filled the glass up with ice and soda water and took a sip. Aargh, it was like the ghost of a white wine spritzer, like the drink had died and here she was at its funeral, trying to relive the good times.

But no pain, no gain. She was going to smoke less and drink hardly anything, if it killed her.

Several days later, she was holed up in her tiny office at Merris lost in thought, staring at the graphs on her screen, when her mobile trilled.

She was irritated at the disruption and cursed herself for not putting it onto voicemail.

'Hello.'

'Hello, Bella Browning?'

'This is she.'

'Hello, it's Declan here.'

Her mind was blank. Declan?

'The midwife.'

'Oh yes. Hello, sorry about the other day. I'm really fine, I don't know what . . .' she felt embarrassed.

'Bella, chill out, will you? We need to talk, is now a good time, or should I call back?'

'Now is fine. What is it?'

'We've had the results of your blood tests and I'd like you to come in and discuss them.'

She felt the hairs stand up on the back of her neck.

'Jesus Christ,' she whispered. 'I'm HIV positive.'

'Um, no, I don't think so.' She could hear him turning pages over. 'No, you're not, actually.'

'Oh thank God.' She slumped back in her chair with relief.

'It's the screening test. Look, you really need to come in and see me,' he said.

'Please Declan, just tell me now.'

'Well, it's come back with quite a high possibility . . .' he trailed off, then added, 'I'd really prefer to see you.'

'How high?' she said immediately.

'One in 50 chance of Down's Syndrome.'

'Two per cent? That's small, in fact statistically insignificant,' she replied, trying to convince herself.

'Well, we consider it higher than it should be for your age. There are some steps you can take to check. You can have an amnio or a scan. It would be best if you came in and talked it through.'

'I can't, Declan, we'll have to do this on the phone.' He sounded so serious it was making her scared.

'Well, OK, I'm going to give you my mobile number. I'm on duty tonight anyway, so when you get home and you've put your feet up and chilled out, call me and I'll talk you through it.'

'Thank you.'

'OK, I've got to go now,' he said. 'I'll speak to you later.'

'Bye.' Bella clicked the phone off and looked at

the screen again. The figures were wobbling around and for a moment she couldn't think why. She was about to cry. Quickly she put her head back so the tears wouldn't trail mascara down her cheeks. A 2 per cent chance of Down's Syndrome. What did that mean?

There was a tap at the door, so she pressed her fingers under her eyes to blot the tears away. 'Come in,' she said, hoping she looked normal.

'Hi.' It was Mitch. She waved at the spare seat.

He sat down, then looking at her properly, said, 'Are you OK?'

'Yes, fine. My eyes are tired from looking at the screen all day.'

'No wonder. You are allowed out of here, you know, you can have lunch, you can take your smokes out to the atrium where you will find other, live people.'

'I know. But I have a hell of a lot of work to do. I'm starting to panic I won't get it done in time. I don't want the contract extended.'

'Are things here worse than you expected?'

'I don't know if it would be professional to comment,' she said.

'Can I level with you?' he asked. 'My wife is expecting our third baby in the spring and I'm not a UK resident. If I'm going to need a new job, I want to know so I can start looking now.'

Why was he asking her this? It wasn't fair. It crossed her mind that he was wired up and testing her out for his bosses.

'I really won't know the full situation until I've completed a thorough assessment, then I'll report in detail to the board.'

111

'Good grief, you sound like a corporate robot. I'm asking you for your opinion.' He looked tired and stressed. He was a nice guy, not the type to get involved with industrial espionage. God, she was getting paranoid.

'Well . . .' she paused. 'Let's just say if Merris was a racehorse, I wouldn't be taking it round the back and shooting it in the head just yet. And that's all I'm saying.'

Mitch burst into relieved laughter. A little too relieved, she thought. If Merris was a racehorse, she'd certainly not be placing any bets on it and she'd be phoning the vet to ask if there was any hope. But then, she was the vet. She was the one who would be recommending either some very expensive treatment or the bullet. The responsibility of her job bore down on her.

When Mitch had gone, her phone rang again. It was Don.

'Hello,' she said. 'I'm getting bugger all done today.'

'Shall I go?'

'No, no I want to talk to you. It's the baby, I got the test results and there's a chance it might have Down's Syndrome.' The words tumbled out.

'What? What test?'

'A blood test they do. There's a 2 per cent chance of Down's Syndrome. They're suggesting we do more tests.'

'OK . . .' he said slowly. 'It's OK. I'm sure it's going to be OK . . . We need some more information about this, don't we?'

'I'm speaking to the midwife tonight.' She realized her heart was beating fast and she was feeling really panicky. 'Can you try and get home early tonight? I'm going to leave soon.'

'Yeah, no problem. I'll be there just after seven unless there's a last-minute hitch. Shall I get some food?'

'Yes please.'

'What do you want?'

'It doesn't matter, Don.'

'OK, see you later, hon. Don't worry – it'll be fine.'

Why did men always say that? He didn't know if it was going to be OK any more than she did.

'Thanks, Don,' she managed. 'Bye.'

She struggled on for another hour, trying to work but finally she powered down the computer. She'd had enough for the day, she couldn't concentrate, her hand was resting on her faint tummy bump. She felt scared and protective and confused.

By the end of the evening, she and Don had reached a decision. She was not going to have an amnio test. Declan had told her it was the only way to be sure the baby was OK but she had argued back that it was madness to assess a 2 per cent risk with a procedure which carried a 1–4 per cent risk of miscarriage.

They would go to the hospital tomorrow for a detailed scan which had an 80 per cent chance of giving them an accurate result.

The next morning, Bella climbed into the limo, said hello to Geoff, then slumped into her seat, too tired and preoccupied to bother with the paper. The awfulness of the decision they could be facing later in the day was too terrible to think about, but she couldn't stop herself.

She felt her stomach flutter in a strange way . . . nerves. It fluttered again and she just knew it was the baby moving. It was one of those magical first time experiences, like a first kiss, first aeroplane ride, first Valentine.

She looked out of the window to make sure Geoff couldn't see the tears welling up in her eyes. She was expecting a baby. A real live little person. It was as if it was dawning on her for the first time.

What if the baby had Down's Syndrome? Was that so bad? Would she really want to give it up? She knew what that meant. An induced labour and giving birth to a tiny, stillborn baby, an unimaginable horror.

'What do you think about these East Asian technology ISAs then?'

'Hmm?' She was startled out of her thoughts by Geoff who was looking at her over the edge of the paper.

'Well, if you've got a few quid spare, sling it in,' she answered. 'Stand back and watch it mushroom to forty times its original value or be wiped out. They're still pretty high risk.'

He didn't say anything else. Just went back to the personal finance page.

Christ, thought Bella, if he spent as much time worrying about the company's finances as he did about his own bank balance, Merris wouldn't be in such a sorry state.

And it was, too. Every day, she ran more figures through the computer and uncovered new areas of decline. The company was running beautifully, smoothly and efficiently but it was going nowhere.

Because it provided pensions, life assurance, illness cover and so on, the coffers were full of mountainous funds, but it barely seemed to have registered that in the past two years the number of new customers had dropped off dramatically. There were no plans in the pipeline to remarket or recreate the financial products Merris sold, no plans to get on-line, and the growth of the fund itself was barely acceptable. With all that money in the bank Merris should be doing something stellar.

She was also seriously worried about a group of pension holders who were taking Merris back to court on appeal next year. If they won this case, the company would be utterly screwed.

This wasn't just her first solo job, it was the first time she'd worked with a company in such bad shape. It was making her very nervous. The whole place was run on such a no-change culture, how could she even begin to chip away at it? She picked at a cracked nail in need of attention.

She'd arranged to meet Don outside the main entrance of the hospital at two o'clock that afternoon. It was ten to two as she stepped out of the cab but, thank God, he was already there.

His coat was buttoned with the collar up against the wind. He was trying to read a broadsheet but it was getting blown about and he was struggling to fold it. She watched him for a moment as he tucked it into a quarter and carried on reading. Then a scowl crossed his face and he took his ringing mobile out of his coat pocket.

At that moment, she absolutely loved him, this tall, capable, independent, clever man.

He spotted her and came running over, mobile still clamped to his head.

With an arm round her he said into the phone, 'I'm sorry, this is important. You'll just have to cut me a couple of hours of slack here. Yup, I'll come back in at five, we'll sort it out then. Right, bye.'

He put his phone back into his pocket, then turned on a smile for her: 'Hello, Bella.' He kissed her on the mouth. 'It's nothing, don't worry about it, some panicking tosser back at the office. Let's just concentrate on this, shall we?'

She was so glad he was there. She had contemplated doing this on her own, but he had insisted on being with her. She slipped her arm through his and they went in, making their way through dreary, fluorescent lit corridors to the ultrasound department.

In the large, institutional beige waiting room, packed with people, an old man was lying on a trolley, the chairs were crammed with heavily pregnant women and slightly pregnant women. In the corner a girl of about 18 or so was sobbing. Three women in green overalls and long white coats were bustling about behind the chaotic reception desk.

Welcome to the hell on earth otherwise known as the NHS, Bella thought grimly.

She handed over her appointment card. It was taken wordlessly and put in a tray on top of a bundle of others.

'If you could take a seat and drink plenty of water, please. You need a full bladder for the scan.'

The woman didn't even look up at her, just carried on writing.

Bella knew this and had already glugged back a bottle of Evian on the way over. Her bladder was full. She looked at the room packed with waiting women and realized she might have made a mistake there. Should she go for a pee and start drinking water again? Or wait with her legs crossed and hope it wasn't going to take too long?

She sat down with Don. There was nothing they could say that wasn't going to be of minute interest to everyone else sitting silently in the room.

'I've got all the papers in my bag. D'you want one?' He held her hand and patted it with his fingers. 'It'll be fine,' he added in a whisper.

She reached in and came out with the *Daily Mail*. She was half-heartedly reading through: 'Why I gave up life in a palace for passion with a plumber' when her name was called out.

Her heart jump-started and she felt both cold and sweaty at once. This was really happening, they were going to know in a few minutes. She stood up with Don and gripped his hand.

Her mind was racing. She and Don were in a hospital together – already a first – and they were about to see their baby on a screen and possibly be told that it was mentally handicapped, or special needs, or whatever term you were supposed to use nowadays, before it had even been born. This was unreal. She walked along the lino corridor clutching Don's hand with her heartbeat hammering in her dry throat.

She was ushered into a curtained cubicle with a little bed. A short, smiling Filipino nurse said hello then gestured to the bed. Bella lay down and unbuttoned her blouse and her skirt.

Don seemed to be awkwardly filling up all the available space left. The curtain was hanging over his shoulder and snagging along the rail whenever he moved.

Bella lowered her waistband and was preoccupied with the prospect of Don turning suddenly and bringing the whole flimsy little contraption down.

'OK, we just put some gel on.' The nurse smiled and squirted a huge quantity of ice cold blue gunk onto Bella's stomach. 'Now we take a look at baby.' She moved the grey handset into place and started sliding it along Bella's greased navel, staring intently at the screen by the side of the bed.

Bella could hardly breathe. Don fixed his eyes on the screen, which was just out of Bella's view. For several long minutes, the nurse looked and slid her handset and said nothing. She pressed a button and the screen made clunking noises.

'I'm just taking some cross-sections for a better look.' This was not reassuring.

More agonizingly long minutes went by. Bella fixed her eyes on Don's face and he broke off from the screen to give her a wan smile.

Finally the nurse turned to look at her: 'I'm sorry' – the word hung in the air and everything after that went into slow motion. Bella watched her lips form the next words: 'Sorry to take so long. I wanted to be sure.'

Bella could feel the blood draining away from her head and cold beads of sweat break out in her armpits.

'Baby looks absolutely normal,' said the nurse. 'We can't guarantee from the scan, but I can see no cause for concern. Let me talk you through it.'

She swivelled the screen to face Bella and Don moved round the bed to stand beside her. She felt for his hand and squeezed it. He squeezed her back. She was trying to feel relief, to run the words 'absolutely normal' over in her mind again, but she still felt a residue of panic.

The nurse ran the handset over her stomach again and a grey and white grainy image flashed up. It looked like the surface of the moon and Bella could see a little astronaut moving about dreamily.

'There is baby, bouncing up and down. You can see the legs and arms.' She pressed a button: 'This is a cross-section of the heart. The four chambers are all normal.'

Amazingly up on the screen was a tiny pulsating heart, contracting and opening at a relentless pace.

'This is a cross-section of the brain, again normal.'

A grey expanse filled the screen. Bella was looking inside the head of her baby before it was born. She felt in awe.

The nurse clicked back to the lunar surface view again. The little astronaut was turning about, carefree and gleeful.

'OK, that's it.' She turned off the monitor and handed Bella a wodge of tissue paper to wipe down her stomach.

'I'll put the report in your maternity book, take it to your midwife who'll go through it again with you, but there's no obvious cause for concern. The Ladies is second on the left,' she added.

119

How could Bella have forgotten? The dull ache in the pit of her stomach was a bladder shrieking to be emptied.

When she came out after a marathon pee, she and Don hugged hard.

Then he took her arm and led her down the corridor. 'That was one of the most amazing things I've ever experienced,' he said.

'I know,' Bella replied. 'Thank God everything's OK.'

'What would you have done if it wasn't?' asked Don, seeing how pale and shaken she still looked.

'I don't know. I'd like to think we'd have been big enough to say "This was meant to be, let's have this baby" but I don't know.'

'That's OK,' he said and squeezed her round the shoulder. 'I didn't know either. I think we should go and get a drink.'

'I've got to get back.' Bella sounded gloomy.

'Me too, but I think we owe ourselves one.'

'OK.'

Looking down the road in front of the hospital, they could see a pub sign 50 yards ahead.

'That will do.' Don steered her along at a hurried pace and they opened the door on a cosy little pub, quiet after the flurry of lunchtime drinkers and before the evening rush kicked in.

Don went to the bar as Bella sat down on a sofa. She fumbled in her bag for her cigarettes, but just guiltily held the packet in her hands.

Don came back with a glass of white wine and what looked like a double whisky with ice.

'Here we go.' He sat down close beside her and

she could smell on his breath that he'd already tossed one back at the bar.

'Should you be smoking?' he asked.

'I'm not. Should you be drinking quadruple whiskies?'

'Aha, caught again. Damn.' He took a sip from his glass. 'I was pretty worried, you know. Up until today, this has been so abstract. You've hardly even got a bump.'

After a pause, he added, 'Christ, I just can't imagine us with a baby, Bella,' and gave a long sigh.

She didn't say anything, so he took another slug of whisky then carried on.

'I'm so unprepared for this. I've never pushed a pram or changed a nappy or held a bottle or even a baby, I don't think. Then suddenly there's all this worry about whether it will be OK.'

'We never asked,' said Bella suddenly. 'We don't even know if it's a girl or a boy.'

'No. Well, anyway. There's all this worry and I realize I am worried. I'm frightened for a baby who hasn't even been born yet but who does exist.'

She put the cigarettes back in her bag. 'I feel that too,' she said. 'But let's not panic. The baby is OK. We will be too.'

She reached for her wine glass and allowed herself a hefty mouthful. It sank straight into her stomach and settled the nervous jangling. She closed her eyes, swallowed again and saw with horror that the glass was empty.

'Better have another,' said Don.

'No. Lime and soda, hon, I really mustn't.'

He came back with a tray loaded with another

double whisky, her soft drink and a second glass of wine, just in case.

'We can't just sit here and get plastered,' Bella reminded him.

'It's solved a lot of problems for me in the past.' Don was smiley and relaxed now, leaning back on the sofa beside her. He unbuttoned his coat, ran his fingers through his hair and looked at her with one eyebrow raised.

'Oh don't give me that look,' she said.

'What look?' he asked, eyebrow still cocked.

'That "I'm sooo bad, you know you want to misbehave with me" look. I said I'd be back.'

'OK, go outside, phone them, tell them you're stuck in traffic and you'll be in early tomorrow.'

'No. No. No. No.' She was smiling at him now.

'OK, I know, we'll have a lovely, relaxing hour here, then we will get in our cabs, go back to our tosspot offices and say we were delayed by aliens who forced us to drink in a faithfully replicated pub in outer space.'

'Go order my cab *now*.' She said it firmly but she wasn't angry with him.

'You're no fun, Bella. But that's why I married you, to stop me degenerating into a drunken bum.'

'I am fun. But only at the right times in the proper places.'

'See?' he said.

He went over to the bar where she heard him say: 'Can we have two cabs in twenty minutes, please? One going east, the other to Hammersmith. Cheers, mate.'

'Twenty minutes?!' she said when he got back.

'Shame to waste these. Cheers.' He drained his whisky, as she sipped her soda.

'Are we going to fight over the last one?' He gestured at the wine glass.

'You total soak,' she laughed at him. *Damn!* How could they have forgotten to ask for a picture of the scan?

'It's really time we told our folks about the baby,' he said, halfway down the wine.

'Yeah, I know,' she replied.

Chapter Ten

'Hello?'

'Tania, it's me.'

'Bella! How are you doing?'

'Good, fine. What about you, darling?'

'Oh, surviving. Are we going to meet this weekend? Please say yes.'

'Yes, that's why I'm phoning,' Bella said, 'Can I come round? I've got a dress panic.'

'Really?'

'I've got two Christmas parties to go to this week and I can't get into anything I own without showing off a suspicious bump.'

'Don't tell me no-one knows yet!'

'Well, I'm still only four months, and a little bit.'

'You are such a wimp. So, you're pretending to be sweet but actually you're wanting to borrow a fat frock from your fat friend.'

'Don't say that. You're not fat, you have better clothes than me.'

'Yeah, in a size bigger. Bella, does this mean you still haven't told your parents about the baby?'

'No, I have told them. It went OK, surprisingly OK.'

'See,' Tania couldn't help adding.

The parent phone calls had happened a few evenings ago. Don's mother, Maddie had of course been thrilled and had spoken to Bella at length about morning sickness and backache and warned her to take it easy. She'd made a lovely fuss and couldn't wait to see them both at Christmas.

Then Bella had put the receiver down and toyed with dialling her parents' number for so long that finally Don had picked up the handset and punched it in himself.

'I do spend most of my day making awkward phone calls and persuading people to talk to me,' he told her as the international ringing tone began beeping in his ear.

She'd fled to the other end of the room and sat listening to Don's side of the conversation with a mixture of horror and relief.

'Hello, Professor Browning,' he'd begun. 'This is Don McCartney, Bella's husband. How are you?'

'No, no, she's fine. She's really well. In fact, she's expecting a baby and very nervous about telling you!'

At this point, Bella had buried her face in her hands. It had been excruciating.

'Well, you know,' Don had given a little laugh. 'What with the two of you refusing to meet me and so on . . . I think she's feeling a little awkward.'

There had been a long pause then as Don listened and Bella wondered what the hell her father was saying to him.

Then Don had said: 'I hope so . . . I think it would do us all good to meet up. When are you next over here?'

Bella had looked up to see Don giving her the thumbs up and she heard: 'Great, OK then, I'll put Bella on now,' before the receiver was thrust at her.

'Dad, hello,' she'd managed.

'Hello darling, congratulations,' her father had said, sounding genuinely pleased. 'Is it going well?' he'd asked. 'How far on are you?'

'Four and a half months.'

'Well done, Bella,' he'd said.

There was a little pause and she was grateful that he didn't ask why she hadn't told them sooner.

'Your mother is going to be thrilled,' he'd said.

'Is she, are you sure?'

'Yes, darling . . . She'll phone you as soon as she gets back in.'

Then after a small hesitation, he'd added: 'You know, maybe we've made a bit of a misjudgement . . . about your husband.'

'Don.'

'Well . . . he sounds like a good guy.'

'He is, Dad,' she'd told him and for a moment pictured her father, mother and Don all together round a table chatting, eating, hanging out like a normal family. Maybe it would happen.

But her mother's phone call later in the evening had felt like a dampener. Celia had of course gushed that she was delighted, but had immediately listed the reasons why they couldn't come over until the baby was there: so busy, a lecture tour, building work on the house, looking after the neighbour's property when he was away, etc., etc.

'Maybe you and Don could come and visit us?' she'd asked after what sounded suspiciously like Bella's father talking to her in the background. 'What about Christmas?' she'd added.

'Don's mother is coming here.' Bella was grateful for the excuse. 'We'll see, Mum. We haven't got a lot of time off before the baby's due. But you will come then, won't you?' she asked, wondering what on earth that would be like.

'Of course,' her mother had gushed. 'A grandchild, how exciting!'

But to Bella, even this had sounded somehow insincere.

On the night of the Merris Christmas party, work wound up at 4 p.m. so that everyone could go home and get dressed up. The annual party had always been a ball at the Dorchester for employees, clients and various guests. Bella had been somewhat taken aback to learn it was going ahead this year, but she supposed the board were making every attempt to quell rumours that the company was 'in difficulty'.

Just before she left the office she rang Don, who assured her he was going to get away on time. She was still soaking in the bath when he arrived home, so he came into the bathroom and perched on the loo seat.

'Hello, hon.' He took his glasses off because they were misting up and she could see the tired circles under his eyes. But he still looked lovely, she thought, smiling at him.

'You're gorgeous,' he told her. Her hair was piled on her head, her shoulders were peeping out of a vat of foam and she pointed a toe, with perfectly painted pink toenail, in his direction. He took her foot and began kneading it.

She sank back into the bath and closed her eyes. Don massaged her foot, then leaned over to stroke up her calf. He knelt by the edge of the bath and let his hand run gently down her thigh into the water.

'Don.' Her eyes snapped open, her legs shut. 'We haven't got time for this.'

'There's always time to enjoy yourself,' he smiled.

'Well, I'm not in the mood.' She stood up and reached for a towel.

'Nope, you're certainly not. We haven't had sex for ages,' he muttered.

'Yes we have. We had sex last weekend,' she said as she wrapped the towel round and stepped out of the bath.

'No we didn't.'

'OK, the weekend before that.' She was a bit surprised herself.

'Oh well, that's all right then,' he said irritably.

'I'm sorry, I've been very tired, what with work, being pregnant, the baby scare.'

He was instantly contrite. 'I'm sorry, hon, come here.' He held out his arms and she snuggled in.

'It's OK.' She gave him a light kiss on the lips. 'Come on, let's get ready to party.'

'I'll jump in the shower.'

'OK.'

Tania had lent her a long gold slip dress, which clung to her every curve and bump, but it came with a wonderful floor-length gold taffeta coat she didn't intend to take off, which hid everything.

128

She put on a pink underwired bra, tiny black knickers and hold-ups, then pushed her hair up and applied full-on glamour make-up.

The dress coat was on and she was just sliding into her shoes when Don came through.

'Wow.' He moved in.

'Don't touch, don't kiss or crush.' She pushed him away playfully. 'The cab will be here in fifteen minutes, will you be ready?'

'Yes, ma'am.'

She gave him the once-over as they got into the lift. His dinner suit was secondhand and a bit shabby, he was wearing a not perfectly ironed shirt with a not perfectly tied bow. But that was why he looked so sexy, the aura of just having got out of bed and just dying to seduce you back in clung to him more than to anyone else she'd ever met.

'I totally love you, Don,' she said.

'I totally love you too,' he answered. 'You look fantastic – not at all pregnant.'

The lift doors pinged open and she walked to the taxi, obsessing about whether that meant he wasn't going to find her fantastic when she did look pregnant.

They arrived at the Dorchester just after nine to find a lavish party well under way. Champagne glasses were pressed into their hands and one of the senior execs came over to welcome them.

After the 'hello, how are you? lovely you could comes', they were alone again.

'I think I'll take up a seat at the bar, that's where my type hang out,' Don said.

'Sad old alcoholic soaks,' she teased.

'Ha ha. Now, you go off and network like a good

girl. I think that crowd of boring old farts in the corner are praying that you will go over and talk filthy facts and figures to them.'

'Bella,' one of the men in the group Don was indicating stood up and waved her over. It was Mr Merris himself.

'See you later, hon,' Don said as they parted.

'Bella, I want to introduce you to some of my old cronies,' said Merris. He went round the group making introductions as Bella shook everyone's hand.

'This is Bella Browning, our troubleshooter. She's not just absolutely ravishing, she's also damn clever and that is a compliment, coming from a man who's never put a woman in a top position before.'

Loud chortles from the group. Oh bloody hell, thought Bella, welcome to Jurassic Park.

'Well, we're all equals now, Tony.' She flashed a megawatt smile and deliberately used Merris's first name – something she'd never heard anyone do before, in fact, his first name was Anthony, maybe no-one *ever* called him Tony. That would shut them up.

'Yes, yes of course.' He was even more impressed with her now: what an extraordinary nerve!

'So, you're the type who comes in, has everyone over the age of 40 fired and then calls it a cost-cutting efficiency drive?' asked one of the dinosaurs.

OK, they clearly weren't going to be happy with a nice little chat about sure bet investments or property prices.

'Something like that, except we now prefer to fire everyone over 20 because teenagers are so cheap these days and so good with computers, you'll find they can do everything you need.'

Startled silence, then finally laughter. Phew.

Now she went into her gentle pitch for business, handed out a few cards, then patted Merris on the arm to draw him slightly to one side.

'I'd really appreciate the chance to have a chat with you before the Christmas break. It's very important,' she told him.

'No problem. Now go off and enjoy yourself.'

So she did. She swanned round the room chatting with the people she'd got to know at the company and their guests. She glanced over to the bar where raucous laughter was emanating from the small group which had gathered round Don and was about to go over when Mitch came up and introduced his hugely pregnant wife. Her enormous bosom was cantilevered up close to her chin and the big round belly billowing underneath her ballgown made her look like a large green velvet Easter egg.

'When is it due?' asked Bella.

'February,' said Mrs Mitch.

'Gosh.' Bella was going to be this big in three months' time, it was a terrifying prospect.

'Baby number three, I seem to get bigger and bigger every time. Stomach muscles stretched to the limit, baggy pelvic floor.'

Whoa, this was far too much information.

When she went off in search of the loos, Bella was directed down a shiny yellow corridor with little glass cabinets of expensive trinkets set into the walls. Her heels tapped along the marble floor. This was *such* a plush hotel.

She rounded the corner and walked into Don.

'Hello,' they both said at once.

'How's my corporate dynamo?' He sounded nicely pissed.

'I think at least another two jobs are in the bag.' She looked flushed with her own success.

'How sexy. Well, I've got about ten stories. Five usable, two libellous and three utterly unprintable.'

'Have you been talking dirty to the ladies again?' She leaned in to kiss him.

'No, but I can if you want me to.'

He bent down and put his lips over hers. After a long, probing kiss, he moved to her ear and whispered, 'There are no attendants in there, you know.'

'Are you serious?'

'Oh yes.' He kissed her again, scooping her up against him. She could taste champagne on his warm, familiar mouth and she couldn't deny it, she was turned on, but maybe even more importantly she wanted to make up for his 'no sex' crack earlier in the evening.

'Not the Gents, too many people I know might go in there,' she whispered.

'Go and see if anyone is in the Ladies,' he urged.

She opened the pale beech door onto a whole, shiny, peachy little world. It was empty.

She beckoned him in and they rushed into one of the cubicles and banged the door shut. They turned to face each other and burst out laughing.

'I'm getting you back for the bra changing room,' he said, kneeling down in front of her.

'Oh boy,' she replied.

He parted the front of her coat, lifted the filmy gold dress up and let it fall back down over him. Bella shut her eyes and leaned against the wall as

132

she felt him push her tiny knickers to the side and put his mouth against her crotch.

She giggled and he started to lick.

'I want you inside,' she said after a few moments, partly because she did, partly because she didn't want to hang around the cubicle too long.

He stood up and wiped his mouth on the back of his hand before kissing her.

She put one foot up on the edge of the toilet so he could slide in easily.

He felt very good; I might even come, she thought.

'Too much champagne,' Don said by way of explanation as he startled a serious-looking company wife by striding out of the ladies' loos straight into her path. He smiled his extra-dazzling charm smile and she smiled back.

On Friday evening, Bella was getting dressed up again. She wondered why she was feeling anxious. This was office Christmas party night with Susan, Kitty, Chris and Hector. There was to be dinner, champagne, the works and they were all going to behave, especially her.

She was wearing the gold taffeta coat again, but this time with black trousers and boots. It looked surprisingly glamorous and very bump disguising. Don wasn't there to give his opinion, he'd gone to the gym after work.

She had seen Tony Merris in the morning for the private chat and she couldn't really tell how he'd taken her news. She'd listed all her concerns but it had been hard to gauge his reactions. He'd listened carefully and even made a few notes but she couldn't honestly work out if he was surprised by what she was telling him or not.

When she'd suggested that the pension holders might win their appeal case and bring the company to its knees, he had told her that 'friends in the right places' had assured him this would not happen. It was only when she told him that she was going to recommend implementing an emergency action plan well ahead of her full report that he began to look slightly concerned.

'What were you hoping to achieve by calling me in?' she'd asked him.

'Well, I'm very happy with the way the business is run, but I'm aware it's not growing.'

'So you'd be surprised if I told you it is in fact declining and fairly rapidly at that?'

'Hmm.' He'd raised his eyebrows. 'I'd need to see some figures.'

'No problem.' She'd reached into her files and slapped a folder on his desk.

He hadn't picked it up. She'd glanced round the room and noticed the large formal portraits on the walls. 'Your father?' she'd asked, pointing at the one above his desk.

'Yes and that's his father beside him. I'm the third generation in charge here,' he'd said gravely.

'They look pretty fierce,' had been her reply.

To her relief, he'd smiled and said, 'Yes, they were rather. Both naval men, liked to run a tight ship.'

'You run a very tight ship here. Very tight, very formal, very old-fashioned.'

'Is that a problem?' He'd raised his alarmingly bushy grey eyebrows.

'It might be hard to change things.'

'Hmmm,' was his reply.

'May I ask you when you're planning to retire?' She had held her breath and almost crossed her fingers for his reaction.

'Well, that's a little bit presumptuous, young lady.'

'Have you not thought about it at all?'

'I've thought about it, but I haven't decided.'

'It's just . . . please stop me if I'm going too far, but real changes are needed in the organization and I just wonder if you'll be here . . . well if you're going to be . . .' Jesus, should she really be telling the chief executive, the chairman, the grandson of the founder to consider his position?

'Am I the right man for the job? Is that what you're asking me?' He gave a little laugh. 'Well you certainly don't stand on ceremony, do you, Ms Browning?'

She smiled a little and felt she had said enough. She didn't really need to risk her position by spelling out to Anthony Merris that it was time to appoint a new chief executive and sod off to the upper echelons of non-executive directorship.

'I know what you're getting at,' he'd said finally. 'I will give the matter careful thought.'

He had drawn the meeting to a close by suggesting that she draft him a confidential memo on all the matters she'd raised, so he could mull it over during the Christmas break. She'd spent the rest of the day writing it up and making it as bleak as possible in an attempt to spur him into action.

Glancing at her watch now, she saw she still had a little time, so she smoothed down the taffeta

135

coat, lit a guilty cigarette and sat down on the sofa.

She hadn't seen anyone from the office for several weeks now, so she was looking forward to the party, but then the pregnancy secret was a bit of a burden she still did not feel ready to share.

She could see her cab in the street outside, so she flung the cigarette packet into her bag and headed out of the door. They were meeting for dinner in a big, smart restaurant in the West End. She was the last to arrive and was greeted with a chorus of hellos by the gang of four, already seated at the table.

Everyone was dressed up: even Hector wore an unusually impeccable black suit. She sat down, felt instantly relaxed and realized how lovely it was to see them all again, her little office surrogate family.

'Bella! Looking lovely as usual.' This from Chris.

It would be fun to flirt but absolutely nothing else, no way, she promised herself.

Susan was on her right, Hector then Kitty to her left and she was opposite Chris. It was a round table, just slightly too big for everyone to have one group conversation, but that was a good thing. Hector and Kitty were chatting – Kitty trying not to drool – and she, Chris and Susan were no doubt going to talk shop for a while.

Susan wanted to know how Merris was going and Bella outlined the worst of it.

'We can't just tell them that they're in decline,' said Susan. 'You'll have to think of a way of making it look more positive. A shut-down and new start-up, a whole new direction for the company beginning on a small scale, maybe even a takeover or merger. If you're telling them they're on a ship that's going down, in the next breath you'll have to throw them a life raft,' she added.

'I know,' said Bella, 'and I'd really appreciate some input from you. I thought we could maybe meet up over the Christmas break so I could go through it with you and see what ideas you have.'

'Yes, fine,' Susan answered. 'But it will have to be tomorrow, I'm off on my Christmas cruise the day after.'

'Oh lovely,' said Bella thinking, yuck and she'll come back looking all deep brown and leathery.

'Why don't we meet in the office at ten, go through everything, then have a nice lunch?'

'That would be great,' Bella answered.

'Maybe Hector should be asked to have a look. He might come out with some unexpected genius,' Chris put in.

Bella and Susan didn't say anything.

Chris added: 'He's brilliant. Still a bit disorganized . . .'

'And lacking in basic mathematical skills,' Bella added quietly, so Hector couldn't hear.

'But brilliant,' Chris said again. 'He is going straight to the top.'

Bella felt rattled by this. *She* was meant to be the up and coming office star, not barely-out-of-university-unbearably-pompous Hector. Not being childish at all, are we? she ticked herself off and drained her glass. Oh no, now what was she going to drink? Mineral water would be a bit suspicious. She accepted a refill.

'How are you, darling?' She turned her attention to Kitty.

Kitty, squeezed into a tiny silver sequined dress

137

with her hair cut in an extra-short spiky number, was looking sexy, cheeky and hardly bizarre at all.

The mood was mellow. Platefuls of wonderful food arrived as Hector and Chris held court, trying to outdo each other with client anecdotes. Even Susan seemed quite relaxed. There was a nice buzz, Bella thought; Kitty still lusted after Hector and Chris still fancied her. How nice. Now on a third glass of wine, she was starting to feel just a little bit tipsy.

Hector leaned over and whispered in her ear, 'I've brought some stuff with me if you want a dose. Remember the laugh we had last time?'

She giggled and turned back to him, leaning up close to his neat little ear and thinking how nice he smelled, smoky but with an undertone of expensive aftershave and laundry.

'Thanks but I really shouldn't, now that I'm pregnant,' she whispered and they looked at each other in utter amazement: Hector astonished at what she had said, Bella astonished that she'd said it.

'*What??!!*' said Hector, then, 'Did you lot know this?' before she could stop him.

Everyone looked at him. 'Bella's up the duff,' he announced.

Could three people have looked more shocked? She took in the expressions one at a time: Kitty looking delighted-shocked, Chris looking stunned-shocked and Susan looking absolutely furious-shocked.

'That's fantastic!' Kitty spoke first.

'How long have you known?' Chris asked. Hardly surprising.

'When is it due?' from Susan.

138

'Umm, I'm really sorry about this. I didn't mean to say anything until after Christmas. It just slipped out.' She was seriously flustered and glared at Hector, but it was rather lost on him.

'I'm almost halfway there. The baby is due early June . . . ummm.' She was totally rattled, looking at them all staring at her, open-mouthed. 'Don is really pleased,' she added, then, 'And . . . so am I. We had a scan last week and it's looking fine.'

'Boy or girl?' said Kitty excitedly.

'Don't know yet.'

'I just can't see you with a baby, Bella. It's unbelievable', this from Kitty again. Obviously everyone else still didn't know what to say.

'Congratulations,' finally Chris spoke again. Well could she be surprised he was a bit taken aback? By now he'd probably worked out she'd been pregnant in Birmingham.

'Well, we'll have plenty to talk about at lunch tomorrow,' said Susan and made it sound ominous.

Somehow the meal carried on without revolving entirely round Bella and her news. She made it pretty clear she didn't want to talk about it much, politely brushing off Kitty's clumsy questions about maternity leave and what she was planning to do afterwards.

By midnight she was a little drunk, over-anxious and exhausted. Gratefully she clambered into a cab and headed home, wondering how the hell she was going to handle Susan tomorrow.

Chapter Eleven

The square mile that formed the City of London, one of the richest square miles in the world, was eerily deserted on Saturdays. The shops, cafés and bars were closed, the pavements filled Monday to Friday with suits were empty, and the office towers abandoned apart from security guards and the odd weekend visitor like herself.

Bella had dressed down – just a little bit – for the meeting with Susan and as she tapped in the entry code at the front door she wondered nervously how this was going to go.

She was fifteen minutes early, but Susan was already there, in her office with her chair turned to the window. For once she wasn't on the phone.

Bella gave a tentative hello.

The chair swivelled to face her. 'Hello Bella, come in.' Susan's voice was neutral but Bella wondered if she'd made a wardrobe mistake when she saw her boss was in full office gear, with a beige rollneck sweater instead of a blouse as her one concession to informality.

'Hi,' Bella added, somewhat needlessly.

'Sit down.' With a faint smile, Susan gestured to a chair. 'Well, that was quite a bombshell you dropped on us last night. Still, at least you don't have a weight problem.'

What was that? An attempt at a joke? Bella didn't smile, just launched into her planned pitch: 'Susan, I love my job. I love working for you. I'm planning to take a couple of months of maternity leave and come straight back. This is what I've always wanted to do.'

'What, have a baby?' Susan asked.

'No, consult, for the best team in the country.' Bella paused, then added, 'You know I didn't want children when I joined. But I met Don, we got married and my feelings changed. I hope you can understand that.'

'Well, I don't want to be messed around, Bella. Here you are promising me you'll be straight back to work, working just as hard as you do now, but is that realistic?' Susan snapped back.

'I'll make it realistic,' Bella answered.

'We'll have to take you off Danson's.'

Not without a fight, you won't, Bella felt her hackles rise. 'I brought that job in, Susan. They want me to do it. Tell them 1 August and I'll be there. Surely you owe me that?'

Susan tapped long beige nails on the desk and finally said, 'OK August the 1st, but you'll take Hector on the job with you as your number two.'

'Fine.' It was not fine at all, but August was months and months away. She'd worry about that nearer the time.

'OK, well, I'm impressed by your commitment,' said Susan. 'We'll see how it works out.'

141

The subject appeared to be closed, so Bella opened up her files and they began talking about Merris Group.

She listened to Susan and learned. Her boss was as brilliant as ever.

Bella had two whole weeks off for Christmas. She wasn't due back at Merris until 3 January, whereas Don was off just for Christmas Day and 1 January, but she would be too busy to notice, she told herself.

She had drawn up a typically ambitious 'to do' list for her holidays: buy Christmas presents, maternity clothes and a house (well, at least start looking). She also wanted to change hospitals. The ultrasound department had helped her make that decision with its third world waiting room and totally harassed staff. Sod that, she was going private.

Bur first of all, she needed some relaxation, so Tuesday was going to be shopping day. Tania was awarding herself the day off so they could hit town together.

'There's this fabulous maternity shop around here,' Tania assured her when they met for coffee at the start of the day. 'I've already been looking for you.'

Bella took in her friend's recent chunky toffee highlights and bang up to the second manicure. She was the best possible person to take shopping: 'I'm half French,' Tania would declare. 'I don't know the meaning of post-retail guilt. We *need* these things! We *need* to look lovely!'

'Let's do the other stuff first, I just can't see

maternity wear shopping as fun,' Bella said, gloomy at the prospect of getting even bigger.

So they went to Selfridge's and got the Christmas shopping well under way, buying picture frames, candlesticks, rugs, bed linen and books.

Bella cheered up at last when she started shopping for Don. She'd planned to buy him a jumper, but got carried away and bought him the jumper, plus a shirt, plus a new black cashmere overcoat. 'He only ever wears his battered oilskin thing,' she told Tania. 'Oh hell, I'm going to get him a new briefcase as well. It is Christmas.'

'How are we going to carry all this?' Tania asked.

'In a cab,' said Bella.

'Are you as rich as you're making out?'

'Christmas bonus,' grinned Bella.

'Ah-ha, City bitch,' Tania teased.

They hit the maternity shop and wandered round the racks fending off shop assistants.

'Let me just look around for a bit,' Bella told them grumpily. 'God, everything is so twee,' she complained to Tania. 'It's all pink tie cardies and lilac pinafores. I can't turn up for a board meeting in a cardie.'

Bella went to the changing room and was brought one outfit after another.

She flatly refused to try on any pinafores or dungarees: 'Hello, dungarees??' she said sternly. 'They look cute on the under twos. And *no*, I cannot go to work in a pinafore.' She was given a grey jersey skirt suit. It was stretchy, it had no lining, no tailoring, no shoulder pads. It looked like a track suit masquerading as a suit and Bella's gloom deepened.

'Well, it's the only type of suit they've got,' Tania told her. 'Try it with this white smock thing. It might not look too bad.'

And it didn't look too awful, she had to admit, although the skirt was a sad, sad, elasticated thing with a front that looked like an empty carrier bag.

'OK, one polyester suit in grey and one in black. Two smock things – one white, one pink. What else can I wear for work?' Bella asked.

'What about this?' One of the assistants brought in a perfectly acceptable long black Lycra tunic with a deep V neck. There was a matching knee-length skirt to wear underneath.

'This is more like it.' Bella slipped it on. She didn't look too bad at all, sort of sexily pregnant. Her desired intention.

'OK, what other colour does it come in?'

'Grey,' said Tania, her image consultant skills rather stretched to the limit.

'Black and grey? This is pregnancy, not mourning. Well, I'll take them both. So, any maternity leather trousers?' This was a joke.

'Yes, as a matter of fact there are,' the assistant surprised her.

'Hurray! I'll have them please. Plus some of the fitted body things and hell, maybe even a pink cardigan.'

She tried everything on again for Don when he got home.

'It's not so bad, is it?'

'I don't know about the suits.'

'You have a point.'

'Have you been whacking your credit cards?'

he asked, but not disapprovingly; it was her money, after all. Well, actually it was Mr Visa's but . . .

'Just a bit, but I got my Christmas bonus. It was very good and very deserved.'

'Well don't go over the top with my present, because I don't get a bonus.' He sounded sulky now.

'OK,' she said. Oops too late, she thought.

'Where are we going for Christmas lunch? Do you want to take me and Maddie out somewhere posh?' she asked him, taking a sip of her white wine spritzer and trying to pretend that it tasted nice even though it had only a millimetre of wine in it.

'What about here at home?'

'No no, we're not doing that whole plum pudding and turkey thing just for the three of us sitting at home. What will we do all day?'

'We'll have fun. I always have fun when I'm with you and Mum,' he smiled at her.

'I want to go out. Let's go to a really nice restaurant for Christmas lunch.'

'OK, if you like,' he answered.

'Does that mean you wouldn't like it?'

'I don't mind, Bella, you choose.' He was lying across the sofa and looked like he was about to reach for the TV remote control.

'We have to have a house talk, Don. We are still going to buy a house, aren't we?'

'Yup, that's the plan.' He didn't sound that enthusiastic.

'It's a good investment. I think we should spend as much as we can. We can use the savings for a deposit and furniture, decorating and stuff. Well, we'll have to borrow a bit extra for all that, I suppose.'

She was treading as carefully as she could – note use of 'the' savings, not 'my'. It was a tricky subject because he earned less than her and did not like to be reminded of it. She didn't know exactly how much he earned – they had separate bank accounts – but she knew his tax code. And she knew for a fact he had no savings at all – part of his 'life's too short, I'm still young, everyone's so materialistic' philosophy.

'So how big a mortgage do you have in mind?' He looked up at her.

'Well, we could do four times my salary, but I've found someone who's prepared to lend us three times our joint.'

'So how much is that?' Don asked.

'Well, I'm guestimating for you because I know how coy you are but I'd work it out as . . .' she suddenly felt awkward about coming out with it, so she scribbled the figure on the little pad of Post-Its beside her and passed it to him.

'Da-na,' she tried to make a joke of it.

'Bloody hell,' he said, sitting up. 'That's not far off half a million pounds. What the hell would the monthly repayments be?'

'One and a half times our rent. I've found a very good deal.'

'Bella, I don't want you to bite off more than you can chew. Especially with a baby on the way.'

God, that sounded patronizing.

'Yeah, I know, Don. But I am planning to go straight back to work and I'm expecting them to make me a partner next year and I really want to have a house of my own . . . our own,' ouch, she corrected herself immediately.

'Oh please cheer up.' She went to sit on the sofa beside him. 'This is such an exciting time, new house, new baby. Aren't you excited about it all?'

She cuddled up to him and turned her face to kiss him. He kissed her lightly on the lips then, to her surprise, broke away.

'Bella, I've had a few really stressful days, I'm very tired and I think I'll head off to bed,' he said.

'Oh OK,' she sighed. 'Good night then, I'm going to stay up for a bit, if that's OK.'

'Yeah fine.' He nodded vaguely and stood up to go.

She suspected he was suffering from a classic case of income-related impotence. Never mind, he'd get over it. So she earned a bit more than him, well quite a lot more with bonuses. So what?

She stretched out on the sofa and reached over for her cigarette pack. She shook out the last one and lit up.

Lying there quietly she put her hand on the bump and thought about the baby. She knew there was something perverse about the fact that she only really had the peace and quiet to concentrate on the baby growing and existing inside her when she paused for a cigarette break.

'I'm doing the best I can,' she whispered to the little person down there. 'I'm down to five a day, extra mild, sometimes just two. I really, really hope that's OK with you. I'm very sorry I can't give up for you.'

She breathed the smoke in and out several times, then added: 'You are definitely going to be much smarter than me and not smoke. Mind you, I hope you're not too much smarter than me because I'm pretty clever and I don't want you to be one of those mad, genius types.'

Oh God, she laughed at herself, not that I'm going to be a pushy mother or anything.

Chapter Twelve

On 3 January she was back at her desk at Merris Group. It had been a good holiday, bar a small tantrum over her Christmas presents to Don.

He had given her a pair of small diamond earrings, then been a little less than grateful when she'd given him all her gifts.

He'd said 'Bella, you really shouldn't have,' and meant it. She'd ended up yelling at him, when Maddie was out of the room, that it was her money and if she wanted to spend it on him, she should bloody well be allowed to. They'd smoothed it over later, but it still bothered her that he was upset at her generosity. She hadn't been trying to prove what a big fat wage earner she was or anything. She'd wanted to spoil him, remind him how much she loved him.

Over her fortnight off, her bump had suddenly swelled into a definite, undisguisable entity. She was not going to get away with skirts safety-pinned at the waist and jackets worn open any longer. As she'd stood in front of the wardrobe that morning, she'd had to face the fact that she was going to have to put on one of the horrible jersey suits and break the pregnancy news at Merris.

Not that it would cause any problems; her contract would be over well before her maternity leave kicked in. But it embarrassed her, having to bring her personal life so blatantly into the office, it seemed kind of unprofessional. But what else could she do? Leave the baby in an incubator at home?

Strangely, conference was postponed to the afternoon, so Mitch was the first person to come into her little office and wish her a Happy New Year.

'Hello, Bella, did you have a good holiday?' he asked sticking his head round the door.

She swivelled round in her chair. 'Hello.'

'You look different,' he said. 'What's different about you?'

'I ate too much Christmas pudding,' she said putting her hands round her bump.

'Oh my God, you're pregnant!'

'Well you should know, you've seen it all before.'

'Congratulations. And who may I ask is the lucky man?'

'Mitch! You can ask that at engagements, not conceptions. I'm a happily married woman.'

'There are hidden depths to you I would never have suspected,' he said with a grin.

'I brought Don to the Christmas party.'

'You had sex with *your husband* in the toilets? You are unbelievable.'

'What are you talking about?' She put on her most perplexed and wounded face, but was horrified she had been found out.

150

'The rumour sweeping the office is that you lured a mysterious dark-haired stranger into the ladies' loos at the party.'

She gave her best impersonation of outraged laughter.

'I'm sorry,' Mitch said. 'No-one really believes it. Never mind, the news that you are with child will nip it in the bud. No-one's going to believe that a pregnant woman would have sex with her husband in the toilets even if her life depended on it.'

'Quite.'

'Anyway, I'll catch ya later.'

'Bye.'

He could not get out of the room fast enough. She could practically hear him running down the corridor shouting: 'News just in: Bella in toilet romp pregnancy shock.'

She turned back to her screen. Susan's advice had been to let the board have as much of the bad news as early as possible, along with plenty of practical solutions. That way things should already be improving slightly by the time her final report was due in April.

She scanned through her e-mails and saw one in there from Chris.

Bella, hello. We've not had the chance to talk at all since the Christmas party. I just wanted to congratulate you on your news and tell you I think it's wonderful (OK I'm a little bit surprised, I have to admit. Especially after our . . . well, I know I'm not supposed to mention it.) Anyway, I'd love to have a drink some time, we can talk about how things are going to work while you're away / when you come back etc. Hope you're keeping really well and don't let the buggers get you down. Chris

Chris. She hadn't thought about him for weeks. A good thing. But it was nice to hear from him and know he was on her side. She typed back:

So glad to hear from you. How about Wed / Thurs night? Bella

Ah yes! There was something else she had to kick off today. She rootled about in her bag for the card she had put in there and soon was deep in conversation with an estate agent.

'And I'm in a real hurry to move,' she added. 'Baby on the way, hectic work schedule, all the usual.'

OK, board meeting, board meeting . . . time to concentrate, she told herself, once she'd put the phone down.

An e-mail dropped from the finance department. The latest reports she had asked for were 'unavailable – files out'.

This was ridiculous, she would have to find out from the finance director himself what the hell was going on. Preparations for the interim report meeting she was holding with the board kept her in the office for almost ten hours, so Don got home well ahead of her.

She messaged him as she climbed onto the tube, so dinner would be ready when she got back. When she finally made it to the flat, he was in the kitchen stirring up chicken with peppers, soy sauce and rice.

'Mmm . . . very macho new man,' she told him, kissing him hello.

'I'm wooing you tonight,' he warned her, smiling and stirring frantically.

'How nice,' she said, thinking, Please no, I *have* to go to bed.

They ate dinner then he insisted she lie down on the sofa while he peeled off her stockings and massaged her feet with oil.

'This is perfect,' she said to him closing her eyes and feeling herself sink to the brink of sleep almost immediately.

'How's work?' he asked.

'It's pretty tough.' She didn't want to elaborate.

'You're doing really well, you know,' he said as he stroked her bump protectively.

'Thanks,' she said, struggling against a yawn. 'I'm sorry I'm so tired all the time.'

'It's OK.' After a pause he added, 'Are we going to get a place with a garden?'

'I hope so,' she said.

'I like the idea of reading the papers in a garden with our little baby playing on a rug.'

'You'll have to mow the lawn,' she warned him with a smile.

'That's OK, I'll mow the lawn. I'm getting very domesticated in my old age.'

'You're really adorable, you know.' She put a hand against the side of his face and watched his eyes. 'Please don't go off and shag anyone else, will you?' She'd meant this to sound jokey but it came out a little pleading.

'Don't be silly, Bella, you're the one.' And when he said things like that, dead serious and holding her gaze, it still made her stomach flip and it renewed her faith that this love affair could last for a very long time.

Chapter Thirteen

Sitting in her tiny office at Merris several weeks later, Bella could feel pinpricks of sweat break through under her arms. Her hands were shaking just slightly. This was it, the interim report, the first meeting with the board to outline her findings.

She was delivering bad news, probably much worse than they expected, but she hoped they would trust her. They had to be sure she was right and that she could get them out of this rapidly accelerating decline.

Her outfit had been carefully chosen that morning to project maximum authority and gravitas: hard to do with a comical bump protruding from your middle. She'd gone for the black fitted skirt and flared top ensemble, along with diamond earrings and gold necklace, then she'd added serious make-up and piled her hair up on her head in the hope that she looked a lot older than 28.

The figures, the reports and the spiel she was going to give them had been replayed over and over in her mind, but she mentally ran through the intro once again.

'You're just nervous,' she told herself, guiltily stubbing out the second cigarette she'd smoked since she got in.

A glance at her watch told her it was eight minutes to nine. Time to get down there. She gathered up her sheaf of papers and left her office.

Once everyone had settled down round the conference table, Merris went through the introductory formalities, then Bella stood up and took in the attentive eyes turned in her direction: 'Gentlemen,' she began, then gave it to them straight.

She started by demonstrating that the funds were showing negligible growth and moved on to show how new business had virtually dried up.

Arms were crossing defensively, mouths were being drawn into tight little lines and she could even hear irritated sighs. She carried on, unfazed, in a quiet, firm voice. Why were there no plans to set up anything on the net? To meet new regulations head on or to prepare for the pension holders going back to court? she asked.

Now everyone, apart from Merris, who'd already heard all this from her, was looking furious and somewhat shocked.

OK – time to swoop down and cheer them up. She started to outline her solutions: new financial products, new marketing initiatives, an on-line service and better strategic planning to deal with the other problems.

'I've spoken to all of you individually and heard a lot of great ideas. It would not take long to get Merris Group back on course,' she said encouragingly. That was mainly a lie, but she might as well try and be a little bit nice.

'But I'm sure you are all wondering how this can be financed?' Several heads were nodding vigorously at her.

'Well . . .' She knew her number one suggestion was not going to be popular, 'I think Merris Group needs to bring in a partner or a parent company.' In other words merge or get bought over.

There was a collective wave of shocked inbreaths.

She ran through the other options, not looking up much because she knew their faces would be horrified. Yup – she glanced down again – like patients faced with a rectal examination.

When she'd finished, she sat down and looked squarely at Merris himself.

'Thank you very much, Ms Browning,' he said in an entirely neutral tone. 'Does anyone have any questions?' he added. Surprise, surprise noone moved. If this bunch had any courage in their convictions, they weren't about to reveal it now.

'Well, perhaps it would be best to discuss this amongst ourselves, and Ms Browning – we'll call you back in if any clarifications are necessary,' Merris said.

'OK.' She stood up, gathered her papers together and tried not to feel hurt. What had she expected? A standing ovation?

Quickly she walked out of the silent room and headed back to her office to wait. This was horrible. Either she would be told 'thank you very much, but we won't be requiring your services further' or the Merris Group executives were going to have to bite a very hard and unpalatable bullet. She sucked down another cigarette, hating herself for it, drank a cup of coffee and waited.

Finally the phone buzzed.

'Hello, Ms Browning?' It was Merris's secretary.

'Yes,' she answered, feeling her heart hammering high up in her chest.

'You're wanted back in the conference room to discuss your report.'

'Thanks, I'll be right there.' She walked along slowly and calmly, not wanting to jump to any conclusions. This could be OK, oh God! Surely they weren't going to ask her back in to fire her? But it was OK. The executives were still in shock and she wasn't sure if they really believed her yet, but at least they were prepared to listen some more.

One of the few uplifts in the very long week that followed was an excited phone call from the estate agent, who promised Bella he had found her new home.

There was also a message on her mobile from Declan, informing her: 'Bella you f***ing useless cow, you haven't been for a check-up for a month. Drag your arse in here next week or you are in so much trouble.'

On Saturday morning she and Don got into his Jeep to go and view the house. She opened the car door, climbed up and surveyed the scene. It was disgusting. The back seat was strewn with news-papers, empty coffee cups and sandwich wrappers. In the front was a tangle of wires – computer exten-sions, mobile chargers – the ashtray was overflowing and ash was scattered all over the floor and the seats.

'Bloody hell,' said Bella. 'Have you been entertaining again?'

'I tell you what, we'll go via the garage and I'll smarten her up,' Don said.

'Go via the skip, I think you mean.'

'Come on, woman, get in, stop fussing, at least you'll be able to stretch your legs and enjoy the view.'

'I'm perfectly comfortable in my car,' she said clambering up, thankful she was wearing the wipe-clean maternity leathers.

They roared off all the way to the first red light. Don loved to drive fast, which was a bit of a thwarted desire in London. He certainly indulged on the motorways and, even in the tank he drove, seemed to have ratcheted up enough speeding points to be clinging onto his vital licence by a thread.

After a wash and vacuum at the garage, they were running slightly late as they whizzed through north London and into the not very glamorous borough they could soon be calling home. Looking out of the window, Bella took it all in. The high streets full of kebab shops and launderettes, the gloomy tower blocks and council estates which loomed round almost every corner complete with small groups of moody adolescents. Rows of Victorian housing, looking shabby and unloved.

'This can't be right?' She looked at Don.

''Fraid so, we're the second on the left here.'

He turned the car into a long street of tall Victorian terraces which looked grey and grimy. Then they turned left at the bottom and suddenly they were in a lovely little crescent.

The houses here had repainted windows, elegant wooden shutters and brightly coloured doors. The brickwork had been spruced up, railings had been repaired and there were even some jaunty window-boxes.

Bella clocked the cars: a range of new Scenics, Espaces and Golfs. Well, it looked a bit more promising.

Towards the bottom of the road was the large FOR SALE sign.

'This must be it,' said Don, pulling up.

As they got out of the Jeep, the driver's door opened on a car parked right in front of the house.

'Hello, you must be the Brownings.' A young, smartly dressed man was coming towards them with his hand outstretched.

'Bella Browning,' said Bella, shaking his hand, 'and this is Don McCartney, my husband.'

'Hello, I'm Stephen Rennie, so . . . shall I show you round?'

They walked up the steps, Bella noticing the big windows on the basement floor and the glossy wine-coloured front door.

'The owners are away for the weekend, in case you're wondering,' Stephen told them as they entered a vibrant orange hallway. On the left was the big living room painted such a deep navy that it looked strangely dark and old-fashioned despite the huge bay window and multicoloured rugs over the sofas.

In its favour, the room had a lovely old wooden floor. Everything had been neatly tidied and stacked away, but there were obvious kiddie bits all over the place: big boxes crammed full of toys in the corner, a pile of dog-eared books on the coffee table, stacks of Disney videos on a rack beside the TV. The windows at the back of the room overlooked a tiny patch of garden with high ivy-clad walls and a bright swing moving in the breeze.

Bookshelves had been set up in the back of the room and at a glance Bella spotted cookbooks, gardening manuals and more children's books. There was a comfortable armchair beside the open fireplace.

'The fire does work,' said Stephen, following her gaze. 'It looks like it's been used quite recently, in fact.'

Bella heard herself asking all sorts of efficient questions. How old was the central heating system? Would the windows need work done? All that sort of thing. But she felt a strange mixture of excitement and sadness.

She loved not just the house but the whole lifestyle it suggested. It was a warm, family house, cuddly but groovy. It was all kids and dogs and orange and navy. It was a stay-in-bake-cakes-go-out-get-muddy kind of home and although she knew she was never going to be that kind of person, some tiny part of her longed for that.

Oh get a grip, she told herself. Must be the nesty hormones coursing through my bloodstream.

They went up the stairs which were worn and bumpy underneath the blue runner carpet.

The main bedroom was bright pink with an ornate wooden sleigh bed and a beautiful chest of drawers. There was a white fitted wardrobe bulging with clothes. Framed and unframed pictures of two adorable blond boys and their smiley, Sloaney parents were dotted all around the room.

'That's the owners, in case you're wondering,' said Stephen, apparently driven by a need to fill in the long silences as Bella and Don looked around. 'They're moving to the country, Cumbria I think.'

'Hmm,' said Bella. Of course they are, so they can do dogs and wellies and I think I'm going to cry.

'It's a good size of room,' said Don, not risking anything too controversial.

Bella headed into the next-door bedroom. It was a smaller room with a bunk bed, obviously shared by the boys. Everything was brightly painted. Two of the walls were light blue, two were yellow. The chest of drawers and the wardrobes were painted in yellow and blue stripes. Shelves bulged with stuffed toys, trucks, Lego, books and games.

She was feeling very odd now. Here she was looking into other people's lives and she felt a weird combination of regret and longing. She wished she had grown up in a warm, colourful house like this and she wondered if she and Don could ever have such a happy, cosy family life.

The bathroom on the same floor was a cramped sink, loo, shower-in-bath affair. The blue floor carpet was tatty and so were the black and white tiles on the walls, but the bath was a lovely old salvage job.

After looking round the plain third bedroom, they went up a narrow set of creaky stairs to the loft conversion. 'Ah-ha, the home office,' said Don, who got there ahead of her. He was giving nothing away.

The sunny yellow gabled room was crammed with books, pictures, photos, files, papers, all sorts of strange knick-knacks, including an old stuffed salmon – bizarre – a knackered pram and lots of big brown cardboard boxes. There was a long desk with two state of the art computers on it.

Although it was chaotic, the room was totally charming.

'What do the owners do?' asked Bella.

'I'm not quite sure,' Stephen answered. 'Something creative . . . graphic design, media, something like that. So . . . all the way down to the kitchen and the garden now. Shall we?' he asked.

The basement kitchen was just as Bella imagined it would be – antique pine, orange walls, Aga, large round pine table, plants under the windows. It was a country kitchen in the city. Double doors led out into the garden and four pairs of wellie boots were lined up along the wall beside the door.

'And the garden . . .' Stephen unlocked the doors and they stepped out into an unremarkable patch of lawn fringed with untidy bushes and plants. The swing dangled in the chilly breeze. Bella cast her eye round the toys close to the wall of the house: the sandbox shaped like a frog, the faded plastic trike and dirty bucket and spade.

They all looked at each other.

'Is there anything you'd like to see again?' asked Stephen.

'Let's go up to the sitting room,' said Bella.

All carefully wiped the clumps of garden off onto the kitchen mat and traipsed up the rickety stairs. Bella and Don strode round the sitting room, looking out of the windows. The entrance to the park was just four houses along at the end of the road.

Bella sat down on one of the sofas, hoping another angle on the room would reveal something more.

'We'll talk it over then give you a ring,' she told Stephen as they walked down the steps from the front of the house. They said goodbye and Bella and Don climbed back into the Jeep. They watched Stephen manoeuvre out of his parking space and start off down the road before they said anything.

'So,' Bella turned to Don. 'What did you think?'

'You're asking me to go first?' he answered.

'Yup, definitely.'

'OK, well, I'm going to take a chance here and tell you that I really liked it.'

'Don! The whole place needs replastering, repapering, painting, the wiring looks dodgy, the bathroom has to be replaced, there's probably hundreds of other things wrong . . .' she paused to look at him, 'but I love it. Let's buy it!'

He broke into a smile.

'Unless you think we're rushing into it and we should look at some other places first?' she added.

'Well, this isn't going to be the first thing we've rushed into together, is it? And so far, so good.'

They grinned at each other.

'How much is it?' he asked.

She told him and he said 'Fuck me,' but softly. 'Are you sure you don't want to buy a French château instead?' he added.

'I think the commute might get a bit boring.'

'You're right. Crumbly Victorian terrace in the outer reaches of north London it is, then.'

'There's a tube station just two streets away, you know.'

'Well, that's settled then. Phone Stephen up.'

So she did and by the end of the afternoon their offer had been accepted, lawyers and surveyors had been contacted and there was talk of decorators and moving in by the end of next month.

Bella just hoped their bank accounts could take the strain.

Chapter Fourteen

The mobile text message which read: 'Your baby is going to be on the social services register before it's even born if you don't come and see me NOW!' shook her somewhat.

She picked up the phone and booked herself into Declan's next surgery, then she messaged him back with a simple 'Sorry, love Bella.'

Two days later she walked into his little office.

'Hello stranger,' he said with a friendly grin.

'Hello, someone is losing hundreds of pounds' worth of valuable consulting time while I sit here and have you check my blood pressure,' was her stressed idea of a greeting.

'Calm down, will you. Let's just have a little chat first.'

She told him she was feeling a lot better than the last time they'd met and slightly more tuned into being pregnant. The booze and fags were under control.

He pushed a small pile of books and leaflets towards her. When she groaned, he asked, 'How many centimetres have you got to dilate before you can deliver?'

She had no idea what he was talking about.

'See,' he said. 'Someone as smart as you needs to be informed, so you know what's happening every step of the way, so you don't start swearing and raging at everyone in the delivery room and demanding to speak to your lawyer.'

She laughed at him then and he did the tests. Blood pressure fine, urine fine. He let her listen to the baby's thunderous heartbeat with his stethoscope.

'Any piles yet?' he asked.

She raised an eyebrow.

'You know, on your bottom, causing pain, itching, resulting from constipation.'

'All right, all right, I'm constipated and I've got piles. There, I've never said that to anyone before.'

'Piles are the scourge of pregnancy that no-one tells you about. Everyone has them, no-one mentions them and wait until you've given birth, you'll have a bunch of grapes hanging out of your arse,' he told her with some relish.

'Lovely.'

He advised fibre, lots of water and regular exercise.

'Oh God, isn't there just a cream I could use?'

'Why are you such hard work?' he almost shouted, but with a smile. '*Yes*, but you have to do the other stuff too. Now, we haven't talked about birth or hospitals.'

'Well, I was going to tell you about that.'

'Aha . . .'

167

'I'm going to go private. I've got an appointment at the posh place down the road next week.'

'Oh.' He looked genuinely disappointed.

'I'm sorry,' she said. 'I really like you, Declan. But I couldn't believe the state of the hospital when I went in for the scan. It is filthy and run down and chaotic.'

'The labour ward is a bit better,' he said.

'Oh come on,' she replied. 'If your sister was having a baby and money was no object, you'd send her to the posh one.'

'No, it would be against my deeply held socialist principles. But . . . well . . .' he sighed. 'If you're asking me should every hospital in the country have facilities like the posh one? I'd say yes.'

'Thank you.'

'Well, I suppose that's us then. I hope it goes really well and that you have a lovely baby. You've got all my numbers. If you need any help or you change your mind, just ring or make an appointment here.'

'Thanks, I really appreciate that.'

They said their goodbyes and she stepped out, relieved he hadn't tried to change her mind, but a bit sad that Declan wasn't going to be looking after her any more. He'd been great, he was probably a very good guy to have around during labour.

The following Monday, she had another half-day off to go to her appointment at the private hospital. One advantage of everyone knowing she was pregnant was that she didn't have to make up excuses for the endless time off that being pregnant seemed to involve.

She got into the car – sod the shortage of parking

spaces at Merris, she was driving – and looked herself over in the mirror. Her skin was peachy, sixth month 'bloom', but her hair had gone weird, kind of dried out and a touch wiry. She applied some red lipstick carefully.

The hospital was beautiful, a reception gleaming with marble tiles, gold fittings and whispery staff, just like a smart hotel. But the service had been strangely hotel-like too. A brisk blond midwife had gone through her medical and pregnancy history. She was very efficient, but Bella somehow couldn't see the phrase 'bunch of grapes hanging out of your arse' coming from her lips. In fact, this midwife hadn't mentioned piles once.

She'd had another scan and although it had been lovely to see the baby again, she was passingly annoyed that it had been sprung on her so there was no chance to have Don there.

'We like to have our own report, rather than use data from another hospital,' the midwife had told her. But Bella suspected it was so they could add a few more figures to their already ludicrous bill.

She'd also briefly met the consultant who would be delivering her baby. After a quick preamble, he'd recommended an epidural, telling her, 'For most women, a first labour is more pain than they have ever experienced in their lives, it can be quite a shock.'

Not very reassuring.

Back in her car and about to set off for work, she rummaged around in her handbag for some food. Mmm, a packet of cashew nuts, a bag of ready-to-eat prunes, two cereal bars and a large bottle of water. This constituted lunch. The prunes, which she now tried to eat every day, were actually quite good, but they hadn't had any effect on the piles.

G-strings were now totally out of the question, the damn things bit into her raw, itchy flesh like a torment. She was beginning to learn that at around six months, you had to ditch all efforts to remain sexy and move into F-cup maternity bras and large white pregnancy pants. She thought of the pale pink G-strings in her dad's pocket and shuddered.

Chapter Fifteen

Finally she and Chris were meeting for their dinner. He had blown her out twice and she had cancelled once, but he'd confirmed at six o'clock today that it was still on, so she had taxied into the centre of town to the elegant address he'd chosen.

The waiter led her to a table where Chris was already seated, looking through a stack of documents.

'Bella!' He jumped up when he saw her and gave her a kiss on the cheek. 'Are you drinking?' he asked as the waiter hovered to take an order.

'I'm going to have one glass of Chablis and that will be it,' said Bella, rummaging in her handbag for a cigarette. She lit up, took a long drag and relaxed back into her chair, sighing the smoke out.

'Still smoking then?' said Chris.

'Oh God, please don't,' she answered. 'This is my one cigarette of the day. From now on I'm only going to smoke locked up in the loos.'

'Sorry. I'm still really surprised you're actually pregnant. I mean, you must have been pregnant in

Birmingham.' He lifted his brows and shot her an intrigued smile.

'Of course, I forgot, pregnant women are not supposed to have any interest in sex,' she snapped back, irritated now. 'Bloody men, you think you're so liberated but at the end of the day it's all virgins, mothers and whores and anything in between just confuses you.'

'Er . . . I'm sorry,' he said again. 'You're probably right.'

'You're just repressed, Chris.' She was smiling at him now. 'You only fuck attractive single women you don't know very well. You need some variety.'

'What are you suggesting?' he asked and God, he was so good-looking, he was dangerous.

'Well, maybe a married, heavily pregnant woman you know very well would be a start, but . . . hey, I'm not offering. I've practically given up drinking and smoking, now is not the time to take up infidelity.' She held his gaze for a moment, then looked down at her menu.

'How's work?' he asked.

'Things have just recently got much better,' she answered. 'Merris has told me on the quiet he is going to set up a merger deal soon, so they'll have money to do all the things that need to be done and he's going to hand over to a new chief exec and move into a back seat. About bloody time.'

'Sounds good.'

'Yup.' She blew out a small wisp of smoke. 'Fun this job, isn't it?'

'The best,' he said.

'I'm not giving it up, you know, for the baby.'

'I think you've made that pretty clear. But you might find you can't devote quite so much time to it.'

'I've thought about that. I'm just going to have to be better in the hours that I am around. I think you should up my rate, so people can't afford me ten hours a day.' There was no way Bella was taking a pay cut or going part time after birth: she wanted to put that message out loud and clear.

'Hmm, interesting idea.'

She was annoyed by that: 'Come on, Chris, don't say you don't think I deserve to be a senior partner by the time the Merris job is over?'

'I think you do. You're doing it brilliantly, but . . .' he trailed off.

'But? Susan doesn't agree?'

There was a pause. Bella wondered if she had overstepped the mark. Chris and Susan were partners after all.

'She's very angry with you,' Chris replied. 'She's unreasonably angry. But she is the boss, you'll just have to wait it out and give her a chance to calm down. You might even need to wait until you're back from maternity leave and can prove to her you're just as good as before.'

Bella was about to launch into an angry tirade, but suddenly thought it wouldn't be best politics.

'Let's eat, I'm starving.' She picked up her menu and decided that the business part of the evening was over.

Bella was feeling stressed and in a fairly lousy mood as she drove to the hospital two weeks later for yet another check-up.

173

In less than three months' time the baby would be here, and it felt like pressure, not pleasure. The house sale still hadn't gone through. She wasn't sure if she could wrap Merris up in time, she hadn't read the pregnancy books yet, or the labour guide, or bought any baby stuff or, NAMES, they hadn't done anything about names.

She was so busy playing it all down, telling everyone she was rushing back to work, it wouldn't change her at all . . . blah blah, she kept pushing the whole thing to the back of her mind. Denial – not just a river in Egypt, as they say.

She put one hand on the bump as she whizzed her car into the hospital's car park. There was a lot of movement down there now, she could feel kicks and prods and a weird twirling motion when the baby span around.

Sweeping in through the hospital's gliding doors, she marched over to reception and was told to go straight through. As she turned from the desk, she saw another woman approaching. With long blond hair and an expensive cream trouser suit, she looked vaguely familiar, but Bella couldn't place her and carried on towards the corridor to her appointed consultation room. When she got there, she shook some of her reports out of her briefcase and began to read them.

After thirty-five minutes had gone by, she was extremely irritated that she was still being kept waiting. She could hear someone walking down the corridor but they stopped just short of her room and opened a neighbouring door.

'Was it really her? From *EastEnders*?' said one voice.

'Yes, she's really nice, very down to earth,' came the reply.

'She was a bit early, wasn't she?'

'Yes, but we saw her straight away.' The voice dropped low, but Bella could still hear: 'The other woman just had to wait a bit . . .'

It took Bella a moment to realize the midwives were talking about her, then she felt the blood rush to her face. She pushed her papers into her bag and strode to the doorway.

The midwife standing at the other door swivelled round and looked at her with dismay.

'Well, I've waited quite long enough today, thank you very much,' Bella said sharply. 'I'm sorry my labour won't be featured in *Hello!* magazine. I thought you'd be too professional to care about that. But obviously not.'

Bella might have changed her mind about walking out of the place for good if the nurse had at least apologized, or said something, but she just stood there absolutely silent. So, Bella turned on her heel and marched out down the long corridor, every step ringing in her ears.

At reception she said curtly: 'Due to the treatment I've *not* received today, I'm cancelling my booking with this hospital. Can you send anything outstanding to my home address? Thank you.'

Back in the car, she was surprised to find herself bursting into tears.

What was she going to do now? She'd signed off from the NHS and now she'd pulled out of the private hospital. What was she doing? She was six months pregnant and she hadn't even had the check-up.

She tried holding her head back so the tears wouldn't ruin her make-up, but it was no use. She put her hands over her face and sobbed. She knew there were some takeaway napkins somewhere in the car, she would just have to do a clean-up operation afterwards.

Several minutes of hard sobbing later, she decided to phone Don, who was of course out of town overnight.

She rang his number and after an age heard a very faint, crackly 'Hello?' at the other end.

'Don, Don? Hello. It's me.'

'Hi, Bella.' He sounded lovely, which made her cry again.

'I've just fallen out with the hospital and I'm not going back and I don't know what to do.'

'What?'

Once she'd explained it all to him, he told her he'd ring her back in a few hours from his hotel when he could talk properly. She knew this was the best plan, but she felt gutted. God, why was she being so pathetic? Must be the hormones.

She dialled Tania's number.

'Tania, it's Bella.'

'Hello darling, how are you?'

'In a bit of a state. Can you sneak off for lunch? No-one's going to miss me at work, they're all too busy figuring out how to avoid bankruptcy,' she sniffed hard.

'Antonio's? 1 p.m.?' Tania answered, sensing the urgency.

'I love you,' Bella answered.

'Likewise.'

Bella clicked the phone off and looked at her face

in the rear-view mirror. Much worse than she'd hoped. Big red nose, panda eyes, rivulets of mascara and foundation running down her cheeks. She searched for the napkins and her make-up bag and began a repair job.

Lunch with Tania was inspired. In a comfortable Italian restaurant, Tania poured her red wine to 'fortify' her and let her smoke two cigarettes, soothing, 'You go right ahead, you've had a very upsetting morning.'

By contrast, Tania's morning had been very good. She'd finally landed the big account she'd been after for weeks and Greg had booked a trip to Venice to celebrate.

'Maybe this will be it, the big proposal!' she giggled at Bella.

'Oh God, don't you dare come back all depressed if it doesn't happen. Why don't you ask him yourself?' said Bella.

'I can't.' Tania sucked on her cigarette and blew out smoke with the words: 'It's just the one last bastion that I, as an independent woman in charge of my own destiny, can't overcome, storm . . . whatever it is you're supposed to do with bastions.' They burst into laughter together.

'So, how does it feel now, to have this big tummy, this big baby thing sitting in front of you like that?' asked Tania. 'And by the way, you still look unbelievably slim, you cow. You've got lovely big boobs and a glamorous bump and everything else is just the same. Your bum still looks pert, for God's sake. It's disgusting, it should not be allowed. You better have dessert or I'm not paying.'

Bella snorted with laughter again.

'I feel tired and heavy and fat and tearful,' she confessed. 'My hair is all weird and wiry and I'm going to have to start wearing flat shoes because I can feel my spine starting to buckle with all this forward pull—' she cupped her hands round her bulge.

'Are you getting excited about the baby?' Tania asked.

'I don't feel I've really had the chance, at the moment it just feels like a hassle. Work, maternity leave, the bloody hospital. It's causing problem after problem rather than giving me any cause to celebrate,' was Bella's truthful answer.

'Will you let other people deal with some of the problems for a change, Bella? How's Don?' Tania asked, obviously meaning 'why isn't he helping you?'

'He's been away a lot. I think he wants to do all the foreigns he can, while he still has the chance. I don't know, we feel a bit out of touch right now.'

'And what is sex with a bump like?' Tania asked, twirling a forkful of pasta.

'Let's just say there's less sex.'

'Ah.' Tania looked across at Bella, but the subject appeared to be closed. 'I've got a very good idea,' Tania said suddenly. 'Why don't you come down to my parents' house at the weekend?'

'Yeah?'

'Yeah. We'll drive down on Friday after work and we'll have fresh air and pampering. Mum is desperate to see you, now that you're pregnant. She's hoping you're going to make me broody. Anyway, she knows everything about hospitals

178

and midwives and stuff, she'll know what you should do.'

Bella agreed, deciding maybe it would be nice to let someone take care of her for a couple of days.

By 9 p.m. that night, Don still hadn't rung. She'd tried his mobile several times, but only reached the messaging service. She wondered if she should be worried about him but she couldn't get worked up to it, not after just one evening.

She went to bed soon afterwards but half an hour later was woken by him calling from a noisy bar.

'I'm asleep,' she told him grumpily.

'Sorry,' he said. 'It's only 10 p.m.'

'Yeah, well . . .'

'Sorry, Bella. Don't worry, everything's going to be fine.'

'Easy for you to say . . . you aren't carrying around a six-month bump and wondering how the hell this is all going to work out.' She felt angry now.

'Look, go to sleep, it won't seem so bad in the morning. Good night, hon.'

'Bye,' she said and slammed the receiver down.

Chapter Sixteen

Bella had forgotten how fantastically opulent Tania's family home was. It was in the heart of stockbroker belt Kent, a big country house in its own small woodland.

They arrived there in the evening and as they drove up to the house, gravel crunched under the car wheels and vast lit up windows welcomed them in.

Tania's mother, Valerie, was at the door to greet them, hugging and kissing warmly. Ronald was in the enormous sitting room, drinking gin and tonic. He kissed Bella hello and insisted she sit down beside him, because he wanted to hear her City gossip. He was the one who had fired up her enthusiasm for consulting in the first place.

'You are not allowed to talk with Bella all evening, *chérie*. I want to hear all about your pregnancy darling,' Valerie warned from the door.

'Now, what are you drinking, girls? We've got mineral water, cranberry juice, apple, all sorts of soft things in for you, Bella.'

Bella and Tania's eyes met. Valerie was a

respected alternative health writer, it was not going to do to get caught drinking and smoking in your third trimester in her house.

'Cranberry, please,' said Bella.

'Gin and vermouth with a twist,' said Tania.

'Ha ha,' Valerie answered. 'You'll have a white wine and be grateful. In fact you should probably have a cranberry juice and a handful of milk thistle capsules for all the abuse you do to your liver in town.'

It was lovely to be there. Valerie mollycoddled Bella all evening, listening to the story about the hospitals with a great deal of sympathy.

'Well, I have a possible solution for you,' she said when Bella told her she still hadn't made any new arrangements. 'Home birth. I've just interviewed a woman who runs a group of independent midwives in London. You hire the midwife for the whole pregnancy, and in labour she comes to your home.'

Bella was somewhat taken aback.

'God. Is that safe? Is it legal?'

'Oh darling, go read the statistics. Let me get you a book.'

She came back with book, her article on the midwives and the phone number.

'Think it over. Now, tell me all about your new home.'

So Bella did and once Valerie had got over the shock – 'That's how much houses cost in Holloway, darling??' – they got into a whole decorating conversation along with Tania, who lived to decorate.

'I love this room,' said Bella, taking in the rugs,

antiques, luscious plants, paintings and all the polished, gleaming things which glittered in the firelight.

'Oh, it's very boring,' Valerie assured her. 'Nice floorboards, very expensive curtains, everything else is white – white walls, white sofas and then all the plants, paintings, things one seems to accumulate.'

'Not very minimal though, is it?' said Tania. Every available space was crammed full and the walls were so laden with paintings, Bella hadn't even registered they were white.

'We've lived here for thirty years, Tania,' said Valerie.

'What makes you think I'm going to be minimal?' Bella asked Tania.

'For a start, you're a mathematician, they're always anal. And secondly, you haven't got any stuff. Your house is going to be a temple to Zen unless you do some serious shopping.'

'Don has stuff. I made him throw out boxes and boxes of stuff before he was allowed into my flat.'

'Yeah, he's got a sofa and a bookcase left, I've been to your place,' Tania teased.

'Well, I was planning to buy a few things,' said Bella.

'You'll have to take me with you. In another month, you are not going to be in a fit state to go alone. By month eight you'll have lost your marbles completely.'

'No I will not!'

'Tell her, Mum.' Tania sounded like a teenager.

'Well, there are so many things to think about,'

Valerie soothed, 'and so many oestrogens and oxytocins buzzing round the system, mental calculations go down the priority list before and after birth.'

'Oh great,' said Bella. 'Like I haven't got enough to worry about.'

'When do you stop working?' Valerie asked.

'I'm working right up to labour day, I hope, then taking about two months off.'

'For a first baby, this is not enough,' Valerie told her rather bluntly.

'Well, I've got a client waiting for me in August and my boss is not exactly brimful of understanding right now,' Bella answered.

'Oh, you are pushing yourself very hard,' Valerie added. 'Just like Tania. Maybe you should take a step back and think about this in the long term. Is a few extra months off now really going to make such a difference to your career in ten years' time? I don't think so.'

Valerie could see by Bella's stormy face she had said too much.

'Think about it, Bella, please.' She patted Bella's arm then stood up and announced: 'Dinner's ready, let's go and eat.'

'Christ, Don, did it ever occur to you that you might have got shot?' she asked, having listened to Don's latest exploits at work when they got together again on Sunday evening. 'And in Bradford, not even Beirut.'

'Well, yes, but I kept telling myself that it wouldn't happen because I've got such a ludicrously big life insurance policy.'

183

'Have you really? I think I should be told,' she asked teasingly.

'God, that's a point, Bella. In my will at the moment, everything goes to Mum.' He scooped up the last of the sauce from his plate with a piece of bread.

'Better get that changed,' she said. 'I don't want Maddie swanning off to retire in Bermuda while I'm left destitute to care for your infant.'

'*You* destitute – that I would like to see. By destitute, I suppose you mean down to your last technology fund ISA.'

'Ha, ha,' she answered, wishing that were true. They were soon to be mortgaged to the hilt and the very last of her savings were going to be spent on decorators.

'Let's go snog on the sofa,' he said to her when the meal was finished.

'Well, OK, but I'm going on top.'

'Snog, I said. Don't assume I want to go all the way,' he was teasing now.

'One minute of my practised tongue technique and you will be desperate.' She got up from her chair and kissed him all the way over to the sofa where he flung himself down.

'No, not working yet, I think you'll have to try again.' He pulled her over.

She was uncomfortable trying to lie on him and kiss him over the heavy, cumbersome bump. 'Let's go to bed,' she said. 'I can't manoeuvre here.'

They walked through to the bedroom where Don sat down on the edge of the bed and pulled her close. They kissed for a long time then began to undress each other. Neither felt frantically turned

184

on, but there was tenderness in their movements.

Don felt round her outfit for an opening and realized he would have to pull it over her head. He
yanked her top clumsily off and left her standing
messy haired and rumpled in the most hideous
white bra and low slung pants he'd ever seen.

'I know,' she said picking up his disconcerted
look. 'Why don't I change into something less
comfortable?'

'No, take it all off, I want to see you.'

She unhooked the bra and her heavy breasts
dropped down unsupported. The nipples had
grown large and a dark raspberry colour.

Her stomach swelled out in front of his face with
a strange-looking stretched belly button punctuating the middle. The deep blue veins on her white
breasts and stomach were prominent. She pulled
off her pants and her pubic hair was tucked away
under the bulge, which suddenly flickered.

'God, it moved,' he said anxiously.

'Of course.' She couldn't believe she hadn't
shown him this yet. 'Give me your hand,' she said.
She put his hand flat against one side. They waited
silently for a few moments then he felt a surprisingly sharp blow underneath his palm.

'My God, that is so strong and it's just there, right
underneath your skin.'

'Yup,' she smiled.

'That's amazing,' he said. 'It doesn't hurt at all?'
She shook her head. 'This is OK, isn't it? Having
sex,' he asked.

'Well, let's try.' She smiled at him, sitting there
in his boxer shorts, socks, shirt and tie. She knelt
down and pulled his shorts and socks off, then

leaned into his lap and put her mouth on his erection.

When she pulled herself up to kiss him, she tried to straddle his lap but the bump was in the way.

'Lie down,' he whispered.

She lay on her side and he tucked in close behind her, putting a hand between her legs. She reached back for his cock and slowly worked it inside.

He took hold of her hips and began to move in deeper.

'Oh God,' she gasped, not entirely in pleasure. 'I just don't know if there's room. This feels weird.'

She felt utterly full with him inside and worse, the baby's sharp, solid parts were being pushed about and rearranged. She felt like a sink full of crockery clattering about as someone tried to push more plates in – not exactly passion-inducing.

'Do you want me to come out?' asked Don.

'No, just go really slowly, don't do anything sudden.'

He moved very carefully and it wasn't unpleasant, but it wasn't really sex.

Chapter Seventeen

Completion date on the house had arrived one week earlier than agreed – a minor London miracle, Bella couldn't help thinking as she and Don went to pick up the keys and make the journey up town to their new home. She felt nervous. Christ, they'd just spent an absolute fortune buying property in an area they'd *driven* through.

Don looked relaxed, breezy almost.

Bella was wearing the most glamorous maternity clothes she could muster, black leather trousers and soft white tunic underneath a new grey fur-collared coat. But a seven and a bit month bulge was no longer elegant. She was starting to feel very heavy on her feet and it was some effort to clamber up into the Jeep.

They were visiting the house in the morning, then she was meeting the independent midwife for the first time this afternoon to discuss the home birth option. She'd ummed and ahhed about having Don at the meeting, then decided no, that would probably horrify him more than he deserved at this stage.

He would now look so pained whenever she mentioned birth that she was beginning to worry that he was going to back out of attending her labour.

'Don! You've reported from battlefields,' she'd told him in one heated exchange.

'I've seen people give birth in fields as well,' he'd shot back. 'And it is not pretty. I just don't know if I want to see you in so much pain.'

It was still an unresolved point.

They drove up through town. It was a grey March morning, cold and raining slightly. Her pet hate weather in the world. When they got to the street, it looked much greyer and gloomier than it had done on the day they'd looked round.

Don parked up and got out of the car first. Bella took a few moments to clamber out and lumber up the street after him.

They unlocked their front door and went inside. Don flicked on the hall light and the walls looked unrelentingly orange now that the place was empty and stripped bare. In the dark, sombre navy sitting room there were patches on the walls and on the floorboards where pictures and furniture had been.

Bella looked out of the back window at the rain-sodden garden where yellow flattened grass marked the spot where the swing had been. 'God,' she said to Don. 'It does need some cheering up, doesn't it?' She was trying to sound upbeat, while silently thinking, What have we done?

Upstairs looked no better, especially the pink bedroom, savagely pink now that it was empty, and the children's bedroom with its mismatched walls.

'It feels empty and lonely,' she said to Don, with a slight wobble.

'It'll be fine,' he assured her. 'We need to decorate and put in our own things.'

'Do you still think we've done the right thing?' She needed to hear him say yes.

'Yes. It's a good choice. It's a lovely big house. It's going to be great.' He put his arms around her, 'You're going to feel a lot better once we've christened the place,' he smiled and kissed her nose.

'Now I know you're kidding!' she laughed and pushed him away. 'The only thing I'm going to christen right now is the loo.'

The bathroom was much shabbier than she remembered and cold too. The family must have moved out several days ago because the house was chilled to the brick.

Back down in the kitchen, Don leaned against the Aga as she outlined her decorating plans.

'I want to keep it simple because we've not got long now.' She stroked over the bump. 'I think replaster, paint everything white, strip down and revarnish all the floors, put in a new bathroom and new kitchen.'

He looked at her incredulously. 'That's simple? Bella! That's about eight months of work!!'

'No! Stephen has put me in touch with a team of people who say they can do it in a month,' she answered.

'Can we afford all that on top of the mortgage and an extra month or two renting?' he asked.

Not to mention the deposit, the solicitor's fee, stamp duty . . . she couldn't help adding it all up and the answer was 'No, not really', but she couldn't stand the thought of bringing the baby into a messy, unfinished house. She wanted it all sorted out. She'd get the promotion to partner when she went back to work and then it would be OK. This was just going to be a bit of a struggle for a few months.

'We'll be fine,' she answered. 'I'm going to be a partner by the end of the year,' she assured him.

'This is making me feel strange,' he said, folding his arms across his chest.

'Don –' she was beginning to feel exasperated now – 'You're paying half of the mortgage and we're a couple now. What's mine is yours. Don't say I can't spend money on our home, please.'

'Well, if you're sure it's what you want to do . . .' He looked her in the eye. 'Just don't spend every last penny, Bella, or you'll end up a sad old git like me who has to rely on his wealthy wife.'

'Don!' she smiled. 'Come on, we've got to go. The hippie midwives are coming to see me in an hour.'

'The what?!'

'Sorry, that's what I keep calling them. The independent midwives, the ones who are going to look after me from now on.' She had not had the home birth talk with Don yet. She hadn't made up her mind, so what was the point in worrying him?

'Ah . . .' Long pause. Please don't ask, please don't ask . . . but he did: 'So where are you having the baby now, Bella?'

'Let me speak to them and then we'll go through the options tonight, OK?' She put on her most relaxed, smiling, everything's fine face.

'OK, let's go then.' He glanced around the kitchen which looked dingy and forlorn in the grey

190

light. 'This is a great house, I can't wait to move in.' He was only lying a little bit. It would be fine once it was repainted.

She kissed him on the cheek. 'I love you.'

'Me too,' he said. And they headed home.

Twenty minutes after the arranged time, the doorbell rang. Bella went to the intercom and told Annie Mellor to come up to the third floor. She opened the door to a pleasant-looking, 30-something woman with mousy brown hair gathered into a long waist-length ponytail. She was wearing strange patchwork baggy trousers, suede desert boots, a knee-length anorak and had a straw basket over one shoulder. Bella felt her heart sink: this just really wasn't what she'd expected.

'Hello, I'm Annie.' Annie held out a soft white hand and Bella shook it firmly.

'Come in,' she said, trying not to sound as un-impressed as she felt.

She led Annie into her large sitting room where she perched on one of the two black leather sofas.

'Gosh,' said Annie. 'This is big, isn't it?'

'Can I get you a tea or a coffee?' asked Bella.

'Have you got anything herbal?' Annie asked.

'No.'

'Just water then, please.'

Bella returned with a tall glass of iced water and a cafetière of extra strong, super-caffeinated coffee for herself. She was tempted to have a cigarette as well but decided that would probably scare Annie off completely.

'OK,' said Bella, plonking her tray down on the coffee table. 'I'm considering using your service, so I want you to tell me all about it.'

191

'Well, basically, I will do all your antenatal care . . .'

'Can you come to my office?' Bella chipped in.

'Well, I don't see why not,' said Annie calmly.

'Right.' That was a major Brownie point.

'And then when you are in labour, I'll come to your home and deliver the baby.' This sounded too easy, too much like 'I'll come to your home and deliver your parcel.'

'So . . . how much experience do you have?' Bella asked.

'I'm a fully qualified senior midwife, I've been doing home births for about fifteen years now.' Annie fixed her with a slightly stern look and Bella saw the network of tiny lines around her eyes and mouth and realized she was much older than she at first looked, probably mid-forties.

'Right. And what happens if anything goes wrong?' Bella asked.

'Yes, everyone asks that,' said Annie. 'Obviously, if it's major we rush you to hospital in an ambulance. But our transference rate is about 10 per cent, mainly requests from the mother. Ninety per cent of our babies are delivered naturally without any intervention or even pain relief. You should compare that with the figures at the hospital down the road.'

Aha, figures. Bella was starting to relax.

'We find that women labouring at home with a midwife they know and trust deliver much more safely than if they are whisked off to hospital where all kinds of strangers are prodding and poking at them, strapping them to machines,' Annie said.

192

'So you don't give any drugs at all?' Bella asked.

'We prefer not to. We have a TENS machine on hand but we prefer aromatherapy massage, hot baths or a birthing pool and natural remedies.'

'Well, I've read a home birth book,' Bella said. 'A friend gave it to me, but I just wonder if it isn't all a bit idealistic. It's all smiley happy people having a back rub while babies pop out. What about all the screaming and blood and agony?'

'Well, there's a bit of that too – but birth is not half as bad as they make out on *ER*,' Annie smiled. 'If you're in a good atmosphere with people you know supporting you, it can make all the difference.'

Bella noticed how slight Annie was. Her thin legs were crossed and her desert boots gaped at her bony ankles. She just didn't look strong enough to be a midwife.

'So what do you need for a home birth?' Bella asked. 'We're moving house next month, by the way.'

'All pregnant women are moving house or decorating. It's a rule,' Annie smiled again and Bella smiled back. She was warming to her . . . a little bit.

'First of all we need to talk about your health,' said Annie. 'Truthfully!'

'Right.'

Annie read her way carefully through Bella's maternity notes.

'Are you still drinking and smoking?' she asked.

'I've cut right down.' She did not need another lecture.

'Well you've got to stop, Bella. I can't over-emphasize how bad it is for the baby. Are you doing any exercise?'

'I ran every morning till about month six, now I'm power walking and going to the gym once or twice a week.'

Annie looked a touch horrified and recommended an antenatal yoga class.

Then she asked: 'When do you stop work?'

'I was going to work right up to wire, but the project I'm on might wind up a week or two early, so I might have a bit of extra time off.'

'Good,' Annie said. 'I think you need it, because you've not really had the time to give this baby much thought yet, have you?'

This was said kindly, but Bella felt a little bit stung. She knew it was true and she did feel ready to slow up a bit now, read the books, mooch round the nursery shops and think about names. There and then she decided she was going to give Annie a go. She would get regular antenatal visits in her office, sign up for the yoga classes and mull over a home birth.

Once Annie had left, Bella called Tania for a second opinion.

'You don't think it's just a bit alternative and hippie?' Bella asked.

'Home birth?' Tania answered. 'No, it's ultra modern and cool. *De rigueur* in Notting Hill. The NHS is too PC, private is "Too posh to push", so everyone's having their baby at home.'

'Oh well that's OK then,' Bella said, heavy on the irony. 'God, Tani, this is birth not a fashion statement!'

'Bella, you live in central London, they can get you to hospital in ten minutes flat, I'm sure it will be fine. How's your new house?'

'We went there this morning, it looks empty and sad and depressing.'

'You need to decorate. When can I come and look round?'

They fixed up a date for the weekend.

Bella and Don were eating out with Mel and Jasper that night, so they drove across town crammed cosily into Bella's car.

'I can't believe you can still get into this thing,' Don teased as they sat almost cheek by cheek in the low seats. 'Isn't driving a bit difficult now?'

'No, it's lovely . . . I can whiz around and duck and dive and forget that I'm a great big huge pregnant whale when I'm on dry land.'

'Any more metaphors you'd like to stir into that cocktail?' he teased.

'Oh shut up.' She fired up the engine and reversed out of the space. 'I'm the mathematician, you're the wordsmith. Can we leave it at that?'

'So, who are we going to name our child after?' he asked once they were on the road. 'Wordsmiths or mathematicians?'

'I don't want to name him or her after anyone,' she said. 'I want something totally unique.'

'Oh no . . . not Bellabel Ginseng Algebra Browning!'

She snorted with laughter.

'What about your heroes?' he asked. 'Maybe Benito?'

'Who??'

'Mussolini, of course . . .' he carried on over her protests. 'Woody? For Woody Allen? And what's Einstein's first name again?'

'Frank,' she answered. 'Frank Einstein,' then over his laughter, she asked, 'You want Dylan, don't you? After the great Bob?'

'Yes!' he answered. 'Please, can we?'

'NO! Absolutely no way!'

'Well if we're doing musical heroes, I suppose you'll want Robbie or maybe Ronan . . . or Posh,' he said, so she whacked him on the arm.

'How about Karl . . . after Marx?' was his next suggestion.

'Mark . . .' she said. 'Markie McCartney. Hey! I like that.'

'Hmmm,' he answered. 'And girls?'

'It won't be a girl,' she said with a grin.

'No?'

'No, I just know.'

'You sneaked a peak at your last scan, didn't you?'

'I'm not saying!! I just know.'

'You are a totally devious, cheating woman, Bella,' Don was teasing but stopped when he saw her expression change abruptly. 'What's wrong?' he asked urgently.

'Nothing, nothing . . . sorry. Anxious baby thoughts, that's all. Sorry,' she said, gluing her eyes to the traffic lights in front of them and willing the big hit of Chris guilt to go away.

'It's going to be great,' he said soothingly.

'I hope so,' she answered.

Chapter Eighteen

'Bella, Bella, wake up. Your alarm's been beeping for ages.'

She opened her eyes and looked at Don wearily.

'Oh Christ.' She rolled onto her side and pushed herself up off the bed.

She was heavy and extremely tired. It was impossible to get a full night's sleep now. She had to empty her bladder at least twice a night and despite having pillows between her knees and under her bulge, it was hard to get comfortable.

Still, she had to keep going. It was already April, she was in her eighth month and the Merris deadline had to be met before she could entertain any thoughts of dropping this little load. She cranked herself up and put on her dressing gown, tying the cord over the bump so she looked like a walking Easter egg. She waddled to the bathroom, pinned up her hair, washed her face, slapped some make-up on.

Back in the bedroom she put on large white bra, pants, black maternity support tights, which practically came up to her armpits, then a flapping white shirt and the grey polyester suit and flat shoes.

Don was looking at her from the bed.

'Don't say anything,' she warned him, 'I look like shit, I feel like shit too. The stylish, sexy woman you married has turned into a monster.'

He laughed, but she didn't.

'I hate this, Don, I feel like a whale. I know you're going to make lots of nice reassuring noises but I am a whale.'

Don said: 'I'm your whale mate, then.'

The doorbell rang. It was the taxi. She and Geoff now took a shared minicab to work. It was a posh minicab – plush Rover with driver who could speak English, drive and get them there – but still a minicab, not a limousine.

Geoff didn't say anything to her at all now, just 'Umm' for Good Morning then hid behind his paper.

It always got like this towards the end of the job. Everyone hated you because your criticisms of their work were made public and acted upon. This was the toughest part. It was the natural human 'shoot the messenger' response and she tried not to take it personally, but she always felt a bit hurt when it kicked in.

The baby rolled round in her stomach. She hadn't had time for breakfast and a hard lump of heartburn was stuck in her chest.

'Geoff, I hope you don't mind,' she said. 'We're passing a café in a few moments, I'm going to ask the driver to pull over so I can get something.'

'Ummm.'

'Do you want anything?'

'Ummph.'

God Almighty, she hadn't faced this kind of behaviour since primary two.

She was glad when she was finally in her little office, closeted away from the growing panic enveloping the company. The merger had just been announced, along with Merris's resignation from the chief exec position. Everyone now knew the changes were happening and the anxiety was palpable.

Bella Browning, 28, first solo project, had set this all in motion. She felt badly in need of some re-assurance, so she decided to phone the office.

'Good morning, Prentice and Partners.' She felt better just for hearing that on the other end of the line.

'Kitty, hello, it's Bella.'

'Bella! How are you? We haven't seen you for ages. You must be huge by now. Promise you'll come for Friday drinks?'

'I'll see. I don't know what's happening on Friday yet, I'll try. I've missed you all.'

'It's been so quiet, no-one's been in the office apart from Susan.'

'Is she in now?'

'Yup, I'll try the line, but come and see us on Friday.'

'I'll be there if I can.'

She held for several long minutes. She had barely spoken to Susan since Christmas and she now felt a nervous twinge about it.

'Bella, hello, how are you?' Susan's voice was crisp and professional.

'I'm OK. Well, actually I'm having a bit of a

confidence crisis about Merris. I'd really like to talk you through my final report before I give it, just to make sure it's all right.'

'Of course it is. I have every faith in you, Bella,' Susan answered.

'Is there a good time to phone you later today? I'd really like to just take you through an outline,' Bella persisted.

'That's fine. How about 3.30? But Bella, don't worry, I'm sure it's very good work.'

'Thanks, Susan, I needed to hear that.'

'I'll speak to you later then.'

'Bye.'

She had made the call on her mobile – it was time to be very careful. Now her desk phone was ringing. Janice from Merris's office wanted to know if Bella could go in and see him now.

'I'll be there in ten minutes,' Bella answered thinking *AAAAAArgh* and scrabbling to get some papers together. She could feel her heart thud in her chest and the baby churned around inside her stomach.

She didn't know what this could be about and felt panicky. She took her ten-pack of cigarettes out of her briefcase and lit up with shaking hands.

By the fifth drag, she was starting to feel steady, by the seventh she was toughening up again. Her analysis had been correct, her suggestions good – there was nothing she needed to worry about: if the chairman wanted to hear it from the horse's mouth first, ahead of the board – he was bloody well going to.

Janice showed her into Merris's office. She'd forgotten how old-fashioned it was – wood

200

panelling, portraits of horses and ancestors on the walls, him behind a vast desk in an over-upholstered swivel chair.

Merris, as ever, looked like a dapper politician in a dark three-piece suit, complete with watch chain and tiny yellow carnation bud in the buttonhole. His grey hair was combed back neatly and he fixed his pale blue eyes on her. 'My word Bella, you have torn through us like a hurricane, haven't you?' was his opening gambit.

'No not really,' she said, settling down in the chair he indicated. 'Hurricanes are destructive, I want to help you build something strong for the future.'

'Yes, I appreciate that,' he said, then added: 'I'm very pleased with the merger.'

He told her the very big price he'd achieved. She whistled and he laughed at her.

'Do they know about the appeal case?' she asked.

'They know it's a remote possibility. You're very concerned about that, aren't you?'

'If you lose, it would be a disaster. Well, less of a disaster now you have new partners,' she said.

'We won't lose,' he replied and made it sound like his final word on the subject.

'So,' he continued, 'I'm moving upstairs, which makes me feel a touch sad, but thank you for reminding me that chief executives can't go on for ever. I don't know who's replacing me yet, our new partners will want to have a say in that, but I've called you in here, Ms Browning because I'd like to recommend you for the post of financial director.'

He paused for her reaction, but she didn't make one. She was thinking about Geoff, the current financial director, tutting at her in the taxi and wondered where he would be going, so Merris named his price.

She whistled again.

They looked at each other, then finally she said: 'That's a very generous offer, Mr Merris. But I've got a lot to think about at the moment. I'm five weeks away from giving birth for the first time and to be frank, well, I'm not sure if I have the experience yet.'

That was the clincher. A financial directorship would be very nice and would certainly pay the mortgage but it wasn't in the career plan just yet. She had a lot more consulting to get under her belt first.

But Merris said: 'I wouldn't ask you if I didn't think you could do it,' then added, 'Well I don't expect an answer straight away. Feel free to come back to me any time.'

She smiled at him.

'Now,' he said, 'I am looking forward to your report because I'm expecting you to tell us that the merger and strategies we've put in place, thanks to you, are going to have a very positive effect.'

'Yes,' she said, 'I hope that will encourage everyone.'

'Excellent. Now we may not have the chance for another personal chat before you leave, so I want to tell you how grateful I am for your work. I'll be telling your boss that too. But I'd rather you came and worked for me than anyone else.'

'Well, I'll give it some serious thought.' She smiled at him.

She stood up with the feeling that the meeting was drawing to a close.

'Now—' he opened a drawer and brought out a small exquisitely wrapped box. He stood up and walked round the desk to hand it to her: 'This is a token of my appreciation.'

She took it from him thinking, Jewellery from a client, oops. It struck her as somehow inappropriate.

'Please open it,' he said.

'Right.' She wondered how to handle the situation.

She tugged at the ribbon and lifted the lid on a white teething ring attached to a large solid silver bear. It was quite the most ridiculous gift for a baby ever, but she was still touched at the sentiment.

'Thank you, Mr Merris,' she said, holding out her hand for a businesslike handshake.

'You can call me Tony,' he said shaking her hand firmly and patting her arm. 'In fact, you already have once.'

She blushed slightly.

'Yes, I have, sorry . . . I can be a bit . . .'

'Don't apologize,' he cut in. 'That's what I like about you, Bella. You've got guts. I'm surrounded by yes men and look where it's got me. I think it would do me good to have a "no woman" around.'

'A "no woman", I like that,' she smiled. 'Thank you so much for your support. Now, I'd better go and put that report together.'

'Yes,' he said. 'I look forward to it.'

She swanned out of his office and back to her own, smiling all the way.

At 3.30 p.m. she telephoned Susan to tell her about the latest developments.

'It's gone so well, Susan, he even offered me a job.' She said this lightly to imply there was no question of her taking it.

'And what did you say?' Susan asked.

'I told him I had a lot on my mind right now and I'd get back to him. But I'm with you, Susan. I want to let you know how committed I am, despite the baby.'

'Despite the baby' – she didn't like herself for saying that. Having a baby was not something she should be apologizing about. Hello, this is century 21.

'I appreciate that,' Susan replied. 'Are you handing in the report and finishing up there next week?'

'Yes, probably on Wednesday/Thursday.'

'Well, next Friday we're taking you out for a maternity leave party and as of then you are off. Don't count it as official leave, have the three weeks extra on us. You deserve it.'

Bella felt touched now. 'Thanks,' she said. 'That means a lot.'

The report smacked onto Mr Merris's desk at 8 a.m. the following Wednesday. The eight days it had taken to finish off had passed in a blur and she had worked like a dog.

Most of the weekend had been spent in her dressing gown at the computer compiling the vast amounts of data needed to prove that her recovery strategies were already working, but could be further improved on. She'd barely seen Don, who had been working late as well.

It had been a grind with momentary flashes of inspiration. She wondered about the future of Merris. They were getting an injection of new money and new talent but she did not know if it was going to be enough to really change the thinking there. And she still couldn't be as blasé about the court case as everyone else seemed to be. What if the pension holders won? Merris would be forced to make enormous payouts and its reputation would fold overnight.

Mitch crossed her mind. She had more or less told him it was safe to stay, but now she just didn't know.

On Wednesday afternoon she made her presentation to a surprisingly large audience, not just Merris chiefs but also executives from the new partner company. Her thrust was encouraging but cautious because Merris Group was not out of the woods by a long shot.

She felt horribly self-conscious as she stood in front of them, ridiculously pregnant, bulging at the seams of her foul jersey dress. Could she have been any more of an outsider? Would they take her at all seriously? At the end of the day, that was their problem. She'd done the job she'd been paid to do, she kept reminding herself.

Afterwards, there was a small drinks party, so everyone could shake her hand, ask more questions and thank her for her efforts. Later she was back in her little office, emptying her drawers and packing up, when there was a knock at the door.

Janice came in weighed down with a big bunch of flowers.

'These are from Mr Merris, with compliments,' she said, passing Bella the enormous bouquet. The note attached read: 'Well done, we'd still like you aboard, Tony.'

She was standing in the room, unsure where to put the flowers when there was another knock.

Mitch appeared.

'Whoa, who is your secret admirer?'

'Tony.'

Mitch looked blank.

'Tony Merris.'

'Oh. Really? I'm impressed.' Then he added, 'I'm sorry you're leaving, mainly because all hell is going to break loose here now. I hope.'

'Yeah, I hope so too. It needs a good shake-up, but there's going to be lots more room for good people like you.'

'I hope so.' Then Mitch voiced the concern she expected: 'Do you still think I should stay?'

'I can't answer that. It depends who's doing the reorganization, I've asked them to bring in a lot more new talent. And I'm still worried about the court case . . . if they lose, that's a lot of money.'

'Hmmm.' He didn't give anything away. 'Well anyway, I've got you a present.' He handed her a squishy, wrapped parcel.

'Oh you shouldn't have, now I'm really embarrassed because I haven't got anything for you.'

'It's for the baby,' he added. 'Open it.'

She unwrapped a small, perfectly adorable, blue velvet frog.

'It squeaks and it's machine washable, dads know about that sort of thing.'

'Thanks very much.' She was surprised to feel tears pricking at the back of her eyes. 'How's your wife?' she asked.

'She's doing good, she's very tired because she's got two other little people to run after all day and the baby. But she's well and we're really glad to have got a girl.'

There was a brief silence; they smiled at each other, comfortable with the pause.

'Give me your card, Bella. I'll keep you in touch with what's happening here.'

'Of course.' She dipped into her bag and handed him one.

'Well all the best then,' he said and they shook hands warmly.

'Take care,' she said as he left the room.

So, that was about it. She'd packed up, she'd said her goodbyes. She buzzed reception to get her a cab, then headed out of Merris laden down with bump, bags, laptop, briefcase and the flowers.

As she flopped into the cab seat, Bella took one last look at the revolving swing doors and impressive marble front. She swallowed down the urge to cry as the taxi moved off.

Friday night was much more emotional.

She went out with Susan, Chris, Kitty and Hector for dinner and they made baby jokes and lovely appreciative noises about her all night long.

Finally, as dessert and coffees arrived to the maelstrom of empty wine bottles and overflowing ashtrays on the table, Chris made a jokey speech about her which ended with a silly poem. Everyone collapsed in pissed-up giggles. Fortunately, Kitty brought out a large parcel from under the table.

'Open it,' she urged.

Bella cleared a space and undid the wrapper. Inside was a small mountain of exquisite baby clothes: orange and blue velour babygros, beautiful striped and decorated jackets, rompers, tiny suede shoes, a multicoloured hat with ear-flaps and a bobble and a mobile of little stuffed clowns on ribbons.

'Oh my God,' she said quite overwhelmed. 'You found all these lovely things.'

'Me and Susan,' said Kitty. 'Took a whole after-noon.' That surprised Bella, she tried to picture Susan in a baby shop.

'Oh thank you, thank you so much.' Bella looked up at each of the four faces in turn. 'This is absolutely wonderful. I'm going to cry now.' And she did. At first able to stem the flow with her napkin, then needing to bury her head in Kitty's shoulder for a serious howl.

'Oh God, this is so embarrassing,' she said when she surfaced. 'It's the hormones, I'm starting to go completely mad.'

It was after midnight when she finally kissed them all good night and climbed into a taxi to go home.

Lights were on in the flat and she hoped Don had waited up for her. He was leaving early tomorrow morning on another foreign assignment which he'd promised would be very short as the due date was getting close now.

'Hi,' she called out, opening the front door.

'I'm in here,' he answered and his voice sounded incredibly serious. She walked into the dark sitting room, noticing two large holdalls next to the front door as she passed.

Don was sitting on the sofa in silence, no TV, no music on. He didn't look up at her as she came in. 'I've just found out about the baby,' he said.

'Hello?' she said, wondering what the hell he meant. 'I thought I told you months ago. What on earth do you think this bump is?'

'I'm just so angry with you. How could you do this to me?' He looked round at her now and she saw he was furious.

'What are you talking about??' she asked, totally confused.

'Well, let me explain,' he said. I was having a quiet evening in with not much to do and I happened to see your maternity notes on the shelf. I was just curious, didn't see any harm in reading them . . . didn't have any idea I'd be uncovering your big secret.'

'What do you mean?' she asked, feeling very nervous now.

'Well, either someone's made a mistake, or you intended to get pregnant all along, without bothering to tell me.'

He thrust the booklet out at her and she could clearly see the tick in the 'planned' box. She also saw the handwritten note beside it, 'Folic acid taken for four months before conception.'

'Four months before conception,' Don read out. 'And it never occurred to you, for one moment, to even mention this to me?'

'Jesus,' she whispered. That all seemed so long

209

ago now, she'd completely forgotten about it. 'Can I try and explain?'

'No. Not right now. I'm too angry. I always thought there was something strange about *you* having an accident.' He stood up and rounded on her: 'How could you lie to me about this? Why couldn't you just trust me, like I've always, always trusted you?

'It's so manipulative,' he added furiously. 'You've got it all figured out, haven't you? And I'm just supposed to fit into your big plan.'

'No. Don, I'm sorry, I just didn't think you'd want to . . .'

'No, you know what? I've got to get out of here. I can't listen to this right now,' he cut in. 'I'm going to get a cab over to Rod's and we'll go to the airport together in the morning.'

He stood up and walked past her to the door.

'Don!' she pleaded, she put out a hand to stop him, 'Don, please—' but he brushed her off and went into the hall. He picked up his bags, then walked out without another word, slamming the door.

She slumped down onto the floor, burying her head in the parcel of baby clothes she was still holding, and wept.

Chapter Nineteen

The next morning Bella woke late but felt relieved that at least she had something planned for the day – her first antenatal yoga class.

She felt a lurch of fear whenever she thought about Don and needed distraction from the situation. When it was time to go, she packed her mobile into her bag, just in case he should ring, and drove off to the address she'd been given.

It was a small church hall. In the vestibule she saw a row of socks and shoes leading to an open door where a group of women, many just as pregnant as her, were chatting.

She took off her trainers and socks, and went through to join them.

'Hello, I'm Bella,' she said when everyone looked up at her, 'and I definitely can't put my feet behind my ears.'

Lame gag, but there were smiles and hellos back. This felt very strange. It occurred to her that she had not hung out with other pregnant people before.

The teacher, a slim, wiry-haired woman, took her

details and they settled down for the class. They 'breeeeeeeathed' a lot, they stretched, they practised relaxation techniques and Bella felt that at last she'd found a way to slow down and stay still.

When the two hours was over, she felt calm, happy, rejuvenated. The teacher passed round drinks and biscuits and everyone chatted about babies, birth plans, breast feeding. She suddenly felt fascinated by it all, by the reality of this whole pregnancy state.

'I'm Red by the way,' said the extraordinary-looking woman sitting next to her and Bella said hello, finding it hard to take her eyes off her. Red had skin the colour of chocolate caramel, liquid brown eyes with a halo of gold round the pupil and wild, corkscrew dreadlocks which were unexpectedly ginger.

'When're you due?' Red asked.

'In three weeks,' Bella answered.

'Oh me too . . .' Red cupped her hands round the enormous bump Bella somehow hadn't noticed. 'Not long to go, thank God.' Red added, 'My feet are almost totally flat!' They both smiled.

Back in the car, Bella feeling serene and full of happy, pregnant, yoga thoughts, tried Don's mobile.

It rang for a long time, then diverted to message: 'Hello, Don,' she said. 'It's me, I'd really like to talk to you. I'm so sorry about this. Call me . . . bye.' She clicked off the phone, disappointed.

By bedtime, she was really disappointed. She'd left another message and he still hadn't phoned back.

By Sunday morning, she felt totally depressed.

There was still no reply on Don's mobile. She lay in bed and couldn't face anything, not even making breakfast. She just lay still, staring at the ceiling, wishing she could fall asleep again.

When she finally dozed off, she drifted in and out of dreams of Don and Don holding babies. An insistent hammering and shouting was punctuating the lovely dream; she tried to ignore it and hang onto the image of Don beside her with their baby. But the picture faded and she gradually woke up to the realization that someone really was hammering at the door and calling her name.

'Bella!'

'Bella, are you in there?'

'Are you OK? For God's sake, *Bella*!'

She levered herself slowly out of bed and waddled to the door. She opened it up to see Tania standing there, looking exasperated but hugely relieved.

'Thank fuck for that,' Tania said, 'I thought you'd died or gone into labour or something . . .'

Bella stared at her.

'You weren't at the house. Or answering any of your bloody phones. And I knew you were alone this weekend and . . . when I saw the curtains shut, I just panicked.' Tania was beginning to feel embarrassed now.

Bella was still staring at her.

'The house at twelve. We were supposed to meet there.' Tania held up her hands in total exasperation.

'Were we? Oh God, I completely forgot,' said Bella listlessly.

'Pregnancy, look what it's done to you?' Tania

213

was teasing now. 'You're in bed at 1 p.m., you look absolutely awful and now you've lost your marbles.'

'Yeah, and maybe my husband,' Bella added.

'What!' Tania followed her into the flat and shut the door. 'What the hell's happened?' she demanded, steering Bella into the sitting room.

'We had a huge row. Well, actually . . . we didn't. He's just stormed off on a work trip and not called. I don't know what's going on,' Bella said, wondering why she felt so numb.

'You seem really strange, Bella, are you OK?'

Bella could feel a wave of pins and needles move over her face. She parted her lips and whispered, 'I think I'm going to . . .' before she swayed dangerously. Somehow Tania managed to move Bella backwards into the sofa before the full weight of a fainting eight-month pregnant woman felled her.

Trying desperately hard not to panic, Tania looked at her friend, lying unconscious and deathly white with her huge stomach moving ominously.

She heaved Bella over onto her side and opened up her buttons. Vaguely remembering something about feet needing to be up, she propped several sofa cushions under them. Then at a total loss, Tania stroked Bella's damp forehead and told her it was going to be OK. Bella's eyelids began to flicker.

'Bella? Can you hear me?' Tania asked.

'Yes,' came the whisper.

'Are you OK? Are you in any pain?'

'No, I'm fine. I think I need something to drink.' Bella still wasn't opening her eyes.

'God, you're scaring me,' said Tania. 'Do you think we should phone for an ambulance?'

'Give me a moment, then we'll ring the midwife.'

This reassured Tania slightly, so she brought Bella a glass of water and held her head as she sipped it down.

Once Bella was able to sit up, Tania made her drink milky, sugary tea and halfway through the mug, Bella realized she was ravenously hungry, so Tania made her toast slathered in butter. As Bella ate and drank, she started to feel better. She rang Annie, who promised to come and check on her later in the afternoon.

When Tania started to quiz her about Don, Bella, somewhat shamefacedly, confessed to the whole 'accidental pregnancy'.

'Is that such a big deal?' her friend asked.

'Well, yeah really. Obviously,' said Bella.

'What do you want to do now?' Tania asked.

'I want to sort it out, I need things to be OK between us again.'

'Is there other stuff going on?' Tania asked.

Bella gave a deep sigh and tried to put the vague unease she'd been feeling lately into words: 'I think he's still a bit terrified of all this. Marriage is one thing, but a mortgage and fatherhood is scaring the shit out of him. And I've been really preoccupied, with work, with the baby . . . with all this house move stuff. I haven't really noticed what's been going on with him or with us.' After another sigh, she added: ' You know Don's dad left when he was tiny. I'm terrified that's what he's programmed to do, on some level.'

'Bloody hell,' said Tania. 'How are you going to fix this?'

'I'm not really sure,' Bella answered. 'But I'm going to have to try.'

Tania smiled encouragingly at her.

'Would a cigarette be totally out of the question?' Bella asked, still horribly pale.

'Yup, I'm afraid it would,' Tania answered.

'Will you smoke one for me, then?'

'Well OK, but I'm opening the window and you can't sit right next to me.'

'Spoilsport.'

On Wednesday morning, Bella got up very early, put on the most glamorous pregnancy outfit she could muster and drove to Heathrow to meet Don's 7 a.m. flight, which was, of course, delayed. She wandered round Terminal 3 in a tired daze. With her current bladder situation, drinking a string of café lattes was not an option.

Checking herself over in the bathroom mirror, she was instantly depressed at how enormous she looked, not even her groovy get-up could detract from that. In fact the outfit looked bloody ridiculous, a brightly coloured sarong, high-heeled ankle boots, ouch, and a low-cut clinging top, what was she thinking?? Over this she'd slung her one fantastic item, a brand new mock croc brown leather coat.

She'd gone to town yesterday intending to buy baby things, but it had been way too gloomy. It made her want Don with her even more. They should be choosing cot blanket patterns and types of pram together. So, she'd tried to cheer herself up with the coat.

When the plane finally landed, she stood at the arrivals gate feeling the nerves from hell and scanning every face that went past.

At last she saw him striding along, bag and coat over his shoulder. He was talking to someone else. Damn! She'd forgotten he wouldn't be alone. She couldn't decide whether to wave or wait until he got closer. Then he spotted her and a look of surprise crossed his face.

'Hello Bella! What on earth are you doing here?' He sounded matey, jokey almost. He leaned over and pecked her cheek and she couldn't say any of the things she'd planned, because his colleague was being introduced to her now.

'Rod, this is my wife Bella.'

'How d'you do?' said Rod, shaking her hand.

'Hi,' she answered. 'Good trip?'

'Yeah,' they both replied.

There was an awkward pause, then thankfully Rod said, 'I'm going to shoot off then. Nice to meet you, Bella, see you tomorrow, Don,' and he was gone.

They were left facing each other.

'What are you doing here?' Don asked again.

'I'm your fucking wife, what the fuck do you think I'm doing here? I didn't just happen to be passing.' So, the speech she'd had in mind was undergoing some hasty revisions, as she turned into Reservoir Wife.

'OK,' he said steadily.

'Just how long were you planning to sulk?' she

217

demanded. 'Were you going to come home today? Or were you going to carry on pretending that I don't exist?'

'I hadn't really got a plan,' he said, still very calm. 'Some of us don't plan every little thing to the nth degree.'

She looked him straight in the eye and felt all her anger dissolve. She loved him and just wanted this to be over, just wanted him back.

'I'm really sorry, Don. I should have told you. It was a really shitty thing to do.' Quietly, she added: 'I'm sorry . . . I really wanted us to have a baby and I was sure you'd say no if I asked.'

'But maybe I'd changed my mind, Bella,' he answered. 'I should have at least had the chance to consider it. Don't you think it would have made a difference, if I'd known how much you wanted this?'

'I'm sorry.'

'I feel you don't trust me.'

'I'm so sorry,' she said again and tears began to slide down her face.

He put his arm on her shoulder. 'What do you want to do, Bella?' he asked.

'I want us to go home,' she sounded tired and sad, 'I want everything to be OK.'

He looked down at the ground: 'I'm sorry I've upset you.'

'Don, I'm eight and a half months pregnant, the theme tune to *Emmerdale* upsets me,' she managed a smile.

He smiled back and they both relaxed a little.

'Please come here,' he said and they hugged as best they could over her huge bulge.

'Shall we go and get a coffee?' he asked into her hair.

'Yeah, OK.' Bladder be damned.

When they were sitting down, he confessed to all the anxieties Bella had suspected.

'I'm sorry.' It was his turn to apologize now. He took a swig of his coffee and she saw how tired he looked: 'It still seems so soon,' he said. 'We've only known each other for a year and a half, now we're buying the house, having a baby. You're charging into all this and I'm wondering if I can handle it.'

'I didn't expect the pregnancy to work out so easily,' she said, 'I thought we'd have to have a few goes. You know what my mother went through.'

He nodded.

'I'm not going to be able to do this without you, Don.' She couldn't bear to meet his eyes, so just stared at the layer of foam dimpling in her untouched cup.

'I know. And I promise I'm going to be here for you, I've been thinking about you non-stop, I've missed you so much,' he squeezed her hand.

'But you didn't even call!'

'I know, I know. I'm so sorry. Once I'm on my high horse, I can never see a way of getting down again.'

'Don! How long would you have left it?' she looked up at him now and tried to smile a little.

'I don't know, Bella. It's terrible. There are some women out there who are still waiting to hear,' he gave a half smile but she looked serious.

'We're about to become parents, Don, we need to tackle all this difficult stuff head on. Even though it's really hard.'

'OK, we will. I promise.' He moved his chair over so he could put his arm round her. 'Come here,' he pressed his mouth against hers, tasting her for what felt like the first time in months. She flooded with relief.

'I love your coat,' he said when they finally broke off.

'Thanks. Can we go home now?'

'D'you think I'll get all my stuff in your car?' he asked as they followed the signs to the car park.

'Oh, I brought the Jeep,' she tried to sound casual.

'You brought the Jeep! You must really love me.'

'Yeah, I do,' she answered.

When they got home, they closed the curtains and went to bed for a very tender fuck, lying side by side.

He moved carefully inside her moving his hands over her heavy breasts, enormous taut stomach and down between her legs. She was tensing and trembling against him and just as he came, she cried out 'Oh my God!' and moved his hand onto her stomach where he could feel waves pulsating across it.

'Shit! Are you in labour?!'

'No, I've just had the most incredible orgasm ever. I'm still having it. Whoa . . .' the rippling was slowing down now. Don kept his hand on her stomach for a long time, until it finally stopped.

'I love you,' he said, settling his head back on the pillow but still curled up close behind her with his arm resting on her side.

'I love you too,' she answered.

'I'm going to love the baby,' he added.

'Me too.' She felt tears prick at the back of her

eyes. Not again! She blinked them away and closed her eyes.

Moments later they fell asleep and for the first time in days, both of them slept soundly without any troubling dreams.

Chapter Twenty

As soon as they clapped eyes on the genuine Land Rover three-wheeler, complete with real tyres, sheepskin lining and handbrake, they both knew that this was the pram for them.

'I cannot believe how much money we have spent on a small, unborn baby.' Don was looking fazed in the lift. He had taken a few days off, so they could spend a long weekend finally moving into the house and shopping for furniture and baby things.

One tiny baby seemed to require a mountain of stuff – cradle with all the trimmings, a bath, changing table, towels, vests, rompers, cardigans, assorted clothes Bella could not resist, a car seat and finally – the only thing Don could get excited about – the baby's set of wheels.

'Yeah, well hold on tight, we're going to the kitchen department now,' Bella told him. Poor Don, he had no idea about all that was on her list. They'd rented for years, now they had to furnish a whole house.

The kitchen was granted an enormous stainless steel fridge, a washing machine, a dishwasher, crockery, pots, pans, cutlery, glasses and wine glasses, which all went through on Bella's card as Don began to pale at the running total.

A taxi ride later and they were buying maple wardrobes for the bedroom, an incredibly Parisian-cool leather armchair and a distressed beech kitchen table with six chairs.

'Not half as distressed as I'm going to be when my bill comes in,' Bella joked to Don, as she signed the card slip, and instantly regretted the gag when he didn't smile back.

'Right,' he said as they headed out of the shop. 'That's it, you're not spending any more money. What else do we need?'

'Well, some lamps, some rugs, a coat stand. A new sofa?' She knew she was going out on a limb here.

'OK.' He sounded reasonable. 'Well, I'm getting them.' Before she could object, he added 'No, no, no . . . I don't want to hear it. Bella it's my home too. I'm not your kept man.'

'Can I come with you?' she asked. If he was going to go off and rack up a whole load on his credit card, she felt she should at least guide his choices a little bit.

'No, you have to bundle yourself off into a taxi and get home for your check-up with Annie.'

'OK . . . OK, Don. But you don't have to get everything today,' she told him, kissing him goodbye. 'You know, if you don't see anything you like . . .'

'You mean if I don't see anything you'd like,' he grinned at her.

'No, no, it's your home too.' She tried to really mean this.

223

It was a sunny May afternoon and she was heading back to her new home. She felt happy in the back of the cab, but very tired. Buying the baby clothes had made her feel weird. What was this going to be like? She had spread one of the tiny babygros over her bump and it just didn't seem possible that a real, live baby, this size, was going to come out of there in a matter of weeks . . . *Weeks!!!*

Mostly she felt strangely relaxed about labour, but occasionally she woke up at night covered in sweat having had a dreadful nightmare about blood and agony.

She had pitchforked the home birth issue around and around her mind until she had just had to leave it alone as a decision made which should not be unmade. She repeated the statistics to herself like a mantra and took some solace from the intelligent, reasonable women at the yoga class who were nearly all doing the same. The yoga class was fun. It was nice to be surrounded by other pregnant women and moan about varicose veins, stretch marks and, bugbear of her life, piles.

The front door was open, as usual, because there were always decorators in. Almost every room had now been replastered and painted dazzling white. The floors had been sanded and varnished and the house looked huge, empty and new.

She walked through the hall and upstairs to the bedroom to dump her bags. The mattress they were sleeping on was still unmade from this morning and boxes full of clothes lined the walls. A bulb hung from the ceiling and there was only a sheet pinned over the window, so they kept waking up early with the light.

The new shower, toilet and sink were in the bath-room, plumbed in and working but the walls were still bare plaster and the lino had been ripped up, leaving stained plyboard underneath.

Two of the decorators were replastering in the baby's room. She put her head round the door to say hello.

'Hello, Bella,' said the younger one. 'Bill's down in the kitchen if you want to talk to him.'

Not really. She wanted to lie down flat out on her bed, but she thought she'd better go have a chat. She braced herself for the three flights of stairs down to the kitchen and began waddling.

Bill and two other men were drinking cups of tea when she came in.

'Hello, Bella,' Bill greeted her. 'Don't go giving birth early, this is going to take another week or so. Hopefully we'll get the bathroom finished off at the same time.'

'Well, I think you're safe,' she answered. 'The baby's head hasn't come down yet.'

There was a collective gulping of tea. This was obviously too much information.

She hoped the Aga would look OK in the new stainless steel kitchen. She hadn't had the heart to rip it out and replace it with a steel range. That was the thing about Agas: built-in nostalgia for kitchens you didn't grow up in but kind of wished you had.

Finally lying down on her bed, she called Don. 'Hi, how's it going?' she asked.

'Fine,' he answered. 'Leave me alone, I can handle this!!'

'All right! I'm just checking! Will you bring dinner home? All our kitchen stuff isn't being delivered until tomorrow and anyway, I'm too tired.'

'OK, is Annie there yet?'

'No, she won't be long though.'

'Take care.'

'Bye.'

When Annie arrived and began doing the routine checks, she was concerned at Bella's blood pressure. 'It's slightly up,' she said, looking at Bella lying in an exhausted heap on her bed. 'It's been rising gently, but this is a little bit of a blip. You've got to take it really easy.'

No wonder her blood pressure was up, Bella thought, she'd done more damage to her collateral today than Black Monday . . . ha, ha.

She could feel slight palpitations just at the thought of it.

'Are you OK?' Annie asked.

'Yes, I'm fine. I've definitely overdone it today. I don't think I'll leave the house again.'

'Well, a little walking is fine and your yoga poses, but really nothing more now. It's getting very close.'

'Not in the next two weeks, though?' Bella asked anxiously. 'The kitchen won't be finished.'

'Well, let's hope not. There is running hot and cold in the bathroom if things do start early, isn't there?'

'Yes,' said Bella looking panic-stricken. 'God, Annie, is this really about to happen? I'm not ready.'

Annie smiled at her. 'No-one is ever ready, Bella. You can only be prepared. Prepare to be knocked over, amazed and filled with awe. This is going to 'bowl you over like nothing ever has done before.'

'Oh no, you're giving me the hippie stuff again, aren't you?' Bella smiled. This had become a standing joke between them. Any time Annie started spouting her natural birth philosophies, Bella dealt with it by teasing her.

Annie wasn't sure what to make of Bella's attitude. She was having a home birth, so on some level she must believe it was a good idea, but she hadn't bought into the whole active birth idea at all. There was no birthing pool, no raspberry leaf tea, no aromatherapy oils burning in the house, no partner learning breathing or massage techniques. Annie hadn't even met Don yet.

'Why did you choose a home birth, Bella?' she asked, venting her curiosity.

'Because it's statistically safe and I wanted a midwife I knew, who could come to my office and home. And . . .' little pause, 'I kind of fell out with the private hospital.'

'Ah.' That explained a bit.

When Annie had gone, Bella took her tiny pack of ten Ultra Super Mega light cigarettes out of her handbag. She propped herself up on pillows and prepared for her three minutes of what used to be happiness but now was a necessary indulgence hugely spoiled by guilt. She clicked on the lighter and inhaled, firing up her cigarette. The yoga breathing had at least been a help here, she could now fill her lungs right up to the brim and get the maximum benefit out of the paltry amount she allowed herself to smoke.

Despite all the compulsively interesting birth books she'd read, squatting in front of the Aga in the small hours of the morning, labour was still a mystery. She felt incredibly well informed, but strangely clueless.

She knew exactly what and why an episiotomy was – OUCH – but no book seemed to offer any description of what labour would actually be like. And she still didn't know the first thing about babies apart from you 'put them to the breast' whenever they cried.

She liked the idea of breastfeeding. She imagined lying in bed beside Don with their little baby between them nuzzling at her breasts. And what the hell was sex going to be like after birth? There was no useful information about that either, just warnings to exercise that pelvic floor.

Don wasn't revealing any details about his shopping trip when he got home that evening and would only say she had to stay in and wait for a delivery the next day.

The van arrived soon after 11 a.m. and three men were needed to haul the most enormous pale tan L-shaped sofa into their sitting room. Jesus! It must have cost a fortune. This was made from a whole herd of Italy's finest designer cows, my God. She was stunned. She hadn't really known what to expect from Don, but certainly something a lot cheaper.

Three very chic lamps and a vast cream sheepskin rug were also delivered. She was really impressed now.

She phoned Don at work.

'Hello?'

'Hello, darling, guess what I'm lying on?'

'Bill, the decorator?'

'NO!!! A hugely expensive, wonderfully luxurious *sofa*.'

'Ah-ha. It arrived then. What do you think?'

'Amazing, fantastic . . . bankrupting!' she told him. And not exactly baby-friendly, but she left that out.

It did not take long for Bella to set up home on the sofa. Just days from her due date, she had decided it was finally time to stop working, exercising, trying to look nice, even shopping and nesting. She was too tired, too heavy, too huge. She had put on almost three stone in seven months and her home outfit was shapeless black maternity trousers and one of Don's washed-out tartan shirts. Her feet would only fit into a pair of old sheepskin slippers she'd found behind a wardrobe when they moved.

Prone on the sofa, glued to crap TV or reading decorating magazines, surrounded by grape stalks, digestive biscuit wrappers and empty water bottles, was where Don now expected to find her when he came home from work.

So he was surprised to find the house strangely dark one evening. In a total panic, he realized he could hear something in the bedroom. He ran up the stairs two at a time, heart pounding, convinced he was going to find his wife about to give birth in their brand new bed.

He opened the door and saw Bella lying with the duvet over her, sobbing into the pillow.

'What's the matter?' He rushed over to her side.

'Oh, Don.' She looked up at him with streaming red eyes and nose.

'What's wrong?' he asked urgently.

'I've ruined this house,' she sobbed.

'What do you mean?!'

'It was so lovely. It was full of character and the two lovely boys and two lovely parents and I've ruined it.'

'Oh hon, what's made you think that?' He put his arm around her comfortingly.

'I've stripped it and gutted it and now it feels white and soulless. And our baby's going to grow up in this white soulless place and we'll probably break up because it's so white and empty and it's all my fault,' she sobbed almost hysterically against the pillow again.

'Bella –' he lay down beside her and stroked her hair – 'Bella, you've gone completely bonkers.' He said this as gently and as soothingly as he could. 'The house looks great. It looks airy and light and at the moment any kid would love it because they can charge around without knocking anything over.'

He was hoping to make her laugh a little, but she was still crying hard, so he added: 'If you think it's too white, we'll get the painters back to change the walls. It's not a problem, hon, it's not a problem.'

She looked up at him and he saw how swollen her eyes were with crying.

'I love you,' Don said.

'Are you sure?' she wobbled. 'Are you really going to stay here with me and the baby?'

'Of course I am.' He folded her up into his arms. 'Of course, please don't worry about that. I'm so sorry if I've made you worry about that.'

'But our dads . . .' she tried to restrain her tears

230

long enough to get the words out. 'Yours left and mine shags around. It's not exactly promising, is it?'

He hugged her harder and didn't say anything for a while, then he answered: 'No-one turns out exactly like their parents, Bella. Let's just give ourselves a chance. You can't promise this will work out and neither can I, but we both really want to try and that's enough.'

'I feel so vulnerable and dependent,' she said in a frightened voice. 'And I hate it.'

He held her for a long time, then kissed her fore-head. For a moment she was calm, then she put her face against his chest and burst into tears again. 'Oh God and then there's the kitchen!' she sobbed.

'Bella, it can't be that bad!' he said.

'It is, it's terrible. Come and look.' She heaved herself up and shuffled into the appalling slippers she seemed to wear all the time.

They went down the stairs slowly, Don following his lumbering wife. At the bottom was the kitchen, finished that day, a gleaming, brushed steel tribute to modern kitchen design. A glassy black granite surface glittered in the light of the tiny overhead spots. The walls were crisp white, bordered with a splashback of more glossy black tiles.

The Aga looked a little uncomfortably un-fashionable.

'Wow,' said Don. 'I'm impressed.'

Bella just burst into tears again.

'What don't you like about it?' He put his arm around her back.

'I want the old one back. It looked like the kind of place where mums make soup and kids eat biscuits and play with their toys on the floor . . .'

her voice trailed off into another volley of sobs.

'Bella,' he was smiling as he hugged her awkwardly over her mountainous bump, 'you're going to be a great mum. You don't have to bake cakes . . .' Another sob, so he added: 'Unless you want to.'

What should he say next?

'Do you want to replace the doors?' he suggested. 'Maybe you could get wooden doors like the old kitchen?'

'That's a good idea.' She sounded slightly brighter. 'Maybe you're right,' she sniffed. 'Wooden doors.'

She wiped her nose on the back of her sleeve. 'Oh God. I'm sorry,' she said. 'I've got to go and blow my nose and wash my face, I've got to get a grip.'

Chapter Twenty-one

Two days later, all the delivery vans had come and gone, the house was almost complete and Bill had been back personally to change the kitchen doors. He had seemed a bit bemused, but never mind, Bella was deliriously happy with the results.

'It's fantastic,' she told him. 'I don't know what I was thinking of with the stainless steel, so cold and impersonal.'

'Quite tricky to clean too,' he told her. 'You'll be getting grubby little handprints on everything soon.' He gestured to her stomach, now an eye-popping mound which looked far too heavy for her frame to support.

'Any day now then, is it?' he asked.

'It's actually due tomorrow, but the first ones are always late, aren't they? Just as well, there's still a few things left to do.'

She ran through her mental checklist: curtains for all the rooms, more towels and sheets. Don was taking her shopping at the weekend for the final baby bits: nappies, cotton wool, vests.

Bella felt quite sad to see Bill go. He had been

knocking around the place with his workers ever since she moved in. As he drove off in his little blue van she realized it was the first time she'd been alone in the house during the day.

After lunch she fell asleep on the sofa and when she woke up at about four she lay still, feeling the baby stir inside her tummy. Suddenly it made a big movement, almost a roll which came with a loud clicking noise, more like a clunk. She couldn't believe she had just *heard* the baby! What the hell was that? A joint flexing?

She heaved herself down off the bed and stood up. There was a very odd sensation between her legs, like a hard ball pressing down from inside. She took several steps, but it was still there, she had to waddle with her legs apart. The weight was incredible, like a great big pendulum. The baby's head had obviously moved right down, ready to go. But she knew it could still be days away.

When Don got home that night he found Bella in her by now regular position on the sofa, in the black trousers and tartan shirt.

'Hello hon.' She held her arms out to him. 'We have to celebrate tonight, the decorators have moved out and the place is finally ours,' she said.

'Well, I've got chilled white wine, microwavable duck and noodles, ice-cream and about a kilo of grapes,' he said, holding up his shopping bag up.

'I could grow to love you, Mr McCartney,' she answered.

She went to bed early feeling tired and heavier than ever. Her stomach was tingling, there were little ripples of contractions passing up and down it and she could feel it go hard then relax again.

At about four in the morning, she stumbled out of bed to go to the loo. As she sat there she was aware of a strange trickling sensation. Investigating with toilet paper, she found an alarming quantity of mucus spilling out from between her legs.

She had expected 'the show' to be a 'plug' of mucus, not vast bucketfuls of stuff.

The birth was going to happen some time in the next day or two. She felt a small thrill take hold of her, mixed with panic. *Now?? Not yet!!*

She couldn't feel anything – no contractions, nothing different – so she went back to bed.

Just before 6 a.m. she woke to small stitchy pains travelling across her stomach. She lay in bed watching the numbers stack up on the digital alarm clock. The pains lasted just a few minutes. Then at 6.23, they were back . . . and again at 6.57.

Just after 7 a.m. she woke Don.

'You're having a day off today,' she said, amazed at how calm and relaxed she felt.

He opened his eyes and smiled. 'Really?'

Then he sat bolt upright. 'Oh my God, you mean . . . Has it really started?'

'I think so!'

Chapter Twenty-two

'I've got tons of things to do Don, come on, let's get up.' Bella threw back the covers and hauled herself out of bed.

'What do you mean?' he asked nervously. 'You're in labour.'

'Oh God, it won't kick in properly for hours. The bathroom needs a good wash down. All the baby things need to be washed and dried, they're still in their packets. *God*, you have to go out and buy *nappies*!'

He was looking pale with terror.

'For God's sake,' she said, lowering herself slowly down to hug him, 'I'm the one giving birth, remember.'

'Aren't you at all worried?' he asked. She looked at him: stubbly, dishevelled hair, putting on his glasses. Why? As if that would help?

'God no,' she was incredibly calm, 'I weigh so much, the stairs buckle under me, my fingers look like fat sausages, I've had this great mass hanging in front of me for months. I can't wait for it to be out of here—' she pointed at her stomach.

'But it's got to come out through . . .'

'Don! Shut up!'

She pulled on the massive maternity bra and pants: 'Two more things I won't miss about being pregnant,' she said and then as she hoisted herself into the black trousers and tartan shirt, he added: 'And two I won't.'

She padded all the way downstairs to make breakfast in her new kitchen.

The stitchy pains were so mild, she could almost ignore them as she got on with juicing oranges, cutting bread for toast and boiling up a big pot of tea.

She could hear Don showering. When he came down, barefoot, in chinos and a denim shirt, he made a quick call to the office to tell them his paternity leave was starting *now*.

She could tell by his smiles his boss was teasing him mercilessly.

'That's enough,' Don said. 'I'll ring you later . . . yeah, thanks, mate.'

'Do you really think it will arrive today?' Don asked. 'On the due date?'

'Well, it's starting. Who knows how long it will take?'

'That would just be so like you to give birth on the right day. Not early, not late, just exactly on time,' he said and they both laughed.

'Have you called the midwife?' asked Don.

'Let's have breakfast, then I'll speak to her, then we'll clean the bathroom.'

'It's clean, Bella!'

'I want the bathroom and the bedroom extra clean.'

'Well, leave it to me.'

'No, I want to help. Otherwise I'll have nothing to do, just hours and hours of mild labour. Anyway, I feel so energetic!'

'Good grief . . .' he went into TV reporter mode: 'A woman gave birth on her bathroom floor yesterday still clutching a scrubbing brush in her hand. "I just wanted my house to sparkle," said management consultant, Bella Browning, who is currently in talks with the Flash marketing department.'

'Ha ha,' she said and went off to phone Annie.

She had expected Annie to play it cool and offer to come round later. But in fact, she said she would be there in an hour. Bella felt mildly irritated. What would the three of them do all day?

'Honestly, Annie, don't come before twelve. I'll phone you if anything changes,' Bella told her.

They cleaned the bathroom and the bedroom and the kitchen, then Bella made Don hoover the whole house.

The baby clothes were put through the wash and chucked into the tumble drier.

'We haven't got nearly enough,' Bella told Don. 'You'll have to go and buy some more when the baby's here.'

'How will I know what to get?' he said anxiously.

'Just go into baby shop looking clueless and say "newborn baby, about this big." They must be used to it,' she giggled at him.

He kissed her on the mouth. 'This is it, Bella, our last few hours as a couple. It's about to change for ever.'

'Well a shag is out of the question,' she said.

'I know, probably for months.' He hoped this was a joke.

'About six weeks, actually,' she answered.

'Oh my God!'

'Are you sad?' she asked. 'I don't mean about the sex, obviously you're devastated. But about the changing for ever.' She scanned his face.

'No. Well, maybe a bit. I've loved every moment of the two of us. I just hope the three of us is going to be as good.'

'Of course it will be.' She put her arms around him and leaned against his cheek. 'I hope it is too. I love you, Don.' After a pause, she added, 'You are going to get me through this OK, aren't you?'

'Of course.' He stroked her head.

Not long after Don had come back with the nappies and other essential groceries, Annie arrived laden down with bags.

'Hello. Hello, Bella and you must be Don.' Out of breath, she plonked one enormous bright yellow bin bag on the doorstep, then offloaded the holdall she'd had slung over her shoulder.

'Good grief, what is all this stuff?' asked Bella.

'You'll see,' Annie said.

Don picked up the yellow bag.

'If you take that one upstairs, I'll get set out first. Bella, you put the kettle on.' She saw the look on Bella's face and added: 'For tea!'

Annie had asked for a table up in the nursery and she laid out all her equipment there.

'OK,' she called down the stairs, 'Bella, if you can come up, we'll do a little check-up.'

Blood pressure, urine sample, baby's heartbeat, then it was time for the internal. Bella stripped off her trousers and pants and felt uncomfortably exposed as she lay down half naked on her bed. She watched Annie don thin latex gloves and take out a tube labelled VAGINAL EXAMINATION JELLY . . . urgh.

'No-one in the world likes these, do they?' Bella asked, trying to make small talk.

'You'd be surprised,' said Annie. 'Now, just relax.'

'Of course. Why should I be at all tense at the prospect of you jamming a great big latexed hand up my fanny?'

Annie looked at her quite sternly, Bella thought.

Ouch, it was surprisingly painful. She wasn't prepared for that. Either Annie was the clumsiest internal investigator ever or it was something to do with labour.

'OK,' said Annie. 'Only two or three centimetres, so we've a long way to go. Why don't you come down and we'll have a light lunch.'

Annie had brought a flask of homemade vegetable soup, which she was advising Bella to eat. She also filled the teapot with camomile tea bags before pouring the hot water on top.

Don ignored this spartan regime and made rounds of toast smothered in melted cheese with pickle, and strong black coffee.

'Goodness,' Annie couldn't help herself. 'Don't you worry at all about stomach ulcers?'

'No,' said Don with a grin.

Bella's face winced slightly with the pain of another contraction.

'How are you doing?' asked Annie.

240

'It's OK actually, just like a sharp period pain, but then it goes away completely.'

'What would you like to do after lunch?' Annie asked. 'Maybe a walk, or we could do some yoga stretches. Or maybe there's a video you'd like to watch while I give your shoulders a massage?'

'That's a good idea,' said Bella.

'I've brought a lovely video with me called *Birth Lines*.'

'Oh God no, how about Woody Allen?'

Annie said 'Of course,' and Don rolled his eyes.

Bella sat cross-legged in front of Annie who massaged her shoulders with wonderful smelling oil as all three of them watched *Manhattan*. Don kept getting up to pace about the house on some supposed errand or other and Bella would occasionally clutch at her sides and say 'Ohhh, that was sore.'

By the end of the film the contractions were coming every ten minutes and Bella was finding them painful.

Annie ushered her upstairs for another check-up, which revealed a dilation of about four centimetres, then sent her for a hot bath. Don moved a stool inside the bathroom, so he could sit beside Bella and Annie stayed in the nursery so she was around, but not too obtrusive.

After twenty minutes in the bath, Bella got Don to help her out so she could sit on the loo for a bout of crampy, painful diarrhoea.

'Look on the bright side,' she said weakly, climbing back into the bath and turning on the hot tap. 'At least I won't need an enema.'

Don was starting to feel more nervous. This was

really happening. He'd watched women give birth before but in squalid conditions, shouting out words he couldn't understand and it had been like watching a film.

This was Bella, here in the bathroom, in the bath.

Annie came in with a little ball of Plasticine. She stopped up the bath overflow and ran the hot tap again. She tipped in a little oil and the room began to smell of warm summer holidays.

All three of them breathed deeply and felt a little calmer.

Bella was squeezing Don's hand: the pains were shooting up her stomach. She screwed up her eyes and gasped with the intensity of them. But the water was hot and comforting and she tried to relax in between contractions.

Already it was 5 p.m. and soon Annie wanted her out of the bath to do another set of checks.

Bella was irritated by this. Somehow she lumbered out and Don and Annie wrapped a huge towel round her and supported her to the bed. Don went down to the kitchen to throw some food together while Annie performed another painful examination.

'Ouch,' said Bella loudly. 'Can't you be more gentle?'

'I'm sorry,' Annie said then prodded just as hard again. 'OK, about five centimetres now.'

'Five centimetres? Are you sure?' Bella said grumpily. 'This is going to take for ever.'

'Calm down, Bella, some women are slow at the start, then it all rushes out at the end. Just go with the flow. The baby's fine and so are you.'

'It really hurts now,' Bella said.

'Let's try the TENS machine, then come down to the kitchen and have a change of scene.'

Annie dried her thoroughly, then stuck the electrodes onto her back and gave her the little control panel to hold.

'OK, you just push those buttons when you feel a contraction coming on. It stimulates endorphin production,' said Annie. 'Give it a whirl. If you don't like it, we'll take it off.'

Bella pushed down the button and felt a mild flicking on her back. She pressed again and the flicking increased to a sort of stinging pain. She couldn't really see how that was going to help, but at least it was something else to think about. All this waiting was driving her demented.

She was just waiting, waiting for the next contraction and the one after that and for the next hour to pass so she could be a bit closer to getting this over with.

Down in the kitchen, she huddled in an armchair with her control panel and watched Don cook pasta with bolognese sauce.

'Are you going to have some?' he asked Annie.

'I don't eat meat,' she replied.

'Have the pasta with butter and grated Parmesan then. We've got fantastic tomatoes too,' Don said.

'OK. Thank you,' said Annie.

Fantastic tomatoes? thought Bella grumpily. How the hell could he think about tomatoes when she was in this much pain?

'Bella, what can I get you?' Don came over and asked her so kindly, she forgave him immediately.

'Just some apple juice please.' She screwed up her face against another contraction and zapped up the counter-effect on her machine. It seemed to block out the intensity by pummelling small electric shocks all over her back.

The pains were bad now: they clamped right round her stomach and back. But then they released and everything felt fine again, felt good in fact.

She was starting to count in the moments when her eyes were screwed up against the pain and she knew the contractions were getting longer. How long could this all go on for? It had been about ten hours since the first twinges. Most first labours took about 12 hours, so there could be as little as two hours to go. Hallelujah!

Two more hours of Annie fussing about and prodding her with those awful latex gloves was about all she could take.

'AAAAAArgh, here comes another one,' a great vice-like grip moved round her stomach and felt as if it was going to squeeze the life out of her. She pushed the button to whack over her back and slowly counted five, four, three, two, one, zero, minus one, minus two, minus three . . . finally the contraction let go of her.

Don was staring at her, fork frozen in mid-air. Annie was eating on blithely. 'We'll finish our supper, then maybe you'd like another massage?' she asked cheerfully. 'Walk around the room a bit, it might help.'

It's all very well for you to say that, you hippie ratbag, Bella thought. She was beginning to feel helplessly furious with the pain, the indignity and most of all with Annie.

Another fierce contraction began and Bella dropped onto all fours on the kitchen floor.

'Owwww!' she felt so stupid, crawling there helplessly.

Don rushed over to her side. 'Hon, are you OK?'

'Of course I'm not fucking OK. It really, really hurts.'

'Come on, Bella,' Annie said briskly. 'Let's get you upstairs, I'll give you a nice relaxing massage.'

'I don't want one,' Bella heard herself say petulantly. 'I want this to stop.'

Somehow, pausing for the contractions that were coming every few minutes, Don and Annie got Bella upstairs into the bedroom.

'OK, let's have another quick look, please,' said Annie lying Bella back on the bed.

Bella groaned.

'Still about five centimetres,' Annie said withdrawing the dreaded glove.

'Jesus,' Bella exclaimed in frustration. 'We're just not getting anywhere.'

'We've got to help you relax and open up. What would help Bella?'

'Less pain,' she snapped. 'Here comes another one . . .' There was a catch of fear in her voice.

She grabbed Don's arm and clung to him, groaning.

'I'll go and get some music,' Annie said, and went out of the room.

When the contraction had passed, Don and Bella's eyes met. He looked anxious to her and she looked frightened to him. That made them both even more worried.

'I'm really scared, Don,' Bella whispered. 'Most

245

women dilate at a centimetre an hour. That's another five hours to go before I'm ready to push. I can't do this for another five hours.'

Her face looked stricken again: another contraction was on its way. It seized her violently round the middle and gripped her with a pain hotter and more intense than anything she could ever have imagined before this ordeal began.

She was kneeling on the bed with her elbows up on the bottom bedstead clinging to Don who stood on the other side of it. Her face was buried in his chest, her eyes were closed. Then the contraction let go and she breathed again.

Annie came in with a cassette player in one hand and a steaming mug of tea in the other. She went out again and came back with candles, matches and an aromatherapy burner.

The next contraction set in and Bella buried her head in Don's chest again.

When she closed her eyes and felt the pain grip, she knew this was what it was like to be tortured on a medieval rack. Lashed down on a frame, she was being cranked and stretched apart, wrenched open bit by agonizing bit. She was waiting to hear the crack and snap of ligaments being torn apart.

Medieval was the word that kept running through her mind. It was the twenty-first century, but she had chosen a medieval way to give birth. She could have been in hospital with an epidural anaesthetic coursing soothingly through her central nervous system but instead, when she opened her eyes, she saw that Annie had turned down the lights and was lighting candles.

There was the cloying smell of incense in the air

and awful New Age music. Bella began to feel panicky.

Her hair was sticking to her face and neck, droplets of sweat were trickling off the ends and into her eyes, she could feel sweat running freely down her sides, between her breasts.

The contraction was over and Annie was coming towards her with the mug.

'Here we are dear, have a little camomile tea, it will help you to calm down.'

That was too much for Bella: 'Camomile fucking *tea*?' she screamed. 'Do you seriously think that is going to make any difference?'

There was silence in the room. Then Bella moaned because she could feel another contraction cranking up again. It began low down like the cramping pain of a terrible stomach upset and radiated out until she was helplessly overwhelmed by it. She clung to Don and tried to stay afloat.

Suddenly, there was a terrifying bursting sensation and Bella felt as if something had exploded out of her in a rush. Her legs were soaking wet and for a moment she thought the baby must be there.

'That's good,' said Annie. 'The waters have broken.'

Bella came out of the darkness of the contraction to find Annie mopping at the puddle on the bed with a horrible beige, plastic-backed mat.

She laid another mat over the back of Bella's legs. The plastic clung to her sweaty calf muscles, but before she had time to be irritated and move it, another contraction was bearing down on her.

In the depth of it, Bella heard a low animal-like

247

groaning and wondered what the hell it could be before she realized she was making the noise herself. Christ, this was awful.

Annie went out of the room and as Bella surfaced from the gripping agony and drew in breath, she spoke to Don in an urgent voice. 'Get my handbag, quick.' She pointed at the bag in a corner of the room.

'You can't smoke now, Bella,' Don hissed at her.

'No, no,' Bella said urgently. 'Get the bag!'

He handed it to her and Bella rummaged for her address book. The next contraction was already welling up, she had to be quick.

'Pass the phone,' she urged Don, who in disbelief handed it to her.

'What are you doing?' he asked.

She dialled in the number – Answer, ANSWER – the pain was spreading from the pit of her stomach. The receiver was sliding in her hand, wet with sweat.

'Hello, caller, please leave your message after the tone.'

'Declan, Declan, it's Bella, you've got to help me.' She could hear the groan of pain start to enter her voice, she tried as hard as she could to continue . . . 'Please come round, bring drugs, 18 Park Crescent. I'll pay you whatever you need.'

She dropped the phone and grabbed hold of Don's shirt. He put his arms round her back and hugged her. He had no idea how they were going to get through this. He was starting to feel very afraid.

Annie came back in with a bowl and a face flannel.

When the storm of the contraction had passed, she offered to wash Bella down.

Bella realized how much she needed this. The large T-shirt, all she was wearing, was totally sodden and clinging to her. Her hair was completely wet now with salty beads streaming into her face. Her legs were soaked and the plastic mat was sticking claustrophobically on top of them.

Every pore in her entire body was running with sweat.

Annie helped her take the T-shirt off and sponged her face with cool water. She moved on down over Bella's back and legs.

'I'm sorry, Annie,' Bella was wailing now, 'I can't trust you to do this. I don't want this any more . . . candles and shit . . .' Her eyes were swimming with tears and she could feel the low pain starting up again.

She felt like vomiting and began to retch. Racked with fear, she was beginning to think she might die. She buried her head in Don's shirt again and started to concentrate on getting through the pain.

When she closed her eyes, she saw a black ocean swell and her own head bobbing in the enormous bank of water, trying to stay afloat. She was just trying to keep her head above the water and survive, but she had no idea how long she could hang on for.

There was no sign of help and she was so tired of swimming and only very vaguely aware of Don and Annie talking. Way in the distance, she thought she could hear the phone ringing, but it all seemed like a dream she was having while she paddled desperately in this ocean against the black mountainous waves that were trying to drag her down.

At last, it was time to open her eyes and breathe again. The bedroom window had been opened and the sheet was billowing in front of it, sending a cool breeze into the room. The incense and candles had gone, replaced by bright sidelights.

Don was stroking her hair and Annie was prodding about between her legs and listening to the baby's heartbeat with a stethoscope.

'You're both doing fine,' said Annie in a soothing voice. 'Look Bella it's absolutely OK with me if you want someone else here. Just do whatever you need, whatever you want. You have time to go to hospital if you like, Bella, but it will be a very uncomfortable journey.'

'Is Declan coming?' Bella looked up at Don.

'Yes.'

'When?'

'Very soon.'

'Oh thank God.' She was vaguely aware she might be hurting Annie's feelings somewhat but she knew she couldn't really care about that right now.

Declan was coming. The fresh air hit her and she began to feel slightly stronger and thirsty.

'Annie, could I have a drink? There's apple juice in the fridge.'

'Of course.'

Annie bustled out and Bella sat back on her heels and tried to rest and breathe but the pain was there, cranking up again.

'Oh Don,' she moaned and held out her arms so he could gather her up and somehow get her through this.

She was amazed at how much agony her body

could endure. Hours ago she'd thought the pain was as much as she could bear, but each contraction since then had upped the level again and yet again and harder and longer, trying to squeeze the life out of her and still she was surviving somehow. It was becoming a relentless storm with no clear beginning or end to the contractions. It felt as if hours had passed yet it also seemed barely twenty minutes since she had been in the bath thinking labour was OK.

Outside it had grown dark and she was aware of more people coming into the room. At one point she opened her eyes and saw Declan, or was she just imagining it? She managed to smile at him but had to close her eyes and groan again.

But it was him. He was really talking to her in his lovely Irish accent.

'Bella, hello, how are you doing? Come on my love, open your eyes and look at me for a moment.'

With enormous concentration, she prised open her eyes.

Her arms were still wrapped round Don, but Declan had his hands round her face now and looked into her eyes.

'Bella, you're doing fine. It's just taking a long time to happen, so you're getting tired and a bit discouraged. Now I'm here, with my good friend Zena, to help you. Annie is here too and together we're going to help you do this. You are a strong, tough old girl, Bella. I know you can do this. You've got your lovely husband here holding onto you for dear life. We are all here for you. We are not going to let you down. OK?'

'OK,' she managed to whisper.

251

'Now, gas and air. I promise this will really, really help.'

He passed her up a flat white plastic tube. 'Put this in your mouth and take a deep breath,' he said.

A blast of cold parchingly dry air hit the back of her throat. She wanted to cough but sucked in again and again.

She pushed the tube away as her face now felt strangely numb and she felt sick to the pit of her stomach.

'No, no, no . . . I feel sick,' she wailed.

She could hear Declan: 'Keep going, I promise, it will be fine.'

She put the tube to her lips again, everything was starting to blur in a dark red melting pot of pain. Declan's reassuring words felt like a repeating mantra which had been going on for hours.

She knew it was night time, but there were flashes of bright light when she opened her eyes. When she closed them, she was in a sea of hot red liquid pain.

'We've got to get her up.' Declan's voice sounded far away in the distance, she was still focused on the tiny head, bobbing in the waves, dipping under in the hot sea. God, she just wanted to rest, just wanted this to be over.

She felt strong arms under her armpits wrenching her out of the sea.

They were trying to make her stand on dry land, but her legs weren't working.

'Bella! Bella!' It was Don with a hint of panic in his voice. She thought she would like to see Don, where the hell was he?

252

There was cool water on her face and running down her back. She opened her eyes.

Don was standing in front of her, holding her up, Declan was at her side.

She opened her eyes wide and was aware of the terrible, clear pain. They were holding her up, defying the force between her legs, which was dragging her down. She felt her knees buckle with the effort, but still they held her up.

She made a primeval, guttural scream as she felt an enormous weight crash down against the whole band of muscle from her belly button down round to her anus. An irresistible force was urging her to push it out although it went against every instinct of pain avoidance and self-preservation. Her hip joints were screaming at the very edge of their sockets.

And she had to push, knowing it was ripping her in half. Her anus was being pushed inside out. There was a wrecking ball inside her pelvis crushing and destroying everything in its path.

It was coming down, it was coming out.

She was squatting on her knees despite Don and Declan hauling against her.

She could hear roars and screams of agony, which she knew she was making, but her mind was in a small still place. She was alone and quiet in the eye of the storm. Small logical thoughts were forming there: This is it, the baby is coming out. It's almost over. We're nearly there. I've just done a crap on the bedroom floor. I hope someone's put plastic sheeting down.

The arms pulled her up so she was kneeling on

the bed, Don was in front of her, so she automatically flung her arms around his chest. Everyone else was bustling about behind her. There was an immense burning and a tearing sensation so violent she thought she heard it, then the pain peaked – white hot searing pain and silent screaming. And then it was over.

She sank forward into Don. Oh thank God, thank God, thank God. It was over, she was still alive, she'd got through it.

Don was hugging her head into his chest.

'Oh Bella,' he sounded croaky. 'There's the baby.'

God, the baby, she'd totally forgotten about the baby. She turned her head and saw an enormous purple baby, with two little tubes in its nose, which Declan was deftly manipulating.

She collapsed into an awkward heap on the bed, blood spilling out from between her legs and was handed this big, slippery solid baby.

She just looked for a long moment, then managed to whisper, 'Hello.'

The eyes opened and Bella looked into them and somehow in the same moment noticed she was holding a boy. He smelt briny, as if he'd been plucked from the sea.

'Hello there,' she whispered. 'Hello Markie.'

Don's face was next to hers and they were both gazing at this extraordinary new person.

His dark eyes latched onto hers in an unblinking, steady gaze. They were the deepest, darkest pools of wonder she'd ever looked down into. She was just astonished they had managed to make something so perfect.

The baby put a tiny hand up against his face and

254

Bella took in the fingers with perfect little purple nails and wrinkles round the joints and dimples on the knuckles.

'My God Bella, he's just amazing,' Don whispered beside her.

Bella looked round and noticed three other faces close by watching them quietly.

She smiled and they all smiled back at her.

She looked back at the baby. 'Just perfect, so perfect,' she said falling back in elated exhaustion against the pillows someone had propped behind her.

Chapter Twenty-three

'OK, Bella, we've still got some work to do here.'
Declan sounded brisk.

The cord was cut, then Declan handed Markie over to Annie for a wash while he busied himself with delivering the placenta.

When the enormous lump of raw liver slid out from between her legs, Bella saw she was sitting on a damp and bloody plastic sheet. She was naked and her legs were smeared with blood, dried blood and traces of shit. Her fingernails were dark with dried blood, her hair was soaked, blood was pooling between her legs and she was beginning to shiver.

Don was over by the baby bath taking pictures.

'I'm really sorry, Bella, but we're going to have to do stitches now,' said Declan.

'You're kidding,' she managed.

'I'll hand you over to Zena, a wonder with a needle. We'll give you a jab first, then you better have the gas and air to hand.'

Bella sucked furiously at the gas cylinder as Zena

cleaned then began to stitch at the long tear on her perineum.

Bella's face contorted with pain. She could not believe how much she'd had to endure in one night. A deep stoic resignation began to settle over her. If someone had come in and said they were here to pull out her back teeth, she would have accepted it as her lot.

'You know why it's called labour now,' said Zena in a gentle Caribbean accent as she worked away on an interminable number of stitches. 'It's women's work, no man would be able to take this.'

Bella smiled at her weakly in between gulps from the gas cylinder. She wasn't sure if the gas helped at all but at least it gave her something to do other than scream.

Finally it was over. Markie was dried and dressed and Zena helped Bella hobble into the bathroom for a warm deep bath.

Bella sank into it. She looked down at her body. Somehow, on the edge of the deepest exhaustion, she found the energy to be pleased that her stomach was so amazingly flat.

OK it looked like a strange wrinkled, deflated soufflé, but it was flattish. She could see over it, she could bend. Her breasts were absolutely enormous, especially in comparison to this flat stomach.

Between her legs everything felt oddly sensationless and tightly strung together. How the hell was she going to pee? Let alone . . . she didn't want to think about that. There were piles the size of houses rubbing painfully between her buttocks.

She could hear vigorous crying coming from the

bedroom, so she raised herself carefully out of the bath, she dried off with a towel and slipped on the clean nightshirt hanging on the back of the door.

The bedroom had been transformed. New clean sheets and pillowcases were on the bed, Markie's little cot had been brought through. The lighting was dim with just one sidelight and a few candles.

Zena was tying up plastic rubbish bags and Declan was scribbling in Bella's maternity note-book, while Don sat on the bed holding the crying baby.

Bella went over and picked Markie up awkwardly, letting his head loll back. 'Sh, sh sh,' she soothed.

'OK,' said Declan. 'Let's help you get him latched on.'

She sat back against the mountain of pillows and opened her nightshirt. Markie immediately turned to her breast. Very matter-of-factly, Declan pinched up her nipple and pushed it into the baby's little open mouth. He sucked vigorously.

'Well, he's off,' said Declan. 'No problem at all. Your only trouble might be making enough milk for that baby, do you know how much he weighed? Ten pounds and three ounces. For your build, that is enormous. No wonder we had a job getting him out.'

Bella watched her son's little mouth chomp up and down on a breast bigger than his head.

'It was absolute hell. I am never, ever doing that again,' she said, at last feeling just a little bit like herself again.

Declan laughed. 'I've heard that before. The second one is always easier.'

'Yeah right,' she said. 'You just say that to keep yourself in a job.'

She looked at Don: he was exhausted with huge damp patches under the arms of his shirt. 'I'm sorry hon, we can never ever have sex again, even in six months' time, when the wounds have finally healed,' she said.

'Nonsense,' said Declan. 'Give her a month Don, then put on your best gear and she'll be gagging for it. But lubricate,' he added.

'Enough!' said Bella in horror. 'I'm never having sex again. That is final.'

As she leaned over and kissed Don, the baby unlatched and scrabbled frantically to get his lips back round the nipple.

'Oh no,' said Bella, breaking off her kiss. She turned Markie round and let him have a go at the other side.

Don kept an arm round her. He had never felt so relieved in his life. Bella and his son were alive. They were safe and well in the bend of his arm, and he didn't think he would ever feel so grateful for anything ever again. It had been terrifying. About twenty minutes before Markie was finally born, Don had heard Declan make the calls to check that an ambulance was available and to warn the hospital that an emergency C-section could be on its way.

Annie came in with tea but Don said, 'Bugger tea, I've got champagne downstairs,' and he set off to get it.

'I'd really like the tea first,' Bella quietly told Annie.

'I'm sure, dear. And there's a big jug of diluted

apple juice here for you as well. Do you want some toast or something?'

Bella thought about the hideous piles and said 'No, thanks. And, by the way, I want to say thank you, I'm sorry I was so awful to you.'

'Bella, it's fine. I got worried too that nothing was happening and I think you felt that. You did the right thing and it's all worked out.'

Annie looked down at the little face buried deep in Bella's breasts.

'Look at that,' she said with a smile. 'Hopefully he'll sleep for a long time tonight and give you both some rest.'

'What time is it?' Bella asked.

'Three-thirty in the morning. Markie was born at 2.15 a.m. precisely. So you were in labour for about 21 hours. That's a long time.'

'Damn right,' said Bella.

Several glasses of champagne later, it was time for everyone to go and leave the three of them alone together. The three of us: Bella kept trying the words out in her mind. They sounded strange.

Declan had left her a huge bottle of extra-strong painkillers after insisting she take two. Annie had disapproved and promised to come round in the morning with a breast milk friendly alternative.

Bella had taken the pills. Her whole genital area was starting to throb and painful contractions still racked her stomach. She longed for sleep.

Don came up to the room after he had seen everyone out of the door.

He looked at the picture before him of Bella and baby and felt his heart swell to encompass this.

Bella was a mother and they had a new baby to care for.

The baby had fallen asleep in her arms. 'The baby' – he still seemed too new to have a name.

Bella put him down in his cradle at the side of the bed.

Don undressed and pulled on a T-shirt and some shorts. He climbed into bed beside Bella and held her close. 'I am so proud of you,' he said.

'So am I,' she answered with a smile. 'That was hell on earth. I thought I was going to die.'

He didn't say anything, just wrapped his arms around her even more tightly. Finally, he leaned over to switch off the light and realized how enormously tired he was.

Bella rolled over so she could lie looking at her tiny son in his little crib beside her. Her son: the word resonated in her mind.

In the gloom she could see that he wasn't sleeping any more, his eyes were open and fixed on hers. She felt overwhelmed with love. Don was on one side of her and this wonderful new baby was on the other. Nothing had ever felt so perfect and so complete before.

She tried to sleep, but felt too overcome. She kept opening her eyes just to check on the tiny person lying brand new beside her.

And it seemed to Bella that every time she opened her eyes, those small dark ones were looking back at her, gazing in wonder at her and this whole new world.

Chapter Twenty-four

Don made all the phone calls and handled the hourly delivery of flowers while Bella lay in bed like a worn-out princess with Markie snuggled up beside her.

'Tania's coming round later,' Don said, poking his head round the door, amazed to find Bella finally awake: 'There's no stopping her.'

'Oh, it's OK,' Bella whispered, 'When I said no visitors today, I meant apart from her.'

'And Mum and your parents have sent the most amazing flowers. D'you feel up to calling them? They're all waiting by the phone.'

'Yeah, of course,' Bella answered, feeling guilty that she would rather speak to Don's mum than her own.

Don went over to look at the baby again. He was lying on his back fast asleep with his head turned to the side and his arms up beside his ears in a still life Highland fling.

He had a white cotton hat on with a knotted top but his face looked too old for such a babyish thing.

He looked like an ancient Buddha, not sleeping, merely closing his eyes in meditation.

'Has he been awake again?'

'No,' said Bella. 'Not since seven. I think they do that for a day or two, sleep it off.'

'How are you?' He looked at her pale face and the deep dark circles round her eyes.

'Not too bad. I'm exhausted, I can't walk, I'm still getting contractions and my tits feel like lead balloons but these are keeping me happy—' she nodded at the big bottle of hospital-strength painkillers Declan had left her.

'Remember to hide them when Annie comes round or she'll take them away.'

'Over my dead body.'

'Have you changed his nappy?'

'God no!' Bella looked appalled. 'It's been on for hours.'

'OK . . . what do we need?'

They set up a towel on the bed. Don brought in a bowl of lukewarm water, cotton wool balls and a new nappy as instructed.

He lifted Markie onto the towel and he and Bella fumbled with the hundred tiny popper buttons on his babygro and the velcro on his nappy straps. Markie was disgusted to be so rudely awoken. He balled up his tiny fists and began to howl so violently that his body shook and his face changed from red to purple.

Bella opened the tiny nappy: it looked bone dry, so she peered down more closely and was aware that her cheek was wet. She moved back in surprise as Markie's teeny willy sprayed about in all

263

directions. In an elegant arch he wet the duvet, his babygro and his own face. This made him cry even more frantically.

Bella and Don were in a horrified panic. He dabbed at the baby's face with the edge of the towel and Bella picked the little bundle up and cuddled him to try and stop his piteous wailing.

'OK,' she tried to sound calm. 'We'll need a new vest and babygro.'

Don brought them in to Bella on the bed and they looked at each other with apprehension. Markie was still purple and crying fiercely.

Two grown-ups, one who had covered wars, the other who had fought in her fair share of boardroom battles, were just beginning to get an inkling of how truly helpless they were in the field of baby rearing.

Changing Markie for the first time ever was horrific. He battled with his legs and arms and roared at them in terror. His parents, terrified they were going to break him, touched him gently and gingerly but he acted as if he was being tortured. Finally, when it was all over, Bella lifted him up to her breasts and let him nuzzle. At last there was silence.

'Oh my God,' Don sighed, then he looked at Bella. After a moment of relieved silence, they collapsed into giggles which got more and more hysterical.

'He peed in your face . . .' roared Don in between belly laughs.

'Your expression, when you came in with the vest . . .' Bella was laughing so hard that Markie lost his grip and squawked until she'd latched him on again.

'How does it feel?' Don gestured to his son

clamped tightly onto his wife's breast, when they had finally calmed down.

'I don't really feel anything apart from his little jaws going chomp, chomp, chomp.'

'How do you know he's getting enough?'

'Because Annie told me he'll howl the house down when he's hungry, not lie in his crib asleep – normal survival rules.'

'I'm glad you're so sussed,' he told her.

'Oh God, I'm so not, Don. I'm terrified! But we'll just have to muddle through, learning the ropes on the job.'

'Are you sure you don't want anything to eat?'

'Believe me if your exit points felt like mine, you wouldn't want anything either.'

He didn't need to know more.

'OK,' she said when Markie had drunk his fill, 'Let's call the folks.'

Don sat up on the bed beside her as she punched in her parents' number.

'Hello Mum, it's me,' she said when her mother picked up.

'Bella! How are you? We're so proud of you.' Well that was a first, Bella couldn't help thinking.

'Just spare me the details,' her mother added. 'Don said it went on for hours. I don't want to know, I really don't . . . but then you would insist on doing it at home. But you are OK now, aren't you? And little . . . Mark?' She said the baby's name in that 'Please tell me I'm wrong' sort of voice.

'Markie,' Bella answered.

'Oh yes, I'm sure he's a little Markie now, but later . . . anyway, is he utterly lovely and perfect?'

'He's beautiful,' she said and slipped her hand

into Don's. 'You should come and see him, Mum.' She held her breath for the reply.

'Well . . . it will be hard for me, Bella' – and here we go, Bella thought. 'I've had nothing to do with babies since you were small because of what I've been through,' her mother continued. 'I know it's going to trigger a lot of difficult feelings. I've bought a book about becoming a grandmother and I'm trying to prepare myself for the rush of emotions. All the pain and sadness of losing five little babies, it's all going to come flooding back.'

As she listened, Bella thought how strange it was that her mother seemed so emotionally open and yet only ever managed to push her away. Whatever Bella did, her mother could only experience it in terms of how it affected her – even giving birth, for God's sake.

When the call was finally over, Bella banged the receiver down, relieved that her mother had given herself an excuse not to visit for months now and furious with her for it at the same time.

After that, it was a pleasure to have Don's lovely mum, Maddie, on the other end of the line saying all the right things.

'Well done, Bella, Don is so proud of you, I've never heard anything like it. And so am I . . . Markie, what an adorable name, goes so well with McCartney . . . I'm coming down as soon as I can sort out some cover and only if you want me. Maybe you want a little time to yourselves first of all? . . . Now back to bed, make sure you rest as much as you can.'

She fell asleep again not long after. Her last image was the bank of purple, yellow, pink and white

266

blossom forming in the bedroom. Don had run out of vases and was now using buckets, bowls, whatever he could lay his hands on. It reminded her of the night she'd told him she was pregnant.

Her last thought before falling into the doze was: Twenty-one hours! Ten pounds and three ounces! Bloody hell, it was little short of a miracle that they were both alive.

Tania arrived much later when the sun was starting to set on Markie's first day. She rushed into the bedroom and woke Bella with a kiss.

'Oh congratulations, you fantastically clever girl,' she gushed, leaning into the crib and trying to get a good sniff of the sleeping bundle inside.

'Look at him, he's absolutely gorgeous.'

'No he's not,' Bella said groggily. 'He looks like a miniature Chinese Winston Churchill.'

'Actually, now you mention it . . . Shut up, Bella. He's adorable. I'll have him if you don't want him.'

'If you think I went through all that just so I could be your surrogate mother . . .' Bella was smiling now.

'Was it really bad?'

'*Bad??!* I'm sorry, I'm not joining in the postnatal mum conspiracy to keep childless women in the dark. It was appalling, it was awful, it was much, much more excruciating agony than I could ever have imagined. Went on for much longer than humanly bearable and is just barbaric in every way. Next time – Caesarean or at the very least, the full epidural works.'

Tania looked at her in horror.

'Oh my God, you're not pregnant are you?' Bella asked.

'No,' said Tania. 'But I might reconsider that plan now,' then she burst out: 'But he's so gorgeous, I want one!!'

She rustled around in the glossy shopping bags she'd brought and pulled out a huge, plush teddy bear. They both burst into laughter.

'Oh my God,' said Bella, 'it's so big, he'll be frightened of it.'

'He'll grow into it. It's so cute. And look at these.' She tipped out an array of jewel bright baby clothes.

'Baby Kenzo,' she said. 'Aren't they fantastic?'

'Oh wow,' said Bella. 'You really shouldn't have.'

'Nonsense. I'm his fairy godmother. Now for you, fairy princess . . .' She opened another bag and out slid a huge, fat bottle of lavishly expensive aromatherapy foam bath.

'Thank you very much,' said Bella. 'As soon as the stitches have healed, I will indulge.'

Tania pulled a face: 'How many?'

'An unspeakable amount. I've told Don we can never have sex again.'

'Oh God. That means you won't need my final present.'

Bella laughed, curious now.

Tania brought out a shoebox. Inside were pale green strappy snakeskin shoes with vertiginously high heels.

'Good grief,' said Bella shocked at Tania's extravagance.

'Well, I worried you might not get back into your clothes just yet, so I thought these would make you feel foxy again.'

Tania was surprised to find her friend choked with tears.

They put their arms round each other and Bella sobbed.

'I'm sorry,' Bella said as soon as she could. 'It must be the hormones. Thank you very much.'

'It's a pleasure, honey,' Tania smiled and got paper hankies out of her handbag. 'I brought supper as well, Japanese . . . sushi, broth, all your favourite things. I'll go down and heat them, then Don and I will come and eat by your bedside with you.'

When a steaming bowl of noodly broth was put in front of her with a large hunk of buttered bread, Bella realized she was ravenous. She was going to have to eat and worry about passing the consequences when it happened.

'My mum says you have to have someone come and stay and look after you for a while,' Tania said biting down on a piece of rice and sushi. 'She says she's going to come if you haven't got anyone else!'

Bella laughed: 'That's very sweet. I think Maddie's visiting soon, Don's mum, so that will be good. But Don is off for two weeks, so we'll be fine. I'm sure I'll feel back to normal by then.'

She heard herself saying this but wondered if it was true. She was shocked at her condition and her injuries. Just two days ago, she could clean floors, walk round the block, make love: now she was barely able to shuffle to the bathroom. And she was in so much pain. Her breasts ached, her uterus was still contracting in sharp spasms, especially when the baby breastfed, and her stitches and piles . . . well, best take another painkiller and try and forget about it.

She felt as if the entire area between her legs had

been stapled shut. It was bruised and swollen and an exploratory feel of the damage had not been reassuring. In between a dense weave of hair matted with congealed blood were hulking great stitches, which, thank God were supposed to dissolve rather than need tweezing out when the wounds had healed.

She had torn almost to her anus; only a large bulbous pile seemed to have stopped the path of the rip. And she hadn't been prepared for the bleeding either. Annie had brought round maternity pads the size of mattresses earlier in the day and told her to bathe in water with lavender oil when it all got too uncomfortable.

Jesus, Bella had just never expected this amount of damage. She felt injured, war wounded and everyone was smiling and sending flowers and congratulating her as if she'd just won an award. Get well cards and sympathy would be slightly more appropriate. Maybe she should design a new range: 'It's a boy! Fifteen stitches, wow you must be feeling sore!'

But she had her reward, didn't she? Markie was sound asleep in his bed again, oblivious to the chat going on around him in the room.

Tania was stroking his downy head and watching his chest rise and fall and Don was gazing at him too as he spooned noodles into his mouth.

The baby was a magical presence, no doubt about it. They were all transfixed by this tiny being whose beautiful blue-veined eyelids were fluttering in sleep like butterfly wings.

Chapter Twenty-five

It was close to 2 a.m. when Bella was ripped out of deep sleep by her baby's ferocious wailing. She turned on the sidelight. Don had woken up too.

She lifted her screaming son out of his crib and put him against her breast. He sucked like hell and it really, really hurt. She gritted her teeth and watched his jaw moving up and down. 'Oh God—' she turned to Don. 'This is so painful. I don't think I can let him drink much more.'

Her bleary-eyed husband mumbled something sympathetic.

Bella put her finger down to Markie's mouth to break the suction and took him off. He burst into desperate screams again. Quickly she put him back on her other breast. She watched the little face working up and down and tried not to think about the horrible rubbed raw pain coming from her nipples.

After about three minutes, she swapped sides again, then several minutes later she swapped back. She couldn't take it any more. Surely, he must have had enough by now. She broke him off again and was horrified to hear his anguished cries.

She rocked him a little bit, then put him back in his crib. Maybe he was just tired and needed to go back to sleep now.

He screamed furiously at her down there and balled up his little fists. Maybe he needed a new nappy. She picked him up and stumbled through to the bathroom with him, she undid the rompers and opened the tiny nappy while the pink legs kicked against her and Markie screamed so hard that his jaw was trembling.

In the nappy was a small solid black mess. Bella filled with relief. OK, as soon as this was changed he'd settle down and feel much better.

She fumbled her way through the nappy change and headed back to the bedroom. Don was already half asleep. Bella put Markie into the crib and he screamed even harder. She patted him and spoke gently to him, but he was inconsolable.

'I don't know what it is,' Bella turned to Don.

'Turn out the lights, I'm sure he'll settle down,' Don mumbled.

In darkness they lay listening to the anguished crying. Bella felt so tired she could barely move and yet the crying pierced her to the core and it was impossible to just lie there and listen to it.

She leaned over and scooped Markie out of his crib again. She rocked him in her arms – no change – she hauled herself out of bed and began to hobble painfully round the room holding Markie up against her shoulder and patting his back.

An age later, he finally stopped crying against her shoulder. She leaned over the crib to put him down and the wailing started up again.

'Oh no!' she cried in desperation and sank onto the bed, 'I can't feed him again, it's too sore,' she wailed. 'And I've got to get some *sleep*!'

Don dragged himself out: 'Let me have a go.'

He picked up the screaming baby and walked round the bed with him, then he started singing something indecipherable and astonishingly tuneless. Bella watched the digital minutes stack up on the bedside clock. It took sixteen minutes, until 3.08 a.m. before Markie was asleep again.

Don eased him into the crib, then collapsed back onto the bed. Less than three hours later, they were woken again by the wail of a hungry baby.

After four more nights like this, Bella began to wonder how she was going to survive. She felt dizzy and ill with tiredness. Her head was pounding and more than anything else in the world she wanted to sleep, but she felt so desperately needed by this tiny, helpless baby. Her nipples hurt excruciatingly as Markie drank and she was balancing him awkwardly against her as she couldn't even sit up properly because her stitches and piles were so painful.

Don had fallen straight back to sleep beside her and it was impossible not to fill up with rage. Bastard, she thought, how dare he not have to stay awake and breastfeed? He could damn well wind and change the nappy and then change the outfit which usually got puked on just when the nappy changing was over.

She looked into the little eyes which were wide open and fixed on her and at the furrowed brow and tiny, perfect fingernails and she knew she was completely, helplessly, hopelessly in love. Markie was making her life utter, utter hell but she loved him, adored him, felt totally captivated by him.

Oh great, she thought. Just the kind of dependent relationship I've been trying to avoid for ten years and here I am desperate to please a needy, greedy, ungrateful little man.

She stroked his cheek: 'You are,' she said gently, 'a needy, greedy, ungrateful little man.' The baby sucked contentedly.

She took Don's advice and went back to bed in the middle of the morning once Markie had been fed again and gone back to sleep. As she walked up the stairs, she had to face the fact that finally she was going to have to go to the loo, and not just for a pee.

Christ. What if the stitches ripped? Or everything tore? Or she passed out with the pain? She was going to have to be brave and find out what the score was.

She sat herself down on the toilet seat and waited. She was hit with an absolutely searing pain but within seconds it was over. Hardly childbirth then, she thought to herself. She wiped and was surprised to find the toilet paper covered in bright red blood. She looked into the bowl and the white porcelain sides were splattered with blood droplets. Oh God. Gingerly she felt down. Stitches all seemed to be in place. Anus was ringed with a bleeding spongy mass. God, there must be something she could do about this. The technological advantages of living in the twenty-first century had to include not having to put up with horrendous post-partum piles.

She went into the bedroom and collapsed on the

bed. She felt as if she had only just fallen into a jumbled sleep when Don was at her bedside holding a red, screaming Markie.

'What's the matter?' Bella asked, shaken out of exhaustion by anxiety about her baby.

'He's just hungry. He's been awake for about forty-five minutes, but I've been carrying him around, trying to distract him so you could sleep for longer.'

'Thanks, Don.' She glanced up at him. His eyes were ringed too and he was sprouting a healthy coat of stubble. 'Why don't you go for a shower while I feed him?' she said.

'OK. Then I'll make some lunch, shall I?'

'Yeah, thanks.'

She didn't look up again, he noticed. Her eyes were fixed on Markie as she lifted her T-shirt and placed her nipple in the ravenous mouth.

Don was ashamed to feel a wave of jealousy pass over him. He was jealous that Markie had all Bella's attention but also jealous that Bella was everything Markie needed. He felt left out of the intimate circle of two. It was also strangely arousing to see his son's tiny lips suck at the large rosy pink nipples. Bella looked beautiful. Buxom and blossoming and just perfect. How was he ever going to last another . . . *five and a half weeks* without sex?'

'Oh God,' he groaned.

'What's the matter?' She asked while the baby suckled on, unperturbed.

'I've just remembered how long it is before we can have sex again.'

She laughed now for what felt like the first time in days. 'Forget it, Don! We are never having sex again! They've stapled me shut and even if they hadn't, I am never, ever going through childbirth again. So I'll need medical documents to prove your vasectomy has been a complete success before letting you near.'

They both laughed now and wondered how much of that was true.

Don made lunch and later on, he made supper. He was a pretty domesticated man, but the household was deteriorating round them fast. The bedroom laundry basket was overflowing with tiny vests and babygros stained bright yellow with baby crap. How could something so small produce so much vivid waste product? he wondered, taking care to handle the clothes by the edges.

The kitchen was grubby and cluttered with dirty dishes; everywhere needed to be hoovered.

Don could hear Markie upstairs in the bathroom wailing all the way through his evening bath. That was bound to upset Bella. He suddenly felt exhausted and decided to nip out and finally get some newspapers in. The walk would clear his head.

Chapter Twenty-six

Bella had her laptop out and was trying to engage her brain just long enough to write her New York friend, Jenna, an e-mail.

My dear darling Jen, My seventeen day old baby is finally asleep and I have just enough energy left to sprawl out on the sofa and type you a note. Thank you so much for the lovely outfit which arrived yesterday. It's just gorgeous, perfect . . . thank you. Markie has worn it for about 20 seconds but now it's back in the wash basket covered in projectile vomit. Ah the joys of motherhood!

I'm sort of hanging in here – battered, bruised, a bit weepy and totally, totally beyond the limit of human endurance tired. I have never been so tired.

I am going to hit the next person who tells me 'don't worry, the first six weeks are the worst' because I'm thinking SIX WEEKS – I cannot survive another six DAYS of this!!

Breastfeeding – lovely concept – hurts like hell, plus I look like a chunky, frumpy, brunette Dolly Parton. Only industrial size painkillers are getting me through the stitches, post-partum piles situation but, hey, I don't want to put you off or anything . . . are you still brooding on the broody question?

How is Ritchie doing? I hope you are considering a visit soon so I can inspect this man and you can come and worship at the shrine of Markie.

Don is OK, despite me turning into the baggy shirted, slipper wearing harpy from hell who nearly screamed the house down when he suggested going off to Italy for a week to 'work' on some football tournament.

Markie is of course adorable, adorable, just a million times lovelier than I could ever have imagined. But so much work, much worse than expected . . . I'm such an amateur it terrifies me – I can't even steer the buggy properly. I feel a bit helpless and out of control and I'm very worried about how I'm going to make all this work. But I keep telling myself I'll figure it out somehow . . . hopefully soon. Take care cupcake, love you, Bella xxx

She hit send then closed up the computer and tried to fall asleep.

By the afternoon, she felt strong enough to take Markie out for a walk when he was fed and ready for a sleep. She put him into a new nappy, sleepsuit and cardigan, then laid him down in the buggy. That had only taken about forty minutes – a new world record time.

She dragged the buggy down the front door steps, cursing every single one of them. This had all been much easier when Don was around. But he was already back at work.

It still felt strange to walk along the road pushing this great big thing along. The sun broke out from behind a cloud and Markie, dazzled, began to cry. She pulled up the hood and it only partially covered his face, so she moved him gently up the pram until he was in shade again, still crying. She spoke to him soothingly as they moved on down the road and finally he fell asleep and she felt herself relax a little.

The nearest high street was shabby and run down with a grotty-looking shopping centre at one end, then a handful of chain stores, interspersed with kebab shops and taxi offices. Scabby market stalls selling cheap handbags and underwear were pitched up against the pavement.

She went to Boots first where she headed for the aisle with nappies and all the other postnatal products.

Wow, I'm an entirely separate consumer group, she couldn't help noticing. Extra-large sanitary towels, cracked-nipple cream, nipple guards, haemorrhoid cream, she piled the lot into her basket. Add a packet of super-strength painkillers, a bottle of wine, and maybe she would get through the evening after all.

As she paid at the till, Markie started to stir. By the time she got back outside, he was bawling miserably and she knew she had to feed him . . . where?? There was no bench or seat in sight and anyway, would she really be happy whipping up her top here? Plus there was the wind chill factor to consider. She headed for the baby shop at the far end of the street.

Markie was red in the face and howling by the time she got there. She hurried through the shop straight for the tweely labelled 'Mummy's Room' which had a bench, several changing mats, a sink, a grotty cartoon character frieze on the wall and an overpowering stench of dirty nappies. No wonder new mums got depression, this looked like the perfect venue for a postnatal suicide.

She bent over the buggy to lift out her screaming son and as her fingers reached behind him, they slid into warm wetness. She lifted him up and he and the sheepskin-lined buggy were covered in slimy yellow crap.

'Oh God,' she cursed under her breath.

She hadn't brought anything with her: no wipes, no change of clothes, no cloths, it was another Amateur Mum moment.

She put Markie down on one of the changing mats. He was waving his fists and bawling. No wonder, starving and covered in poo, not a good scene.

Stay calm, she told herself. There was a drum of paper towel on the wall so she pulled off about six feet from the roll and bundled Markie up in it. That would do while she fed him; they would begin the damage limitation exercise afterwards.

The staff were somewhat bemused to see a harassed and obviously brand new mother come out of the changing room holding a baby swaddled in yellow-stained paper towel.

Bella scanned the shelves and got vests, babygros and a large box of wipes. She picked out a black duffle changing bag, paid for the lot at the till and went back into the Mummy's Room for some time. When she came out again her baby was re-dressed and lying in his buggy on a wad of paper towel. The bulging duffle bag was slung over her shoulder.

On the walk home she tried to laugh about it but she felt hopeless and weak. God, how useless was she? She couldn't even take her baby round the block without turning it into a major crisis. She could feel tears welling up at the back of her eyes. This was just nothing like she'd imagined. All her baby daydreams had been about sitting in a sunny garden with a darling baby fast asleep in his pram. Instead the weather was cold and grey and he cried most of the time and she felt shattered and totally wound up.

Her mobile trilled in her pocket.

She clicked it open and was astonished to hear Kitty: Kitty asking her if she wanted the mail accumulating in the office to be sent to her or if she was coming in. It felt like greetings from another planet and served only to ignite her anxiety about the countdown on her time with her son.

She had six more weeks of being with her gorgeous little boy 24 hours a day and then she had to hand him over and get back to work, or else she would lose her place and anyway they had a mountainous mortgage now which they could not pay without her salary.

Chapter Twenty-seven

'Hello?' Don's voice sounded irritable.

'Don?' Bella was in tears again and there were frantic screams in the background.

'What's the matter, hon?' He tried to sound sympathetic.

'He won't stop crying,' she sobbed. 'I don't know what to do, I've fed him, I've changed him, maybe there's something wrong with him.'

'Have you winded him?'

'Of course.' She was beginning to sound angry now.

'Maybe he's just tired, Bella. I'm sure he's fine.'

'Tired?' she shouted. 'Of course he's bloody tired, he's been up since 6 a.m. and it's now eleven but he'll only sleep with my nipple in his mouth. I can't take any more of this. I need to tidy up, I need to have a bath, I need some sleep, I'm going to go insane.' She was practically screaming now.

'Bella,' Don's voice was angry too, 'I'm at work, I can't help you right now, calm down, go for a walk or something. I've got more important things to do than listen to this.' Shit, he regretted the words as soon as he'd said them.

All he could hear was his son's inconsolable wailing then a venomous 'Fuck you' before Bella slammed the phone down. 'Go for a walk' – she was too exhausted to walk the length of the room. She threw herself down on the sofa and howled with her baby.

Don sat at his desk wondering what to do. Was his wife bashing his son's head against the wall right now? Should he phone her back? Should he phone social services? He decided to phone his mum.

'I think it's definitely time for you to come down and help, Mum, if you can,' he said as soon as the fond hellos were over.

'Don, I'd love to, I've been dying for you to ask, I didn't want to impose.'

He was already feeling much calmer at the sound of her voice.

'How are you both getting on? I've been worrying about you.'

'It's absolute murder,' he was surprised to hear himself say.

'Oh dear,' Maddie said sympathetically. 'How's Bella coping?'

'Not very well right now,' Don answered. That was putting it mildly.

'Well, she's been such an independent girl for so long now. It must be a shock to be at the beck and call of a baby.'

'When can you come?' he asked, thinking she'd probably missed the last flight out of Inverness today. But maybe he could get her on the first plane in the morning.

'When do you want me?'

'Tomorrow? I can organize a flight.' He knew how desperate he must sound and felt a bit embarrassed.

'Don't be ridiculous, Don. You need to warn Bella. I'll come at the weekend. Are you phoning from work?' she asked sharply.

'Yes.'

'What on earth are you doing there? Your son isn't even three weeks old.'

'I had to get back.'

'What utter nonsense,' she said. 'Take the next three days off and I'll be there on Saturday. In fact, if you don't take the next three days off, I'm not going to come, is that clear?'

'I'll see what I can do,' he mumbled.

'Don McCartney, you should be ashamed of yourself.'

Once the call was over, Don arranged the time off, despite the news editor's raised eyebrows, and he left work that evening as early as he could.

He still hadn't dared to phone Bella back and wasn't quite sure what to expect when he opened the front door.

Bella was obviously giving Markie his evening bath, because there was frantic crying coming from the bathroom. Don went into the sitting room and flicked on the TV to the championship match he'd been hoping to watch.

He took off his shoes and glanced round the room. It looked extraordinary. There were cloths and pieces of kitchen towel in little heaps all over the floor. In one pile he spotted a yellow stained vest and several yellowish rolled-up nappies. Plates, one with a half-eaten cheese sandwich, and mugs half full of cold tea littered the area round the sofa. The beautiful leather sofa had an unmistakable yellow stain on it. Christ.

It was time to go upstairs and say hello. He took off his coat and carefully hung it up in the hall before heading up the stairs.

Opening the bathroom door, he saw Bella had Markie cuddled in a towel on the changing mat. He was shrieking and she was trying to talk to him soothingly as she struggled to put on a nappy.

She looked awful, her face was pale and blotchy with red-rimmed eyes, her hair was lank and fixed up messily on her head. She was wearing his old tracksuit bottoms with the hideous tartan shirt. The shoulders were stained with white patches of vomit and he could see patches of damp around her breasts when she turned round to look at him.

'Hi,' he said gently.

She didn't say anything back.

'I've taken the rest of the week off so I can help you, and Maddie would like to come down at the weekend.'

'Fine,' she said simply and turned back to Markie.

'Does he need a feed now?'

'Yes, no doubt,' she snapped back.

'Well when he's finished, why don't I take him and you can have a bath or a nap and I'll order some curry in if you like.'

'OK.' She didn't add anything more or look round at him again.

'All right, I'll go downstairs and tidy up a bit.'

She still didn't reply, so he left the room.

About forty-five minutes later, Bella came down with Markie. He was nuzzled up against her shoulder looking dreamy.

'OK, you're in charge,' she said, handing him over gently to Don.

She went out of the room and Markie started to grizzle. Don put him up against his shoulder and started to walk round the room trying to keep one eye on the football match – bloody hell, a penalty kick.

He stood still to watch the kick and could hear the soft choking noise which meant his son was puking on his shoulder. With some distaste, he looked over at the lumpy white vomit on his best work shirt. Where were the cloths?

He searched the room and realized he had tidied them all away, he would have to go into the kitchen. From the hallway he could hear the cheers, damn, a goal. Damn, damn, damn, he should be there. He should be in Italy right now, not dealing with baby sick.

Bella was standing naked in the bathroom waiting for her bath to fill. She looked at herself in the full-length mirror and the sight was utterly depressing. Her breasts were huge sagging marrows with silvery stretch marks streaked across them. Her stomach was unmarked but it looked deflated with crinkly skin covering a horribly large mound of wobbly flab. She turned around and saw with horror that her bum appeared to have dropped by five inches and there was a layer of unyielding cellulite sitting all round her thighs.

She sighed and tried to think happy thoughts. A bath, a long, hot, relaxing bath and she would feel better. She opened the bottle of fantastically expensive bath foam from Tania and leaned over the taps to tip it in.

The liquid hit the running tap water and bounced, spitting a blob back, which landed squarely in her right eye. It stung like hell. She rushed to the sink and tried to wash it out. AAARGH, her eye was smarting. She rinsed and rinsed then looked up in the mirror to see her eyeball, bright red and watering.

For a moment, she thought she was going to dissolve into tears for the millionth time that day, but she suddenly saw the funny side and began to laugh hysterically. She could feel her stitches strain as she drew breath and laughed again.

God, this was a nightmare. No wonder nobody warned you, no-one would have children.

She crawled into the bath and leaned back to relax, but now that the water was off she could hear Markie howling downstairs. OK, from now on baths were out, she would have to relax in the shower, where she wouldn't be able to hear him.

With a heavy heart, Don had decided to abandon the football entirely and take Markie for a walk outside. He had finally managed to work the little howling bundle into his zip-up suit and then into the buggy when Markie vomited again all over his clothes and the buggy.

Oh God, Don groaned to himself, how do people do this? How do they manage with a baby, with a toddler, with two children . . . three? This baby was going to be dependent on them for the next sixteen years at least. Sixteen years!! He pictured Markie as a little schoolboy, as a 12-year-old, as a sulky teenager and he felt gripped by a vague panic, he didn't know if he could handle this. Was this what he wanted? To go through all that stuff again: swings, sandpits, playground bullying, school football matches, homework, first dates, wet dreams, driving lessons, but this time as a dad?

He looked at the baby, crying now with vomit in a pool beside his face and on his jacket. God this was going to be really, really hard.

For a moment Don thought about his own dad and wondered what part of it all had caused him to walk out of the door for ever.

Chapter Twenty-eight

Maddie's visit was life-saving. She breezed in on a cloud of Crabtree and Evelyn Gardenia and diagnosed the cause of Markie's long screaming sessions at once: 'He's absolutely starving, Bella. He's enormous. You can't possibly feed him all by yourself, not until you get some proper rest.'

Bella was happy to agree, so Maddie had barely dropped her bags in her room before she rushed out to buy baby milk, a sterilizer and bottles.

Once Markie had drunk Bella dry, he greedily sucked down several ounces of bottle milk and fell into a deep sleep which was to last for an astonishing six hours.

'You see.' There was no note of triumph in Maddie's voice, she was just happy she could help. It had been a shock to see Bella looking so exhausted and unwell.

With an enormous pot of tea, Maddie held court in the sitting room: 'I know baby care nowadays is very different from my day and just as well, I was in the maternity hospital for a month and only allowed to see Don every four hours and not at all during the night but, if you ask me, it's gone too far the other way now, it's all home birth and breast-feeding on demand and doing things naturally and that's all very well if you're a tribeswoman with a whole tribe to support you—' she took a breath.

'But Bella, you poor dear, you can't even walk properly yet. You need total rest and relaxation. Don't you dare feel guilty about giving Markie a top-up of bottle milk. Now I'll make some more tea and then off to bed with you.'

Maddie went back down to the kitchen and Don and Bella were left on the sofa looking at each other. Markie was in the carrycot in the corner of the room still sound asleep.

Bella smiled.

'She's quite a girl,' Don said, smiling too. 'You better do what she tells you.'

'I feel awful,' Bella confessed.

'You look awful too,' Don added, but kindly and with a grin.

'Thanks a lot.' She considered hurling a sofa cushion at him, but didn't have the strength. 'If I could wish for one thing in the world right now, it would be for you to have the breasts, so you could feed him 24 hours a day and see just how hellish it is.'

'You're doing a great job, Bella.'

'You lie. I'm the worst mother on the face of the planet, I was starving my baby and I wouldn't even have known because I haven't had the strength to take him to the baby clinic yet. He's probably already on the at risk register.'

'Bella! Go to sleep, hon,' Don ordered. 'Just go now!'

290

'Thanks,' she said. She got up and walked to the door.

He looked at the baggy grey tracksuit trousers, drooping round her bum. God, she had to get some new clothes, this was depressing.

'Don, give the girl a chance!' Maddie fired back at him when he mentioned it to her. 'She needs rest, more rest and your love and care and attention – not to be told she's looking frumpy. For goodness sake, give her time to adjust to this. You hardly look like Kirk Douglas yourself. A shave wouldn't go amiss and maybe you should think about reacquainting yourself with the ironing board. There's a stack of housework to be done and you will be the one doing it when I go back home.'

'How long are you going to stay for, Mum?'

'A week. I think that's as long as any woman wants her mother-in-law around.'

'OK. That's great.'

'Right.' She drained the last of her cup: 'The whole place needs a good hoovering, so Don, you do that while I dust, then we're going to tackle the windows.'

He'd had six hours of fragmented sleep the night before and was desperate to join Bella upstairs in their cool, white haven of a bedroom, but his mother was right, the house was a mess.

Markie didn't wake up until close to six o'clock. Don distracted him for a little then brought him upstairs to Bella.

She was curled up in the bed, still fast asleep. He placed Markie down on the duvet close beside her so that the baby would be the first thing she saw when she woke up. Markie lay on his back and gave a little gurgle. Bella's eyes opened and focused on the baby. She smiled an intensely loving smile that gave Don a lump in his throat.

Then she looked up and saw him standing there and smiled the same smile at him too.

'You've been asleep for hours,' he whispered. 'You look much better.'

'Thank God. I feel better. Has Markie just woken up?'

'He woke up about half an hour ago, but he's starting to get hungry now.'

'How long did he sleep for?'

'Almost six hours!'

'That's amazing!! Have I been asleep for five then?'

'Yeah, Maddie and I have renovated the entire house and she's now busy making a "nourishing stew for tea",' he mimicked her singsong Scottish accent.

'How sweet of you both.' Bella still sounded dreamy.

She sat up in the bed and held Markie in her arms. She lifted her T-shirt and Don glimpsed the luscious creamy white breasts with big, pert nipples before Markie hungrily clamped on. He sat there watching and inhaling the milky, sweaty, sweet smell coming from them and realized he was totally turned on. He could hear the baby sucking noisily at her breast and God, he wanted her. He sat close beside her and kissed her on the cheek as together they watched the baby's jaw moving up and down.

'Where are you going?' Bella asked as he finally got up to leave the room.

'For another cold shower,' he joked.

She gave a little laugh. Men. Absolutely obsessed with sex. She stroked her son's tiny, downy soft head and tried to remember what sex was all about, but she just couldn't.

Maddie cleaned and cooked and looked after Markie for as much time as she could, but it was hard to wrestle him away from Bella.

'Go to your room!' Maddie would order Bella. 'I don't care if you're not sleepy, go and read a magazine, file your nails, have a bath . . . just rest. You'll be sorry when I'm gone.'

'I will be very sorry,' Bella told her one morning over what felt like her seventeenth cup of tea. 'I've got so much to organize, I haven't done anything about finding a nanny, or a cleaner. We'll really need a cleaner when I go back to work.'

There was a pause and Maddie looked up, surprised to see Bella's eyes filling with tears.

'Whatever's the matter, dear?' she asked gently.

'I'm really confused about it all. Oh it's nothing,' Bella sipped at her tea, fighting back the urge to cry. 'Just the hormones, isn't it? Makes you feel like this.'

'It's normal to feel worried about going back to work. Of course it's normal, you're handing over your precious little boy to someone else,' Maddie said.

At that Bella couldn't hold back any more. She burst into fierce sobs.

'I don't want to do it, Maddie. I want to be here with him . . .' Maddie put an arm round her.

In between sobs, Bella said: 'But I loved my job, I don't want to give it up. I just want the impossible

. . . I want Markie to not exist for the time I'm working then be here when I get home. I can't bear the idea of him crying and needing me when I'm not around, how will I be able to work thinking about him?'

Maddie cuddled her close and asked, 'Can you take a bit more time off to work this out?'

'Not really, no,' Bella answered, thinking about the Danson's contract for the first time in weeks.

'Can you do some work from home? Or maybe go part-time for a bit?' Maddie asked.

'I don't think so. Anyway we need the money. The mortgage on this place is astronomical and Don's never going to get a pay rise and we've borrowed loads of money to do it up and furnish it. Oh shit, shit, shit.'

Maddie hugged Bella hard and tried to sound comforting, but she felt worried. She'd never seen her daughter-in-law like this before. Bella always had everything figured out, this was so unlike her.

'You've got to find a lovely nanny Bella, that's your top priority,' Maddie said. 'And get comfortable with her before you go back. Then go back with an open mind and see how it goes. If you hate it, have a rethink. You can change jobs or move to a smaller house, whatever is going to make you all happy.'

Bella wiped her tears and Maddie added, 'Have you talked to Don about all this?'

'No, he's terrified as it is, if I tell him I'm scared, he'll just take off altogether.' Damn, damn, Bella could have kicked herself.

'Just because his father walked out on us does not mean Don is going to do the same, Bella,' Maddie said. 'I've brought him up to be a good man and he won't let you down, but be careful not to shut him out.'

There was an uneasy silence at the kitchen table, then Maddie decided to change the subject. 'Well, the two of you are going out on Saturday night. I won't hear any objections, you are going to scrub up and go off somewhere nice.'

Well, it was a reasonable idea, although the prospect of having to scrub up was making Bella feel mildly panicky. She went upstairs to look in the wardrobe. There was no way she was putting on her maternity clothes again, that would just be admitting defeat, but she was never going to get her enormous bust or flabby stomach into any of her old things.

There was still the Heathrow outfit. A sarong didn't technically count as a maternity skirt and she could wear the green sandals from Tania.

She decided to give her friend a call.

'Bella, hello! How's the little pooky pie?' Tania asked.

'He's fine. He cries a lot and feeds non-stop and goes through 200 nappies and items of clothing a day.'

'And how about Markie?' Tania joked.

'Ha ha. How are you? And Greg?'

'I'm fine, he's the same old . . . gone off to see his parents *again*. I still haven't met them . . . live in the country somewhere. You know, I don't even have their address or phone number.'

'How do you speak to him when he's there?'

'On the mobile . . . when he remembers to turn it on.'

Bella was beginning to wonder how long Tania, Greg and the no-proposal situation could go on for.

'You need to ditch him, find a nice man and have babies, Tania,' she joked, realizing as she said it how much she needed a friend with a baby right now.'

'Hmm. Anyway, are you chatting or do you want to arrange something?'

'Do you want to come and cuddle and kiss with my baby next weekend?' Bella asked.

'But I don't fancy Don at all!' was Tania's answer.

'Ha, ha. Actually, that's a real shame because he's gagging for sex and if you could just service him for a few months I wouldn't consider that infidelity at all because you're family.'

'Better incest than infidelity, that's nice.'

'Please shut me up, my mind has gone since birth.'

'What's 84 times 169?' Tania asked her.

'14,196,' Bella shot right back.

'Is it? Well if you're right, that strange bit of your brain is still working, so good, you still have a job to go to.'

'I hope so.' She said this cheerfully, but wondered if she meant it.

Chapter Twenty-nine

They took a cab to the restaurant and Bella felt weird and uneasy leaving the house without Markie. She'd given him an hour-long feed before they left, barely leaving herself enough time to get changed and made up.

He hadn't been asleep but had snuggled quite contentedly in his granny's arms.

'Just go,' Maddie had shooed her away. 'He'll be absolutely fine, he's going to fall fast asleep and if he wakes up before you're back, I'll give him some bottle milk. Now *go* and *enjoy yourselves.*'

Sitting in the back of the cab, Bella looked down at her outfit. God her boobs were enormous, but they didn't look glamorous, just matronly, trussed up in a nursing bra closely akin to scaffolding.

At least her feet, in the shoes from Tania, looked sexy and so did her husband.

She smiled at him and folded her arms under her breasts. 'I look like the Queen,' she said mournfully.

'You look great, just calm down,' Don said, looking round at her. 'I love your hair.'

'What? Washed and brushed?'

'It looks nice.'

When they got to the restaurant and were shown to their table, Bella's unease had blossomed into full-blown nervousness. She took her mobile out of her bag and placed it on the table, checking there was a good signal.

'What are we going to drink, then?' Don said cheerfully, picking up the wine list.

'Well, I can't have much, goes into the milk, and anyway, I've got to get up later.'

Don didn't say anything. He watched her fiddle with her phone and cutlery and wished she would relax.

'Do you think we should ring up and check?' she said finally.

'No,' Don answered firmly. 'Maddie will phone if there's a problem. We'll probably just wake him up if we call.'

'Mmm.' Bella looked round the room distract-edly.

'Bella,' Don took hold of her hand and looked at her face. 'Bella, look at me. I'm here with you tonight, this is "us" time, Markie is fine, can you please stop worrying, just for a little, tiny bit?'

'Yes,' she said. 'Yes, you're right, what shall we eat?' She picked up the menu and tried to concen-trate although her stomach was churning and she couldn't imagine how she was going to eat anything.

When the first course arrived, she asked Don about his work because she knew he would talk and she could pretend to listen.

By the time the main course was there, she could feel her heart pounding, she was so anxious.

'I'm going to have to phone, Don,' she said suddenly, interrupting his story.

'It's OK, I'll do it,' he said. She was relieved she hadn't seen any flicker of annoyance cross his face.

'I'll go into the lobby where it's quieter.' He got up and walked over to the double doors.

Moments later he came back to the table, smiling. 'He's still sleeping, he fell asleep ten minutes after we left and he hasn't stirred. OK, are you going to start enjoying yourself now?'

He poured himself another generous top-up of wine but didn't offer her anything as she had barely touched the glass in front of her.

Halfway through her plateful, she wondered if Don had phoned at all. God, what an idiot she was, he'd probably stood in the lobby and not even bothered because if Markie had been crying, well it would just have spoiled the meal, wouldn't it?

'Bella, for God's sake. By the look on your face, you'd think our son was in hospital not snuggled up in his bed.' Don sounded exasperated now. 'Why don't you just have a cigarette or something? Christ, I thought this would be fun.'

She had not had a cigarette since Markie was born. Her conscience had finally overridden her urge to smoke. 'I don't want nicotine in my breast milk,' she said.

'It never worried you when you were pregnant,' Don answered sharply.

'But he's here now, he's not an abstract baby, he's a real one, I couldn't do anything that might hurt him.' She felt her eyes fill with tears and she just longed to hold her baby. Her breasts were tingling strangely, she wanted to be with him, feeding him

299

and cuddling him. 'I want to go home,' she said, a tear spilling over onto her cheek. 'I'm sorry, I'm just not ready for this.'

Don knocked back his glass and refilled it, draining the last of the wine from the bottle.

'OK,' he said 'I'll get the bill.'

They were home at 10 p.m., just an hour and a half after they'd left. Bella went straight upstairs to bed, and took Markie, who was still asleep, up with her.

Don stayed downstairs with his mother and opened a bottle of whisky.

When Markie woke at 1 a.m., Bella sat up, switched on the sidelight and fed him. As the baby suckled, Bella watched Don fast asleep beside her. He had not even stirred whereas Markie's smallest cry woke her from deep sleep.

At 6 a.m., when Bella was woken up by Markie again, Don still slept on soundly. Markie wasn't ready to go back down straight away, so Bella got up. As she put on a dressing gown, she looked over at her sleeping husband and felt a fresh wave of resentment break over her. She had thought they were going to be ultra modern and share the parenting equally. But it was obvious to her that breastfeeding was letting Don off lightly.

Don was already back at work, he slept soundly all night and wanted to go out for dinner and have sex and the relationship they'd had before the baby. She was the one who felt that everything had changed for ever and she felt bitterly angry that he couldn't see that.

She and Markie were the couple now, Don was the third party. It was Markie she was attuned to,

Markie she wanted to make happy and needed to be with. Don felt like just another demand on her time and emotions and she was so physically exhausted, she could barely cope with the baby's demands.

Right now, she couldn't feel anything apart from the mildest affection for Don. Whereas for the baby snuggled against her shoulder she felt the fiercest, most possessive love, passion and need.

She took Markie downstairs. Maddie joined them soon after 7 a.m. and put the kettle on.

'I've had a lovely time, Bella, but I bet you're looking forward to having the house to yourselves again.'

'Not really,' Bella said with a smile. 'You've been wonderful. Thank you so much for coming down.'

'I'm sorry if I packed you off for a night out before you were ready for it,' Maddie added.

'Don't be,' said Bella. 'You weren't to know, neither was I really. I think Don's a bit angry with me though.'

'Och, he'll get over it.' Maddie poured boiling water into the teapot and brought it over to the table. 'But don't leave it too long before you go out again,' she added. 'You and Don need each other too.'

'Hmmm. Shall we take a walk round the park after breakfast?' Bella tried to sound breezy. 'It's not too bad, a bit of greenery at least,' she added. This was about the nicest thing that could be said about the park. It was a dismal stretch of urban grassland bisected with tarred paths and furnished with grimy benches, concrete litter-bins and piles of dog dirt.

She had wheeled the buggy around it several times and it never cheered her up, in fact it made her depressed. Litter blew about the grass, she had once spotted a used condom lying under the bench and she had never seen any other mothers or children playing there. People just came to the place to shag and let their dogs crap.

It continued to amaze her that so much money had only bought her a house in this unremarkable part of town. OK, the houses in her street were lovely, but the high street was dire, the park was a pit and there was nowhere to go. No coffee shops – ha, that was a joke – no bookshop, no cinema, no duck pond, no swings for Christ's sake, just a branch of Mothercare. Is that what she was supposed to do all day now that she had a baby? Go to Mothercare and Boots and hang out?

She and Maddie put on their coats, bundled Markie into his pram and opened the door on another unseasonably grey and cold June day.

'Goodness,' said Maddie as she helped lift Markie's pram down the steps. 'It's like November out here.'

Chapter Thirty

Bella sat at the kitchen table watching the cold wind shake at a bush in the garden. Tears were streaming down her cheeks but she didn't care, didn't even really notice. She was exhausted but couldn't imagine going back to bed. Markie would wake up as soon as she fell asleep anyway.

She'd been up since before 5 a.m., feeding, changing, winding, sterilizing bottles for the top-up feeds, tidying up the house, feeding, changing, winding, feeding, changing, winding. It was one long endless cycle. Markie was crying less, but not sleeping for the luxurious long naps he had settled into when Maddie was here. Bella blamed herself, what was she doing wrong? In the four days since Maddie had left, Markie had somehow wound himself up again.

Her nights were wildly interrupted and she was barely making up for the lost sleep with catnaps during the day. As soon as Markie fell asleep, she rushed round the house, tidying up, getting dressed, doing all the things she didn't have time to do when he was awake. Then just as she lay down and started to relax, he would wake up again. It was like living with a ruthless torturer, except she loved him hopelessly, was driven to despair when he was unhappy. The most sophisticated torture of all.

Why could she not get this together? Christ, she was still in her dressing gown at 2 p.m., she should probably eat something . . . She brushed the tears from her face and wondered if there was anything in the fridge she could face.

Then she heard the doorbell. Who on earth was that? There was no time to change, she would have to answer it as she was.

She went upstairs and considered looking through the peephole first, but then decided 'oh bugger it, who cares?' and swung the door open.

There on the step was Red from the yoga class. Bella had totally forgotten they'd swapped numbers and addresses and said they'd keep in touch.

'Hello,' Red said, cracking a wide smile which showed beautiful white teeth against her dark skin. 'I thought I'd come round to show mine off and see yours.'

She looked just jealous-making lovely, in a tight sports top and wide-legged trousers and trainers, her long ringlets fanning out in the wind. She had a tartan papoose strapped across her front and Bella could just see the hat on the little baby snuggled inside.

'Hello.' Bella smiled broadly back, surprised at how glad she was to see this woman. 'Come in, the place is a mess . . . I'm a mess, sorry.'

'Sorry?!!' said Red, incredulously. 'Don't ever

apologize. The first six weeks are an absolute hell. Just be thankful everyone's still alive.'

Bella burst out laughing.

'Don't,' Red said, laughing as well. 'The pelvic floors can't take it yet, we'll pee ourselves.'

This just made them laugh even more. Bella began to feel quite hysterical, tears were forming in the corner of her eyes and oh God, she was about to cry *again*.

She started to sob and Red put an arm round her. 'I'm so sorry, I wish I'd come sooner,' she said.

'Don't be silly,' Bella managed after a few more moments. 'We don't even know each other very well.'

'Well, yeah, but I've been here before and I should have thought about you.' She squeezed Bella's arm affectionately. 'Come on, let's get some tea. Gorgeous house, by the way.'

'Thanks,' Bella said gratefully and they headed downstairs.

'This is Ellie.' Red patted the little hat buried deep down in the papoose. 'Born May 25th, 10.32 a.m., six pounds, nine ounces, after a four-hour labour, epidural, no tear, thank you God, but second babies are easier,' said Red.

'Oh yeah,' Bella said. 'I'd forgotten you already have another one. How old is . . . ?'

'He. Jamie is three,' answered Red. 'He's with his dad this afternoon,' she said as she settled into a chair. 'Come on, I want all your gory details.'

Bella busied herself with the kettle and realized she was starving: 'Do you want a sandwich?'

'Oh yes please,' said Red. 'Isn't breastfeeding the

305

best? An excuse to eat even more food than when you're pregnant.'

'Brie, ham, pâté or peanut butter?' said Bella looking into the fridge.

'Yes please,' said Red with a giggle.

When they were sitting down with tea and big plates of food in front of them, Bella gave Red her labour low-down and didn't spare any little detail. It took about half an hour. Bella was amazed the babies were still sleeping.

'It was so much pain,' she said. 'I could never have imagined how much pain it was. I didn't feel I'd been warned either.'

'I don't think anyone wants to tell pregnant women, in case they spend nine months in a state of panic,' Red said, then added: 'Well actually, I could have told you. I did the all-natural home birth thing the first time, but it was so Godawful I told Sandy I was only going to have another one under general anaesthetic. The epidural was our compromise,' she said in between big mouthfuls, 'and it was fab, no comparison with bloody gas and air. I think they give you that mouthpiece just to stop you screaming. It doesn't have any effect at all.'

They both cackled.

'How are you doing now?' Red asked.

'I'm just so tired,' Bella confessed. 'I didn't know I'd be awake most of the night, every night . . . because feeding takes so long and he doesn't want to go back to sleep afterwards.'

'I know,' Red added. 'You've just got to sleep in the day, sod the housework, sod the cooking, let the whole place fall in around you. You must sleep! Or

306

else you will go loopy loop, stare at the walls, crack up big time.'

'I think I'm already close,' Bella answered.

'You're back at work really soon, aren't you, you brave woman. What do you do again?' Red asked.

'I'm a management consultant. I'm supposedly back in three weeks' time, but I haven't done anything about a nanny. I don't know where to start and I can't face it.' Bella sounded almost tearful again.

'It's OK,' said Red. 'Everything you're feeling is normal. You'll be fine.' She gave an encouraging grin. 'Just give yourself some time.'

'That's the one thing I don't have.' Bella stared down into her tea. 'What do you do?' She looked up at Red.

'I'm an accountant . . . part-time accountant,' said Red. 'Well, when Jamie was born, I went back to work full time, but I found it impossible. I hardly saw him, I hardly saw Sandy because he was working so hard and all three of us were exhausted.

'We struggled on for about half a year, then jacked it in and downsized,' she continued. 'We sold the house, got a little flat round here and Sandy and I now run our own business together from home. He does most of it and I help out when I can.'

Red took a gulp of tea then added, 'I've told him absolutely nothing doing until Ellie is at least five months old. I really believe in breastfeeding, it's good for the baby, establishes immunity and everything but it's *terrible* for the mother, so exhausting and such a bind. You can't leave them for more than four hours max and even then you worry all the time. How are you managing with it?'

'It's getting better. I give Markie bottle top-ups as well,' Bella told her. 'I'm just hoping he'll take bottle milk in the day and breast milk at night when I go back to work.'

'Good for you,' said Red. 'I've never managed to get one baby to take as much as a sip from a bottle. But don't you dare feel guilty if you have to give up breastfeeding once you're back, you might find it's just too much. I mean, I was a lunatic, working all day, breastfeeding all night!'

Bella felt a surge of relief to hear someone else being honest about how hard this all was. It felt wonderfully bonding and conspiratorial.

Red added: 'I wouldn't say it's impossible working full time in London with a baby but it's really, really hard. What does your partner do?'

'Don's a journalist,' Bella answered.

'Oh yikes!' said Red. 'So not around very much?'

'Well, it's not too bad. Long hours, but he's not usually out of town more than a week every month.'

Bella could see the little lights rising on the baby monitor. Markie was starting to stir and she leapt up to get him.

'Oh God, he's enormous,' exclaimed Red when Bella brought him down to the kitchen. 'I'm amazed you can sit down.'

'Only on cushions!' Bella laughed and began feeding him.

When Ellie started to stir, Red didn't even take her out of the sling, just deftly lifted her top, twanged open a patterned, colourful, actually quite pretty nursing bra, Bella couldn't help noticing –

and her hungry baby latched on, leaving Red with both hands free to cradle her cup of tea.

'I like your outfit,' said Bella. 'I can't get into anything apart from Don's old stuff. I refuse to wear my maternity things again.'

Red laughed: 'Go buy yourself some new sports gear, that's my tip. It's very stretchy and covered in logos and stripes which detract from all the lumps and bumps. And I think it looks a bit more racy than leggings and a T-shirt, the uniform of new mums across the western world.'

It was Bella's turn to laugh: 'And what about work clothes? What did you do when you went back?'

'I did wear some maternity things, cunningly disguised,' Red confessed. 'But I bought a couple of suits, two or three sizes up and then just had them altered when I got back to normal.'

'I don't know if I'll ever get back to normal,' Bella said looking down at her stomach ruefully.

'You're joking, right?' said Red. 'You are about to become the busiest woman on the planet. You will never sit down, eat properly or get the chance to laze ever again. The pounds will fall off, in fact you'll have to try and eat extra if you carry on breastfeeding.'

Bella didn't really believe her, but it was nice to hear it anyway.

'I'm going to have to go,' Red said finally. 'This is my address and phone number, in case you've lost them—' she handed Bella a bright red business card. 'Just come round or phone, any time, I'd love to see you.'

They headed upstairs and as Bella opened the door she felt childishly pleased when Red gave her an affectionate kiss on the cheek as she left.

Markie had fallen into a doze again and Bella went upstairs, inspired to find a new outfit. But there was nothing in the wardrobe she could hope to get into so she donned the tracksuit trousers and tartan shirt again. Depressingly hideous.

But she washed her face, brushed her hair, put on lipstick and felt surprisingly better. OK, sod the housework, the most important item on the agenda was finding a nanny. In the sitting room, she found the phone book and began dialling.

Several phone calls later, she was totally disheartened again. Everyone she had spoken to had been appalled she'd left it so late. She basically wanted a nanny who could start in two weeks' time. All said they would put her on their lists, but could promise nothing.

She punched in another number.

Instead of a deep sigh in response to her request, a slightly more human-sounding woman said, 'Oh dear, has someone let you down?'

'Yes, I'm afraid so,' Bella fibbed.

'You poor thing, it's so awful when that happens. Luckily for you, we prefer to keep a waiting list of nannies rather than mummies. Do you need someone this week?'

'Well, no, the start date would be in two weeks' time. I go back in three weeks' time, but obviously I want to find the right person.'

'Of course. We've only got one girl experienced with babies ready to start at the moment, but let me tell you all about her and we'll arrange a meeting.'

Bella felt a wave of relief and anxiety pass over her. OK, she might be able to solve the nanny problem after all but that meant she really could be going back to work in just *three weeks*.

She thought about her little son sucking contentedly at her breast and felt an overwhelming sadness at the thought of giving him up. Her eyes were pricking, Christ, she was not going to allow herself to cry again. Heading back down to the kitchen, she tried to keep Maddie's words in her mind. She would go back with an open mind and see how it went. If she had to change her plans, so be it.

Chapter Thirty-one

Bella was dimly aware of the alarm in her dream for a long time before she managed to drag herself back to the surface and open her eyes. Her sleep was so fractured now, every nap led to the deepest, most complicated dream sequence.

Don had taken Markie downstairs after his 6 a.m. feed to allow her to sleep in until eight. But now she had to get up and get ready. Today was nanny interview day.

After she'd washed and leaned over the top of the stairs to make sure she couldn't hear frantic howling, she came back to the bedroom. The usual problem of what to wear loomed large today. It had only occurred to Bella this morning that this wasn't just about her liking the nanny: the nanny had to like her too.

She opened her wardrobe but closed it in despair after a few moments and tried Don's. There she found a white shirt, which did at least button up over her chest, and a pair of camel-coloured jeans. She pulled them on, rolled up the bottoms and looked at herself in the mirror. Frumpy but not hideous, it would have to do.

She added earrings, her diamond pendant, lipstick and even a squirt of perfume. It was a slight improvement.

'Bella!' said Don with a smile when she came into the kitchen. 'You look nice.'

'No, I don't,' she snapped.

'OK, nicer,' he said. 'Christ, I'm just trying to be friendly.'

'Nicer than what?' She was so tired, she didn't have the energy to be anything apart from irritable.

'Well, nicer than in my old track suit. Look I'm not saying any more. Everything I say just seems to make things worse.' He turned to Markie who was lying on his sheepskin rug on the floor gurgling.

'I'm sure he smiled at me a minute ago,' Don said, waving a rattle over his son.

'Did he?' Bella rushed over. If Markie was going to start smiling, he damn well better smile at her first. 'Hello hon, how are you today?' she cooed at him. Markie locked eyes with her and smiled.

'*See!!*' Bella and Don said in unison, then laughed.

'Wow, he's smiling at five weeks, I think that's early,' Bella said, gazing at her son.

'Oh no,' Don groaned. 'He was supposed to have your looks and *my* IQ!'

Bella managed a laugh at this, then sat down and ate some cereal, her mind on all the things she wanted to do in the house before the nanny arrived at 10 a.m. She was glad Don had taken the morning off to help her make this decision.

Bella was still breastfeeding in the immaculately

tidy sitting room when the doorbell rang at ten to ten.

Don jumped up to get the door and Bella could hear polite hellos before Don ushered the nanny into the room.

'Hello, I'm Joanne,' said the solidly built girl heading towards her with an outstretched hand.

Bella juggled Markie for a moment, then managed to reach Joanne's hand.

'Hello, Bella Browning, pleased to meet you. Please sit down.' She was surprised at how quickly her brisk, business tone had kicked in, even with a baby clamped onto her nipple.

'And this must be Mark,' said Joanne sitting down on the edge of the one armchair.

'Markie, we call him Markie,' said Bella, glancing down at the fuzzy little head nuzzling at her.

Looking up again, she took Joanne in. She was unredeemably plain, squarely built with pale, freckly skin, watery blue eyes and short mousy brown hair. She had a large nose and thin lips and was wearing no-nonsense navy blue trousers, a white blouse and a navy blazer with gold buttons.

Well, look on the bright side, Bella thought to herself. Don isn't going to shag her.

They spoke about Joanne's last job, which was perfect previous experience, two years looking after a little boy from babyhood until he went off to nursery.

Then Joanne asked Bella questions while Don made coffee.

'Have you got him into any sort of routine yet?' she asked.

'Errrr, well, he wakes up at about 6 a.m. for a

feed,' Bella answered. 'And he's usually awake till about eightish, then we both go back to bed for a snack feed then a nap. From about 10 a.m. he feeds every two and a half to three hours and his naps in between feeds vary from none to the full three hours . . . umm . . . he has his last feed at 9 p.m. when I go to bed, then Don looks after him till he falls asleep about an hour later.' She knew this was not a routine, just daily chaos.

'He wakes up at about two and then six in the morning . . .' she added, 'and then off we go again. It's not much of a routine yet, I know . . .' Bella trailed off.

'Well, it's not bad for . . . five weeks he is now?'

'Yes.'

'So you're managing to get enough sleep?'

'Well, just about enough to keep sane,' Bella smiled.

'And does he take a bottle as well?'

'Yup, he got a lot of top-up feeds from a bottle until a few days ago, then suddenly he didn't seem so hungry.'

'So we'll have to get him really happy with the bottle before you go back. Are you giving up breast-feeding?' Joanne asked.

'I don't want to just yet. I think I'll try and do a morning and evening feed for as long as I can,' Bella replied.

Joanne looked doubtful. 'It makes it very hard for the baby to detach from you,' she said matter-of-factly.

I should bloody well hope so, Bella thought, I don't want him to detach.

'Well, I'm not setting anything in stone, I'll have

315

to see how it goes,' she said, suddenly anxious that Joanne was going to turn them down.

They covered some more ground. Joanne was slightly taken aback by the hours: 8 a.m. till 8 p.m. Monday to Friday.

'That's a 60 hour week,' she pointed out.

'Well, most nights I hope to be here at 7.30 p.m. but I want to make sure I'm covered if I'm later,' said Bella.

'I don't mind doing those hours to start with until we're all settled in, but then you'll really have to think about giving me a three-day weekend and finding someone else for Monday or Friday,' Joanne said, then added: 'And I won't be able to do any regular evening babysitting.

This was not the attitude Bella had expected at a first interview. She thought about her own first job and how she had worked almost every waking hour.

'It's a very tiring, demanding job looking after a small baby,' Joanne said by way of explanation.

Well yes, thought Bella, but not so bad if you've been able to sleep the night before.

Don returned with coffees and put Joanne more at ease with general chatty questions about where she was from and how she got into being a nanny.

He followed that up with: 'Can you cook?'

'Yes,' Joanne answered. 'But obviously that won't be one of my duties here, will it?'

'Well, it could be,' Bella wobbled. 'If you wanted it to be . . .'

'I'd rather not,' said Joanne with unarguable finality.

'Will I have the use of a car?' she asked.

'Not immediately,' Don answered, trying to imagine Bella letting someone else drive her Mercedes. 'But we'll look into it for the future.'

Bella was horrified. She didn't want Markie to be driven anywhere without her.

It was time to wind this up, she decided.

'It's been lovely meeting you Joanne,' she said with a slightly forced smile. 'We're going to talk this over together, call your references if we may and I will get back to you on Monday, if that suits.'

'Yes, no problem at all,' said Joanne, picking up a bulging navy handbag and standing up. She shook hands with them both and bent over to gently stroke Markie's head before leaving the house.

As soon as the door had shut, Bella and Don turned to each other.

'Well, what did you think?' Don asked first.

'No way. Just no way,' Bella answered.

'You're joking?' Don asked, exasperated. 'I thought she seemed really nice.'

'What!? She wasn't going to stick her finger out one little bit. I can't have someone who works to rule looking after my baby. What if he's awake for an hour longer in the day than she'd estimated, would she just ignore him?'

'Bella, what are you talking about? She wanted to clarify her hours, which are bloody long, and make sure she doesn't get lumbered with all our house-work and cooking. I think that's fair enough.'

There was a pause as the two looked at each other.

'She seemed like a nice, caring person and she certainly knows what she's letting herself in for,

317

she's done this before,' Don said. 'Anyway, have you got any alternative?' he added. 'Your start date is less than three weeks away and this is your only candidate.'

Oh no, Bella was looking tearful again.

'Look,' he said putting an arm round her. 'Why don't you phone the family she was with before and ask them before you make a decision? Then, if you like, you can put her on trial for a month. If it's not working out, look for someone else when you're back at work.'

Bella sniffed hard.

'You should be enjoying this time,' Don hugged her against him, 'not filling it with anxieties about nannies and going back. I'm sure it's going to work out fine,' he added. 'You kept telling me when you were pregnant that this was what you wanted. It'll be fine.'

'I don't want to leave him,' Bella heard herself wail against Don's chest. 'He's so small and he needs me and I just haven't figured this whole thing out yet.'

Don held her tightly and didn't say anything for a while. Then in his most soothing voice, he said, 'Bella, just suck it and see, hon. Go back and see how it works out. You loved your job, I just don't believe you'd be happy without it. You've got to start thinking about how you're going to make this work, not blow every hurdle up out of all proportion.'

She knew he was right, but she was still crying.

Chapter Thirty-two

Joanne was hired on the basis of the absolutely glowing report from her last employer and Bella now had one last week on her own with Markie. Next week, Joanne would start and the week after, she would be back. Back at Prentice, starting on the Danson's project. It seemed unreal.

This morning, Bella had woken up with an agenda. This was be nice to Don day. She was going to do the supermarket run, very superficially clean round the house, cook him dinner and who knows, they might even have sex. It had been six weeks, after all.

She packed Markie into his car seat and left him rocking in the hall while she to-ed and fro-ed to her tiny car with all the equipment: one bottle of warmed milk in a thermos, one bottle of cooled, boiled water in case he got thirsty, a change of clothes, sunhat, parasol, nappies, wipes, muslin cloths for wiping up vomit, the changing bag, her handbag, buggy, sunscreens for the car windows . . . this was a nightmare, how was she going to fit all this in?

She crammed the buggy into the boot, squashed the changing bag into the space under the passenger seat and piled the extra nappies, bottles and dummies into the glove compartment and squeezed it shut.

When she went back for Markie, she smelled the unmistakable smell of dirty nappy and with a groan felt her determination to go out draining away. But she changed him, put him back in the car seat, fumbled the seat into the car and *finally* they were off, Bella, like every half-demented brand new mother, driving with one hand on the steering wheel and the other shading her howling little son's eyes from the sunshine.

When Don came home that evening, he found his wife and his son out in the garden, enjoying the last of the day's sun, Bella in a deckchair, Markie lying on his sheepskin rug. They were both freshly bathed and changed. Bella's hair was still wet, but she looked nice, in a clean white T-shirt (his) and a sarong and sandals.

The kitchen was unusually tidy and it actually smelled as if something was cooking.

'Hello!' he kissed them both, adding, 'Have I walked through a time fault and come out in the 1950s? Baby on the lawn, the wife in a skirt, dinner in the oven.'

'Ha, ha . . .' Bella answered, 'I'm being nice to you – for a change.' She smiled at him and he kissed her again.

The evening was so warm, they ate the simple meal of baked potatoes, ham and salad out in the garden. Bella lit candles on the garden table and poured out ice cold white wine.

Markie astonished them both by falling fast asleep straight after his 9 p.m. feed, so Bella carried him upstairs then switched on the intercom so she could go back out to the garden. When she sat back down in her deckchair, Don moved his chair behind hers. He began to rub her neck and rumple her hair, which she loved.

'How are you doing?' he asked.

'Fine,' she said. 'It's nice to see you, I feel as if I haven't seen you for ages. Are you OK?'

'Yeah,' he answered and as she felt his strong thumbs circle at the base of her neck, she let her head fall forward and closed her eyes.

After a few moments, Don said: 'So . . . Markie is asleep . . . and you're not. I don't suppose you'd want to go inside and, you know . . . cuddle up?'

She turned round to look at him and gave a sly grin. 'Don't you mean go inside and hump like an animal?'

'Hey, I'm trying to be sensitive and understanding here!' He smiled back and couldn't help running a finger down her nose and onto her lips.

'Have we even snogged since he arrived?' she asked.

Don shook his head sadly.

'That's disgraceful,' she said and got out of the chair.

She blew out the candles, then took his hand and led him into the kitchen. She turned to him in the open doorway and pulled him close for a kiss. He tasted warm and wine-flavoured; she pushed her tongue deeper into his mouth and moved her hands through his hair.

He kissed back for several long minutes but kept his hands anchored firmly round her waist. He wasn't going up to her breasts or down to her pants without written permission. He held her tightly and concentrated on the kissing.

Then Bella took him by surprise by throwing her T-shirt off over her head. Quickly she unhooked the matronly white nursing bra underneath and tossed it to the side.

He cupped his hands round breasts which felt heavy and solid. 'Are you OK?' he whispered.

'I'm fine, I've missed you . . .' this in a teasing voice as she pulled his shirt out of his trousers.

'Where are we going to go?' he asked in such a throaty I'm-so-ready-to-fuck-you voice that she suddenly flicked from 'this could be fun' to 'take me now'.

Their kisses became long, hot and devouring.

'Kitchen table?' she broke off to say. 'No, I'll get squashed. Kitchen wall?'

'Ah ha.' He steered her until she was backed up against the wall then they kissed again. As she unzipped him, he moved his hands down to the fabric of her skirt.

He felt through the folds to her pants and pulled them aside. Their eyes were open and he watched her closely. 'Just tell me what to do,' he whispered, feeling how encouragingly wet she was.

'Slide your finger into me,' she whispered back. It felt OK, it felt good. She smiled at him and licked his mouth, feeling his stiff hard-on flicker in her hands.

'You're a lovely man,' she said.

She pulled her pants down, unknotted her skirt so it fell on the floor, then guided him slowly inside.

She felt a ring of pain at the opening and nothing but numbness beyond that.

He moved against her and they looked at each other. Where was he?

'Are you really in?' she asked.

'Yeah,' he said.

'I can hardly feel you.'

'Let me move a bit.' He moved his cock almost all the way out and pushed back in again.

'Ow!' Bella's head fell back against the wall.

'Sorry.'

'Oh God, is this it?' Bella asked, sounding upset. 'Is this what sex is going to be like now? It feels like a sharp pencil in a shoebox. No offence, Don,' she added.

'Ermm . . . none taken.'

'Does it feel OK for you?' she asked.

'Well . . . it's different, but it's still good,' he reassured her. 'I take it you don't want me to carry on here?'

'No, no, I'm sorry. I'm totally depressed. It's obviously something else no-one wants to tell you about, having a baby ruins your sex life for ever,' she said.

Don moved out of her and tilted her chin up with his hand.

'Maybe it doesn't, Bella.' He kissed her on the cheek. 'Maybe things move back into place slowly. It's OK. I'm not going anywhere,' he kissed her again. 'Come on, I'm sure it's going to be fine. Anyway, there are lots of other things we can do . . .'

But for her the moment had well and truly gone. 'Yeah, like the washing up!' she answered.

*   *   *

Bella phoned her new friend the next morning, as soon as she had the chance.

'Red, hello, it's Bella.'

'Oh hello! How's it going?' Red sounded glad to hear her, although she was speaking above chaotic baby and toddler noise.

'Fine, I was going to come round this afternoon, if you're about?'

'Yes, that would be lovely. How about 4, 4.30ish, so we can all have a nap first?'

'Perfect,' answered Bella. 'Look there's one thing I have to ask, it can't wait.'

'Yes?' Red was intrigued.

'Sex? Does everything stay this baggy for good?'

There was a momentary pause and Bella suddenly wondered if Red didn't know how to break the bad news.

But then Red broke into cackles of laughter. 'Blimey!' she said. 'I'm impressed. I'm planning to milk it for at least another month.'

'Pelvic floor exercises,' she added. 'That's probably what you need. No-one ever does them and things do bounce back eventually, but I suppose you could use them to hurry it up.'

'So will it really be the same as it was? I want the truth,' Bella asked, hating the fact that she sounded so anxious.

'Do enough exercises and it will probably be better,' Red laughed, 'Anyway, I'll see you later, which will be lovely.'

'OK, thanks. Bye.'

'Bye,' she squeezed in and tried to hold for ten . . . where had those muscles gone?

Chapter Thirty-three

Red opened the door looking just annoyingly good: glowing face, tumbling hair.

'Hello!' she said enthusiastically and came down the steps in her bare feet to help Bella up with the buggy. Bella noticed that her toenails were French manicured – her toenails!! How did she find the time to do this stuff?

'God you always look so well, it's very irritating!' Bella said.

'Thank you, I think! You look much better than the last time I saw you,' Red replied.

'Still room for improvement though.' Bella looked down at her outfit, more of Don's clothes, this time a faded blue T-shirt and grey drawstring shorts. Revolting.

'Oh, he's asleep,' Red said looking down at Markie as they came in the door. 'Shall we leave him in the hall?'

'Yeah, that's fine,' said Bella.

'Come in,' said Red and pointed Bella in the direction of the sitting room.

She walked in and was surprised to find the

quaintest little room this side of *Little House on the Prairie*. The walls were covered in faded flowery wallpaper, the sofa and armchairs were large and chintzy. Dark, antique furniture was crammed into every available space and there were toys and books and balls and cars everywhere.

On the one available square inch of floor, a little black-haired boy was squatting down, drawing.

'Jamie, this is Bella, say hello,' said Red.

'Hello,' said Jamie without looking up.

'He's going through an intense drawing thing at the moment,' said Red. 'Actually maybe we should sit in the kitchen, it's not so calamitously untidy.'

She led Bella into a red kitchen, again crammed to bursting with table, chairs, a pine dresser, bunches of herbs, bookshelves, a drinks cabinet.

Bella pulled up a chair at the table and estimated there were at least fifty little cars and trucks scattered across the surface.

'It's a bit different from your lovely Zen home!' said Red, spotting Bella's wry look at the table.

'Oh no, it's lovely,' Bella said, feeling caught out.

'Believe me,' Red put on the kettle and hunted for clean mugs, 'I would love to live in your house, but it's just impossible, I'd drive Jamie and Sandy insane asking them to tidy up all the time . . . and then both Sandy's parents and my mum died in the last couple of years and we couldn't bear to give their furniture away so we've tried to fit most of it in . . . and we never got round to redecorating after we moved in . . .' she tailed off.

So Bella said: 'Stop it! It looks really homely. I kind of rattle around in my place and worry if it's too white. It will probably look really cold and clinical in the winter.'

'Well homes seem to evolve around you, never quite the way you planned them,' Red said, bumping mugs down on the table in front of them. 'Anyway, how are you?' She sat down and propped a hand under her chin, looking Bella squarely in the face. 'And the truth please, not the "I'm a new mum and I'm coping" version!'

'Not too bad,' Bella answered. 'The nanny starts next week and I'm going back for my first half-day on Friday, then work proper the Monday afterwards. Yikes.'

'I'm glad you found a nanny, is she lovely?'

'Ummm. To be honest I didn't really like her at first but her references were good and I thought, well, we'll do a month's trial and see how we go.'

'Sounds fine. Are you looking forward to going back?'

'Not yet.' Bella sighed, she felt complicated about this. 'I think I'll be OK once I'm there. I'm just so worried about Markie. I worry about how he'll adjust and that he's going to miss me the whole time.'

'You'll have to wait and see,' said Red. 'You'll only know once you're back. Try not to fret about it too much.'

'Right now, I really envy you, Red,' Bella said. 'But don't you miss work just a tiny bit?'

'Well, I do work part time to remind myself how boring accountancy is, but you know what I miss?' she said. 'I miss the whole getting dressed up, going to the office, meetings, colleagues, team effort sort of thing. And I miss the way I could forget about everything else in my life and just work, you never get that feeling when you work part time, especially from home. But as soon as you're a mum, everything becomes a compromise.'

She put the teapot down in front of them and loaded two spoons of sugar into her cup.

'But, you know,' she went on, 'I really wanted to be with my son and now the baby, more than I wanted to be at work, so it made sense to leave. But the flip side is, at the moment I don't have nearly as much money or the "Gosh how impressive" status that went with the job.'

She sipped her tea adding, 'No-one in the world considers motherhood a good job or an important one. How can it be highly rated when most women like us hire someone else to do it for a fraction of our salaries?'

Bella was silent.

'I'm sorry,' said Red. 'I'm being very tactless, you've got me banging on about my favourite topic.'

'Don't worry, I'm interested,' said Bella.

'Well, as I said it's a compromise. I like being at home, teaching Jamie how to draw, reading to him, building sand castles, all those small things that are so important to him, and I'll be able to breastfeed Ellie for ages. But it's a sacrifice to stay at home – financially, careerwise, statuswise. I've just learned to live with that – for the moment,' she added with some emphasis. 'Maybe I'll feel different in a few years' time and want to go back. I just keep telling myself that life is long and childhoods are pretty short really.'

'Right,' Red smacked her palm onto the tabletop. 'Here endeth the lesson for today.'

They both smiled.

'I just don't know how I'm going to have the energy to do it all,' Bella said. 'I'm functioning reasonably at the moment because I sleep for two to three hours in the afternoon. But in a week's time, that's going to be over.'

'I don't know, Bella. Maybe you'll have to get the nanny to stay over, so she can do some of the night feeds,' said Red.

'She's made it pretty clear she doesn't want to do that.'

'Look, try not to worry about it. You'll have to figure out what's going to work for you when you get back,' Red soothed. 'If I have one tip, it's just try not to be too extreme.'

'What d'you mean?' Bella asked.

'I started out a workaholic career mum, put Jamie in the kind of nursery where they teach French and maths from three months and we got through the nights with Calpol abuse. But it made me utterly wretched, so what happened? I went to the other extreme . . . quit work, became the mad organic puree-ing, breastfeeding till he was two, co-sleeping supermum. And surprise, surprise, I didn't feel any better.'

'I'm trying to find a balance this time round. But everyone is different,' she added quickly. 'All kinds of arrangements work.'

'Hmm . . .' said Bella, feeling slightly panic stricken. Did she have any idea what she was getting herself into here?

Jamie came into the kitchen.

'Hello sweetpea,' said Red, and her little son scrambled onto her lap.

'Like some juicy please,' piped the little voice.

'Of course.' Red got up and, holding Jamie under one arm, with impressive biceps, Bella noticed, she deftly rinsed out a beaker and filled it up with apple juice from the fridge diluted with water.

Jamie sat on her lap and gulped it down.

'You've got to come upstairs and meet Sandy,' she said when Jamie had finished.

'Oh, he's here is he?' Bella was certainly interested in meeting Red's other half.

'Yeah, he's always here, slaving away in the office.'

Red led her up the tiny, narrow staircase to the top floor and pushed open one of the two doors.

'I've brought Bella up to say hello,' said Red and a head turned round from the large computer screen which dominated the small floral room.

'Hello,' said Sandy with a wide smile. Well, well, thought Bella taking in this surprisingly young and utterly gorgeous man with dishevelled jet black hair and dark eyes, dressed in chinos and a floppy blue sweatshirt.

'Hello there,' she answered, deeply regretting her outfit, particularly the shorts.

'I'm sorry I'm so busy, otherwise I'd come down and be sociable,' he said and grinned again.

'We'll leave you to it,' Red told him after a few pleasantries had been exchanged.

'I'll meet you properly some other time, I hope,' said Sandy as they backed out of the room.

'Wow,' Bella grinned at Red on the way back down the stairs. 'He's a real dish.'

Red giggled. 'I know and *five* years younger than me. I still can't believe my luck.'

'So don't tell me – he's 25?'

'No,' Red looked incredulous. '29.'

'Bloody hell,' said Bella. 'You are looking good for your age.'

'How old are you anyway?' Red asked, smiling at the compliment.

'Twenty-nine as well and I know, I look ancient.'

Red laughed, then a baby started crying. For a moment they listened, then Bella knew it wasn't hers. Weird, she thought, how you could tell the difference.

They went back into the kitchen where Red fed Ellie and Bella topped up their teas.

On Sunday, Bella, Don and Markie were out together for a supposedly nice, relaxing lunch. But it was not nice or relaxing. Markie had been crying and fussing ever since they sat down.

Bella had fumbled with her shirt and bra and given Markie his first ever public breastfeed – feeling strangely embarrassed considering she was someone who hadn't shrunk from sex in public places – but it didn't settle Markie. As they waited for their order to arrive, he began to howl.

Bella could see irritated customers twitch their Sunday papers and scowl and the worst thing was she knew she'd done exactly the same, in this very café when she used to come here on Sundays with Don from their little flat round the corner.

She felt upset and angry. She offered Markie a drink of water, another feed, but he turned his head away and didn't want anything, just grizzled and cried.

Don sighed, which upset her even more.

'I'll take him out for a bit, maybe the change of air will help,' she said, getting up.

'I'll get them to wait with your food till you come back,' he answered.

'How big of you,' Bella snapped.

After pacing up and down the street for twenty minutes with Markie crying against her shoulder, she decided to go back in and eat something.

'What do you think it is?' Don asked as she came back in.

'I don't know, Don,' she said, feeling totally stressed. 'Maybe he's just a bit tense, like me.'

'Look, you sit down and I'll take him out in the buggy, maybe he'll fall asleep. We can't let him howl the place down.'

Bella felt like a traitor handing over her wailing son. Don tucked him into the buggy and wheeled him out. She felt as if every head in the restaurant was turned on her.

Now, when she glanced around, she saw there were lots of babies here but they were all sitting contentedly in their prams and car seats, gurgling and watching their parents happily. What was the matter with her son? She felt a tear sliding down her cheek. He always needed all her attention, all the time.

She never seemed to be able to just put him down and let him watch happily. Christ, she was obviously the most tense, uptight, crap mother in the world, creating the most tense, uptight and miserable baby in the world. More tears splashed down onto her scrambled eggs and smoked salmon. She wiped them away and tried to concentrate on eating something.

She'd been finished for ages when she finally saw Don coming back into the restaurant. He was pushing the buggy and smiling at her, surely a sign that Markie was asleep.

He wheeled over and sat down wearily in the chair. Bella immediately looked into the buggy to check her sleeping baby.

'He cried for ages, poor little guy, but then he did finally drop off,' said Don. 'Thank God, I can now have a few moments of peace, with my wife.'

He looked at her and put his hand over hers: 'Hello,' he said smiling into her face. 'Remember me? I'm the person you used to spend lots of time with until that little munchkin came along.'

She laughed. 'Don't call him a munchkin!'

'He is, though, all he does is go munch, munch, munch on your breasts – which I never get to play with any more – or waaaaaaaah a lot.

'Poor Bella. Are you OK?' he added.

'I'm tired,' she answered, rubbing her hands over her face. 'I feel like I'm going to be tired for ever now, I'll never ever have enough sleep ever again and I'm worried about what going back to work will be like.'

'It will be fine, Bella,' Don soothed. 'You're you at work, that's your natural habitat. It's the baby part, being at home, breastfeeding and being bawled at all day that's strange to you. That's why you feel so weird.' He smiled at her.

'One week back at the job, axing staff, bloodletting, and you'll be your old self again. I'm expecting you to drop a stone and have worn me out by the end of the month.'

'Right,' she said grimly. 'Remind me to get you

that book . . . What Not to Say to New Mothers Unless You Want to Get Kneed in the Balls Very Very Hard.' She took her hand out of his.

'Bella! I'm joking, but yeah, there's some truth in it. I'm sorry, I want things back to normal a bit. I want you back to normal. You're just so wrapped up in this, there's no room for anything else. Christ, you haven't even bought any clothes that fit you. I can't believe you're wearing my trousers and shirt again.'

'Oh sod off,' she said and looked away. Tears were welling up in her eyes again. God! She hated herself for all this self-pity, but she couldn't seem to stop it.

'I'm sorry,' he said, 'I feel left out. There's just not much I can do for Markie. Walk him about in the pram, that's about it. He's not really at a terribly interesting age, I can't play football with him yet.'

Don thought he was being light-hearted, but Bella took every word as a slap in the face.

'Jesus, Don . . .' she looked at him with eyes brimful of tears. 'You could speak to him and sing to him or carry him around, or hold him in front of flowers in the garden or shake a rattle over his head . . . or persuade him to drink out of a bottle or . . . there's just a hundred things you could do. But let's face it, you're not interested . . .' Her tears were slipping down and she spat out the last words with droplets of saliva. 'You didn't want him in the first place, that's what you really want to say, isn't it?'

'Just calm down,' he said urgently. 'I'm sorry. I'm sorry . . .' he held her arm. 'I'm really glad he's here. I'm really glad you got me to do this. I think he's wonderful.'

334

She felt a little better for hearing him say this so passionately.

But then Don added: 'I'm just a bit overwhelmed at how much things have changed. I feel I haven't got any time to myself at home, you certainly don't have any time and there's just nothing left for us.'

'Well too bad, Don,' she stormed. 'We're adults. I expect you to be able to look after yourself now. Markie is six weeks old, he can't.'

There was an uncomfortable silence.

Then Bella said simply: 'I'd like to go home now please.'

Don motioned to the waiter and asked for the bill.

They drove home in silence. Unusually, Markie hadn't woken for the transition from buggy to car seat and was sleeping in the back. Bella looked out of the window and watched the chic streets of glamorous north London gradually grow shabby as they headed to their part of town, further north-east.

Christ, why had they moved to such a big house so far away from anything interesting? Why hadn't they just gone for a lovely two-bedroomed flat nearer civilization? They'd borrowed an absolute fortune for a Georgian terraced house in urban wasteland. What had she been thinking?

She began to feel even more miserable. What the hell were they going to do for the rest of the day? Just babysit and argue. Nothing was fun any more, just effort.

Chapter Thirty-four

Bella was standing in front of the bathroom mirror, nervous as hell, trying to apply make-up properly – for work. She couldn't believe it had come round so quickly. It was already Friday. And was that a hint of double chin? Good grief.

Nanny Joanne was out for a stroll with Markie, and Bella was heading for the *office*.

She'd decided to go in for an afternoon catch-up session with everyone before she moved straight into the work at Danson's on Monday morning.

She saw her hand trembling as she applied mascara and she had a dry feeling in her mouth. She couldn't decide if she was nervous or excited. She was looking forward to seeing everyone again and hearing the gossip. If only she could shake the guilt and anxiety about leaving her baby.

In the bedroom, she changed into one of the new, size bloody 14, suits and shirts she'd bought yesterday in the two hours Joanne had forced her to go out of the house and leave Markie alone.

She put on the dark knee-length skirt and white shirt, no point wearing the jacket, it was

27 degrees outside. God her bust was enormous. A post-partum bulge sat uncomfortably below the waistband of her skirt. She looked like every other out of condition mum and it made her deeply depressed.

She put on stockings and her highest heels, shocked at how excruciatingly uncomfortable they were, but in her eyes it didn't make up for the lumps and bumps. At least her hair was gleamingly clean and neatly put up. She decided on diamond earrings for morale, and she'd put on red lipstick in the car.

OK, almost ready to go. Bella looked through her briefcase, untouched for two months. She poked about inside. Everything she needed was there and ah ha, in the zip-up compartment at the side was a packet of Marlboro Lights and her gold lighter. Suddenly she felt as if she was looking at the answer to her prayers.

She picked up the bag and ran down to the garden. Perching on the edge of the iron table she pulled out a cigarette and lit up. The smoke filled her mouth and touched the back of her throat, oh yes . . . yes . . . yes, she'd definitely missed these more than sex. She spent a few dreamy moments enjoying every breath of smoke then finally stubbed the last inch of cigarette out with her heel on the lawn and went back into the house to pick up her bag, car keys, jacket.

Right, she thought, checking herself out in the hall mirror, this was it. Goodbye maternity leave, hello working mother.

She shut the front door and locked it, feeling a momentary panic about whether or not Joanne would have remembered her keys. Oh shut up, she told herself, are you trying to become the most neurotic woman on the planet? Of course Joanne has her keys.

She walked to the car enjoying the click of her high heels on the pavement and the clunk as she opened the car lock. She clambered in awkwardly, totally unused to the skirt, and damn, smudged oil onto her leg. Automatically she leaned over to the glove compartment and popped the button.

A pile of nappies cascaded to the floor, followed by a baby bottle full of water, a squeaky toy and a dummy. For a moment she had to blink very hard, but the tears were averted.

No, there was not a single pair of stockings left in the drawer. She re-examined the smudge. Well, it wasn't so bad, she could live with it.

She fired up the engine and drove out into the street. It felt good to be driving on her own again, without a bump or a baby. Actually, it felt brilliant. She dodged into the traffic, put on her sunglasses, buzzed the roof down and flicked through her CDs. Girl guitar rock with the volume up loud.

It was of course Kitty she saw first when she walked out of the lift and through the double doors into the office.

'Hi,' Kitty, in something fluorescent green, mouthed silently with a big smile, waving excitedly, because she was on the phone.

No-one else was in the reception area and for a moment Bella couldn't decide whether to knock on everyone's doors or go into her own office.

She decided to check out her room first.

She pushed open the door and was amazed to see Hector sitting in her chair with his feet up on the desk as he chatted on the phone. The room smelled like a café, so obviously he was using her coffee machine too. Coffee!! She'd somehow forgotten about coffee and spent her entire maternity leave drinking tea.

Hector's eyebrows shot up when he saw her.

'Actually,' he said into the receiver, 'something rather urgent has just come in, I'm going to have to call you back. Sorry. Bye then.'

He put the phone down, stood up and smiled at her, holding out his hand. 'Hello, Bella, welcome back,' he said, 'I do hope you'll forgive me for using your office while you were away.'

'And my coffee machine,' she cut in, noticing how well dressed he was; he was obviously sharpening up big time.

'Oh no, is that yours too, I am sorry,' he replied. 'Makes wonderful coffee, though. In fact, would you like a cup?'

'Piss off, Hector!' She was trying to joke off the irritation she felt at finding a usurper in her office space. 'You just moved yourself in, the moment my back was turned!'

There was a small silence and she began to wonder what else of hers he'd moved into.

'I'm looking forward to Danson's,' he said. Hell, she had totally forgotten Susan's decision months ago that she would have to take Hector along with her on the job.

'Oh yes,' Bella managed to say.

'The project manager on Danson's side was at Cambridge with me. I've had lunch with him to talk about it, sounds very interesting.'

This was even worse news.

'Hmm,' she said. 'Who else is in today?'

'Oh hasn't Kitty buzzed everyone for you?' Hector asked.

'Yes,' came Kitty's voice from the door.

'Hello Mummy,' she said holding out her arms to Bella. As Bella hugged her, she could see Susan and Chris coming out of their offices to greet her.

'Hello, darling,' said Chris when it was his turn. He squeezed her in his arms and kissed both her cheeks.

'Hello. Well done,' said Susan and for a split second they stood facing each other without moving, then Susan leaned forward and gave her a dainty hug and peck on the cheek.

'So,' said Susan, 'tell us all about him. Is he cute and adorable and I hope you've brought pictures.'

Well, this was an unexpected show of interest.

'Well, funnily enough . . .' said Bella opening up her bag, and everyone laughed.

She'd been very restrained and had only brought an envelope of about ten pictures.

'Oh he's gorgeous,' said Kitty.

'Lovely eyes,' said Susan. 'Looks like you, Bella.'

The boys were more sheepish.

'I'm sorry, he looks like Chairman Mao in this one,' said Chris holding up a photo of Markie's face.

'Chris!' Kitty smacked him on the arm.

'So, Susan, has anyone got any work to do or are we adjourning to the pub?' asked Chris.

'We are adjourning,' said Susan.

'But it's only two o'clock,' Bella reminded them. 'I *want* to do some work!'

'But this is a very special day,' said Chris. 'We've got our hot shot back.' He put his arm round her and added, 'And can I just say, fantastic breasts.'

Another round of laughter.

So the office phones got diverted to Kitty's mobile and they went to the pub across the road for drinks and work gossip and a bit of baby gossip too. She didn't want to make their eyes glaze over, so stuck to horrific labour details served with a slice of humour.

'And then, when I'm in the most pain you can experience without passing out or dying or something, Don and the midwife – *Declan* – start discussing which match they thought was the best they'd seen that week. Was it the Man U last minute equalizer or the Bayern Munich v. InterMilan championship decider?' she joked.

'And pretty soon after that I gave birth to something the size of a sofa. All I can say girls is "don't try this at home" – next time I'm doing the drugs.'

She sipped her white wine and soda and drew heartily on her fifth cigarette. She felt relaxed and civilized and back to normal, as Don had told her she would.

But by six o'clock, she was feeling twitchy about Markie and Joanne. This was the longest Markie had been without her and her breasts were enlarging by the minute. Chris had barely been able to keep his eyes off them. They were starting to feel hot and sore: it was time to go home.

She said fond goodbyes and headed for the car

feeling happy and light-headed. This was going to work, it was going to be fine.

When she got back home at 6.45 p.m. Markie was asleep and Joanne was straightening up the kitchen. 'Hi,' said Bella, plonking her bag and keys down on the kitchen table. 'Give me the full rundown.'

'He was fine,' said Joanne. 'He's not really happy with the bottle yet. He drank a little milk and spent some of the time feeling unsettled, but he fell fast asleep about an hour ago. Don't worry, we're getting used to each other and it's going to be OK.'

'Thanks,' said Bella. 'Thanks for doing the kitchen. Do you want a drink or something? I'm going to have a glass of wine.'

'I'm fine,' Joanne answered. 'I'll be off if that's OK with you? Do you want me here a bit early on Monday, as it's your first day?'

'That would be great. That's very kind of you. About 7.45 a.m. would be perfect.'

'OK, see you then. Bye, Markie,' she said leaning over the carrycot.

'Bye Joanne,' said Bella.

She poured out the wine then stood over her son's cot. He was curled up on his side fast asleep with his little fists bunched up close to his mouth.

She couldn't resist picking him up. He stirred, turning his head instinctively to her breasts, so she undid her blouse and bra and he latched on and began to drink, not even opening his eyes.

She stroked his cheek tenderly. He was just perfect, and this was going to work.

Chapter Thirty-five

Hector and Bella were in a glossy little office buried in the heart of the Danson's Corporation having a celebratory coffee. They had just pulled off a very slick presentation together and felt they deserved to pat themselves on the back.

The Danson's job would be fun, provided Hector wasn't too major a pain in the arse. It was a healthy, profitable company just wanting to trim back costs, get some fresh ideas and step up turnover. The kind of thing Bella could wrap up in two months, tops, but still very lucrative for Prentice and Partners.

'You look tired,' Hector said.

'Tired? Ha! Tired is for wimps.' She inhaled the steam coming from her coffee. 'I'm just going to have to get used to functioning on this level of sleep deprivation. I went to bed at 9.30 p.m. last night. I was up at 12.30, then 3 a.m., then got up at 6.30. Only women are tough enough to take this on a nightly basis.'

'Are you missing the baby?'

'Markie? In a funny way, no,' she answered. 'Because I don't associate him with work at all. But when I think about him, then I just want to be with him. It's like when you're first in love, you know, when you want to hold someone and look at them and be with them and make them smile all the time and watch them sleeping. Yeah, I'm obsessed.' Shut up now Bella, she told herself.

'Hmmm,' Hector answered.

'Anyway,' she said, trying to snap back into work mode. 'This morning went really well. I think they love us.'

'Yeah,' he said. 'This should be a nice easy one for you to get back into the swing of things.'

'I'm not out of the swing of things!' she exclaimed.

'So what new ideas are we going to hit them with then?' he asked.

As well as all the usual cost-cutting and evaluation, she wanted to tackle the levels of stress and poor communication in the company with lots of 'touchy-feely' stuff . . . a shorter working day, breakfast stations, informal brainstorming meetings, parental leave and even a crèche.

'Are you sure you're not letting the baby get to you here?' Hector asked.

'No,' she told him. 'I'm not the only person in the world with a child, you know.'

Hector didn't make any further comment, so Bella outlined the first round of data to be analysed.

After several hours of steady work, it was obvious she was going to have to deal with the excess milk now starting to leak out of the zeppelin-like breasts sitting in front of her. She was also going to have to phone home, she couldn't hold out any longer.

'I'm off to pump out breast milk for a bit,' she told Hector. 'I hope you don't think that's too weird.'

'Right,' he said.

Perched on a chair in the ladies' loo, she undid her bra and cupped the pump over a solid, throbbing breast. She squeezed the trigger steadily and watched the pale, bluey-white milk spurt out into the bottle.

Of course she was thinking about her son as she did this. She wondered what he was doing right now, was he asleep, curled up in a dear little huddle? Was he looking round, flickering smiles? Or was he drinking out of a bottle, wishing he could cuddle up and feed from his mummy? With that thought she felt tears prick the back of her eyes. God, she did really miss him.

Work felt surreal, like it was no longer the real thing, but an elaborate game, a way to spend time before getting back to reality. Markie was reality for her now, not coming up with money-saving schemes and gimmicks for some multimillion-pound organization.

She rinsed her gadgets, packed them into the black bag and dialled home on the mobile as she walked back down the corridor.

'Hello.' Bella heard Joanne's voice, then listened closely and could hear Markie crying in the background.

'Hello, Joanne, it's Bella. I wanted to see how everything was going.'

'Well, he's a bit unsettled. He's barely taken anything from the bottle all morning and now he's hungry and tired.'

'Oh dear,' Bella's heart sank to her shoes at the

sound of the pitiful wailing in the background.
'What are you going to do?' she asked Joanne, not
sure herself what would be best.

'Well, I think I'll take him out for a bit. Hopefully,
he'll fall asleep then feel more like drinking something later when he's had a nap.'

'OK, just phone me if there's anything I can do,'
Bella said, but she felt helpless.

'Don't worry about him,' said Joanne. 'We'll get
settled down and into a routine soon.'

'OK . . .' she tried not to sound as anxious as she
felt. 'OK, I'll try and be there about six-ish. See you
later.'

'Yeah, bye,' said Joanne, hanging up.

She kept a brave face through lunch with Hector
and several Danson's execs, but by the afternoon,
time was dragging and she was desperate to go
home.

At five, she told Hector she was going to have to
go: 'I'll take some of the sheets with me to do on the
computer later and I'll be on my phone if you need
me, but I really need to go, it's Markie's first day,'
she explained.

'Yes, of course,' he told her. 'It's a shame though,
I'm meeting my friend, you know Peter Garvy, for
a drink after work, and he'd hoped you could
come.'

'No, drinks after work are going to be out of the
question for a while, tell him I'll do lunch this
week,' she answered, trying to firmly squash
down the feelings of guilt this conversation was
inducing.

Hector's friend was not the trainee she'd expected, he was one of the senior members of their

liaison team at Danson's. She really did not want Hector having cosy little meetings with him while she was seen to be leaving the office at five. Shit. But she had to go.

Once she was in the car, she told herself to get a grip. She was the senior person on this job and she remembered her fighting talk to Chris when she was pregnant. She'd aimed to up her day rate so people wouldn't want her hanging round their offices for too long. She and Susan really needed to have that talk about her promotion to partner or, at the very least, a pay rise.

She hadn't spoken to Don all day, so speed-dialled him on the mobile.

'Hello,' he answered almost immediately, sounding terse and stressed as usual.

'Hello, Don, it's me.'

'Bella. Hello, what can I do for you?'

'Don! It's my first day back at work. Aren't you going to ask how it's going?'

'Oh God! I've been really busy, hon. I've been in court on the Mitchell trial.'

'Oh.'

'How is it going?' he asked.

'Well, fine for me, but I don't think Markie is having a very nice time. When I phoned at lunchtime, he was howling his head off and he hadn't drunk anything all morning.'

'He'll be fine,' Don said. 'Try not to worry about him.'

'I'm heading home a bit early to see him,' she said.

'OK. Why don't you sort yourself out for dinner? I'm going to be late, about nine, ten-ish.'

'Right. I might not see you then, I might be in bed,' she said, feeling annoyed about this.

'Let's speak later hon, I've got to go.'

'OK, bye then.'

After a frantically impatient drive home, through snarled-up roads, Bella ran up the steps to the house, desperate to see her baby. She opened the front door and could already make out his wailing.

Rushing into the sitting room, she found Joanne cradling her son who was red-faced and inconsolable. She scooped him up into her arms and plonked herself down on the sofa. As she struggled with her buttons and bra hook, Markie was already quietening down and had turned his head towards her to drink.

Only when he'd latched onto her breast did he open his eyes to look at her for the first time.

'Has he been like this all day?' Bella asked.

'I'm afraid so. He had a good long sleep in the afternoon, but he's been crying almost non-stop since four.'

'Oh God.' Bella flooded with guilt.

'I can't get him to drink out of the bottle. Well, no more than a few sips. He won't even take water. I'm worried he'll dehydrate in this heat.' Joanne sounded rattled.

'What about the survival instinct?' Bella said. 'I thought babies were programmed to eat or drink something when they were hungry.'

'You'd have thought so,' said Joanne.

'He's not going to starve himself to death without me, is he?' Bella asked.

'No, I don't think so,' said Joanne. 'But he's going

to have some very uncomfortable hours waiting for you to get home.'

'Oh God,' Bella said again.

'Look, things will probably be much better in a week or two. We can't give up yet.' Joanne's sensible and reassuring tone kicked in. 'Why don't I make you a cup of tea before I go? You must be tired.'

'Thanks,' said Bella. Yes she was tired. Sunk deep into the sofa, she wondered where she was going to find the strength to get up.

An hour later, with Markie cuddled up to her, dozing and feeding on and off, she knew she did not have the strength to move. She ordered in a Chinese takeaway from the phone beside her and clicked onto a TV news channel to wait. She was planning to eat dinner, have a bath with Markie in his carrycot beside her, then go straight to bed with him. Sod the work she'd brought home from the office.

She'd decided Markie should just sleep and feed next to her all night, it might let her get some more sleep than switching on the light, getting him out of his bed for a proper meal of both breasts then trying to settle him back down to sleep, which always took ages.

Her head hit the pillow just after 9 p.m., ridiculously early, but she felt as if she was finally crawling to bed at 2 a.m. after a hard day's work and a night on the town.

It was a very disturbed night. Don woke her up when he came to bed at midnight. Markie then seemed to wake her almost hourly to feed.

Finally at 6 a.m., there wasn't any point in

pretending to be asleep, so she decided she might as well get up. She looked at her husband, so sound asleep in bed he didn't even stir, then picked up her baby and headed to the sitting room. Together, they watched the news and had breakfast.

By the time Joanne arrived, Bella was ready, made up, hair up. She had changed into her suit at the very last minute in case of baby vomit. Don was still in bed.

'Just ignore my husband wandering around,' Bella told Joanne. 'He's probably got a late start or something.'

'Markie looks happy today,' said Joanne, seeing him gurgling on the sitting room floor.

'Yeah and he's full of food, because he's been stuffing his face all night.'

'Oh dear,' said Joanne. 'That's a bit hard on you.'

'Hmm. There's plenty of breast milk in the fridge for you to try with today. And he needs a change and some new clothes. I just haven't had the chance, or the energy,' she confessed.

'OK, off you go. We'll be fine, don't worry about us.'

Bella picked her son up and kissed and held him. 'Goodbye sweetheart, see you soon.'

As soon as she put him down again, he began to cry.

She left the house with a wrench.

Chapter Thirty-six

Bella called home on Friday morning and could once again barely listen to Joanne for the sound of her son's raw howls in the background.

All week Markie had cried for most of the time she wasn't at home. He was refusing to drink anything at all now and she had the eeriest feeling when she came home at night that he was withdrawing from her. He seemed to turn away, he wasn't looking at her for as long, he merely ate and slept when she was around, he didn't seem to want to interact with her and he hadn't smiled at her since Wednesday.

Joanne sounded tense and harassed now, she obviously no longer knew what to do to try and distract this baby from his misery.

'Why don't you bring him in to see me?' Bella asked now. She knew it was not a good idea, not a practical one, but she hoped that somehow they could all wring some relief from it. Markie and Bella could have some breastfeeding time, then Markie would sleep all afternoon because he was full and

Joanne would have the distraction of a day trip to the office.

'Yes, why don't we do that?' Joanne sounded quite cheered up at the prospect.

At 1 p.m. on the dot, Bella was buzzed by reception and she told them to show her visitors up. She'd warned Hector, who had gone off for lunch early so she would have some privacy.

Joanne arrived with Markie strapped up in a baby carrier.

'I hope you don't mind me using one of these, buggies are such a hassle on the tube,' she explained as she came into the room.

'No, no,' said Bella.

'Very nice office,' Joanne added.

'Yes. I'm on assignment here. How's he doing?' Bella looked anxiously over at the little head she could see at the top of the carrier.

'He's fallen into a doze, he's so exhausted with crying, but I'm sure he'll wake up at the prospect of lunch.'

'This is just terrible,' Bella told her.

'He's so attached to breastfeeding,' said Joanne. 'I've never seen anything like it. You should have had him on the bottle from the off. Most women going back to work so soon do that.'

'But breast milk is so good for them. No-one ever warned me that this might happen.'

Bella took her son from Joanne's lap. His hair was plastered against his head with sweat and his babygro was damp. His face looked flushed.

'He's a bit hot, Joanne,' Bella said, cradling him in her arms.

'It's very hot outside and I got hot on the journey.

Sorry, I should have thought of that,' she replied.

Markie stirred against Bella and instinctively latched on. As soon as he started to suck properly, Bella felt herself relax. Maybe Joanne could bring him in every lunch break? Maybe that would be how they could get through the next few weeks. Surely that was all it was going to take for him to get used to the bottle, get used to this new set-up where she wasn't around for most of the day?

She felt the heavy weight of guilt in her heart as she looked at the little cheek moving up and down just a few inches from her face.

Markie fed from both sides slowly. When he was finally stuffed full, he broke off. Bella looked at the white dribble of milk running down his chin. He was fast asleep. She stroked him tenderly on her lap. It felt such a betrayal to be sending him home asleep. He would wake up and not even understand where he had been and where she had gone.

She hooked up her bra and tucked in her blouse. There was a knock at the door.

'Come in,' she said, assuming it was Hector.

The door opened and she was horrified to see Tom Proctor, the group FD she'd had sacked from AMP last year. The one who'd phoned her up just to tell her she was a cunt. God, she still remembered that awful conversation word for word.

'Well, well, it is you again.' There was no hiding the contempt in his voice. 'I didn't think I could be quite this unlucky but there we go, once the shit has hit the fan, it gets everywhere.'

She didn't see why she should reply to this.

'Having a little crèche meeting, are we?' he asked with a sneer.

'No actually, there isn't a crèche at Danson's.' How dare he try and make her feel guilty about seeing her son. 'Are you going to be working with us, Mr Proctor?' She tried to make this sound civil.

'I bloody hope not,' he replied. 'I'm going to do all I can to get you parasites drummed out of the building.'

'And what is your position here now?' she asked, trying to keep the panic she felt out of her voice.

'Yes, I bet you're bloody anxious to know that, aren't you? But I think I'll keep you guessing Mzzz Browning. So watch your back.'

With that he slammed the door and was gone.

Bella looked at Joanne and caught the appalled expression on her face.

'Don't worry about him,' she said, trying to hide how shaken she was. 'He's an arse. I'm sure if he was in any position to get rid of me, he'd have said. He's just trying to rattle me.' She hoped this was true.

We have a contract with them, we have a half a million pound contract, she was reminding herself.

It was time for Joanne to leave. Bella kissed her baby on the forehead and handed him over, feeling like a traitor. Joanne buckled him back into the carrier and he was in such a deep, satiated sleep, he didn't even stir.

'See you later,' her nanny said, gathering up her things and heading for the door.

'Bye and thanks for bringing him.' Bella watched the door shut behind them and suddenly felt a little weak and wobbly.

Her mobile began to ring, so distractedly she went over to her desk and picked it up, just as

Hector came back into the office from lunch.

'Hello,' she said into her phone.

'Hello Bella?' She didn't recognize the voice.

'Yes, who's that?' she asked.

'No, I don't suppose you'd remember.' It was an American accent, clipped and cold.

'Mitch! How are you?' she said fondly.

'How the fuck do you think I am? I've just been sacked. Merris lost the court case and the company's been bought over by a bunch of money-grabbing vultures. No-one is to blame for this more than you and I can't believe you didn't warn me.'

She was stunned.

Mitch continued furiously: 'I asked you Bella, I came to your office to see you. I told you I had a baby on the way. Surely you could at least have warned me?'

Bella felt as if she had been slapped in the face or winded and all the fight drained out of her.

She didn't want to spout all the usual stuff – that the company was going down the pan, that Mitch would have lost his job anyway, that she had been Merris's only chance. Maybe Mitch was right, maybe she had cocked it up for them all. Most of all, she knew she did not want to be the one taking all this shit all the time.

'Haven't you got anything to say?' he asked.

'I'm sorry,' she mumbled, 'I didn't know.'

'Yeah, well it's a bit late for sorry. It's a bit fucking late for that.'

There was a long pause.

'Is that really all you can say?' he asked, even more furious that she wasn't giving him the chance for a proper fight.

'Yes,' she whispered.

Mitch hung up.

'Oh fuck,' she said under her breath.

'Who was that?' asked Hector.

'Someone from Merris Group. He was a bit upset,' she mumbled. 'I didn't know they lost the court case.'

'Yeah. It was big news a couple of weeks ago,' Hector answered. 'Never mind. You should have just given him your famous line – sod off to the country and restore antique furniture,' Hector said with a laugh and was astonished to see Bella bursting into tears.

'Oh come on, Bella, get it together,' he said, 'or people are really going to think you're not up to the job.'

Stung by the remark, she knew at once that Hector didn't think she was up to it and she wondered who else he'd told.

Hiding in the Ladies, she lit a cigarette and took a deep drag. OK, she told herself, two more hours of work then I'm out of here. Maybe Markie won't even have woken up. But when she rang home on her mobile on the way out of the office, the loud screaming in the background told her otherwise.

'Hang on in there, Joanne, I'm getting into my car, I'll be back in forty minutes.'

Except she wasn't, she got stuck in a long traffic jam full of angry overheated drivers blaring their horns and swearing at each other. Her breasts were hard and hot and oozing milk onto her sticky, sweaty shirt. She clicked the button to pull up the roof of her car so she could cry without attracting too many stares. What a complete, fucking night-mare of a day.

Finally she got home and collapsed on the sofa with her baby.

Joanne fetched cold drinks from the kitchen, while Markie sucked frantically. 'I've made us something to eat,' she said, handing Bella a tall iced fruit juice.

'Oh thank you.' Bella felt pathetically grateful. Joanne had tidied the sitting room as well, despite her earlier warnings about refusing to do house-work. No wonder, it had been revolting, dustballs building up in the corner, takeaway dishes from four nights in a row.

Bloody Don, shouldn't he be helping with some of this? Instead he'd come in late every evening and she'd been away before he was up in the morning.

Bella nibbled at her luscious chicken sandwich crammed with slithery tomatoes and mustard may-onnaise and occasionally glanced over at Joanne eating hers. There wasn't much to say. Joanne had had a terrible day, Bella was shattered. They were both hoping things would work out better next week.

'I really appreciate how hard this is for you at the moment,' Bella said. 'I hope it will get easier.'

'Me too, we'll wait and see how it goes,' Joanne answered.

Soon after her sandwich, she left and Bella and Markie were alone.

Bella stroked his cheek and cuddled him close to her. Propped up on pillows on the sofa, she fell fast asleep with Markie in her arms.

It was 10.30 p.m. when he began to cry. Her eyes

357

opened and she was momentarily startled to see an unfamiliar ceiling and set of curtains, then realized she was in the sitting room.

She looked at the baby snuggled up against her chest. His face was pink and marked with the folds of her clothes and he was bathed in sweat from sleeping so close beside her. There was also a telltale feeling of wetness on his back, oh yuck, she could see yellow goo seeping out of his nappy. She decided to take him upstairs where they could both peel off for a bath together before bed.

By contrast, the next day, Saturday, was perfect. Once Don had surfaced from his lie-in, he looked after them both. He did the babysitting, cooking and tidying. Markie was calm and contented all day, he ate well, he slept for long stretches, leaving Bella free to lounge around the house and relax.

She lay on the sofa, watching sunlight stream into the room and she felt pleased with how lovely it looked, snowy white with gauzy curtains stirring in the breeze and big pools of light on the elegant blond floor.

By Sunday morning, she felt so calm and rested that when the call came for Don to go off on a job for a day or two, she took it in her stride. She considered phoning Red or Tania for company, realizing that she hadn't spoken to Tania in weeks. But somehow, the day passed and she didn't get round to it. Funny how the idea of phoning Mel, Lucy or Jaz seemed almost ridiculous now. What would they talk about? Her old friends wouldn't be at all interested in Markie.

She played with her son, dangling things above his head and watching him reach out his little hands. He was so surprised with his hands, he opened and closed them in amazement and startled when they moved back and touched him. Bella watched him with utter devotion and he rewarded her with long, adoring looks and the occasional fluttering smile. By Sunday night, she knew she did not want to go back to work, could not go back for another week like the one they had all suffered.

The work for the next month at Danson's was basic figure analysis, there was no reason why she couldn't do it from home. Hector could e-mail it all over to her daily. He could call her whenever he needed to, hell they could have a meeting every couple of days if necessary, but basically, she would be at home.

She could feed Markie whenever he was hungry and Joanne could look after him while she worked.

The more Bella thought about it, the more perfect a solution it seemed. Why hadn't they arranged this from the start? Just naivety. She hadn't know what a nine-week-old baby was like and neither had her office.

It was time to let them know.

Chapter Thirty-seven

On Monday morning, Bella put on her work suit and high heels and headed for the office. She thought she might as well stick with plan A until everyone knew about her plan B.

In the car at 8.05 a.m. she decided to try Susan before she drove into the morning traffic. She dialled her direct line.

'Hello,' came the reply, before a second ring had sounded.

'Susan, hello, it's Bella.'

'Oh hello, Bella. I've been thinking about you. How are you coping?'

'I'm fine, sort of. Have you got any time today? Lunch or after work when we could have a quick meet?'

There was a pause, Susan no doubt checking her overstuffed diary for a bite-sized chunk of opportunity.

'No, I'm totally booked up. You're speaking to me in the freest moment I'm going to have all day.'

Oh well, here goes, thought Bella, taking a deep breath.

'I'm going to suggest doing my share of the Danson's work from home for the next few weeks. I haven't spoken to Hector or Danson's yet, I wanted to clear this with you first.'

No response. Bella thought she'd better just carry on: 'Hector and I can communicate by e-mail and phone and we'll have regular meetings. I really don't think it will pose any problems.'

'What's brought this on?' Susan asked.

'Well, I have a full-time nanny, but my son is still unsettled, really upset about me being away all day, Susan. He's still breastfeeding and he needs me around.'

She tried not to sound too emotional as she said those words.

Utter silence from Susan. Bella waited a moment then began to wonder if she should say something else.

Finally Susan spoke. 'Well,' she said, 'I have lots of other things you can do for me from home, Bella. But if that's where you want to base yourself for the time being, Hector will do the Danson's job on his own, closely supervised by Chris.'

Bella couldn't believe it. She was stunned, too shocked to do anything but gasp for breath.

'Does that sound OK?' Susan said lightly.

'No it bloody well does not!' Bella was surprised at the anger in her own voice. 'Hector!' she exclaimed. 'I can't believe I'm hearing this. This is a half a million pound contract, which I won for you, remember. I have given up a whole month of maternity leave to come back and work on it and all I'm asking for is a little bit of flexibility here. Hector is the most junior person in the office, he was my assistant on the job.'

Susan's voice came back, calm and controlled. 'Don't have a girlie fit on me, Bella. Yes, half a million pounds is at stake here, I can't take a risk. Hector told me on Friday you didn't seem to be ready to come back yet. He said you were tearful, leaving early, unable to attend key meetings. And there's some senior exec there you have a problem with, apparently.'

Bella was distraught, the little shit had completely stitched her up.

'Go home and think this over for a day or two if you like,' Susan continued before she could challenge Hector's version of events, 'but I'm sure you'll see I'm right. I've got lots of work to keep you busy with, I can't let you risk our reputation by sending you out to clients before you're back to full strength.'

Bella could not believe what she was hearing. She was being demoted to Hector's position and he was waiting in the wings to snatch up her job. Her prized job, the one she had fought so hard to get.

'I should have been promoted after my work with Merris, Susan,' she said, surprised at how calm she suddenly felt. 'Instead, you're going to demote me because I've had a baby.'

'I'm not demoting you,' Susan cut in.

'If you make Hector the number one on the Danson's job, you'll leave me with no option but to resign.' She realized she was deadly serious.

362

'For Christ's sake, Bella, don't be so melodramatic. You're obviously tired and postnatal, don't do anything you're going to regret.'

Bella was speechless with anger.

Susan spoke again, angry too now: 'Resign! Don't be ridiculous. Of course you're not going to resign. This is your dream job, the one you were born to do, you're not going to sit at home pureéing carrots, you'll go up the wall.'

There was a long pause, then Bella began to speak, only recognizing the truth of her words as she said them. 'You know what? I am going to resign. It's not ridiculous. Leaving my two-month-old baby alone all day with a stranger is ridiculous, thank you for helping me to see that.'

There was a long silence on the line, then Susan stormed: 'Bella? Bella? Don't even think about putting the phone down now, Bella. If you hang up, your job here is finished. I mean it, I will not re-negotiate with you . . . Bella?'

Bella held the phone away from her ear and clicked the end call button.

She stared at the little hung-up phone symbol on the green screen in disbelief.

Her message symbol was flashing, so she called it up and looked at a wonderfully inappropriate text note from Don: 'Dn't let the bugrs get u dwn. Luv u D.'

Christ. She dangled her car key in her hand and wondered what to do. She couldn't face going back home just yet, she needed some time to think. She decided to head over to the café beside their old flat.

During the fifteen-minute drive she replayed Susan's words over and over: 'You're obviously tired and postnatal' . . . 'You're not going to sit at home pureéing carrots.' She was so furious, it was hard to drive straight.

But she had *resigned*. She felt her stomach lurch at the full implications. No more Danson's, no more Prentice, no more Chris, Kitty, no more big salary. But on the other hand no more leaving Markie behind . . . well, for the moment. God, she needed to think this through.

In the café she drank a succession of lattes and smoked her way through five cigarettes. It didn't really make things any clearer, but she felt calmer in a sort of caffeined up, nicotine buzz kind of way.

OK, she'd resigned from Prentice, she would take a couple of months off to be at home with Markie full time, then she would get another job. Hell, she could still take up Merris on his offer; well, if he had a company left to run. She shuddered at the thought of the phone call from Mitch.

Suddenly she really wanted to speak to Chris about all this, so dialled him up on the mobile.

His reaction to the news was a hardly surprising: '*What?!!!!*'

'I had a bit of a run in with Susan this morning,' she explained. 'And anyway, I've left.'

'Bella! What the hell happened?'

'All I wanted was to do the Danson's work from home. I thought that would be perfectly feasible. But she said she'd give Danson's to Hector and give me "other things" to do.'

'Oh God . . . so you took the huff?'

'Chris!' Bella felt very defensive. 'I was really insulted she didn't believe I could do it. And she was offering the contract I won to that creep. He phoned her up on Friday and told her I wasn't up to it.'

'Jesus,' Chris let out a long sigh. 'But are you happy about this? Do you really want to leave?'

'I didn't feel I had any choice, Chris. I don't know. I'll have to think about it. I just want to be with my son right now.'

'Look . . . maybe you need some time off, time to think this over,' he said. 'Why don't you leave it a few days then phone her back? I'm sure something can be worked out. Bella . . .' Chris was almost pleading with her now. 'You don't really want to leave, do you?'

All at once Bella felt exhausted, far too tired to deal with all this, so tired she just didn't care any more.

'I don't know Chris,' she managed. 'You're right, I'm not in the best frame of mind to make any decisions. I need to go home, get some sleep.'

'I'll phone you. Take care.'

'OK thanks, you know, you're a really nice guy,' she added.

'Thanks, bye, bye,' said Chris.

'Bye,' she answered.

She had to get home. She paid up and headed for the car then drove back, wondering what the hell she was going to tell Don.

As she let herself into the house, she could hear Markie's desperate cries coming all the way from upstairs but also the TV on in the sitting room. She walked in and saw Joanne lying on the sofa watching breakfast television.

Joanne turned round to her, open mouthed.

'Well, you're fired,' Bella said simply.

'There's nothing I can do with him to make him feel better, I've had to leave him to cry himself to sleep,' she said by way of explanation, quickly getting to her feet.

Bella was white with fury, but controlled. 'I don't care,' she said. 'It's not what I would do and I need a nanny who will do things my way, or Markie will never be happy.'

Joanne's face flushed, she picked up her bag and her jacket. She looked up at Bella, obviously wanting to say something before she left the house.

'You should have bottle-fed him from the start. The situation you're in now is unfair on him and unfair on me,' she said in a raised voice.

'Thank you, Joanne,' Bella said grimly, 'you can go now. I'll settle up with you through the agency.'

Bella stood rooted to the spot in the sitting room until she heard the furious slam of the front door, then she ran upstairs to her son.

He was lying on his back in the cradle beside their bed. His face was red and creased with howling and his furious fists were waving about in the air.

God, how could Joanne have left him like this? Bella scooped him up and slumped onto the bed. Propping pillows behind her back, she hurried to feed him.

Afterwards, they both fell into a doze.

Bella was woken by the trilling of her mobile. Gently she laid Markie in his crib and ran out into the hall. Hell, where had she put it?

The trilling stopped and then the house phone rang.

Aha, she knew what was coming next.

She ran back into the bedroom to pick up.

'Bella?' It was Don, sounding anxious.

'Yes.'

'Is everything OK? I couldn't get you on your mobile so I just tried this number on the off-chance.'

'Everything's fine,' she said. 'I've resigned from my job and fired the nanny, otherwise everything's just fine.'

Don swore. He'd been able to tell from her weird tone of voice that this was not a joke.

Bella held the phone tightly and wondered what was coming next.

'OK,' he said, very tense now. 'What happened?'

Bella gave him a sketchy outline of her quarrel with Susan, then Joanne's dismissal.

'Right,' Don said. 'I can come back this evening, I think I probably should. There are obviously a few things you need to talk through.'

It was the right answer. 'Thanks, that would be really good,' she said.

He promised to be home by seven.

'Drive safely,' she pleaded, imagining him bowling the Jeep all the way down the fast lane of the M6 in his rush to get home.

Don was surprised to come back to such a peaceful house: he'd worked himself up into a state about Bella on the drive home. He'd expected to find her hysterical and on the verge of suicide with a screaming baby in her arms. Instead, she was snuggled up on the sofa watching TV with Markie asleep at her breast. She'd had a bath and her damp hair was coiled up on her head.

They kissed hello. She smelled clean and flowery and milky, whereas he was unshaven, grubby and reeked unmistakably of the greasy café he'd spent the afternoon in.

'You look incredibly calm,' said Don, sitting down on the sofa beside them, 'I was expecting you both to be having tantrums.'

'I am very calm,' she said, smiling at him. 'I need to take some more time off to be with Markie, then I'll have no problem finding another job.'

'Well, OK,' he answered. 'You seem to have made up your mind. Don't you want to keep a slot open with Prentice? I'm sure you could patch things up.'

'Maybe, but not right now. I've got a point to make to Susan.'

'Right . . . and that point is?' He felt irritated by her now.

'That she can't have everything her own way.'

'I wonder who else needs to learn that lesson,' he said quietly.

Bella rounded on him. 'Just fuck off, Don. This is my life. I'm allowed to make my own decisions.'

'Of course you are, Bella,' he retorted. 'I just don't want to see you toss your career away for a few more weeks of playing the good mother.'

'What the hell does that mean?' she asked furiously.

'You worked your arse off to get that job and you loved it. I can't believe you've just thrown it away over a petty argument.'

'Petty? She won't let me work from home. She won't let me be here with a two-month-old baby who needs me.'

'She said you could work from home, just on different stuff,' he reminded her.

'She was going to give Hector my job!' Bella

shouted and Markie woke up with a start and began to cry.

'Oh well that's a perfectly logical reason to resign, wounded pride,' Don replied.

'Just fuck off,' Bella said, for the second time. 'And go and have a shower, you smell revolting.'

Don stormed out of the room and Bella was left feeding Markie again so that he could settle back down into sleep. She was very hurt and angry. She'd taken a huge step, albeit without any forethought, and she needed Don's support. He'd always supported everything she'd done before, made her feel confident and understood and fantastic. Now, she felt unsure and damn furious with him.

Don, standing under a hot, soapy shower, was in no better a mood. He'd been away for two days and quite frankly wished he hadn't bothered coming back. He was nostalgic for the homecomings they used to have. He remembered eating takeaways in bed and fantastic sex. Their relationship was now turning into everything he'd dreaded about married life, everything he didn't want – rowing, screaming baby, chaotic home, sexual frustration.

For the first time ever, he felt bored with Bella. She had always been so much fun – interesting, daring, outrageous. This was all so mundane and now stressful as well. Just how the hell did she think they could afford the mortgage without her salary?

Bella was wondering exactly the same when the phone rang.

It was Tania, but Bella could feel only mildly enthusiastic.

'Hi, how's it going?' her friend asked.

369

'Well . . . I quit my job today.'

'Really? You've had a better offer? You cow, you better not be earning more money than me.'

'Ha ha. No, I've decided to stay at home for a couple of months, look after Markie and get a new job after that,' Bella explained.

'Oh my God! Now I'm really shocked!' Tania laughed. 'What are you going to do all day? And what will you live on?'

'The answer to your first question is a fuck of a lot,' Bella was frosty now. 'And I'm going to live on my savings,' she lied. 'And my husband, if I still have one. It's only two months, for God's sake, just no shopping for a few weeks.'

'How boring,' Tania groaned. 'I wanted to ask you over on Saturday, just you and me. We could have a girlie good time, shop, drink cappuccinos, maybe go for a massage or something. I've had such a stressful week, and I want to talk to you about Greg.'

'Tania,' Bella cut in, 'I've got a small, breast-feeding baby, I can't spend a day without him. Anyway I don't want to,' she huffed.

There was no response from Tania, so Bella said: 'I'm sorry. Why don't you come over? I'll make you lunch, then we can take Markie to the Heath and have a long walk.'

'God, Bella, you're in danger of turning into a surburban housewife,' Tania joked.

'Well at least I'm not some sad Bridget Jones,' Bella snapped. 'Why don't you just phone me back when you've grown up?' With that she slammed down the phone.

She threw herself back down on the sofa and lay looking at her son asleep in his carrycot.

Good going, she told herself. At this rate I'll have no career, no husband and no friends. A little part of her also thought, So what? My son loves me, I just want to be with him.

She stroked the little fuzzy head.

Chapter Thirty-eight

Bella stood up very slowly to move her sleeping baby from her arms into his bed. She put him down with tiny, careful movements, but as soon as his head touched the mattress, he woke and began to cry.

She let out a curse of frustration. Damn, damn, damn. For the third time, she was going to have to sit down and put him back on her breast until he fell asleep, then try and move him. She felt furious with him. Why couldn't he fall asleep without a nipple in his mouth? Why wouldn't he leave her alone for just half an hour so she could do something for herself, clear up the breakfast dishes, take a shower, lie on the sofa in peace. She needed to be left alone, just for a few minutes.

He was so tired, she knew she should just put him down and let him howl until he fell asleep, but she couldn't bear to do it. He had cried and cried and cried the times she had tried before and in the end she had always given in, picked him up and comforted him with her breasts again.

Every single one of the plethora of babycare

books she had surrounded herself with recently had advised her that feeding a baby to sleep was a bad plan, but it had become too entrenched now. Markie was four and a half months old. This was how he went to sleep, morning, noon, night, middle of the night. She didn't know how she could break the cycle. The fact that it was all her fault made her feel even worse about it.

She picked the baby up roughly. 'Damn you!' she shouted. He cried even harder with fright.

'I'm sorry, I'm sorry,' she soothed him up against her shoulder and felt like crying herself.

She lay on the sofa and put Markie beside her so that he could latch on. He had barely swallowed a few mouthfuls before he had fallen asleep again. His lips smacked as they broke off from her nipple and to her infuriation, the noise woke him up and he quickly started to suck again.

Finally, ten minutes later he fell soundly asleep. She didn't dare to move him. If he woke up again, she was in danger of shaking him, smacking him or doing something that she would have found just unthinkable before. Now, with a thousand tiny frustrations heaped on her every single day and night, she knew anyone could hurt their child, if they were pushed far enough.

And she was very close to that line. She was absolutely exhausted. Every day, she was functioning on just six or seven fractured hours of sleep, she had dark double bags under her eyes and her skin looked grey. She had just enough energy to get through the day and nothing in reserve. She had taken on way too much. She was doing all the baby care, all day long, all the breastfeeding, day and night. Don was there to cook her dinner some evenings and he helped out at the weekends, but otherwise, she was totally unsupported.

Right now, she just couldn't see a way out of the situation. She couldn't bear to get any childcare sorted out while she wasn't working because of guilt at the expense and because she still hated the thought of handing Markie over to anyone after the last experience.

But she knew she wasn't going to get any aspect of her life back together until she had some time and some energy.

And what the hell was she going to work as anyway?? She couldn't be a part-time consultant. It wasn't that sort of job and even if she could think of a way of going part time, she might as well throw her ambition in the bin.

Where was the solution?? All these questions and anxieties were whirling round her head in such an unanswerable frenzy, it was beginning to make her very depressed.

The day before, she'd made the mistake of thinking company would cheer her up and she'd met Mel and Lucy for lunch in the City but the obvious gulf between what she once was and what she'd now become had just depressed her even further.

She'd turned up at the smart restaurant in Don's jeans and a shirt, with a changing bag on her back, lugging a baby in a car seat. Mel and Lucy were in exquisite designer suits, with Fendi bags, kitten heels, long nails and tiny mobile phones.

Markie had been perfect. She'd propped him up into the restaurant's high chair – an unexpected miracle – where he'd mouthed on pieces of bread as

Mel and Lucy had cooed over him adoringly, even though Bella forbade them both from smoking within 50 yards of him and Lucy had cuddled him just a little bit too hard so he'd landed a blob of sick on her jacket.

But the questions about what her plans were had been hard to answer because she just didn't know.

'Well, you know, in another couple of months he'll drink from a beaker and eat more solids, so I'll be able to leave him with someone else for a bit,' she'd heard herself say, but she was mentally adding, but not all day, no way.

'God, how are you surviving without a salary?' Mel had asked, genuinely curious.

With a lurch, Bella thought about the mountainous overdraft, the credit cards racked up to the hilt, and said: 'Oh you know, I've got a bit saved up to tide me over for a while . . .'

'Do you spend the day doing lovely stuff?' – this from Lucy – 'Going round parks, art galleries, deli shopping, it must be so relaxing not having to go to work. God, it must be fabulous.'

Bella pictured herself endlessly breastfeeding day and night, dodging dog shit with the buggy, trawling round Boots and dealing with the trauma of a screaming baby when she was out with no place to feed or change him and said, 'Hmmm, yeah,' vaguely.

'Don't you miss work a bit?' asked Mel.

She'd looked at the two of them, perfectly dressed, perfectly made up, about to go back to their vastly well paid jobs, then afterwards maybe on to a noisy cocktail party. On Saturday they could sleep in all morning, read the papers, go out for lunch, see a film, have a facial, buy expensive new clothes, book holidays. Shit. Shit. Shit. She missed it all desperately.

Then Markie happily waved a bread crust in his fat fist; he was giggling and drool was running down his chubby chin onto the bib she'd tied round his neck. She adored him, felt her heart ache just looking at him.

'I don't know,' she sighed. 'I miss lots of things about work, the buzz, the power trip, the money, that feeling of purpose every morning. God,' she managed a laugh, 'I can't believe I used to go jogging *every* morning! But I'm just besotted with him. I don't want to miss anything. I don't want to make him unhappy and I want to do everything right.' As she said this, she wished she could think of a way to somehow have both lives, but it seemed utterly impossible.

'Have you spoken to Susan, since you . . . em?' Lucy asked awkwardly.

'No,' Bella said.

'What about doing two or three days a week. Susan would definitely take you back, wouldn't she?' Lucy asked.

'Ermm . . . I don't know, I keep meaning to speak to her. God, I don't know.'

Lucy and Mel had felt slightly at a loss. This was Bella, the girl who'd always had it all figured out before, who'd got the fab job first, who'd got married first, who'd now had a baby, *first*. It was unsettling to see her like this, looking crap, sounding vague and anxious.

On the walk back to her car, Bella looked round at the streets which had been her backdrop for so many years. She felt like an outsider. Everyone who pushed past her was in a suit and in a hurry, Markie was bumped about in his car seat as the City's workers raced past back to their offices to make more money.

There was a smartly suited couple kissing passionately on the street corner and she watched them break apart laughing as their mobiles went off together. 'Synchronicity,' Don's voice was in her head. That had happened the first night they met . . . about one hundred years ago.

Now, one entirely uneventful day later, she was back at home with Markie finally asleep on the sofa – snuggled right up against the back, so even she, the most anxious mother in the world, couldn't worry about him rolling off. She plugged in the baby monitor and left the room with the listening device in her hand.

Downstairs in the kitchen, she opened all the windows and lit up a cigarette. She inhaled right down to the bottom of her lungs and felt the wonderful tingling buzz, she put her lips round the butt and sucked in again. It was warm and comforting and wonderful. 'Good old Marlboro, that's what I say,' she said out loud in a voice made husky with the lungful of smoke she was exhaling.

'Talking to myself,' she said out loud again. 'An interesting new development. Obviously the first sign that I'm about to go completely bonkers.'

She stubbed her cigarette out in the tiny bronze ashtray and went upstairs to sort out another load for the washing machine.

God, she was bored. She was becoming a slave to an endless round of domestic chores. The washing had to be done, the kitchen sink had to be cleaned, the shower plug unblocked. There were 101 little tasks she could occupy herself with all day long but what for? The clothes and sink would get dirty again, the plug would gum up. It was merely a version of digging holes and filling them in again. A way of making her feel she was busy.

'Oh shut up,' she told herself, 'this is getting very black.'

But then the little voice said: 'You used to get pissed in all night bars, drag strange men home to bed, do boardroom presentations so good they turned you on . . . now you shop for baby vests. SHUT UP, BELLA.'

But it was boring and she was boring.

'He managed to roll over onto his tummy today and he lifted himself up with his arms. He was so pleased with himself, he giggled and squeaked. And he was pointing at me and going "Ah, ah". I'm sure he was trying to say Ma Ma. It's just really exciting,' she heard herself say to Don at supper that evening. She sounded like an idiot.

When she'd finished her bath, she went through to the bedroom and found Don waiting for her on the bed. He looked nice, still tanned although it was the end of autumn now. His thick hair was overgrown and in need of a cut, she liked it like that.

'Hi Bella,' he said gently and she knew that look.

'Oh boy,' she said with a smile. 'You can try, hon, but I'm very tired, it will be like raising the dead.'

'Come here,' he held out his arms. 'Let's just cuddle up.'

'Yeah, you say that, but I know you mean "let's have a shag".'

'Bella! Stop being so defensive and get over here!'

She kept her thick white dressing gown wrapped tightly round her and lay carefully on the bed beside him. He rolled onto his side and wrapped her up in his arms, squeezing her so hard, her large milky breasts hurt.

He aimed for her mouth and kissed her, reaching between her lips with his tongue. God, she struggled against the urge to push him away. She really wasn't in the mood. Why so full on straight away? Couldn't he kiss her neck first? Or her forehead?

She broke away and kissed his cheek, neck, ear, anything to get away from the closeness of a mouth on mouth kiss.

He opened her dressing gown and fondled her breasts, but to her they felt heavy and manhandled. His hand moved down to between her legs as she unzipped him and took his erection between her hands. She'd decided to just do this.

Poor Don, he was a nice guy, he was working really hard and they hadn't had sex for weeks. She would do it for him, she knew it would be quite nice for her too, but she was just a million miles away from being really turned on by this.

He was kissing her on the mouth again, ugh. She broke off and moved down the bed to lick his penis. Bizarrely, that felt much less personal.

She carried on for as long as he would let her, hoping it might reduce the portion of sex coming right up.

Don pulled her on top of him and said breathlessly, 'What's the current contraception situation?'

'Condoms,' she answered, 'In the drawer with KY Jelly . . . the scar is still quite uncomfortable.' Oh the romance.

'OK,' he said, turning to the drawer. She moved off him so he could sit up and fumble about with cellophane wrappers and foil, then the condom and finally the jelly.

'Are you OK?' he asked turning round to her.

She leaned down and kissed his face while he rubbed grease onto his rubber-clad penis. She kissed the small, soft apples of his cheeks and reminded herself that she loved this man. She put her hands into his hair and took him inside her.

It felt good, she felt snug and almost muscular inside, he felt just right again.

He closed his eyes.

She moved to his rhythm, enjoying it but not wanting to lose control. She focused on the bedstead in front of her and felt him cup his hands round her breasts. They felt heavy and sagging. It was painful even to bounce gently on top of him without the ten-ton breasts crashing up and down against her ribcage. She glanced down at her wobbly tummy and immediately regretted it. This was not her body, she just couldn't feel sexy with it.

Don was slowly working up to an orgasm beneath her and, with some detachment, she watched his face change from tension, screwed-up eyes and locked jaw to pleasure and relief.

He opened his eyes and looked at her: 'You weren't there, were you?' He said this kindly, with a smile.

'Well . . . I was there a bit,' she confessed. 'It was nice.'

'Oh God, nice.' He was only smiling a little. 'We've reached the "nice sex" stage. You know what comes next, don't you? The "no sex" stage. The "Not tonight darling, I'd rather have a lovely cup of tea" stage.'

'Don't, Don.' She moved off and lay beside him. 'I'm sorry. I'm not in the mood.'

'You're never in the mood,' he said.

'Please don't. You're just going to have to give me a chance here. I'm looking after a baby 24 hours a day, I'm *tired*. Anyway, we've been together for two years now.' She was starting to sound angry.

'What's that got to do with it?' he asked.

'Well, that's when people go off the boil a bit.'

'Bella, you pessimist!' He cuddled her up in his arms and decided to joke her out of this: 'I'm intending to still fancy you when you're 50. Obviously, feel free to get the necessary plastic surgery and designer corsetry required.'

She whacked him over the head.

'Ha ha. Now leave me alone. I've got to get some sleep.'

'OK.' He kissed her on the lips. 'Good night. Just try and relax, we're OK. You're going to be OK soon.'

She didn't answer. There was no way she was kicking off a discussion about the baby/job/working dilemma right now. She couldn't face it. She did not want to talk about it.

Chapter Thirty-nine

She was curled up in front of the telly, feeding Markie one dreary, grey afternoon when the phone rang. She reached over to get it from the table jammed right beside the sofa arm.

'Hello, Bella?' for a moment she didn't recognize the voice and hesitated.

'It's Red, I just wondered if you were still alive?'

'Oh hello Red, how are you doing?'

'I'm good. How are you? Is this not an odd time for you to be home? I was expecting to leave a message on your machine, or with your nanny.'

'Oh God, have I not told you about all that?'

'No . . .' Red sounded intrigued.

'I resigned . . . and I fired the nanny.'

'Oh my God, really? When did all this happen?'

'Err . . . Markie was two months old and, God, he's coming up for six months now.'

'How come you haven't called me? We could have had lots of lovely baby-mum times together.'

'I'm sorry . . . I just felt a bit, you know,' Bella felt a lump forming in her throat.

'Bored, lonely, exhausted, depressed . . . suicidal? I know.'

'No, I'm fine, honestly. I'm really enjoying being with him.'

'Yes of course, that too.' There was real understanding in Red's voice, which was making Bella's lump even more painful.

'What about coming back to yoga class with me on Saturdays?' Red suggested. 'There's a postnatal class too, you know.'

'No . . . no, I can't go back there,' Bella sounded tearful. 'I was so different back then, I don't want them to see me like this.'

'Like what, Bella?' Red asked. 'Maybe you should come along and see that everyone else is feeling like you – shattered, uncertain about the next move.'

'I can't.'

'Well, another suggestion then. Why don't I come and babysit for you one evening?'

'Thanks, but I don't think that would work.'

'Why not?'

'He falls asleep at the breast and sometimes he wakes up just an hour or so later for a top-up. If he didn't get it, he'd howl himself sick until I came back.'

'Well, just go to the pub round the corner. You've got to get out of the house without him, trust me. You're going to go stir crazy.'

I already am, Bella thought, but said: 'I'll think about it, Red, I promise.'

'OK, sorry Bella, I'm not wanting to bully you or anything, d'you want to meet up or come round?

I've got some free afternoons a bit later in the week. And there's a baby-toddler group we can go to on Fridays.'

'Thanks, Red,' she said. 'How are you anyway?'

They chatted on for a bit and when Bella put the receiver down, she felt a little better. Maybe she would load Markie up into the car tomorrow and go to a park a bit further afield.

She tried to enjoy their park trips, but the truth was, he was just too small still. He sat propped up in his buggy and watched things with interest, but she looked enviously at the groups of mothers sitting chatting on benches in the play areas while they watched their toddlers climb over the slides and dig in the sand pit.

It would be much more fun when Markie was older. The baby stage seemed such a thankless grind. God, she immediately felt guilty at that thought. It wasn't thankless, he smiled at her, he giggled at her, he looked at her with utter adoration and was upset even when she went out of the room. Her son's unconditional love for her was over-whelming.

The following weekend, Bella watched the rain running steadily down the window. The sky was steely grey and even though it was only 4.30, it was starting to get dark. Bloody November, she'd always hated November and she was beginning to hate Sundays too.

All three of them had been cooped up inside the house all day, not able to go out for a walk and not getting it together to go anywhere in the car. She felt as if she and Don had worked split shifts all day long – he had looked after Markie while she slept in, she had kept the baby amused while Don read every paper printed in Britain that day. Then when Markie had his afternoon nap they had tidied the house together, put on laundry and Don had done the supermarket run. God, it didn't come more domesticated than this. She looked out of the window now and watched the rain, feeling bored beyond belief.

What would she give for some time to herself, time away from all this? When she was still a teenager she had backpacked round eastern Europe on her own, now she was stuck in a house in a shitty part of north London. Make that stuck on a sofa, in a house in a shitty part of north London. How had she let her horizons close in around her like this?

She desperately wanted to be alone, but she desperately didn't want to leave Markie. It made no sense that these two emotions should be wrestling in her mind like this. She wanted to un-make him, so that he and his relentless demands didn't exist, just for a weekend.

She fantasized about what she would do: go to an airport and take a flight to New York so she could roam around a loud, noisy, brash city and stay up all night without worrying about the 6 a.m. wake-up call the next morning. Or maybe go somewhere quiet and clean and green. Finland. She'd always wanted to go there.

She wanted adventure and change and above all to be by herself to think her life through. She needed mental free time, time not to think: Are there enough nappies and clean clothes left? Are the pears ripe enough to mash? Is he old enough to try live yoghurt? Will a bread crust choke him? All the million things that took up all her thoughts every day now that just hadn't been there before.

She used to be able to think about work and Don and holidays and the future. Now she was too busy.

What the hell was she going to do next? Up till now her life had run according to the game plan. She had known exactly where she was going and how she was going to get there; now suddenly at 29 she was in freefall.

She was not going back to the 9–5, ha, more like the 8–8. She was not going back to screwing companies for massive amounts of money just so she could get people like Mitch fired. It was too bloody and too soul-destroying and what was she going to tell her son when he asked 'Mummy what do you do?' 'Well, darling, I am the axeman, the bean counter, the cost-cutter, the men in grey suits, the bloodletter.'

But the money had been nice, the power, the status, the respect had all been very nice. She didn't have any of those things now.

'Right, Bella.' Don plonked some sort of noodly chicken concoction on the table in front of her when she came back down from putting Markie to bed. 'We are going to have a proper talk over dinner tonight. I've left you to your own devices long enough and now I need to know what is going on. You've been like a weird space cadet for weeks.'

She sat down, picked up her fork and tasted his meal. 'Hmmm, very nice,' she said, wondering where the hell to begin.

'I know, never mind that . . .' He looked up at her with a serious bordering on angry face. 'Our son is almost six months old and you are still at home, still breastfeeding him all day long, not making any calls, not organizing any childcare, not earning any money . . . you know we can't afford to go on like this.'

Bella looked up at him with big, brimming eyes and did not know what to say. She couldn't begin to express her own wretchedness at the situation: Well Don, the answer is to make Markie not exist for a few days so I can go to Finland and have a rest and come up with some brilliant new plan. That wasn't going to work.

'What's the matter, Bella?' his tone had softened. 'I just don't recognize you. You're so vague and undecided. I don't think you're really happy being here all day long with Markie, but you can't seem to snap out of it.'

'Snap out of it?' She felt angry now.

'Well yes. You're just mooching about here feeling sorry for yourself. You could easily get any other job you wanted, but you haven't tried. You could easily find another nanny, but you haven't tried. Jesus, you haven't even bothered to buy anything that fits you, you just skulk about here in my old clothes. You look awful.' Don regretted that as soon as he had said it. But there it was, he couldn't take it back and anyway, maybe he'd been far too nice to her for too long. Maybe it was time to get tough.

'*Don*, I haven't bought anything because I'm not earning any money,' she shouted.

'I'm well aware of that,' he shouted back. 'What the hell do you think we are going to pay the mortgage with next month? I'm at my overdraft limit and your account must be in meltdown. Just

387

what are you thinking? If you want to spend the next few years at home being a housewife, then we'll have to sell the house and move to a small flat. But that's not why I married you.'

'What is that supposed to mean?' She was furious now.

'I never wanted to be married to someone who stayed home and cooked and did the cleaning and talked about the kids all evening. It's so fucking dull. I thought you were the absolute opposite of that and I feel like I've been tricked.'

'*You've* been tricked?! How the fuck do you think I feel?' Her tears were spilling out now, she was so angry and so hurt. 'I never knew what this would be like. I didn't ask for a baby who would only breastfeed, who would howl the house down whenever I left him. I didn't ask to feel this bad and this tired and this *pissed off* with everything.'

Words suddenly couldn't express her rage and frustration, so she flipped over her dinner plate, spilling food all over the table and ran upstairs.

Lying sobbing on the bed, she heard the front door slam. Good. Don had gone out, she hoped he didn't come back.

Once she had cried herself out, she went and washed her face in the bathroom.

That evening, she started to think about what it would be like to leave Don. Where would she and Markie go? How would she pay for it? Jesus. She could sell the car. She'd have to get a job first. She went into Markie's room and checked on him. He was lying on his back with his hands thrown up and out beside his head. He looked blissfully peaceful.

Far too hyped up to sleep, she went down to the kitchen, opened a bottle of wine and took out her cigarettes.

Two fags down, she felt steadier. She picked up the phone and dialled Tania's number. Unbelievable that she hadn't spoken to her for months now. She'd been so rude to her the last time, and never found the time or inclination to make up.

The answering machine picked up and Bella clicked off her phone. She couldn't leave Tania a message, she'd have to speak to her in person.

Who the hell else could she call? She lit another cigarette and thought for a moment, staring at the telephone keypad,

Aha. Speed dial seven.

After a few rings, that oh-so-missed voice answered.

'Hello?'

'Hello Chris, it's Bella.'

'Bella! Hello. Bloody hell. I thought you'd died or something.' He sounded so pleased to hear her, it made her stomach flip.

'You never wrote, you never called,' she teased.

'No, I didn't. Sorry, that was really, really crap of me. Bad boy.'

'How are things?' she asked.

'Terrible,' he answered. 'Danson's went ape when they heard you were off the job. Threatened to bring you in on a personal contract, then Susan threatened them with breach of contract . . . blah blah. I've been working like a dog, because Hector, well he's just a conceited, scheming bastard. I take back all the nice things I've ever said about him. And we miss you. It's like a leg lopped off, the phone constantly rings with people asking for you and we've all been told to say you're not working for us or anyone else, you're simply not available.'

Bella was amazed to hear all this.

'But that's not true, is it?' Chris asked. 'What are you doing? Have you taken the plunge and set up on your own?'

'Err . . . well, to be honest no. I'm having a bit of a maternity . . . em . . . sabbatical.'

'Really?' He sounded surprised.

'Well, the next move is important for me, I don't want to rush into anything. 'It was funny to hear that sort of career-y, work thing creep right back into her voice.

'No, you're absolutely right,' he said, then added: 'Susan is desperate for you to come back. She's too proud to come to you, but she would bite your hand off if you offered, probably any terms you liked.'

'Partner?'

'I'm sure. I'd probably get sacked to make room for you.'

'Ha ha.'

'How's your son anyway?'

So Bella told him, trying not to go on for too long.

'He sounds lovely,' said Chris. 'Are you enjoying being at home?'

'Mostly. But it's very tiring and I worry a lot that everyone thinks I've dropped off the face of the planet. You know that whole corporate culture of taking your mobile into the delivery room and rushing back to work before your stitches have healed.'

'Don't be silly,' said Chris. 'No-one's forgotten you, Bella. If anything, your mysterious disappearance has got even more people clamouring for your services.'

'Do you ever have any qualms about the job we do, Chris?' she asked, surprising herself.

'Oh-oh conscience time. No not really, we usually do quickly what would have happened much more slowly and bloodily over the long term.'

'Hmmm,' she answered, wondering if she believed that line any more, 'I think it would do me good to see you.'

'I'd love to – when and where? I'm free!'

'No hot dates at the moment then?' she teased.

'No.'

They settled on Sunday, her house, 8 p.m.

'It'll be great to see Don again,' Chris added, because he wanted to know if Don was going to be there, but he didn't want to ask straight out.

'No, you won't see him, he's off to Africa for about ten days, civil war refugees or something,' He was leaving tomorrow morning. She wondered if they would have a chance to make up before then and if she wanted to.

'So just you and me then,' Chris said in a way that made her wonder . . .

'Well, you, me and, hopefully, a sleeping baby,' she laughed.

Chapter Forty

In the morning, she and Don were polite to each other, but there was no big making-up scene. Don had spent the night on the couch after an evening in the pub and woken with a grotty hangover.

He packed his bags as Bella made breakfast for herself and Markie. Don only wanted coffee. Her son was eating porridge with mashed banana and he mouthed at little pieces of bread while she sat down to fresh orange juice, cereal and two slices of toast.

The ring at the doorbell meant Don's taxi was early. She could hear him cursing in the hallway. He went out to say he wasn't ready yet.

Five minutes later he appeared in the kitchen, wearing the long, waxed overcoat she loved him in, with a bag slung over his shoulder.

'OK, I'll say goodbye then,' he said rather stiffly.

He leaned over Markie sitting in his high chair and gave him a kiss: 'Take care my little buddy,' he said. The baby patted him on the cheek.

He came up to Bella and put his arms round her: 'Look after him for me and take care of yourself. I'm sorry we rowed last night, but I can't take back what I said. I think you need to get your head together,' he said. 'I want to help you, but you won't tell me how I can help you.'

'Right, I get the message,' she replied.

'I really don't want to leave on a bad note,' he said. 'But it's work. I have to go and I want to go. I'm sorry.'

'It's OK, Don, I'll be fine, it's just ten days, isn't it?'

'We've not got a definite return date yet, but it shouldn't be more than two weeks.' He leaned down, kissed her quickly on the mouth, and said 'Take care, I'll call you,' then he left.

'Bye,' she said and when she heard the front door slam she wished she'd been big enough to tell him to take care too. Take care wasn't 'I love you', they were both still too angry for that, but it was at least 'I really care about you'.

Two hours later, Markie had finally gone down for his morning nap when the phone rang. Bella rushed over and snatched the receiver up before the ringing woke him.

She was surprised to hear Don's voice.

He'd taken the wrong laptop to the airport. He could still use the one he'd taken, but he asked her to access a file on the laptop at home and pull out the contact numbers he needed for the trip. She found his computer in the sitting room and once it was up and running she called him back.

He talked her through the passwords until she'd opened the right file, then he took down the numbers and said goodbye, telling her to take care again. This time she said it back.

She hung up and decided to e-mail the file over to him and maybe put a conciliatory little note at the bottom.

She prepared her message then plugged the computer into the phone socket and hit send. As it exited the basket, she was left looking at the list of stored mail and she saw 'S.Sewell@nota.Virgin.net re: trip.'

S. Sewell could only be Simone Sewell, the tabloid harpy from hell Don had been seeing on and off over several years until he'd met Bella. She was a news reporter on his rival paper and she'd taken up the L.A. correspondent job not long after Bella and Don's engagement.

Bella clicked open the message, all it said was 'Looking forward to it.' But as she scrolled down, the story unfolded – all Simone's recent messages to and from Don were enclosed on the file.

Simone was back. She'd been made chief reporter on her paper, so now she and Don were direct rivals. She was going on the same civil war story and would be meeting him at the airport. Their first encounter in two years. Simone had sent the tasteful message: 'The child-bride has a baby now, so you must be gasping for a good grown-up shag,' along with a few choice reminiscences of their earlier adventures on the road together.

Bella read through them, thinking that a rain-filled ditch in Cumbria during a police hunt for an abducted toddler wouldn't have been her number one location for a sexual encounter, no matter how irresistible Don was.

She shut down the computer. Her hands were shaking and she could hear blood pounding in her ears. This would not be nearly so worrying if Don had at least mentioned Simone and if he hadn't had to leave home in the middle of a decidedly rocky patch.

'FUCK!!' she shouted out loud, 'Fuck, fuck, fuck.' She had no idea what to do. Should she phone Don and ask him what the hell was going on? Should she bundle Markie up and follow him on the first flight out there? No, that was ridiculous.

Unfortunately, her deepest insecurity now triggered, dinner with Chris was taking on a whole new meaning.

Rifling through the phone book, she booked a hair appointment at one of the most expensive salons in London, then began to make elaborate preparations for Sunday night.

Don opened his eyes and focused on an unfamiliar ceiling. His arm felt numb and he turned to see Simone's bleach-blond 40-year-old head lying on it. He eased it out from under her neck, managing not to wake her up.

Jesus, Simone.

He hadn't seen or heard from her for over two years, yet she had kissed him on the mouth and with her tongue when they'd met at Heathrow and he'd been jolted with a surprise shudder of lust, although the time in LA had not been kind to her.

Her skin was now a dark, dried-out tan, her nails had sprouted to inch-long, candy pink talons and she ended every sentence with a really irritating 'yunno?'

She was still single, of course, still totally neurotic about her career and it was obvious, now she was back, that she had every intention of rekindling their affair.

Their liaison had begun four years ago when she'd joined her paper. It had been a torrid on-off, hot-cold, sex and newspaper centred relationship complete with stealing exclusives from each other and snatching opportunities to fuck on the job. It had been thrilling in parts, immensely stressful, and after just an hour on the plane with her, drinking lukewarm in-flight champagne, he remembered exactly why he'd finally ended it on meeting Bella.

Bella, Bella . . . his beautiful, young Bella, who thought she was so tough and City-slick. To Don she'd seemed fresh, untainted and positively dewy-eyed. All that enthusiasm – for work, for life, for him! Finally, someone who hadn't been fucked up the arse by life one hundred times over like Simone and all the other women he seemed to hang around with back then.

He had listened to Simone cracking her hard-nosed, sarcastic gags on the plane, eaten up with bitterness and totally cynical, and he remembered how she'd laughed in his face whenever he'd tried to say anything really nice to her, whenever he'd tried to get in under that bulletproof shell. He could have become just like that, but thank God he'd met his girl – the gorgeous, sexy, razor-sharp girl asking him for a light. The one who had trusted him enough to let down her guard and fall in love.

Poor Bella. He sat up in bed now and rubbed his hand over three days of stubble. She'd had no idea what had hit her when the baby arrived and he'd left her to it, all the anxiety about money driving him to work harder, longer and away from home. He needed to take a holiday and give her a break.

This week had been hell, covering really grim shit from a place on the very outskirts of civilization. Now it had all turned nasty, and he and eight other journalists were holed up in the last two available hotel bedrooms waiting for a ride out.

He looked at his watch: 8.15 a.m. The plane was due in two hours. If he got good connecting flights, he would hopefully be back in London late, late Sunday, early Monday. He longed to be at home, to wrap Bella and his tiny son up in his arms and tell them it was going to be OK. He was going to make it OK.

Simone was stirring, he looked over and saw her eyes open. She yawned, stretched her arms out over her head and grinned at him.

'There's still time to change your mind, yunno?' she said and under the covers, he felt her hand reach for his belt buckle. 'They're going to say we did it anyway.' She nodded at the two photographers still comatose in sleeping bags on the floor.

'Thanks, but no thanks,' he said and moved her hand away.

'Well, well, respect to the child-bride,' Simone said. 'She's finally reined you in, yunno?'

'Her name's Bella,' Don replied. 'Let's just stick to Bella.'

He threw back the cover and, already dressed in trousers and a T-shirt, he got out of bed and pulled on his boots.

'I'm going to see if I can find some coffee in this place,' he said.

The haircut was fantastic, easily worth the eye-watering bill. Bella's mass of long, dark brown hair had been transformed into a sleek, layered, shoulder-length bob, shot through with ginger and caramel highlights. A heavy fringe had been cut into the front, which managed to make her look 19 again.

By Sunday night, her fridge was crammed with delicious food and very expensive wine, a new outfit was hanging out ready on the wardrobe door and the house was tidy and gleaming, filled with luscious fresh flowers and candles.

She had put Markie to bed early, so she would have a full half-hour to get ready. It still felt strange that he slept in his own little room now, but she'd decided to move him out three nights ago, so she could reclaim the bedroom.

Drying off after a quick shower, she covered herself in fragrant cream, then put on a little make-up. Back in the bedroom, she picked out her best underwear: suspenders, lace G-string, an under-wired bra which she was going to spill out of.

She had no idea if she had the nerve to seduce Chris or not, all she knew was that planning it like this had been the most fun she'd had in ages.

She rolled on nude lace-topped stockings, struggling to see over the cartoon cleavage she'd given herself, and hooked them into place. On top went a new slinky skirt, slit from ankle to mid-thigh, a fitted emerald green shirt, unbuttoned low, and the green strappy shoes.

She had just applied the lipstick, squirt of perfume and checked herself approvingly in the mirror when the doorbell rang. A shot of excitement hit her and she raced down the stairs.

She opened the front door and there he was, still eat-me-with-a-spoon handsome.

'Hello!' She leaned in close to kiss him on both cheeks. 'Lovely to see you.'

'Hi, you look stunning,' he said with a grin, closing the door behind him.

So did he. She'd never seen him out of a suit before, but here he was in cords with an open-necked shirt which showed his smooth olive skin. His hair was longer than usual with a hint of curl and he had a soft navy jumper tied over his shoulders.

'Come in.' She led him into the sitting room.

Chris handed her a bunch of heavy pink roses and a bottle of champagne, so cold the glass was wet. It slid a little in her hand.

'Thank you, you're such a gentleman. Shall we?' She waggled the bottle at him.

'I think so.' He raised his eyebrow, smiled and they held each other's gaze for a long moment.

She watched him peel off the foil and put deft thumbs to the cork. He nudged it out slowly and it made an expensive pop.

'Glasses?' he asked.

'Oh yeah.' She went to get champagne flutes from the kitchen, then curled herself into the sofa, putting her green-sandalled feet up, and watching him carefully pour out their drink.

They clinked glasses and sipped, then he sat down on the other side of the L-shaped sofa, within touching distance of her feet.

'I love your hair,' he said.

'Thanks.'

'Susan knows I'm here tonight,' he said, surprising her.

'Oh really? What did she say?'

'She wants a full report on what your plans are. She knows you're not working. Well, she thinks she'd know about it if you were.'

'And what are you going to tell her?'

'Whatever you want me to, boss,' Chris answered.

Bella took a deep sip from her glass and lit up a cigarette. 'D'you want one?' she asked.

'Think I will, actually.' She tossed him the packet, liking the fact that he smoked only very occasionally, just to keep her company.

As she sat up to light him, he leaned his face close over her hands, so she could feel his warm breath on her fingers. She had to stop herself from touching him.

'So . . .' he said blowing smoke out, 'what are you going to do next?'

'I'm figuring it out,' she answered.

'What do you want to do, Bella?'

'Well, a three-day week for a start,' she said. 'But a three-day week that doesn't kill off all my prospects – something lucrative, but a bit more worthy, and something that feels as if it has a future. I'm sick of batting from contract to contract.'

'That's quite a long list,' he said.

'Every problem can be solved if you spend long enough trying to find the solution,' she said, aware that she didn't have much longer to solve this at all.

'Well . . . I'm looking forward to it,' he said,

then asked: 'What do you want me to tell Susan?'

'That I'm sorry we fell out and I'll be in touch with her soon, when I've got a clearer idea of what I'm going to do next,' Bella replied, deciding it might be a good thing to mend some bridges. 'Will she be OK with that?'

'Yeah.'

They talked animatedly on the sofa, Chris filling her in on all the latest work news, and when the champagne bottle was empty, she took him downstairs for some food.

'What a great kitchen,' Chris said as he stepped down the final stair into the cosy cavern Bella had laboured to create.

The table was laid with crystal glasses, candles and flowers. The lighting was low and the garden lights were on, making the room look far bigger and more glamorous than it really was.

'Thanks . . . take a seat, open another bottle.' Bella handed him the wine and served the first course.

They ate slowly, still talking about work and office gossip. The wine bottle was already two-thirds down and it occurred to Bella that she hadn't drunk this much for over a year, but she felt fine. She felt good.

'I'm not feeling very hungry,' she told Chris. 'Shall we have another cigarette?'

Conspiratorially they lit up together, giggling about it: 'This is what I call the inter-course cigarette,' she joked, feeling herself slip into full on flirt mode.

'We need more wine,' he said and got up to get a bottle from the fridge.

'Oh my God, how come I don't feel drunk yet?'

she asked when she'd got through another large glassful.

'Maybe you're having too much fun,' he answered, tilting his head so a thick lock of black hair bounced down over his forehead and for a moment, she felt slain with lust.

'Are you trying to get me drunk, Chris?' she asked when the power of speech had returned.

'No, no, no,' he was smiling at her. 'Although you're very nice drunk.'

'Oh boy.' She smiled back at him.

'You always know when you really, really fancy someone, because the most unappealing things about them become sexy,' he said, topping up their glasses again.

'Such as?' She knew this was dangerous, dangerous water, but she had her boots on and was wading on out there.

'I'm feeling really quite turned on by those damp patches on your blouse,' he said.

She looked down to see two large wet marks, where her breasts had leaked, and burst out into shrieks of laughter. He began to laugh too and for a few moments, they were overcome with hilarity.

That was when she realized how pissed she was.

'OK, your turn,' he said when they had calmed down a little. 'What's the least appealing thing about me?'

She looked at him closely, trying not to giggle. Two of his white front teeth were snagged . . . adorable. He had a bristling middle eyebrow . . . gorgeous. She looked at him for a very long time and couldn't see anything to complain about.

'You see,' he said finally. 'You really fancy me.'

'Yeah,' she answered.

He leaned over and kissed her hard on the mouth. She opened her lips and let him, thinking only about how strange and interesting a different mouth is, when you've been with one person for so long.

The kiss went on and on. Her eyes were tightly closed and their knees were bumping together. She felt his arms around her lifting her to her feet so they could get closer. He risked pulling her in tightly to him, so she could feel how turned on he was.

Finally, he broke off and looked at her, seeing how pink and swollen her lips were already from the intensity of the kissing.

'Are you OK with this?' he asked.

'Oh yeah,' she whispered and latched onto his mouth again. Then she kissed his neck and felt his pulse throbbing under her lips.

'Where do you want this to go?' she heard him ask.

'The bedroom,' she answered, the head rush of lust and alcohol ruling out any indecision.

They moved up the kitchen stairs and in the hall they kissed, licked and touched each other all over again. He undid the buttons of her blouse and let it fall to the floor. He pushed a nipple out of the tight lace bra and put his mouth against it. Licking round it and biting on the very tip, he whispered: 'It tastes sweet.'

She crashed a kiss onto his mouth and to her horror, he lifted her up and ran to the stairs.

'Chris!' she cried. 'You can't do this!'

She closed her eyes and tried to enjoy the ride.

Chris was struggling as they got to the top of the steps and she had fallen so low in his arms, he was practically dragging her up. He stumbled and fell on top of her.

'Ouch,' she giggled as she lay under him.

'God, sorry.' He saw she was OK and locked his mouth on top of hers. Kissing him hard, she reached for his belt and fumbled to unbuckle it, then unzipped his trousers and felt for his cock.

He put his hands on her thighs under her skirt, then hooked his fingers round her pants and peeled them down her legs. He placed one hand over her naked crotch and held it still, so she could feel the heat radiating from his palm. On the brink of distraction that he wasn't moving it, wasn't feeling her, she pushed down into his hand, meltingly wet.

Their lips were locked together and both her hands were stroking his cock, feeling the long hardness of it, rubbing against the rim and the little opening at the top.

'Come to my room,' she whispered. Of course she'd said 'my room', the thought flickered through her mind.

'Is that OK?' Chris whispered back.

She stood up and led him in by the hand, her heart thudding in her chest.

The room was lit only by the street lamp outside the window, the curtains hadn't been drawn. Snowy new sheets, duvet and pillows were piled up on the iron bed.

Bella pulled off her skirt and sat down in bra, stockings, suspenders and high heels. She enjoyed seeing the effect this had on him. He tugged off his clothes, not taking his eyes from her. Bella looked at the smooth, hairless chest, firm stomach and quivering cock.

Chris knelt at the edge of the bed and pulled her hips to his face.

She closed her eyes and lay back, letting him bury his face between her legs. She could feel herself coming almost immediately, but it didn't do anything to slake her thirst.

'Please fuck me,' she said.

'Do you have anything?' She could hear the urgency in his voice.

'Table beside you, top drawer,' she said.

He pulled out the drawer and found the packet of condoms, open with several left inside. He tore one open and slid it into place.

'You'll need the KY too,' she said, then added: 'Stitches,' by way of explanation.

'Oh,' he said and fumbled for the tube. He squeezed some out into his hand and rubbed it over his condomed penis, which was not quite as hard as it had been.

She stretched out her arms for him and he wondered where to wipe his jellied hand.

He placed it down on the duvet and tried a surreptitious wipe as he carefully crawled up towards her, covering her body with his.

After a long, probing kiss, he noticed how still she was lying, underneath him. He opened his eyes and looked at her face. She was looking at him very seriously. The desire and the drunkenness which had spurred her on to do this was fast dissolving and she was left feeling very naked under a strange body.

'Oh dear,' he said and rolled off onto his side. He propped his face up on one hand and looked at her, lying on her back on the big bed. They were both suddenly very sober and very serious.

'It's OK,' he said.

'It's not OK, it's not OK at all . . .' she sounded angry. 'I thought this would make me feel better, but it doesn't.'

'I'm really sorry, this is my fault,' he said. 'I feel like I've taken advantage of you.'

'No, no.' She was surprised to feel tears forming in her eyes. 'No. I think I meant this to happen . . . I'm really frightened that Don's having an affair. And I somehow thought if I could get even, it wouldn't hurt so much . . . And do you have to be so good-looking?' she added.

'I'm really sorry,' he said again and sat up on the bed.

She sat up too now. 'I've got to speak to him and find out what the hell's gone wrong with our marriage.' She was wiping tears from her face. 'I've been so down, it's hardly surprising he's gone off with someone else.'

'Hey, it can't be all your fault.' Chris put an arm round her, wondering distractedly how he was going to dispose of the condom scrunched up in his other hand.

She put her wet face on his bare shoulder and he felt her breasts brush his chest: 'I'm in love with you, Bella,' he said, taking himself completely by surprise – in fact he didn't even know if this was true.

'No you're not,' she said, but she looked up at him and gave a half-smile. 'You really care about me and you lust after me. And I feel the same about you.'

With some relief, he realized she was right.

'Shit,' she sighed. 'We really shouldn't have done this.'

'No,' he said. 'Well, we haven't . . . not technically. Actually I'm not sure I could have managed.'

'Attack of conscience?' she asked.

'Bella, I've got your husband's condom in my hand.'

Before she could even laugh in response to this, she heard a thin wail coming from next door.

They had woken the baby.

'Oh bugger,' said Bella, reaching for her dressing gown.

Chris stood up and turned away from her, suddenly self-conscious and needing to get back into his clothes. 'I should probably go,' he said.

'Are you sure?' she asked. 'There's lots of food downstairs.'

'Well . . .'

'Go and eat some of the curry, I'll settle Markie down then come and join you.'

Once her son was asleep again, she stripped off her underwear and stockings and let them fall in a heap on the bedroom floor, then in her dressing gown and slippers and went downstairs.

She ate a plateful of curry with Chris and they both drank water. Feeling totally sobered, they talked very safely about favourite curry recipes and cooking until it was time for Chris to call a cab and leave.

'Thanks for dinner,' he said at the door, putting a hand on her shoulder.

'Yeah, and the rest.' Bella gave a wan smile.

'It's OK.'

They kissed on the cheeks.

'I'm really sorry I've loaded all this on you,' she said. 'It's a good thing you're such a nice guy.' She gave him a grateful hug.

'It's really OK,' he said and kissed her forehead. 'Call me if I can do anything and call Susan soon. OK?'

'Yeah,' she said. 'You're a star.'

'Good night.'

'Good night.'

She locked the front door and stood alone in the hallway. God, she was exhausted. She decided to blow out the candles and go straight to bed. She could tidy up in the morning, she had nothing else planned.

In a light, dozing sleep very early the next morning, she thought she heard the sound of the front door unlocking.

She opened her eyes and looked at the alarm 5:41 a.m. She closed her eyes again then heard bags being set down in the hall.

BAGS!!!! Jesus Christ!

She was awake now, bolt upright in bed, her heart pounding. There was the rustle of a waxed coat being taken off and she heard the sitting room door creak open.

She knew what he would see in the sitting room – candles, flowers still wrapped in paper and two empty champagne glasses. She heard Don's heavy tread on the stairs down to the kitchen, where he would find the table still laid out with dinner for two, complete with lipsticked butts in the ashtray and too many empty wine bottles.

He was back in the hall now, probably picking up her blouse. Fuck, fuck, fuck . . . she heard him coming fast up the stairs, two at a time. Frozen to the spot, she saw her stockings and suspenders lying on the floor as the bedroom door swung open.

Chapter Forty-one

'What the hell is going on?' Don's face was stony white.

'Well . . . well . . .' she answered, trying not to panic, 'I was about to ask you the very same bloody thing.'

'What the hell does that mean?' he shouted.

She stared at him in silence.

'Who the fuck was here last night?' he asked.

'And why would you care?' she answered.

'I'm your husband, in case you hadn't noticed.'

'Well, you certainly haven't been acting like one.'

'Just what the hell is going on, Bella?' he asked again. 'Your pants are hanging from the banisters.' His fury was barely under control, especially as he had just seen the pile of lace and stockings on the floor beside the bed.

'Well you start, Don. Did you have a nice little reconnaissance trip with Simone? Simone "you must be gasping for a grown-up shag" Sewell.'

'Jesus Christ, Bella.' For a moment, he looked like he might laugh.

She was slightly thrown off her stride by this.

'I finished with Simone when we met, you know that. But she's back over here, she works in my business, she's a die-hard flirt and you'll just have to live with it. I've made it clear to her I'm not interested.'

'Oh.'

'But just what have you been doing?' he stormed. 'Have you gone out of your mind?'

'Well, what the hell are you doing back anyway?' She threw the question at him, still avoiding his. 'You don't call for five days in a row then turn up on the doorstep.'

'Sorry to spoil your fun. I've just been airlifted out of a war zone by the UN. I thought you'd get a nice surprise!' he shouted.

'Oh.'

Don put his hands on his hips and squared up to her. He looked grey and exhausted, his black moleskin trousers were splashed with mud and his pale green shirt was stained, he hadn't shaved for days. But she saw only the man she loved most in the world and like a dreamer waking up to reality, she realized what a monumental mistake she had made.

'Your clothes are scattered all over the house, there's last night's candlelit dinner for two in the kitchen – am I going to get an explanation? And don't you dare lie to me.' She had never seen him so angry.

She hung her head, she couldn't face looking at him. 'Chris was here,' she said finally, 'We ... things got a bit ...' this was really hard. Fighting the lump in her throat, she said, 'I almost slept with him, but I changed my mind.'

Don turned his head towards the window and swallowed hard. He felt as if he had been kicked in the balls.

'Chris from work?' he asked.

'Yes,' she whispered.

Don folded his arms and kept his gaze fixed on the window.

There was a long silence. She looked up at him and was distraught to see that he was trying not to cry.

'It was a huge mistake,' she pleaded. 'I just felt lonely and unloved and unattractive and I thought you were sleeping with someone else and he seemed like the antidote. Don, I really miss you . . .' she broke off to choke down a sob. 'I miss the way we used to be.'

'Christ. I've got to get some sleep,' was his reply in a strained voice. He turned on his heel and walked out of the room. Bella could hear him take the stairs up to the attic. So he was going to sleep on the sofa up there. The hellishly uncomfortable sofa in that cold, unheated room.

She felt so sorry for him and so full of regret. For a moment she just wanted to howl, but then she decided not to give in to it.

She couldn't feel sorry for herself any longer, this was all her fault. She'd wanted the baby, she'd got pregnant without telling him, she was the one who hadn't been able to handle it all, she was the one who'd pushed Don away, read his mail, seduced Chris . . . JESUS. What a mess. She could hear Markie stirring in his room.

It was late afternoon before Don came downstairs. Bella had already tidied the house and taken Markie out to the park and the supermarket and come back home again. She was stacking the lunch dishes into the dishwasher and Markie was sitting in his high chair messing with the slop of food in front of him when Don came in.

'Hello,' Bella said.

Don didn't answer but bent over Markie in his chair. 'Hi there, little guy,' he said tenderly.

Markie stretched out his gooey hands towards him and Don looked touched.

'Are you eating yourself now? That's very clever.' He picked up Markie's spoon and scooped up a bit of the fruit purée.

'Bella. I've decided to move out for a bit,' he said as he guided the spoon into Markie's mouth.

Bella stood rooted to the spot.

'I think it will give us both some time to think things through and work out where we go from here,' he said.

'No, it will not give me time.' She was furious with him for this. 'It leaves me stuck with the baby 24 hours a day.'

'So, maybe you'll finally sort out some childcare,' he shot back.

'And just where are you planning to go?' she asked.

'To Mike's place, he's got a spare room, it's fine with him.'

How dare he sound so calm about this. 'How is moving to a bachelor pad with your mate going to solve our marital problems exactly?' she demanded.

413

'Well, maybe you should have thought of that before you shagged your boss,' was his furious reply. 'I don't think solving problems was top of your agenda last night, was it?'

'Well, it certainly solved a few problems,' she shouted back.

'And what's that supposed to mean?'

'Oh never mind . . . just walk out Don, just turn your back on me and on your son. Go on, just pack your bags and leave – I hope it makes you feel a whole lot better. You're just selfish and immature and totally unable to deal with any responsibility.'

'What about you?' he shouted back. Markie was staring at them without making a sound. 'You're such a control freak, you can't trust anyone else to take care of our son, yes *our* son . . . not even me . . . no-one else is good enough. What are you going to do, Bella? Look after him every single day until he's torn from your arms to go to school?'

'Just shut up!' she screamed. 'Just shut up and leave us alone.'

'I'll be back tomorrow afternoon to see him. You are not going to take him away from me, Bella.' Don's voice was more controlled and threatening now.

He turned out of the room and headed upstairs, leaving Bella to collapse into the chair beside Markie.

The baby was laughing now, this had all been a big dramatic show for him, not a frightening scene.

'I'm sorry,' she whispered to him, picking up the spoon and feeding him some more. 'I'm so sorry.' Tears were pricking her eyes but she didn't want to cry until Don was out of here.

Ten minutes later, she heard him in the hallway.

'Three p.m. tomorrow, you better let me see Markie or I warn you, Bella, I'm calling a solicitor,' he said loudly from the top of the kitchen stairs.

She didn't answer. The front door slammed shut heavily. Jesus Christ, how had it come to this? She picked her baby up out of his high chair and cuddled him close while her tears fell freely.

The day dragged on and on after that. Markie's routine – changing, feeding, walk, nap, changing, feeding, bath – meant she had to keep going but she felt as if she could break down hysterically at any moment.

God, she had to get out of here, out of this house where everything had gone so wrong. She had fucked everything up – her career, her marriage . . . and how would all this affect her son? She was probably going to fuck him up too. She slapped her hand against the wall, furious with herself.

She had to get out of here.

Markie was clean and fed, it was 7.30 p.m. so he was getting sleepy. She wrapped him up warmly in snowsuit and blankets and put him in the buggy with the raincover over. She put on her thick winter coat and they headed out.

The street was dark and slick with light rain, but glowing orange in the street lamps.

She walked to the end of the road and wondered what the hell to do. Go to a pub? Were babies allowed? Go somewhere in the car? Where? Where? Where? Christ, she felt on the brink of insanity. If she'd been on her own, she would race off in the car and drink herself to oblivion somewhere very chic and expensive. But she was stuck.

She found herself trudging off in the direction of Red's house, not sure if she really wanted to ring Red's bell at this time of night and dump all this on her. It wasn't like they even knew each other well.

But she didn't really know who else to turn to. Tania had never called to make up . . . Jenna was on the other side of the planet . . . Mel and Lucy wouldn't understand . . . Chris was a whole load of trouble. Jesus. And she never ran into anyone else now that she'd moved. Red was the only person she knew round here.

Christ, no wonder mothers ended up on Prozac and Valium. Did everyone think they'd vanished off the face of the planet just because they'd stopped working and hanging out in bars?

She was in Red's street. She looked down at Markie, who was mesmerized by the streetlights. He was wonderful now. The long, inexplicable screams had finally worn off and he was a giggly delight to have around with his boundless wonder at the world. The lights were on at Red's so she took a deep breath and rang the doorbell.

There was a long wait before Sandy answered the door.

'Hello,' he said with a hint of surprise in his voice.

'Hello,' she said. 'I know it's probably not a good time, I was just passing and wanted to say hello . . . is Red . . . I mean, if she's . . . ?'

'Come in, come in – it's always a good time.' Sandy cut her off.

'Red!' he bellowed from the door. 'It's Bella.'

Bella was just grateful he'd remembered her name.

416

Red called down from upstairs: 'Hello Bella! Sandy, come up and take over, will you?'

He bounded up the stairs and a few moments later Red came down, damp and dishevelled.

'Hi – rescued from bathtime – how nice!' she said, swooping down and kissing Bella on the cheek. 'Your hair looks fantastic, by the way.'

'Thanks,' said Bella. 'Just send me away if it's not a good time.'

'You're fine, let me take your coat, come in. Hello, Markie,' she said peering through the raincover.

Bella followed her into the kitchen, which was as cheerily chaotic as before.

'Tea, coffee or no, let's have wine,' Red smiled and held up an already opened bottle of white.

'Good idea.' Bella unstrapped Markie from the buggy and sat down, holding him on her knee. He immediately put out his hands to reach for the toy cars on the table.

'So, how've you been?' Red asked, bringing out glasses.

'Dreadful, couldn't be worse.' Bella said this with a sort of manic smile.

'Oh dear.' Red sat down and poured. 'What's happened?'

'I'm totally depressed, I've fucked up my career and slept with one of my bosses . . . well as good as . . . and now my husband's found out and left.' She had no idea why she was smiling at Red as she told her this.

'Ah,' Red took a deep sip of the wine. So did Bella.

'So . . .' Red said after a while, 'what are you going to do now?'

417

'Well, I was planning to wallow in self-pity for a bit,' Bella answered.

'No, you'll just get even more depressed. How bad is it on the husband front? Has he really gone? Or can you sort things out? I mean, do you want to sort things out?' Red asked.

'Yeah,' Bella said quietly, 'I really do. But I don't know what he's thinking.'

'When did all this happen?'

'Well, he left today,' Bella sighed and hoped she wasn't going to cry again.

'Oh boy,' said Red. 'You probably both need to cool down a bit.'

'Things just haven't been the same between us since Markie was born,' Bella said.

Red snorted: 'Of course they haven't. There's a big, crying, needy baby between you.' She smiled at Markie, who giggled back at her. 'Isn't there?' she said to him. 'You've got to adjust . . . it takes ages. I used to keep a bag packed under the bed all the time when Jamie was tiny, I was so fed up.' She laughed at the memory of it. 'And the one time I did actually run off to my mum's, she sent me straight back, bless her.'

'Red, I don't think I'm a very nice person,' Bella blurted out. 'I don't think I deserve Don, or Markie, or my brilliant career . . . well the one that I had.' She gave a half-smile, but now she really wanted to cry, or at least smoke.

'Oh boy,' Red topped up Bella's wine glass. 'Don't be ridiculous. You must have worked so hard to get your job and I know how well you've been looking after Markie. Now you just need to turn your attention to Don and yourself. Be nice to yourself.'

'I don't know what there is to like about me.' Bella put her nose on top of her son's head and felt a tear slide down her face, she watched it glistening on top of Markie's hair.

'Bella!' Red was smiling warmly at her. 'When you first burst into that yoga class, you were this sort of infectious surge of energy and determination . . . and you're funny and lovely looking . . . everyone wants a piece of you. You're just a bit down and worn out. You need time and rest and a bit of inner peace, man.'

Bella smiled back at her, lump-in-the-throat grateful for this pep talk. 'I'm very glad I met you,' she said. 'You're so together.'

'Well, thanks but don't beat yourself up about it, it's taken me three years to sort the motherhood thing out . . . a bit . . .' Red drained the last of the wine into their glasses, then got up to look for another bottle.

'What do you really want to do next? Have you thought about it?' she asked.

'Yeah, endlessly,' Bella answered. 'It goes batting round and round my head. I know what I want, I just can't figure out how to get it – a part-time job which somehow pays more than my last one, and is going somewhere, really nice childcare for Markie . . . oh and I want him to sleep through the night and only breastfeed twice a day. Then I want Don back the way he was before we had Markie, but also a devoted father.' Bella gave a small laugh. 'Bit of a long list.'

'Not really,' said Red. 'Don probably doesn't want anything radically different – you back the way you were, working, more available to him, but also a devoted mother. Think of all you've been through as . . . adjusting.'

'But I don't know if he'll forgive me for what I've done,' said Bella.

'Was it a one-off, one night stand?' Red asked.

'Emmm . . . kind of. In my head it was,' Bella answered.

'Well, all you can do is try and explain that to Don.'

There was a pause.

'How long have you been married?' Bella asked.

'Oh for ever,' Red said. 'Six years now. And some things get easier and some get harder,' she added. 'Actually, I think being married and having kids is a lot like eating a healthy diet and going to the gym – you know it's really good for you, but sometimes it's completely dull and you can't be bothered.'

They both laughed at this.

'But it's really hard to get it all right,' Bella said. 'You just need to take your eye off the ball and the whole thing messes up.'

'Mmm,' Red nodded. 'And admit to me, before you were married, you had the lovely wedding fantasy, didn't you . . . You in the dress and flowers and the handsome man at the altar?'

Bella was smiling and nodding.

'Then,' Red continued, 'as soon as that ring was on your finger, I bet you started having the funeral fantasy? You know, the one where you're in a beautiful black suit with a hat and a veil and you're devastated but still young and . . . free!!'

Bella was open-mouthed, feigning indignation: '*Red!!* I can't believe I'm telling you this, but . . . *yes!*'

They collapsed into giggles.

'I suppose it's just human nature,' Bella said finally. 'That grass is greener feeling.'

'Count your blessings, child,' Red said, putting on a voice. 'That's what my mum always said and she had a point. Anyway,' she added, 'I can help with baby things. You can pump me for advice on that.'

So they talked weaning, sleeping through the night and childcare for a bit and Bella agreed to go and meet Red's childminder.

Sandy appeared at the door: 'Red, the babies want a night-night kiss from you.'

'OK.' She stood up. 'Have another glass of wine, Bella, I'll be down in a second.'

'No, it's OK,' Bella stood up as well. 'I've really got to go, get Markie to bed.' He was dozing, almost asleep in her arms.

'What time does he usually go?' Red asked.

'Eight-ish, so this is late for him.'

'OK, well I'm coming round at seven tomorrow so we can sort the sleeping problem out.'

'Oh God.'

'Trust me, I'm a mother!' Red laughed.

The three of them said their goodbyes and Bella headed home wishing she'd accepted Sandy's offer of a lift as the rain began to beat down heavily. She ran the final lap to the house, bouncing Markie about in his buggy. She was soaking wet and laughing when she got into the hallway and feeling much better for the evening out of the house.

When Markie was tucked up in bed, Bella tried to

call Don. She dialled his mobile number and it rang for a few moments but then clicked onto voicemail.

'Don, hon, I'm really sorry,' she said. 'I love you . . .' At a loss for anything else to add, she put the receiver down.

Chapter Forty-two

Red's childminder Sylvia was lovely, as Bella found out when she went round the next day.

Ellie was already there, crawling after a squeaky ball, and Markie wriggled about in Bella's arms until she put him down on the floor, so he could try to crawl after it too.

Sylvia wanted two babies to look after, she said, because they could play together and keep each other company.

'I just want to do one or two mornings a week to start with,' Bella said, barely believing she would be able to do it, leave her son here with this woman who seemed nice but was still a stranger.

'We'll start gradually, that's no problem, you just arrange the hours and pay the hourly rate – then we'll all be happy, won't we?' Sylvia directed this question at Markie who was now up again bouncing happily on her knee. 'When do you want to start?' she asked with a smile.

'Errrr . . . shall I bring him for two hours tomorrow and you can see how you get along,' Bella heard herself say . . . thinking, Oh God, what am I doing?

'Yes, that's fine.'

When she left Sylvia's, Bella felt a euphoric sort of panic. Oh my God, could she handle this?

As she was lifting the buggy up the stairs to her front door, her mobile went off. She scrabbled to get it out of the changing bag, hoping it would be Don.

It was.

'Oh hon,' she said, fumbling to open the door without tipping Markie down the stairs. 'I'm really sorry. I'm really, really sorry . . .' She pushed the buggy into the hall and sat down on the floor.

'Look,' Don said, 'I'm phoning because I'm not going to be able to come today.'

'OK,' Bella said, dreading that this meant he didn't want to see her yet.

'My stupid, stupid fucking job,' he said angrily. 'I was supposed to get some leave, but I've now been given this piece of crap to chase down on the south coast for a couple of days.'

'Oh,' she said, feeling a crash of disappointment. He was going away again, they weren't going to see each other for days and they wouldn't be able to sort anything out.

'I'm still so angry with you,' Don added.

'I love you,' she said, 'I really love you, Don. I can't believe how stupid I've been.' She was close to tears now, he could hear it. 'I couldn't bear to lose you hon, please . . .'

He gave a long sigh, then said: 'I'm going to stay away till the weekend. I think we both need the time to calm down and think things through.'

'If it's what you want,' she said. 'But promise me you'll come at the weekend.'

'OK.'

'Tell me about Markie,' he said, changing tack, 'I really miss him.'

'He's gorgeous,' she said, trying to swallow down her tears. 'He's wearing an adorable red cardigan and woolly hat. He's sitting up in his buggy looking at me. His eyes are going to be dark like mine, I'm afraid.'

'That's nice,' said Don, 'I like dark eyes.'

'I wish he'd got yours, I like yours best,' she said. 'And his new favourite toy is the bunch of house keys which is a bit scary because I keep thinking he's going to drop them in a drain when we're out.'

'We should leave some spares with your friend round the corner.'

'You are so sensible!' she managed a slight laugh.

'Just because you're such a wild child,' he said.

'Don, please, I'm never going to do anything like that again.'

There was a pause before he said, 'OK, I have to go, Bella. I'll call you and I'll be there at the weekend.'

'Take care,' she said.

'Bye,' he answered simply.

She clicked off the phone and unloaded Markie from the buggy, carrying him down to the kitchen. She still couldn't really tell what her husband was thinking. He was still angry, but she took the 'I like dark eyes' comment as a good sign. God listen to me, I'm like some stupid teenager, she thought.

She had mixed feelings herself – she wanted Don back, no doubt about that, but the Don who'd bought out a flower stall for her, who'd rushed her to the register office in a passionate leap of faith, who'd held onto her when she was giving birth and willed her to survive.

At 7 p.m. on the dot that evening, Red arrived to help put Markie to bed without a breastfeed. She had assured Bella that it could be done and he would sleep much better for it. But Bella didn't believe her.

'Hello,' Red breezed in with a kiss and a clinking carrier bag. 'Essential supplies,' she explained.

'My God, I feel like I'm letting a witch into my house,' Bella joked nervously. 'Are you going to put a spell on my son?'

'No!' Red snorted, following her into the sitting room. 'Trust me, I absolutely promise this will work, every night from now on.'

She slapped her coat over the back of a chair and put her bag up on the coffee table, spotting a framed photo there.

'God, your dad is so young looking . . . doesn't he look handsome holding Markie!' she said.

Bella laughed out loud. 'You are about to be so embarrassed!'

'No!! It's not?'

Bella nodded vigorously. 'Oh yeah.'

'Well he's very good-looking, but . . . er . . . quite a bit older than you.'

'Thirteen years,' Bella answered. 'He went grey really young, but I think it's sexy, obviously I have a father complex or something.'

'Right . . .' Red put the photo down and emptied out her bag of goodies: 'For you – a choice of comfort aids: bottle of red, a bottle of white, a family

426

pack of Pringles and ten Marlboro Lights, because I suspect you smoke, am I right?'

Bella nodded.

'Also some lavender oil, to keep both of you calm and finally –' Red fished the last thing from her bag – 'this is for you, Markie.' She pulled out a little beige towelling bunny with long, dangly ears.

'Thank you.' Bella was really touched by all this.

Markie grabbed the bunny with his hands and giggled.

'OK, we've got bath, feed and story time to fit in before bed at eight on the dot. Lead the way,' Red told Bella.

After his bath, Markie was breastfed downstairs on the sofa with the TV on loud and the lights turned up to ensure he didn't fall asleep.

Finally, he'd eaten his fill and was looking dopily tired.

'Now take him upstairs,' commanded Red. 'Read him a nice little book on your knee, then dim the lights, lie him in his cot with his little bunny and say "Good night" really nicely and *leave* when he's still awake. *And no cheating*.'

'He'll just howl the house down and I won't be able to stand it,' Bella insisted.

'We will not leave him, I promise. Trust me.'

'OK, OK, I'll give it a go, but I'm giving in if it gets too awful.'

'OK.'

When Bella settled Markie down in the cot, he kicked off his blanket with a giggle, and looked wide awake again. But she stroked his little forehead and said 'Night, night,' then stepped out of the room, leaving the light on low.

There was silence for a moment, then a surprised cry.

By the time Bella got downstairs to Red, muffled roars were coming from the baby monitor in her hand.

'OK.' Red pulled out an alarm clock from her coat pocket and handed Bella a glass of wine.

'Sit down here for two minutes, we'll time it, two minutes, that's all. Then you can go to the door of Markie's room and tell him it's OK, you're just downstairs, then leave.'

'Right,' Bella said dubiously.

She gulped at her wine then went upstairs again and did exactly as she was told. Markie stopped crying for the few moments she was at the door but bellowed with renewed vigour when she left.

'Bloody hell,' she told Red when she got back down. 'Do you really expect him to fall asleep like this?'

'He will, trust me.' Bella urged her to finish her wine, poured her another glass and opened the crisps. 'OK,' she said. 'You've got to wait five minutes now.'

Bella didn't feel she could argue.

They sat for five minutes, Bella slugging back the wine, munching the crisps absent-mindedly and staring grimly at the monitor. The row of green and red lights rose and fell on the monitor, Markie was screaming his head off.

'OK,' Red said as the clock hand nudged towards the five-minute mark. 'Just do exactly the same again, poke your head round the door and speak to him, then leave.'

Bella was shocked when she saw Markie this

time, he was bright red and his hair was matted to his head with sweat. He looked furious and didn't stop screaming when he saw her. She spoke as soothingly as she could, then came down the stairs quickly.

'Are you sure he's going to be OK?' she asked Red anxiously. 'He looks really hot.'

'He'll be fine, now light up,' Red said proffering a cigarette. 'You've got to deal with the full ten-minute wait this time.'

'Oh Jeez.' Bella drew in a deep breath of smoke. She fixed her eyes on the alarm clock, which seemed to be standing absolutely still.

'You're sure this is working?'

'The clock? Of course!' Red answered.

Somewhere around minute seven, Markie's cries began to grow a little bit less desperate, then abruptly they stopped.

Bella looked at the monitor. She went out into the hall . . . silence. What!? He must be lying in his cot wondering what to do next to get her attention.

Red looked at her and smiled triumphantly.

'He's going to start up again in a second,' Bella told her.

'He is asleep, fast, sound asleep,' said Red. 'Believe me, if he had an ounce of strength left, he'd still be bawling at the top of his lungs.'

Bella turned the monitor up to full volume: she could hear the quiet rustle of her son's breath.

'I don't believe it!' she was astonished that her baby could actually go to sleep without being breastfed, rocked, walked, patted or soothed in some way.

'And I bet he doesn't wake up again till the

morning,' Red said. 'Because he's learned to fall asleep without you.'

'In one lesson?!'

'Well, it might take a few nights, we'll see,' Red replied. 'Tomorrow night, just do the same and soon you'll be able to put him down without a squeak.'

'OK.' Bella was still unconvinced. 'Can I go and check him?'

'No! He's fine . . . OK, you can go in five minutes. Meanwhile, let's not waste the wine,' Red answered.

They drank the best part of the two bottles and Bella smoked seven cigarettes. OOPS. But it was a laugh. It was a girlie laugh, well more a mummy laugh.

They talked organic baby milks, stopping breast-feeding, favourite purées and Bella felt at least some of her anxieties about Markie were allayed.

Then they got more personal and talked about themselves. The origin of Red's unique colouring was explained: she was part Polish, part English with a generous measure of Jamaican.

'So,' Red topped up their glasses. 'When did you meet Don? And how?'

Bella told her, reminding herself what a whirl-wind romance it had been.

'God, you two didn't hang about, did you?' was Red's verdict.

'We just knew it was right and that we were ready . . . I suppose,' Bella answered, then stumbled on, 'Everything has always been really full-on between us. What's happening now is weird. I just don't know what he's thinking.'

'I really hope you guys will be OK,' Red said.

'Hmmm.' Bella took a long drag on her cigarette and thought about her husband. She *had* to get herself together and get him back.

It was time for Red to go. As she slipped on her coat, she asked: 'So is Markie going to Sylvia's tomorrow?'

'Yes . . . I think so.' Bella still wasn't sure if she could bring herself to do it.

'We have to go out, to distract you, otherwise you'll just sit here worrying about him and phoning Sylvia up every ten minutes to listen for wailing in the background.'

'Yes, I suppose you're right. Don't you have work?'

'I can make an exception.'

'Where can we go in two hours?'

'We'll go to the shopping centre and the market down the road,' answered Red.

Bella raised her eyebrows. She couldn't see any reason to go there.

'Bella! You've obviously been far too snobbish to notice the good stuff there,' Red teased her. 'It will be fun, I'll meet you at Sylvia's when you drop Markie off.'

They were at the door now. 'OK,' said Bella, 'I'll see you there, 10 a.m. tomorrow. Thanks for tonight, Red,' Bella said and kissed her on the cheek.

'I'm glad to help, OK!' Red smiled.

Chapter Forty-three

The sound of crying woke Bella – as it had done for the past seven months. She opened her eyes and looked at daylight filtering in through the white curtains. Daylight?!! She leaned over to look at the clock – 7.26 a.m.! She was waking up from the first full night's sleep she'd had since her son was born. Apart from the incredible weight of the full breasts lying on top of her chest like bricks, it felt *amazing*!

She went through to Markie's room and bent down to pick him up out of his bed. He smiled and giggled at her, stretching up his chubby hands. She took him back to bed with her and they curled up together, Markie latching on ravenously to feed.

He gazed up at her with his brow furrowed and she just adored him. This was the only time he lay quiet in her arms now, he had grown into such a wriggly, inquisitive little thing. She would miss feeding him so much.

She spent the next two hours in a mild panic – breakfast, changing, dressing, packing one hundred assorted bits and pieces into Markie's bag, so that he wouldn't be without his favourite drink, snack, toy, whatever else she thought he needed to survive two whole hours at Sylvia's without her. She packed a sheet of paper into his bag with her home number, her mobile, her bleeper, Don's mobile, Don's work number. You're being ridiculous, she kept telling herself. *Relax*.

Finally, they were ready to go. She whizzed Markie, his buggy and the bulging changing bag out of the door and over to Sylvia's house.

Red was there waiting for her and Bella was able to hand Markie over without feeling too awful about it. She babbled out a torrent of instructions to Sylvia about drink times and nap times, despite her impression that Sylvia was listening but probably not going to worry about it too much.

'She thinks I'm totally neurotic, doesn't she?' Bella asked Red as they walked away from the house.

'And who could blame her?' Red teased, then added: 'Don't be too hard on yourself. You'll learn to let go bit by bit.'

Bella fumbled in her handbag for a cigarette. She lit up and inhaled.

'Feel better?' asked Red.

'Yes, a bit. Do you fancy a drive to the high street?'

'Well, it's more environmentally friendly to walk – but if you really want to . . .'

Red was very impressed with Bella's car.

'God! How come I've never noticed this outside your house before?'

They climbed in and Bella revved the engine up.

By the time Bella was parking dextrously in the shopping centre car park, Red was talking about work.

'Couldn't you go part time, or work from home . . . set up on your own like I did?'

'Well,' said Bella as they headed down the grimy staircase towards the shops, 'these things are all possibilities, I'm just trying to get my head round them.'

'OK,' said Bella as they got to the bottom and surveyed the scene: stalls selling limp vegetables, a tatty supermarket, a branch of Woolworth's and a discount jewellers. 'Where do you want to go?'

'We're heading for the café, but not until we've trawled round the amazing clothes shops. Follow me!'

Bella wondered what the hell Red could mean. All she could see were the crappy cheap chains with prices plastered on the windows. Red was making a beeline for one of them. 'You cannot be serious,' said Bella.

'Come on!' said Red.

Once they were in, Red scanned the racks like a pro. 'OK Bella, we are finally getting you out of your leggings and rugby shirt and propelling you into the twenty-first century.'

Bella was looking through the stuff and laughing. 'Sequined denim?? You can't make me do this!'

'Look, perfectly acceptable grey combat trousers . . . £8 on the sale rail . . . padded waistcoat £12, T-shirts, a fiver, customized jeans, denim skirt . . . black three-quarter sleeved shirt . . . blah, blah, blah. Bella you are going to come out of here a new woman . . . for less than 50 quid.'

They went to the changing room with armfuls of stuff.

'Oh my God, it's a size 16,' wailed Bella pulling on a remarkably close-fitting shirt.

'The sizes are wincey here,' Red said. 'That's how they save money – use less material.'

'Yeah that and child labour in third world countries.'

'No, this lot are OK. The stuff's mainly made in Morocco and Portugal.'

'OK, well, I'm leaving my social conscience at the door. How come your stomach is so flat already?' Bella asked, eyeing Red up in the long, narrow mirror installed presumably to make women think they looked long and narrow too.

'Gym twice a week. I've gone since Ellie was tiny,' came the smug reply.

'Ah! I remember the gym. I still have membership for the really poncey one, down in Belsize Park.'

'Well, go!' Red replied. 'If you don't go when you stop feeding, you'll be tying your tits up in a bow. They'll have a crèche, you know.'

'Yeah, I know, I just couldn't bear to leave him in there.'

'But you're getting over that, aren't you? Looks very good,' Red nodded at Bella in the sporty, grey trousers and a tight red long-sleeved T-shirt with a flower on the front.

'Is it mutton dressed as the proverbial?'

'*No*! It's Seattle fashion . . . downsized, home-worker, computer nerd. You've got to get some trainers.'

'What about this?' Red asked, modelling a

435

spray-on denim skirt embroidered with multi-coloured flowers. 'Hot off the catwalk. This is real designer diffusion . . . never mind DKNY, Emporio and all that . . . they're just trying to keep up. This stuff is knocked off and in the shops three days after the shows.'

'How do you know all this?' said Bella, trying on a fuzzy white zip-up jacket made of long curls of acrylic wool: 'Ha ha, look at this. Outrageous!' she laughed.

'This chain is my biggest client,' Red answered her.

'Really!'

'The chief exec made almost a million last year on bonuses alone.'

'Wow. Do you get a discount?' Bella joked.

She liked all the shiny anorak fabric stuff. She was thinking how wonderfully wipe clean it would be and went for it big time, deciding on a pair of beige trousers, the grey ones and a long black skirt, all in the same shiny, crackly stuff with drawstrings and plastic buckles.

Then she got three long-sleeved T-shirts with wild designs on the front and a short silvery grey anorak lined with fleece. Red made her buy an over the shoulder rucksacky thing, teasing her that a mock croc kelly bag just wouldn't go with her new outfits.

The total bill was less then a week's groceries, so Bella paid without any accompanying feelings of guilt.

'Boots next,' said Red, who'd bought a couple of tops.

They went to Boots and browsed about the make-up stands like schoolgirls.

'You can't buy red nail polish. It's the most boring shade in the world,' Red insisted.

'Well, I'm not buying green!' said Bella.

'Why not?'

'It's so teenage.'

'So? You're only late twenties, not 100. You don't need to wear camel and dress like your mother just yet.'

'Hmmm. Well what about silver grey? It will go with my anorak.'

'I think there's a daring side to your nature just waiting to be unearthed.'

'No, believe me, I've spent years trying to bury it.'

'Really! But you always look quite . . . conservative.'

'Yeah, fashion was never my thing, just recreational drugs and casual sex.'

'Maybe you should channel your need to shock into something a little less harmful.'

'Like green nail polish?'

'Try it!' Red laughed.

There was time for coffee in an organic, vegetarian, ceramic mug kind of place tucked round the back of the centre which no, Bella had never noticed before.

'I usually do Mothercare and the cute little baby shop, then I'm out of here.' Her face suddenly looked pained.

'Stop it,' said Red sipping her frothy coffee. 'You were thinking about Markie, weren't you?'

'Yes, but only because I haven't thought about him since we got here.'

'Good.'

'But I haven't even been to the baby shop,' Bella said, picking her phone out of her bag and double-checking for messages.

'They are fine,' Red said firmly.

And when Bella was back at Sylvia's house thirty-five minutes later, it was obvious that Red was right. Markie was fast asleep in his buggy and Ellie was playing with the baby Lego in the middle of the sitting room floor.

'He's been good as gold,' Sylvia told her.

Bella wheeled Markie home while Ellie stayed on with Sylvia because Red had gone home to do some work.

Work . . . Bella mused to herself as she pushed her sleeping baby along the road . . . work?? She couldn't deny she was a bit jealous of Red. She would be sitting in her little office, making calls, using all those cool, logical parts of her brain and earning *money*.

A whole massive part of the stress situation with Don would be eased if she was earning a good whack again. The overdraft was beyond maximum and realistically, if she didn't have a job very, very soon, they would have to put the house on the market. That thought instantly depressed her.

She got in, unzipped Markie's coat and loosened his hat, then left him to doze in the hall.

She took the bags from the morning's shopping trip upstairs and decided to cheer herself up with a quick try on. On went the long skirt, with the deep slit up the front, then she pulled on socks and her gym trainers and one of the new long-sleeved T-shirts. She put the silver anorak on top and laughed at herself in the mirror.

It was very different, but comfortable and kind of cool – she looked at her old clothes lying in a heap on the floor – why had she skulked about in that crap for so long?

Internet geek chic. She looked in the mirror and Red's comment about it being the ultimate diffusion fashion came to mind.

Diffusion, brand names for less . . . internet chic. She had the strange, exhilarating feeling that something was coming together in her head . . . then bing! The pieces slid into place and she had the most amazingly good idea.

'Oh my God!' she said out loud. 'That's it! That is it! Brilliant!'

She sat down on the bed and her thoughts raced. It was so good her hands were trembling and it could not wait. She picked up the phone and speed-dialled three.

A very familiar voice answered: 'Good afternoon, Prentice and Partners, Kitty speaking, how may I help you?'

'Kits!' she almost shouted.

'BELLA! Hello, how are you?' Kitty answered excitedly, then in a whisper added: 'What's happened Bella? No-one will tell me anything. I've just got to say you're unavailable for work right now.'

'You could have phoned!'

'Yeah, well, but I didn't want to impose.'

'*Impose*! I'm rattling round the house with a new baby staving off nervous breakdown central and you're worried about imposing! Jesus, Kitty. What would the sisterhood say?'

'God, I'm sorry, Bella. I never thought about it like that.'

'Well . . .'

'Are you coming back?' Kitty cut in.

'We'll see. How is everyone anyway?'

'Good, same as usual, we've got a new girl and she's a total bitch, 24 or something.'

'Hector isn't a partner, is he?' Bella tried not to squeak.

'Oh God no, he got a written warning from Susan last week.'

'Really?' This was good. She suddenly realized how much she'd missed them and all the daily intrigue.

'How is Susan . . . and Chris?' Poor old Chris.

'Susan is pining for you, I think.' Kitty's voice was conspiratorially low. 'Chris is really quiet, maybe he's pining for you too!'

'I miss you all, as well,' said Bella, feeling a rush of guilt about Chris.

'How's your little son?' Kitty asked.

'Oh he's great. Anyway, I want to see Susan, but turn up kind of unannounced, when she's there and not seeing anyone else.'

'Well . . .' she could hear Kitty tapping her way through Susan's agenda, 'your best bet is early morning, Thursday or Friday.'

'OK, well I think Friday will be best. Will you ring me if anything changes and she's not available then?'

'Yeah sure. But *tell me* . . . what is this about?'

'I can't . . . not just yet. But I promise, you'll be the first to know if Susan goes for it.'

'Bella!'

'I have to go now. See you Friday.'

'OK, be like that then! Bye.'

'Bye.'

Bella took a deep breath and speed-dialled four. There was something else she really had to sort out as well. The ringing tone hummed in her ear, twice, three times, she could feel her resolve draining away, maybe this wasn't a good time . . . maybe she would leave this till the evening.

But then there was a brisk 'Hello?' at the other end.

'Hello Tania, it's Bella.'

'Bella?! God . . . hello!' There was a tiny pause, so Bella launched in.

'I'm really sorry I was so awful, Tania. I don't know why it's taken me so long to phone you back. I'm really sorry.'

'I'm sorry too,' Tania said. 'Oh I'm so glad you've phoned. I wanted to phone too. It's OK, we were both very stressed bunnies . . . you with the baby, me with Greg.'

'Greg? What happened?' Bella asked.

'I can't believe you don't know about all this,' Tania replied.

'About all what?'

'He's married.'

'*What!!!?*'

'Yup,' Tania continued. 'All those weekends with his parents and not wanting us to live together . . . turns out he's already got a wife and three kids.'

441

'Oh my God!' Bella was stunned, even she hadn't seen that one coming.

'Yeah, I found out . . . well it's a bloody long story. I was phoning you that night to tell you how suspicious I was.'

'Oh God,' Bella cut in, 'I'm so, so sorry. I thought I had the biggest problems in the world at the time and obviously I didn't.' Christ, she thought, that was months ago. How had Tania got through all this without her? She was so angry with herself that she hadn't been there, hadn't been the shoulder for her friend to cry on.

'How are you doing?' Bella asked.

'Not too bad. I was miserable as sin for weeks. But on the up side I lost about a stone, so I look good. I just worked like a demon, which kept me busy, and redecorated the flat . . . and bought a new car.'

'No! Not a . . .'

'A brand new, shiny red Ferrari.' Tania cut in.

'Cow!' said Bella then added sincerely, 'I can't believe you didn't phone me.'

'I couldn't handle it, Bella – there you are all married and happy and babied up and I'm starting out single *again*.'

'Oh yeah,' said Bella. 'It's been bliss all the way. I resigned from my job, Don and I are having a trial separation, we're practically broke, but thank God, thank God, my son is finally sleeping through the night.'

'*What*?' It was Tania's turn to be shocked.

'Yeah, it's this amazing thing where you put them in bed awake and they cry at first but then they fall asleep by themselves and . . .'

442

'Not the *baby*!' Tania was practically shrieking now. 'You and Don are separated??'

'Yeah, but hopefully not for long. It's been really, really stressful and I kind of slept with my boss but I hope he might forgive me . . .'

'What! Slow down, you're babbling, girl.'

'Do you have time for the whole thing?'

'Well if you could give me the short version now, then maybe we could meet on Saturday and you can tell me the full saga.'

After Bella's quick outlining of events, they arranged to meet on Saturday morning.

'At the gym please,' Bella said. 'I have to go back there, I still look like a blancmange.'

'Ha, ha, ha, ha – I'm slim and slinky,' sang Tania. 'It's role reversal time.'

'Double cow! What's the point in being friends with you if you're going to look better than me?' Bella said, delighted that she and Tania were straight back in best friend mode again.

'*Bitch*!' Tania shrieked. 'Get your flabby arse in gear. No wonder your man's looking elsewhere.'

'He's not!' Bella screamed down the phone. 'I'm the one who looked and I didn't like what I saw . . . well actually, it wasn't bad . . .'

'Bella! You are a mother now. You have to behave responsibly,' Tania said in mock-shock.

'I'm dying to see you,' Bella replied. 'Shall we say 10.30ish? We'll do a class, then sauna, then long lunch?' She was thinking, Four hours away from my son . . . I can cope, I will cope. Don can look after him . . . he can cope, he will cope . . .

'Perfect. I'll see you there.'

'Tania, I've really missed you,' Bella said.

'Me too,' Tania answered. 'Let's be best friends for ever and ever.'

'OK,' Bella laughed. 'See you Saturday.'

'Byeee.'

Chapter Forty-four

Don called at nine-ish as he had done every evening since he'd left the house. The calls were short and they mainly talked about Markie, who was a neutral, safe topic.

It was the third time she'd put Markie to bed without a breastfeed and he had only cried for seven and a half minutes.

'I'm sleeping like a dog,' she told Don. 'I go to bed at ten and don't wake up until Markie stirs at seven, it's just bliss. I feel like a normal, sane person again, it's amazing.'

'Are you still breastfeeding?'

'Yeah, three feeds a day, which is really nice for us.'

'Good, and the childminder is working out OK?'

'She's really lovely. She's going to take him for two full mornings tomorrow and Friday.'

'Wow, what have you got planned?'

'Totally top, top secret. I'll tell you about it on Saturday. You are going to come on Saturday, aren't you?'

'Yes,' he said and didn't elaborate.

'I'm planning to go to the gym in the morning to meet Tania, because I thought you'd want some time on your own with Markie and then hopefully he'll sleep in the afternoon and we'll be able to talk a bit.'

'That's fine, Bella,' he said, then added: 'You're going to the gym? To meet Tania? Well . . .' he'd been about to say 'you're almost back to your old self' but checked himself. There wasn't any going back, she was becoming her new self. Bella with baby. He wasn't sure how he fitted into that yet, but that was what they had to work out.

'Is that OK?' she asked, as he'd paused for a long time.

'It's fine, it's good. I really miss Markie,' he said. 'I can't wait to see him.'

'Yeah.' She decided not to add 'I really miss you' because if he didn't say it back, she would be heart-broken.

'OK,' he said. 'I better go then, good night, Bella.' She detected a vein of tenderness in those words which comforted her.

'Good night, hon.'

She clicked off the phone and wandered upstairs to see her son. She tiptoed into the room and looked at him in the dim glow of the night light. He was on his side with his hands curled up in front of him, he felt warm and slightly damp to touch, still sweaty from his little cry at bedtime.

His chubby cheeks were rosy and impossibly long eyelashes curled down onto them. She listened to his gentle breathing and leaned over to inhale his sweet, warm butter smell. He was perfect. She'd never felt anything like this, so full up with love. It was calming and grounding and heart-expanding.

Somehow, there was going to be room in her heart for all this baby love and for Don too and for loving her job and her friends and, she really should face it, her parents.

She'd thought at first that Markie was going to use up all her love and there wouldn't be any left for anyone else. But she was learning that Markie had opened up the floodgates. She'd made this incredible amount of extra love in her life for him and now she was going to spread it about. Soften up a bit . . . smell the roses . . . hug trees.

She could feel her eyes grow dim and watery again. I'm turning into a complete sap, she thought . . . and I quite like it.

She stroked her little boy on the head then left the room.

Downstairs, she threw together a quick supper, then went up into the attic office taking her laptop with her. She had the plan, now she needed to research it.

Three hours later, she finally went to bed, tired but very excited. This was going to work.

The next morning Bella drove into town once she had dropped Markie off at Sylvia's. If she was to face Susan tomorrow, she needed to psyche herself up for it. She was going to present a radical new plan so she felt it was fitting to have a radical new image to go with it.

Combat trousers and kaleidoscope tops were fine for home, but the new work look was going to have to be a little more sober.

No more tight skirts, high heels, stockings and cleavage. What did she have to prove? She was married with a baby, she knew she was attractive and damn good at her job. It was time to get on with it. She now wanted sleek, streamlined, professional. There was no reason for her office clothes to 'work' at a cocktail party any more either. Once she'd put in the hours, she was going home.

Anyway, she was online, she was on the phone – why the hell did she need to be at the office all day long?

She put the car into an underground garage and headed out onto Regent Street. It was early December, cold but blue-skied and crisp and not quite ten o'clock, so the shop doors were only just opening and the pavements were quiet.

An hour later, after careful consultation with a good shop assistant, Bella had found exactly the right thing: a long, lean, light grey trouser suit, which looked perfect with her shorter hair. She looked at her reflection in the mirror and couldn't believe how much younger and fitter she looked. The suit shoulders were narrow and unpadded, the jacket skimmed down to mid-thigh and the trousers were fluid without being wide.

Underneath, she had on a grey knitted silk sleeveless top, cut straight at the top. No more cleavage but bare arms instead, it was still sexy but in a kind of sporty way. She decided on the same top in bottle green as well.

Her new coat was a black nylon mac, knee length with a tartan lining. Now she decided on a new briefcase as well – shiny nylon black, big enough for a laptop, mobile, car keys and a few nappies – what else did anyone need?

The whole lot was wrapped up for her in glossy

blue bags. She handed over her card without flinching because as of tomorrow she was going to have a brand new job. She was sure of it.

Several shops later and she'd bought two new pairs of shoes, futuristic loafers in black and grey leather with low, trainer-like moulded rubber soles – cool.

Then came new make-up: sludgy green eye shadow, brownish lipstick. Then new underwear. She explained the still breastfeeding situation to the assistant, who suggested a grey jersey crop top sports bra and matching hot pants.

Bella looked at herself in the mirror and began to see the outline of the figure she'd once had. The breasts were still over-heavy, but the tummy was diminishing. She would get there.

It was already heading for 12.30, so she had time for a quick sandwich before she raced back to Sylvia's for 1.30.

She spent the afternoon playing with Markie, then after she'd given him supper, a bath and tucked him up in bed, she got down to work again.

Poor old Susan, she had no idea what was about to hit her.

Chapter Forty-five

It was time to go for it, Bella told herself, as she strode up to the elevator, which would take her to Prentice and Partners for the first time in five months.

She punched the button and the doors pinged open. Once she was inside, she could feel her hands shaking slightly so she tightened her grasp on her briefcase and tried to slow her breathing right down. This was going to work, there was no way it couldn't.

Ping. She was out on the fourth floor lobby, she walked towards the glass double doors and could see Kitty taking off her coat on the other side. Bella smiled and tried to relax. This was her office, this was her job. It was going to be OK.

She stepped in, it was 8.25 a.m. so just Kitty and Susan should be around.

'Hello,' she said to Kitty.

Kitty looked up and stared: 'My God, you look completely different!'

'But good,' said Bella.

'Yes, very good. Very *moderne*. Gimme a hug, it's lovely to see you.'

They hugged and kissed.

'Is she here?' Bella said this quietly; she didn't want to spoil Susan's surprise.

Kitty nodded and picked up the phone.

'Hi, Susan,' she said. 'There's an unscheduled visitor here for you . . . but I'm pretty sure you'll want to see her.'

After a momentary pause, Susan's office door opened.

For a few seconds, her face registered just surprise, then she smiled, half held out her arms and said, 'Bella, my God. Welcome back!'

'Hang on a minute,' Bella grinned. 'I've just walked in the door. I think we might need to talk first.'

'Yes, of course, come in.' Susan motioned with her arms, then added: 'Kitty, can you bring us some coffee, please? And hold all my calls. Come in, Bella.'

Bella hadn't known what to expect from Susan, but this was a very good start.

She walked into the small office and was surprised to see it had been revamped. There was a compact desk at the window now, with a tiny laptop and silver mobile phone on top and below it nested a small set of sleek chrome drawers on wheels. The room was mainly taken up by three vast brown leather armchairs grouped around a low coffee table.

'It's the new, we're all equals, touchy-feely, twenty-first-century thing, do you like it?' Susan asked, pointing her into a chair.

'It's fab,' said Bella, sitting down in the squashy leather and feeling very at ease in her new clothes. No skirt to ride too high, no uncomfortable heels to hoick up her knees at an awkward angle.

'You look great,' said Susan, perching in her chair because of her skirt and heels. 'I love your hair . . . and is that *green* nail polish?'

'Yeah . . . thanks,' said Bella. She was wondering if she should apologize first or if Susan was going to.

There was a pause as the two women looked at each other and smiled.

'About the way I left . . .' Bella began. 'I am sorry about it, but I think I had a point. I'm not saying I was right, but I was making a point which you should have taken on board.'

'I think that's fair,' Susan replied. 'I didn't want you to go, I'm sorry I reacted so strongly. I don't want you to go, in fact I'd love to have you back.'

'I really want to be back, Susan,' Bella said. 'But not in my old role, I've changed too much.'

Susan didn't say anything; she was waiting for Bella to explain.

'I can't put the job first the way I did before,' Bella continued. 'I think that might be quite hard for you to understand. I mean, I want to do a really good job for you, but I don't want to rule the universe the way I did before.' They smiled at each other. 'My son comes first. If there's ever a choice between work and baby, he's going to win. But that shouldn't mean I can't work.'

Bella looked hard at Susan to try and read her reaction, then carried on with her pitch: 'I'm a very capable person, I've got a lot of ability I know you

452

can use for the hours in the week I'm willing to devote to work.'

Kitty knocked and came in with the coffee, which was perfect because Bella knew Susan was thinking hard about what she was about to suggest – and whatever scenario Susan was imagining, Bella knew her own plan would beat it right into the ground.

Kitty poured out two cups, saying, 'Nice shoes,' to Bella to break the silence.

'Thanks, they're my time management shoes,' Bella joked. 'Instead of going to the gym, I'm going to jog home from work.'

'So,' said Susan, once Kitty had closed the door, 'what have you got in mind?'

'I want to run the new Prentice and Partners internet arm.'

'Go on.' Susan's eyebrows were raised but she was listening.

'Your company is going to run the first on-line consultancy for small businesses. Turnover of less than 5 million a year.

'People will log on, answer a detailed question-naire and get an initial plan of action back from us – for free. If they want more advice, they can have consultancy sessions on-line or over the phone at an agreed rate.

'It's designer diffusion, the Prentice brand off-the-peg for the small guys who really need it. Obviously you can sell advertising on the site to tons of linked financial services – banks, lenders, insurers etc., etc.'

'Goodness,' said Susan raising her coffee cup. 'Do you think it will make money?'

'I'm willing to bet it will make pots of money,' said Bella, hardly able to contain her enthusiasm for the scheme. 'You'll have to employ new staff to keep up with the demand. It's the mass market, Susan, tens of thousands of small hits a year instead of five big deals. It's also incredible advertising for you. You're going to look like the most forward-thinking company in the game.'

'But we're giving out advice for free.' Susan almost winced at the thought.

'I know, scary concept, but the whole lure is that you get something really good for nothing, so you pay for more. Anyway, the advertising will pay for all the people who log on for the free stuff and then disappear.'

'Have you got a business plan for this?' Susan asked.

'Of course,' said Bella with a smile. 'I'll e-mail you.'

Susan laughed, then asked, 'How are you going to have time to run it?'

'Well, I've got a minder for Markie four mornings a week, when I'll log on and do most of the work, from home mainly,' Bella said. 'Because that gives me an extra ninety minutes of time I'd otherwise spend in the car.

'I can log on again in the evenings to keep on top of it and I'll meet people here in the office when it's needed, which isn't going to be more than a couple of times a month.'

'You've got it all figured out,' said Susan with a smile. 'Why do I feel as if I'm going to have to let you have a go at this?'

'Well . . .' said Bella still smiling, 'it's either give

in or I take you to industrial tribunal for constructive dismissal during maternity leave.'

'Ouch . . . that would look bad . . . woman boss and everything.'

'Very bad,' Bella agreed.

'Bella, I'm really proud of you,' Susan said finally. 'You remind me of myself at your age, but I think you've made better choices.'

'Susan!' Bella cut in. 'You're running your own internationally successful company. That was a good call.'

'Yes, but I never had a child.'

Bella heard surprising regret in those words and realized this was the first time Susan had ever told her anything personal about herself.

'I kept putting it off for the next promotion, the next good job, the next big client and suddenly I'm 48 and it's not going to happen now,' Susan continued. 'And you know, on some level I'm quite glad, because I don't think I would have achieved all this with a family. But I'm sorry if I reacted badly to your pregnancy – I'm probably a bit hung up about the whole thing, a bit regretful for myself.'

'I'm sorry,' said Bella. 'We've been fed a whole lot of crap about careers and babies and I don't think you can have it all. You can have some of it, some of the time, if you're lucky and work really hard.'

'You see, you've made good choices,' Susan said, then added with a smile, 'But won't you miss walking into the big boys' offices and telling them it's OK, you're here to sort things out?'

'Ah well . . . probably a bit,' Bella replied. 'But I can always come back to that later. I'd really like to try and make this new idea work.'

'Who do you want to help you set it up?' asked Susan. 'Chris?'

'No. I think Chris and I had better stick to our separate empires for the moment. What about the new girl?'

'Milly? You've heard about her then?'

'Yeah. I'll meet her and see if we can get on. Hector . . . well,' Bella wanted to be ultra tactful. 'He's not my type.'

'I'm not sure if he's mine either,' Susan said. 'Hire someone new if you like, a computer nerd. We could soon need a bigger office,' she added, with what sounded suspiciously like enthusiasm.

'Maybe I'll get another mum who also wants her desk to be at home. Oh and I know this great American guy . . .' Bella suddenly remembered Mitch and wondered if he would take her call.

'Well you choose,' said Susan.

'Err, we haven't discussed . . .'

'Money?' said Susan putting her cup down.

'I'm working fewer hours, but I'm not working part time. I'm afraid this is not going to be a chance for you to slash my wages,' Bella said, trying to sound firm.

'Relax, this is a fantastic new venture,' Susan answered. 'I'll raise you by 20 per cent, make you a partner in our new internet arm and give you a 35 per cent profit share in that department.'

'Forty-five per cent,' Bella said straight away.

'You certainly haven't lost your balls, have you?' Susan replied. 'OK, forty.'

'Done.' Bella held out her hand and Susan shook it, then Bella jumped up from her seat and said 'Yeeeeeeees!' punching the air.

Susan, standing up too now, looked at her in disbelief but Bella clasped her in a hug. 'It's the new, touchy-feely, twenty-first-century thing, do you like it?' she giggled, squeezing Susan hard.

'Oh my God,' Susan gasped. 'Trousers, trainers . . . green nail varnish . . . you've gone completely mad.'

They both laughed, Bella feeling ridiculously happy. This was going to work, she was going to repay Susan a hundred times over for this chance.

'So, when do you want to start?' Susan asked.

'I'll come in and meet the new girl next week and work out if we need to hire someone else. Then I want a couple of months behind the scenes before we do the massive, pull out all the stops launch, say in February/March. Oh and I'm assuming I get the usual Christmas fortnight off . . .'

'OK,' said Susan, raising her eyebrows. 'I'll start paying you in a week's time then.'

'Yes please,' said Bella. 'Otherwise, I'll be repossessed.'

'You better keep in close touch,' Susan warned.

'I will. This is going to be fantastic, I'm really, really excited.'

'OK, keep your cool, I'll hear from you soon.'

They were standing beside Susan's door now.

'One other thing,' Bella added with a gleam in her eye.

'Ye-ees?' Susan was wary.

'I have to take you shopping, Susan, you need modernizing. You know the couture suit, padded shoulder, stiff hair thing . . . it's so over.' Bella crossed her fingers behind her back, hoping she hadn't gone too far.

But Susan burst into laughter. 'We'll see, Bella. Bring me in a bottle of the green nail polish . . . maybe I'll start there.'

Susan's mobile began to trill as Bella opened the door. 'Bye and thank you Susan, from the bottom of my heart and all that. You won't regret this.'

Susan had the phone in her hand and managed a quick 'I hope not! Bye,' before she answered with a brisk: 'Hello, Susan Prentice . . .'

Bella closed the door and was in the main office. It didn't look as if anyone else was in yet.

Kitty looked up: 'So, are you going to tell all? Are you back?'

'I'm kind of back in a week's time, but I can't tell you anything yet,' Bella grinned broadly.

'But you promised, you ratbag.'

'It's so exciting!'

'What the hell can be exciting enough about work to shout out yippeee like an idiot in front of Susan?'

'It wasn't yippeee it was yeeeees,' said Bella, adding, 'I like your outfit,' at Kitty's ripped camouflage trousers and neon orange plastic top.

'Oh my God. You must have had a nervous breakdown!'

'Something like that . . . but I'm starting to feel much better. Really good, in fact. I'll see you soon Kits, take care.' Bella was heading for the front door.

'You can't just go without telling me *anything*!' Kitty called after her.

'Oh yes I can.' Bella smiled mischievously.

When the lift pinged her out on the ground floor, Bella opened her briefcase and took out her packet of cigarettes.

She was shaking one out when she realized what she was doing. She was smoking to celebrate, but then she also smoked when she was depressed, she smoked when she was happy, she smoked when she was drinking, she smoked when she wasn't. Basically, she spent all day long giving herself excuses to smoke.

She crushed the lid closed, crumpling the three cigarettes which were jutting out of the packet and tossed the lot into the bin beside the main door. Then she strode out of the office, enjoying the long, comfortable strides she could take in her trousers and flat shoes.

Chapter Forty-six

Bella and Markie were still sitting at the kitchen table over breakfast on Saturday morning when she heard the front door opening upstairs.

Don called out: 'Hello, it's me,' in the hallway and Bella ran up the stairs to meet him.

She bounded up and flung her arms round him, kissing him on the lips without worrying about whether she should or not.

'Blimey,' he said, pulling back from her. 'You look . . . extraordinary.'

'Extraordinary good . . . or extraordinary bad?' she asked as he held her at arm's length and clocked the trainers, rustling grey nylon trousers and tight pink and silver top with flared sleeves.

'Good, good . . . I think. I like it, I'm getting used to it . . . You look very sexy,' he said finally and couldn't help pulling her in for another kiss.

'And the hair?!' he said suddenly. 'When did you do that?'

'Weeks ago, but you've been too angry to notice,' she answered.

'It looks great,' he said, deciding not to get into the 'why I was angry' discussion just yet.

They were interrupted by impatient squawks from the kitchen.

'He's in his high chair,' Bella explained, so they both went downstairs. She noticed Don didn't have his bags with him and felt a lurch of disappointment, but what did she really expect – that he could have forgiven and forgotten what had happened just six days ago?

Don headed straight for Markie and plucked him out of his chair in an easy movement, swinging him into the air.

'Hello, how's my big boy?' he said, beaming. 'You've got so big, in just a week.'

Markie giggled, stretched out with his hands and landed a long trail of drool on Don's face.

'Teething,' said Bella as Don brought the baby down quickly with a 'Yeurgh,' and wiped his face with his hand. 'Tea?' she asked. 'Toast? We're just finishing up.'

'Yeah, that would be great. I came early because I thought Markie might need time to get used to me again and . . . Mike probably wants the place to himself for the day.'

'Yeah,' said Bella. The moving back question hung in the air, but neither of them dared to touch it just yet.

'How is Mike?' she asked. She liked Don's news editor.

'He's well, he's going to retire,' Don answered.

'Really? He's only 50-odd, isn't he?'

'Fifty-six, but it's a hard job, plus ex-wife number

461

two is back in Scotland with the kids, so he's thinking about moving up there because he never sees them.'

Don had spent most of his evenings this week listening to an over-stressed, late-middle-aged man spilling out his regret at having always put his career before his family. The irony of the situation had not been lost on him.

'Anyway, how've you been?' Don settled into a chair with his son bouncing on his knee, trying to pull off his glasses.

'Good,' said Bella. 'Very good, bought some new clothes, got a lovely childminder, Markie's sleeping through the night, got a new job – busy week.' She turned to pour boiling water into the teapot, so Don couldn't see her smiling.

'Bloody hell,' said Don 'New job?!!' He paused, waiting for an explanation.

Bella brought the teapot and cups to the table, saying: 'OK, sit tight and I'll tell you the whole thing.'

So she did, starting all the way back at the cheap shop with the diffused clothes for computer geeks.

He listened intently with growing admiration.

'So,' she said when she'd finished, 'Pretty good huh? So I'll now be earning more than you but working less. Is that a turn-on or what?' she joked but then quickly carried on talking because she couldn't bear for him not to answer. 'Now, I really have to go or I'm going to be late, Markie's food is in the fridge all anally labelled with when you feed it to him and how much, etc. etc. . . . . Have loads of fun. I've got the mobile for any panics.' She kissed them in turn, picked up her gym bag and hurried to the door, before she could change her mind about leaving Markie in the care of his dad for a whole morning.

Don was left speechless and a bit awed by her exiting whirlwind.

Once the front door slammed, Markie looked up at him and said: 'Da, da,' quite distinctly and Don was surprised to feel tears prick the back of his eyes.

'Hello Markie,' he said gently. 'I love you.' He hugged the tiny boy close.

Right, he thought to himself, time for a walk in the park. Where was Markie's snowsuit? And sling thing? And shoes, did he wear shoes? Should he pack a snack, when did Markie next expect some food? How come he didn't know any of these things?? He'd been a useless git, but that was going to change.

'OK son,' he said and patted the baby's head. 'time for a stroll. Hello there, this is your dad talking. The one who's going to teach you about cars, football, girls, keeping a clean bat . . . that sort of thing.'

Markie turned his big head and blinked; he looked a bit like a baby owl thought Don, but he was cute . . . And he's mine, he thought with a strangely joyous swell of pride.

Bella was just climbing out of her car in the gym's car park when an outrageously bright red Ferrari pulled up not far away.

'Hello darling!' Tania called out of the open window.

'Bloody hell! It's lovely!' shouted Bella as she walked towards the car. Both women were grinning at each other.

'Urban grunge?' Tania shouted back. 'God, Bella, I never thought you'd go for that. A silver anorak!!?'

'It's comfortable and cheap,' Bella countered. 'Anyway, get out of the car, let's see the new you.'

Tania threw open the door and stepped out in high-heeled ankle boots, tight black leather trousers and a tiny red sweater. She had huge sunglasses perched on top of her head.

'Oh my God!' Bella exclaimed. 'It's Liz Hurley.'

'I'm much younger than her!' Tania said in mock horror.

'Of course you are, anyone can see that.'

'Come here,' Bella held out her arms.

They hugged and Bella said, 'I love you.'

'Yeuck,' said Tania breaking away. 'My friend has been kidnapped by aliens and replaced with an American teenager.'

'Shut up, you're so uptight,' Bella laughed. 'Let's go work out.'

'I bet you've given up smoking as well,' Tania said as they headed up the gym steps.

'Yup,' Bella answered.

'Will you stop talking like that? What's happened to you, have you been on-line too long?'

'Yup . . . and it's going to get worse,' she hinted.

After an hour and a half of hard effort, they decided to collapse in the sauna together.

'Has it been really rough?' Bella asked her friend as they lay back in the heat.

'Yeah, it has really,' Tania answered. 'I felt so betrayed and so furious . . . furious with him and furious with myself for being so *stupid*. When I think about it now . . . it just seems so obvious. I mean, I wasn't misreading the signs, Bella, I was walking past massive billboards which spelled it out and turning my head the other way. Jesus. But you know, after two weeks of hysterical sobbing, smoking, insomnia and unrelenting grief, normal break-up rules had to apply.'

'You threw everything out?'

'Yup and sold the jewellery and tore up the photos and erased his numbers from all my files and changed the locks and did everything just right.'

'I'm so proud of you,' said Bella. 'Have you had transition man sex yet.'

'Yeah, actually,' Tania laughed.

'And was it the best ever?'

'Yeah, but I cried in the morning.'

'Well, men who don't make you cry in the morning are hard to find,' Bella said and thought about her husband.

'And how are things with Don?' Tania asked, guessing why she'd started staring off into the distance.

'I think they're going to be OK. I hope so. I really love him and if I've screwed this up, it won't just be me who suffers, but Markie as well,' she answered.

'Oh God.' Tania sat up and looked at her friend. 'I'm sorry, Bella. You'll just have to tell him, you know, how you made a big mistake.'

'Yeah . . . very big mistake.'

'I'm sorry I haven't been around.'

'Me too,' said Bella. 'But I'm sort of glad we fell out though, because we've never done that before and it really, really used to bug me that I couldn't say what I thought in case we argued.'

'What! You want to fall out again?'

'No, I just know now that if we do, we'll get over it, but a bit quicker next time! I mean, if we don't argue, we're just sociable acquaintances, we're not really blood, gut and tears friends, are we?'

'So what have you been longing to say to me all this time?' Tania dared her.

'Oh loads of stuff!'

'Well go on then.'

'You're kidding, you really want to hear this?' Bella grinned.

'Bring it on out, if you think you're hard enough,' Tania teased.

'All right then . . . I thought Greg was really boring and you deserved someone better.'

'OK,' Tania said.

'And I think you sometimes act like too much of a ditz when you're actually a really smart, really great person.'

Tania smiled.

'And I'm so jealous you have a lovely brother . . . and a fantastic mum and dad who gave you enough money to start up your own business and buy a flat . . . and you're obsessed with fashion, which is tedious . . . but you know what annoys me the most, you never think you look good in anything, that drives me up the wall . . . Please stop me now,' Bella laughed. 'See? I could have let this out gradually over the years but now it's all gushing out in one colossal friendship-destroying tidal wave.'

'*Bitch*!' Tania said in mock horror: 'What about you!? Ms Smug Smarty Pants Perfect, you're so good at picking out people's faults and bossing them around, you do it for a living.'

'A damn good one,' Bella interrupted.

'Shut up, this is my rant! And you think your dress taste is so spot on, when in fact it's just really boring . . .'

'Hey, what about the silver anorak!'

'And how dare you get married first and have a baby first and always get every man you've ever wanted just by flaunting your cleavage and dropping your knickers. I hope you've learned your lesson this time, Bella.'

'Ouch,' Bella said soberly.

'And . . . and I was so jealous of you and Daniel at university,' Tania blurted out.

'*Daniel*!!' This was news. 'You can't be jealous of Daniel, we were together for three and a half years, we were a couple, we were in love!'

'Of course I can be jealous. He was so lovely and played Hamlet and let's face it, every girl in the place wanted him and I still can't believe you got him.'

'Oh God, you can't be jealous? We hung out with you all the time, don't tell me you were pining away for him because you weren't! And anyway aren't you forgetting all the trauma at the end of that?'

'You left him,' Tania said, as if Bella needed to be reminded.

'But he cheated.'

'But he wanted you to forgive him Bella, just like you want Don to forgive you.'

'Jesus,' Bella felt irrationally angry, 'it was nothing like this.'

'If I ask you something, do you promise to answer truthfully?' Tania said, after a pause.

'No,' said Bella sulkily.

'Well, I'm asking anyway. Do you love Don as much as you loved Daniel?'

'No,' Bella said without hesitation.

'Oh my God!' Tania was shocked.

'I'm a grown-up now,' Bella said calmly. 'I loved Daniel unconditionally. It wasn't very good for either of us. I think Don and I are better at treading that line between dependence and independence,' she tried to explain. 'Between us it's: "I love you, I want to be with you, but treat me badly and I'll . . . reconsider".' It was hard to say that because she knew Don was reconsidering right now . . . knew she had been reconsidering in the weeks before the night with Chris.

'So why did you play away with someone else then?' Tania was not treading lightly today.

Bella hugged her knees up to her chest and rested her face on them: 'Christ I don't know, because I could . . . because he was there.'

'What's that?' Tania asked. 'The Mount Everest defence, "because it was there" – that's just bloody stupid.'

They both started to giggle, then laugh, then became quite hysterical.

'Come on,' said Tania finally. 'We've got to get out of here, it's so bloody hot, we've probably got heatstroke.'

They had a quick lunch together because Bella was starting to fret about Markie and when they kissed goodbye, Tania wished her good luck and promised her everything was going to be OK.

Bella wished she could be so sure; she felt horribly anxious and stirred up.

When she got back to the house, she opened the

front door as quietly as she could. If Markie was asleep, she didn't want to wake him, so she tiptoed in.

She could hear a football match on in the sitting room, and Don making the odd comment: 'Nice one' and 'You must be joking!'

She looked in to see Don lying full-length across the sofa with Markie propped up against his chest. They were both engrossed in the match. It was just heart-wringingly cute.

'Hello,' she said from the door, and when the two heads swivelled round, she momentarily wondered which face to look at first. She shot a quick smile at Don, then beamed at her little son who was laughing and holding out his arms for her.

'Hi darling, how are you? Would you like a cuddle?'

'Yes, please,' said Don.

She laughed and ran over to pick Markie up. Don clicked off the TV with a 'Rubbish game anyway,' and sat up.

'How's it been?' she asked, cuddling Markie against her and noticing that Don was wearing a different top.

'Good, fine mainly. Don't go into the bathroom just yet, I haven't had a chance to clean up.'

Bella raised her eyebrows.

'I took him out in his sling thing and when we got back, well, there was a severe nappy overflow. My God . . .' Don began to laugh, 'there was crap everywhere, all over Markie, all over the sling, all over me.'

Bella gave a snort: 'Yup, it's a learning curve.'

'But, you know, we've had a nice time. He's a

469

really great little guy. I love the way he flaps his arms when he's excited, which is about three times a minute.' Don smiled.

'Has he had a nap?' she asked.

'He nodded off for about ten minutes in the sling, but woke up when we came back in, so not really,' he answered.

'OK,' she said. 'Let's take you upstairs for a nice feed and a snooze.' She kissed Markie on his chubby cheeks.

'Can I come?' asked Don.

'If you like,' she said, surprised by the request.

In the bedroom, Bella lay down on the bed. Propped up on the mound of pillows she turned onto her side, lifted her top, unzipped her bra and snuggled Markie up close against her full breasts.

Don lay down on the bed behind her and leaned on his elbow so he could watch.

Markie took her nipple in his mouth and began to tug hard, his jaw working up and down. She waited a few moments for the warm, tingling rush of milk and saw Markie close his eyes in bliss as it arrived.

A trickle of milk ran out down the side of his chin.

Don's head moved to rest on her shoulder, so he could watch the little face pressed close against the soft, creamy mound of skin. He felt a gush of love and lust.

As Markie sucked hard against her, Bella felt the distinct connection between nipples and clitoris that made breastfeeding such a pleasure.

Don's warm breath was against her neck and she longed for him. He smelled of unfamiliar soap and clean laundry. He shifted slightly so he was closer against her and his keys and pocketful of change jangled as he moved.

She curved her back so she was pressed against him and he kissed her neck. She shivered and let her eyes close, so he kissed gently again.

Markie had stopped sucking, so Bella moved to loosen her other breast and put it into the drowsy baby's mouth. He began to suck again slowly and Don placed small, soft kisses on her neck and licked at her with his warm tongue.

He laid his hand on the curve of her waist then stroked down her side. She was overwhelmingly happy to feel a hard erection against her.

Don moved a hand to the waistband of her trousers and pulled open the drawstring. Then he felt his way down to her wet, swollen clitoris.

She parted her lips with a sigh as he made contact. Her baby was still sucking hard on her nipple and Don was moving his finger slowly up and down between her legs. It felt blissfully good.

She felt wet and slippery and desperate for him as he slid one finger inside her.

'Is this allowed?' she whispered urgently.

'I don't know,' Don whispered back . . . 'Shall we wait until he's asleep?'

'He's nearly there,' she whispered.

She heard Don unzip his trousers and she felt his warm, hard dick press against her buttocks.

Markie's mouth slid off her nipple and she could see he was sound asleep. She moved him slightly away from her on the bed, then rushed to pull off her trousers.

Don grasped her hips in his hands, pulled her back onto his cock and pushed inside.

He kissed the back of her neck, keeping one damp hand against her clitoris and moving strongly inside her.

'Oh God,' she gasped. 'I'm going to come really quickly.'

'Me too,' he said. 'Is it OK?'

She knew it wasn't really but she couldn't bear to have him pull out the condom box and realize there was one less in there than last time.

'Yeah,' she gasped and felt the warm rush and shuddering of her own approaching orgasm. He thrust strongly through it and she came, trickling breast milk, just before his long sigh of pleasure.

They were sweaty and sated and he threw his arm round her and pressed his face into the back of her neck. 'Oh, that was nice,' he whispered.

'Yeah,' she answered and they lay still for a few moments with him gradually shrinking inside her.

When he had pulled out, she turned around to face him. 'Don?' She looked into his eyes and tried to read the answer to this question before she asked it: 'Do you still love me?'

He placed a hand on her cheek and answered, 'Yeah, of course.'

'What about you?' he asked. 'Do you love me?'

'Yes,' she answered.

'But don't think I wasn't angry,' he added. 'Christ, I was furious . . . but I've come to the conclusion that I can forgive *a little* infidelity here,' his finger brushed her pubic bone, 'so long as there is none here,' he pressed his finger to her breastbone.

'I'm so sorry. You're the one, and I know that now,' she whispered.

'Do you want to be married to me?' he asked.

'I do,' she said.

'Do you want to bring up a baby with me?'

'I do.'

'Will you try and keep me unto yourself, for-saking all others?'

'God yes.' She blinked and a tear slid down her nose and hung on the end.

He licked it off.

'I'm sorry I wasn't more help with Markie,' he said. 'It all got a bit much for you. I'm going to do a lot more, be around a lot more. I'm booking some holiday, for a start.'

She hugged her arms round his back and pushed her wet face into his shoulder: 'I'm sorry I didn't think about you . . . I was so wrapped up in the baby and losing my job and everything . . .' She began to cry against him, 'I love you, Markie loves you too. I promise I'll be so good if you take me back.'

'Bella, it's OK,' he soothed. 'It's not a question of taking you back. I never imagined it working out any other way.'

'I love you,' she said again.

'I love you too,' he answered.

'Are you going to move back in today?' she asked.

'Yeah, my things are in the car but . . .'

'Oh dear . . .' she said. '"But" doesn't sound good.'

'I've probably got another two-week foreign coming up very soon. I'm so sorry, I've already said I'll do it, but I promise, I'm taking two weeks off at Christmas.'

'What do you think about going to Italy for Christmas?' she said, surprising herself.

473

He was taken aback too. 'Don't your parents live there?!' he asked.

'Yeeees . . . I'm not suggesting we go and stay with them for a fortnight. But I think we should visit.'

'OK,' said Don. 'This is something of a break-through.'

She didn't say anything more about it, just smiled at him. They stayed cuddled up on the bed together, not speaking, for a long time.

Finally Bella sat up and said: 'I'm starving, shall we go and make bacon sandwiches?'

'Fantastic,' he said. 'Are you going to put Markie in his cot?'

She looked at him with her eyebrows raised.

'Here, why don't I try?' he added quickly. 'Just don't blame me if he wakes up.'

'But it'll be your fault!!'

Chapter Forty-seven

Bella was ensconced in her little attic office where she had been working hard since Markie went to Sylvia's at 8.45 a.m.

She liked the bright yellow eyrie a lot more now. She'd put in new shelves, a filing cabinet, a desk and chair and a cappuccino maker. Once she closed the door at the top of the stairs, she found it easy to forget about her baby and the rest of the house and slip straight into work mode.

Prentice had given her a spanking new computer with all the bits and a tiny silver mobile just like Susan's. Bella had been amused when everything had arrived in boxes labelled 'Bella's Baby'.

She was concentrating hard on the proposals up on the screen in front of her, when a sharp ring at the doorbell startled her.

Oh God! She really could not cope with another Jehovah's Witness, meter reader or carpet shampoo salesman. She stayed put in her chair, hoping they would go away. There was another long, loud ring. Bugger. She closed the file and stomped down the two flights of stairs.

She turned the catch, swung the door open and saw Don, tired, crumpled, with a large bag over his shoulder.

'Hello gorgeous,' he said with a big grin. 'I've lost my keys.'

'Hello!!' she cried. 'I didn't think you were back till this evening.' They hugged and kissed hard on the doorstep. She hadn't seen him for two weeks and she'd missed him like hell.

'Nice coat,' she said as he stepped inside. She laid her cheek on his shoulder and smelled his neck, then kissed it.

'Yeah, my wife gave it to me. Don't tell her I've come here to see you first.' He grinned and they kissed mouth to mouth again.

'You look really tired. D'you want to go downstairs and have coffee?' she asked.

'No, no, I'm fine. Markie isn't here then?'

'No, he's at Sylvia's until one. How was the trip?'

'Bloody awful, but never mind, it was my last one.' He gave her a teasing smile and twined his hands behind her waist.

'What?' She pulled back to look at him.

'Well . . . I've got something to tell you . . . ' he paused, enjoying the suspense. 'I've just been made news editor.'

'No!!' She was really shocked now. 'You're kidding!!'

'I'm not.' Don looked very pleased with himself. 'I just heard this morning. I told them I wasn't going to do it because the hours are so long, so they came back with an even better offer and said I could do four days a week, starting in January.'

'My God! Are you happy?' she asked, somewhat needlessly.

'I'm bloody thrilled,' he said with a smile.

'No more foreigns, though . . .' she said, sure he would miss them.

But he surprised her by saying 'Thank fuck for that!' with a laugh.

'Well, congratulations. Four days a week – that's amazing.'

'So . . .' he said 'What about you?'

'Well . . . I've got some news too actually.' She locked her eyes onto his, very intently. 'It's going to shock you a bit.' She sounded nervous and he started to feel nervous too.

'I've just found out I'm pregnant again. By complete accident, and that's true this time,' she added.

'Oh my God!' he gasped, then put his arms around her. Resting his chin on her shoulder, he let out a low whistle and said, 'God, Bella.'

'It must have been that Saturday. I was so glad you were back . . . I didn't really think about . . .'

'Oh yes,' he cut in. 'That was very hot.' He looked at her tenderly. 'It's a sign,' he smiled. 'We're meant to be.'

She hugged him close. 'Thank you Don,' she whispered and felt tears well up.

'God,' he said again and wiped her cheeks with his thumb. 'Everything's going to be OK, I promise . . . and I definitely need the coffee now.'

As they walked across the hall to the kitchen stairs, she suddenly stopped him to ask with a smile, 'Just a minute . . . has any news editor you've ever known stayed married?'

'No, but I see that as a challenge,' he answered, smiling back.

'And are you going to be earning more than me now?'

'Just a tiny, tiny bit more, I think. But no bonuses . . . so . . .'

'So that's all right then!!' She laughed and turned him round so she could kiss him on the mouth.

'Mmmm . . .' she said. 'Just you, me, a hallway . . . it's like old times.'

'Just what exactly do you have in mind, Mrs McCartney?'

Unbuttoning his coat and letting it fall on the floor, she answered, 'Why don't I just show you, Mr Browning?'

THE END